ASK ME AGAIN

E. J. NOYES

BELLA
BOOKS
2018

Bella Books, Inc.
P.O. Box 10543
Tallahassee, FL 32302

Printed in the United States of America on acid-free paper.

First Bella Books Edition 2018

Editor: Cath Walker
Cover Designer: Sandy Knowles

ISBN: 978-1-59493-612-8

Other Bella Books by E. J. Noyes

Ask, Tell
Gold
Turbulence

Acknowledgments

Whenever I try to write acknowledgements, it gets harder to think of new and exciting ways to say thank you to everyone who's helped me. So…

Thank you (sticking with old faithful here) to BFF Kate who has some great ideas. Even if I don't agree with them. Come on, read THAT BOOK for me.

Christina, I owe you big time for curing my raging case of firstdraftitis. Thanks so much for your patience and ideas throughout the early stages and then beyond. I can't express how helpful our "antagonist" chat was when I was totally stuck and wanted to throw the whole thing out the window.

Rebecca – if not for you, this would still be called "Sequel Dealio." Lifesaver.

Other Kate, you have the best leaning shoulder and beta eyes. I'm sorry I complained so much during this one. Writing is hard.

Other Christina - you're a great Joe go-between. Thanks for your D.C. knowledge, though I still don't understand why it's not The Metro. I owe you a round of 11 p.m. beer and nachos.

Andy, I'm so grateful for your thoughtful insights, for seeing those hidden things I couldn't, and nudging me to do the thing I needed to. Okay, I guess it's *technically* an epilogue…kinda…grumble.

Massive thanks to the wonderful crew at Bella who work so hard to make things so easy for me.

Cath, you rock! But since we met, I feel like I spend all my editing time whispering to myself, "Dammit, but it made sense to me!" I promise I'll try harder next time. Or try to try harder.

And last but not least (I have to say that even though she probably won't read this for a few years) masses of gratitude to my wife, Phoebe, who has taken to my word hobby with such delight. Thanks for not making me feel like an idiot when I text you to double-check that an adjective means it's a describing word. Darling, you turn all my dark places to light.

About the Author

E. J. Noyes lives in Australia with her wife, a needy cat, aloof chickens and too many horses. When not indulging in her love of reading and writing, E. J. argues with her hair and pretends to be good at clay target shooting.

CHAPTER ONE

Sabine

The closer the Army C-17 flew me back toward the States, the greater my unease became until I wasn't sure if the sickening dread was true anxiety, or anxiety about having anxiety. Who the hell gets anxiety about going *home* from deployment? Apparently me, Queen of the Ridiculous.

I nudged Mitch with my knee. "Scoot out of the way."

He huffed another exasperated sigh, dog-eared his page and unbuckled so he could stand up to let me pass. Captain Mitchell Boyd's Texan drawl became even more drawn out as he tried—and failed—to sound like he didn't want to throttle me for being so annoying. "Sabine, if I'da known you were gonna be up'n down this much, I wouldn'ta let you have a middle seat. Take some goddamned Imodium."

"I already told you twice, I do not have diarrhea!" Midway through my loudly indignant rebuttal, the cabin went silent, leaving that last word to echo through the interior of the massive cargo plane. Perfect. The awkward silence was quickly covered by the sound of laughter and merciless teasing all around.

I raised a hand to acknowledge my socially inept outburst, then turned back to my best friend. "But you know what, Mitch? Your bitching would give anyone the shits." I squeezed past him for the seventh time in the last four hours.

As I picked my way around prone bodies sleeping on all available floor space, I passed my good friend and deployment roommate, Captain Amy Peterson, who slept sprawled across the three seats she'd managed to wrangle. Lucky bitch. Even in this inelegant pose she somehow looked graceful, her honey-blond hair still contained in a perfect bun and beautiful features serene with sleep.

It was an illusion.

The moment her eyes opened, with her mouth following milliseconds after, the Sleeping-Beauty spell would break. Housed in that body, which wouldn't look out of place in a Parisian couture house, was one hell of a surgeon with a filthy mind and filthier mouth. Amy came up with new and creative versions of expletives even I couldn't imagine, chewed with her mouth open—usually because she was talking—and voiced her opinions loudly and without a single care as to who might be offended. I adored her and in all honesty, probably wouldn't have survived the last few deployments without her, and Mitch.

Of course the bathroom was occupied. I fidgeted outside the door, wiggling my toes inside my boots, and glanced down the back to see if the second bathroom was free. Nope. Someone waiting outside that one too. A lifetime later, the door opened and I rushed into the tiny closet of a lavatory and yanked my pants down. Nothing but a trickle, just like the time before and the time before that. Get a grip, you idiot.

I leaned over to rest my forehead against the wall. What the hell was wrong with me? This wasn't my first post-deployment rodeo, but instead of turning excited cartwheels, I felt like I was heading to the gallows. I'd been waiting for this moment for over ten months and now that it was here, I felt suddenly cast adrift.

My extended pity-party was cut short by tapping on the door, and a mumbled, "Kinda desperate to pee here, Fleischer…"

I finished up, flashed an apologetic smile at Major John Auger, another Med Corps surgeon in our team, who was jiggling outside the bathroom and made my way back to my seat. I had to squeeze around Amy's feet which hung over the edge of the seats, boots still on but laces loosened and dangling and begging for mischief. It lacked flair but was too easy to pass up.

There was sniggering behind me as I carefully knotted the laces of her left and right boots together, my eyes on her face the whole time to make sure she was still sleeping. She was, snoring as usual. After rooming with her for two and a half deployments, I found it hard to sleep if she wasn't in the small, plywood-lined room with me. Her glottal vibrations were a gross kind of white noise, helping to block some of the persistent, unpleasant sounds of living at a Forward Operating Base hospital in Afghanistan.

I shimmied past Mitch and buckled myself in, yanking the belt so tightly it hurt. He glanced at me. "You done? We'll be landin' in an hour, think you can hold it 'til we're on the ground?"

On the ground. An invisible hand grabbed the back of my neck, squeezing already tense muscle until it felt like it was burning. In six hours or so I would see Bec, in person, for the first time in over ten months. Three hundred and fourteen days since I'd touched my girlfriend. Kissed her. Made love to her. Felt her talented, knowing fingers—uh, really not the time or place, Sabine.

I closed my eyes and conjured up the mental picture that I'd kept coming back to whenever I thought of *her*. The PG-rated one, that is. The night before I left, Bec had leaned on the kitchen counter, watching me use my laptop at the table. Blond hair loose around her shoulders, begging to be twirled around my fingers. Those ocean-blue eyes creased with laughter. Dimples a mile deep.

That memory triggered the one of what came after—the very much not PG version—where I ducked around the counter into the kitchen, then without a word pulled Bec's shirt over her head. The memory bloomed, replaying whispered pleas and loud moans as she lay spread for me on the kitchen floor, and then segued into the hours in bed where we made love until we were so satiated we could do nothing more than just exist together.

You have the most inappropriate mental timing, Sabine.

I forced my thoughts back to those more appropriate in public. Like…family. Judging by the nonstop emails my younger sister, Jana, was over-the-top excited about my coming home. Mom's constant emails in the last month had laid out detailed plans for the five days Bec and I would spend at my parents' house in Ohio once I'd completed my post-deployment processing. Even Dad, hater of electronic communication, had added a few lines at the bottom of Mom's latest message.

Everyone would be excited. So why wasn't I? Why was I so afraid? More to the point, *what* was I so afraid of? The irrational panic bubbled up again, and the windowless, cavernous space was suddenly so claustrophobic I wanted to tear off my seatbelt and sprint away. But there was nowhere to go.

My nervous bladder sent another false, yet insistent message. This was getting absurd. I loosened my seatbelt and leaned down to where my backpack was stuffed under the seat in front, with Mitch's boot covering it. "Move your hoof."

He obliged and I rummaged in the bag, keeping it half-closed to hide what I was doing as I tapped five milligrams of diazepam from the bottle. Ever nosy, Mitch asked, "What's that?"

The lie fell off my tongue. "Midol." I palmed the Valium into my mouth and swallowed it with a gulp of disgustingly warm bottled water. "…Mom."

"Mhmm, sure." Mitch lowered his voice. "Sabs? You're sweatin'."

"Am I? That's because it's fucking hot in here."

"You're also shakin', angel."

"Well, it's…cold too." Nice comeback, Sabine. I wrapped my arms around my waist and faced forward again.

"How's your stomach?" His concern was part friend, part physician and part someone who's greatest source of panic had always been someone puking near him.

I wasn't going to puke. Not yet anyway. "It's fine," I said forcefully.

"Sabs, I—"

"Please just let it go." I spared him a pleading look. "I said it's fine, Mitch, honestly."

His mouth pressed into a thin line but he nodded and did as I'd asked. A few moments later, a large rough-skinned hand came to rest on my knee. I grabbed it, squeezed firmly and kept holding on. We'd been best friends for almost twenty years and I felt awful for cutting him off. For lying. For shutting him out this time.

But this wasn't the place to discuss my stupid anxiety. And even if it was the place, what was the point? Mitch knew what was wrong, especially after dealing with me and my PTSD that had recurred within the first month back in Afghanistan. Recurred was a stupid term, implying it'd actually gone away in the first place. But…the way I was feeling now had nothing to do with PTSD. Did it? Maybe it really was just the deployment.

I closed my eyes and willed myself to leave the front behind, to forget about all the soul-draining surgeries and the men and women I couldn't save or put back into one whole body again. I begged myself to shed the constant undercurrent of fear I'd had ever since leaving Bec at home. If I couldn't set it all aside, it would slowly eat at me until I was nothing more than a hollowed-out shell. Of course, knowing that's what I needed to do and actually being able to do it were two different things.

The plane ride home should have been a transformation of sorts, shifting my emotions and worries into a hidden place so I could interact with regular people again. Even as I tried to reason with myself, I wondered if I even needed to force myself to be *normal*. Did I really need to draw a curtain over my feelings? Bec wouldn't expect that of me, and she certainly didn't need me to make some magical metamorphosis from Deployment Sabine to Back-Home Sabine.

She knew as well as anyone what it was like over there, what it was like to come back. My girlfriend, Lieutenant Colonel Rebecca Keane, had been an Army surgeon for over eighteen years. She'd even been my boss during her final three years before she'd retired after The Incident.

The Incident.

I hated the way we all called it that, but I suppose "The time Sabine was in a Humvee which was hit by an explosive device that literally cut a man in half, then she and the driver also got shot and it really sucked" *was* a bit of a mouthful.

Bec knew how I'd been affected. But I so did not want our reunion to be full of *How are you?* and *Are you okay?* and that unspoken, underlying question that now seemed to overshadow everything. *How is your PTSD?*

Over two years later and post-traumatic stress disorder is still present for duty, Colonel Keane! I mean…honey.

I scrubbed both hands over my face, trying to dispel the feeling that had settled under my skin. Instead of the borderline arousal I'd felt five minutes earlier when thinking about making love with my girlfriend, my body now felt strange, almost weightless, as though it wasn't really mine. An unpleasant sensation, but unfortunately not a new one. It had recurred intermittently since The Incident. Staring at my hands, touching my forearms, tapping my molars together usually helped bring me back to myself, but the undercurrent could linger for hours. Sometimes days. How was I supposed to be Bec's life partner and equal if I didn't even feel like myself?

For the rest of the flight I curled up with my eyes closed, leaning on Mitch's shoulder while he read. The movement of his arm as he turned pages gave me something to focus on and I found myself counting the seconds between each flip. Mitch was a slow reader and after twenty-four pages lasting one thousand, nine hundred and thirty-eight seconds, I felt the Valium kick in.

My panic was blunted at the edges, making the anxiety at least tolerable. Its gnawing was like rats nibbling my bones, but I no longer felt like I was about to run screaming down the aisle of the plane. Good enough.

When we began our descent, the sounds of people moving rose to match the drone of the engines. I opened my eyes again, blinking away the sudden brightness. Mitch squeezed my hand then let it go. "You good?"

"Mhmm." I straightened up and stretched as best I could with two tall men either side of me and the row of seats in front brushing my shins.

Mitch carefully folded down the edge of his page and set the book in his backpack. "Who's meetin' you? Jana or Rebecca?"

Sister or girlfriend. Neither. I massaged the back of my neck. "I haven't told them. They still think we're back the day after tomorrow."

Mitch spluttered and pushed out a strangled, "The fuck?"

I raised my hands to forestall his rant. "I thought it'd be kinda cool. You know, be settled on the couch with dinner on the stove when Bec comes home from work tonight."

Mitch had been like a puppy the whole time we'd been prepping to come home, and the fact I wasn't doing backflips was foreign to him. He harrumphed. "She's gonna be madder'n a wet hen when she comes home and sees you already there without tellin' her we were coming back."

"No way. Surprised, but not mad." I shuffled, trying to get comfortable. "Besides, she did the same to me, remember?" While I was stateside recovering, anxiously waiting for Bec to give me her firm return date, she'd just turned up at my house one afternoon after separating from the Army. It was wonderful and sweet and had been a perfect gift. Now I wanted her to feel the same.

He said something else under his breath that gave the impression he thought he knew better than me. Then he raised his voice. "Geez, woulda thought you'd be dyin' to get home. And into bed," he added.

I was but was also being smothered by that fear of going home. To Bec. To my safe place. Totally rational, post-deployment jitters, that's all. Keep lying, and maybe one of these days you'll believe yourself. Mitch cleared his throat and gave me the pointed look I knew so well. Stop thinking and speak, Sabine, or he's going to dig in. Before I could think of something to say, the address system crackled. The cabin grew quieter, then the usual incantations echoed through the plane. Prepare for approach, thank you for your service and sacrifice, welcome home and God Bless America.

Mitch leaned down to make sure both our packs were stowed under the seats in front. "You two goin' away?"

Once all our in-processing requirements, screenings and briefings and crap were done, we were all being sent on two weeks' block leave. Two weeks was shorter than usual, but the deployment rotations meant we were needed back at work at our new duty station—Walter Reed National Military Medical Center—ASAP. They'd only just moved the hospital to Bethesda and combined it with the Naval Medical Center, and Amy, Mitch and I would likely stay there until our next orders came through in six or nine or however many months it was until the Army decided what to do with us. "Mhmm. Just five days with the parents then the rest at home doing chores and stuff."

"Boring." Mitch had a week in Canada planned with his boyfriend, Mike. Mitch and Mike, my M 'n' Ms. In the beginning I'd teased him about how they sounded like a sitcom. The original M, Mitch, raised both eyebrows. "You're so domesticated it makes me sick."

"Jealousy is unattractive," I said sweetly. "And get off your high horse. What are you guys doing for the second week once you get home, hmm?"

He blew a raspberry at me, his presumably snide response smothered by a command through the cabin to sit down and belt in. From a few rows forward there was a thud and a loud, "Which of you fucking assholes tied my laces together?" Amy's head popped up over the seats. Her murky green eyes found mine, then narrowed. "Sabine, you shit!"

I affected an innocent look. "Moi? Would I really do such a thing?"

Her response was a middle-fingered salute that was most definitely not in the prescribed military manner.

After a hard landing at Joint Base Andrews in Maryland, we taxied for an eternity until there was parking space for the huge plane. The moment the C-17 became stationary, everyone leapt up and noisily began gathering their kit. I did the same, albeit with less enthusiasm. Amy hopped to her feet and launched herself toward me, arms outstretched for a hug. "Come on, let's get to this bus and get our asses home."

I held her tight, burying my face in her shoulder and absorbing her strength. I wondered if she remembered me from the early days, our first deployment, when I didn't need to lean on her so much. When I was normal and didn't have a meltdown every time there was an incoming enemy fire drill. Or real enemy fire.

She'd had a front row seat to some dark times in our last two deployments—my ex's cheating and breakup from thousands of miles away, my subsequent breakdown, then The Incident and PTSD. And she'd stood firm with me through it all.

Amy planted a smacking kiss on my cheek, gave Mitch the same treatment then rushed toward the rear door, calling for us to *hurry the fuck up*. My friends and coworkers disembarked in a seething mass of combat uniforms and excited chattering, and I was swept up and deposited outside with them. Everyone began to disperse toward the buses, but I was stuck in place, as if my boots had melted into the tarmac.

Ten yards ahead, Amy elbowed her way through the crowd, desperate to get to the transport that would take us to the base where family and friends would be waiting. Waiting for everyone except me. Mitch paused, looked around and when he spotted me, waved me over. "Fleischer! Let's go."

I nodded and tried to move. Couldn't. The only way I could unstick my feet was with a decisive internal count of *one step, two steps…three*. No, stop. Don't do that, not here. You don't need to. Mitch always called my demand for regulation and organization OCD, and maybe it was, but what was happening to me now sat in some uncomfortable gray area. I'd had to admit to myself that after The Incident, certain things made me uncomfortable. Like messy surgical trays, misaligned shoes and walking anywhere without counting my steps. Because, you know…I might need to count them to get back to safety if something happened.

I gritted my teeth and jogged over to him, singing the theme song to *Sesame Street* in my head to override the intrusive mental counting. Mitch's warm, dry hand found mine and he tugged me toward the buses. By the time we reached the vehicles, I could barely breathe. I bent over and rested my hands on my knees, trying desperately to oxygenate and stop the dizziness that threatened to topple me. Mitch's hand moved to my back. Along with Amy, he'd spent this deployment holding my hand, literally and figuratively, whenever I had *a moment* and his solid presence helped push some of the panic aside.

Someone spoke from my right. "Are you okay, Sabine?"

I raised my head. "Mhmm, fine. Thank you, John. Just getting over the flu." Stand up, Sabine. People are staring. I straightened and forced a smile.

Mitch rubbed gentle circles on my lower back, his voice calm and quiet. "You're okay, darlin'. Come on, we're here with you." He gave me a gentle nudge forward. "We're home now and it's all over."

All over, yes, but I still had to get into a vehicle. Nothing's going to happen, Sabine. You're stateside, you're fine. Mitch slung his arm around my shoulder, maneuvered me to a bus and into a seat near the front. My emetophobic friend bravely ignored my anxious dry heaving—another unfortunate side effect of my PTSD—and kept his thigh pressed against mine in his version of a show of support. Turned away from me, the music blasting through his headphones blocked the sound of my gagging and completed his little safety bubble. Reaching over from the seat behind us, Amy massaged my shoulder and gave running commentary on the scenery passing by to help distract me.

The trip to Bethesda took fifty-three minutes in familiar traffic and as the bus finally pulled around, I got my first look at where I'd be working until my next posting. Impressive, even with the cranes and mounds of dirt scattered around the grounds. Weapons and equipment handovers, check-ins and final checks took almost three hours and then we were released out into the world again. It began as an orderly procession but the moment we came within sight of the parking lot, and the view of a few hundred people massed and waiting, everyone pretty much let formation go to shit. Mitch grabbed my hand again, both to pull me along and also to stop me from getting lost, and dragged me toward the crowd.

Amy was tackled around the legs by a red and blue blur who was way taller than the last time I'd seen him. She dropped to her knees, pulling her son into a fierce hug, her hand strafing the back of his head. I recognized her husband, Rick, rushing toward them but didn't wave or draw his attention away from the woman he hadn't seen in months. It wasn't the time.

The parking lot was a staging area for joyous reunions—kids climbing over their parent newly returned from deployment, couples embracing and kissing, parents crying and laughing. And even though I'd planned that nobody was there for me, a vise of disappointment tightened around my chest.

Mitch's step quickened when he spotted Mike and I hung back as he strode over with a gait so excited he was practically levitating. The two men paused, staring at one another for a long moment before Mitch grabbed his partner and pulled him in for a crushing hug. At this distance I could almost hear bones grating. Mitch lifted Mike up off the ground and they kissed sweetly. The repeal of Don't Ask, Don't Tell was a thing of great beauty.

They'd met during our last deployment when they'd both been on a few days' leave in Qatar. They'd conquered distance and DADT until Mike's separation from the Army a few months before we'd left for this, our latest deployment. My boys were so sweet together, and also like oil and water. Six-three of All-American handsome Mitch who thought ball, beer and barbeque were the greatest things on earth. Then bookish, quiet Mike who only stood as tall as his boyfriend's shoulder and loved sitcoms and cooking and painting.

Once they'd finished their polite-for-public-eyes greeting, Mitch called, "Sabine! Stop draggin' yer tail and get over here!"

I rushed over as quickly as I could juggling both backpack and laptop bag as well as a heavy kit bag on my shoulder. I set my gear on the ground, and Mike swept me up into a warm embrace. He smelled faintly of freshly baked cookies and aftershave. "So good to see you, Sabine."

I wrapped my arms around his lean frame. "You too."

Mike released me carefully, not letting go until my feet were on the ground and I'd straightened up. He peered around curiously. "Where's Rebecca?" He slipped an arm around his boyfriend's waist and kissed the underside of Mitch's jaw. Mitch responded with a small rumble of pleasure and brushed his nose through Mike's hair. They were so cute, it'd be nauseating if I didn't adore them so much.

"At home. Or work." I gnawed the inside of my cheek before elaborating, "I didn't give her our updated arrival time. Wanted to surprise her."

Mitch's massive paw landed on my shoulder. "Sabs thinks it's romantic, sneakin' in like this." He jerked me back and forth, knowing full well I hated it.

I shouldered my big bag again, knocking his hand away in the process. "It is." I didn't want to be caught up in a discussion about how I chose to come home, so I backed up a step and punched Mitch's arm, knowing full well he hated it. "Speaking of, you two should get the hell out of here and get all caught up. Don't forget to come up for air."

Mitch laughed. "You can talk." He snatched me up and hugged me so hard I groaned. Then he spun me one-eighty degrees, murmuring, "Love you, darlin'."

I kissed his bristly cheek and squeezed him back. "Love you too, Mitchy."

When he dropped me, he asked, "You want a ride?" The question lacked enthusiasm, and considering his boyfriend was in touching range I didn't blame him.

"Nah, thanks. I'm good. I'll see you back here in a few days." I blew them each a kiss and made shooing gestures.

Mike returned my blown kisses. Mitch rolled his eyes. The boys quickly tossed Mitch's bags into the trunk and drove off with an out-the-window-wave each. I stood on the curb, watching other families drive away until the crowd thinned, and I was one of the few people left. It was almost eleven in the morning and I could be at the front door of our two-story Tudor in the outer suburbs of D.C. in forty-five minutes, if the traffic was good and the cab driver drove like my sister.

But I wasn't going home. I just…couldn't. Not yet.

CHAPTER TWO

Rebecca

Jana whirled through the door a little after seven p.m., still dressed in one of her impeccable work suits, and holding pizza and a bottle of Veuve Clicquot. "Sorry, Bec. Court ran late, then I got tangled up with a client," she explained, and went on to blurt a bunch of random thoughts—an endearing trait she shared with Sabine. "Messy divorces are awful, but they pay so damned well. I'm tempted to buy a bigger condo or even a house, but do I need more than two bedrooms for just me? Oh my God, these new shoes are *so* painful, it's a pity they're so fucking sexy or I'd probably ditch them. Maybe I'll buy a house with a yard and get a dog. I was going to get something healthier for dinner, and then I thought screw it, I'll just do an extra gym class this week. Eating pizza with champagne isn't tacky, is it?"

She dropped her bags on the table, slid everything else onto the kitchen counter and with a happy sigh slipped out of her heels. I had to choose something to respond to, so I smiled and answered her final question with, "No, it's not tacky." I picked up the champagne, which was fancier than what we usually drank with our catch ups. "What's the occasion?"

"We're celebrating, obviously." Sabine's sister pulled two champagne glasses down from the cupboard above the coffeemaker.

"Celebrating what exactly?"

"Sabbie's home the day after tomorrow, and I made it through the day without killing anyone or yelling at opposing counsel." She paused and added a cheeky, "Only just. Plus I got a fantastic settlement for someone who really deserves it while nailing her bastard ex-husband to the wall and I negotiated a custody arrangement for another client that actually works for everyone, kids included. Well, as much as those things can. Oh! And I have another date with Hot Coffee Roaster tomorrow night." Jana left me to open the bottle while she busied herself fetching plates.

Good enough reasons for me and given I didn't have to work for the next four days, a few glasses of champagne sounded heavenly. I'd taken a couple of vacation days to get organized before Sabine's arrival, and to have some uninterrupted time once she came home. Then I had another two weeks concurrent with her post-deployment leave so we could reconnect, and visit her parents and grandparents.

I busied myself with popping the cork and tossed it to the ground for the cat. Titus was a ginger and white blur as he batted the cork around the floor, until he eventually punted it across the room and under the fridge. Game over. Sabine would have been on hands and knees fumbling for the cork, and even moving the fridge if she couldn't reach the insignificant and replaceable cat toy. Innocuous daily events like this were when I was most aware of her absence. I pushed the feeling aside, reminding myself that in less than forty hours, she would be home.

Jana poured champagne, raised her glass and flashed me a smile. "To our last dinner as The Left Behinds." She'd dubbed us this silly name not long after Sabine had gone back to Afghanistan. From the outset, Sabine's family had accepted and enfolded me, but during Sabine's deployment Jana and I had grown even closer, drawn together by mutual sadness. She'd become the sister I never knew I'd wanted. Or needed.

I tipped my glass to her. "Cheers."

After a mouthful, Jana set her glass down and gathered her bob into a ponytail. She had the same hair as Sabine—a shade off black, thick and straight. After tucking a few loose strands back, Jana asked, "Have you heard from her since Monday?"

"No." I couldn't help frowning. Two days without contact was odd but not cause for alarm. "Have you?"

"Nope. Probably just technical issues, work, preps, all that shit," Jana said dismissively. After supporting her sister through three deployments, Jana knew the coming home routine almost as well as I did.

I murmured in agreement and carried the bottle and my drink to the table. Jana brought the pizza and settled across from me, her butt barely hitting the seat before she flipped the lid. Her expression was one of pure delight, as though pizza would solve all her problems. Jana pulled out slices and dropped them carelessly onto plates. "When do you guys go to Ohio?" She studied her thumb then licked it.

I helped with a piece of cheese that was trying to part ways with the rest of the topping. "Two days after she's finished all her in-processing." Sabine would have to complete a week on post-deployment debriefing, and physical and mental evaluations before being allowed her two weeks' leave.

"Time with the in-laws. Lucky you." Jana didn't bother to hide her smirk.

My smile was automatic, and genuine. "I know."

Sabine and her family were extraordinarily close, and at the beginning of our relationship, I'd been consumed by an emotion I could only call envy. My parents died when I was five. I was an only child and my aunt who'd raised me had died eight years ago. Then the Fleischers began to treat me like a daughter, and that envy turned to love and an overwhelming sense of acceptance.

Jana ate most of her slice then set it down with her eyes half-closed and her mouth still quirked into a smile. After a mouthful of champagne she said, "You know she's been sending me emails this whole time making sure that I've been taking care of you." Those last four words were accompanied by air quotes. "I wonder if she's going to make me give her a detailed report."

I swallowed quickly and laughed. "I know. I've been getting the same. Except mine are more along the lines of 'is Jana taking care of you?'"

"Ugh, she's such a control freak," Jana complained. After a moment she seemed to collect herself, and grew serious. "But… she's way different with you than I've seen her with anyone else. Protective of you and of your place with us. You do belong with us, Bec." After a decisive nod, she let calming silence envelop us.

I stared into my champagne flute. Protective. I was eight years older than Sabine and logically, I should be protecting her. It didn't feel as though I'd done a very good job of keeping her safe. Before I retired from the Army I'd broken so many rules to be with her. Then I'd sent her on the errand that led to her being hurt. And I hadn't been able to *protect* her from having to redeploy when she was clearly still struggling with PTSD.

Every time we'd Skyped during our time apart I'd wanted to weep. She'd insisted that going back to where it'd happened would help her move on, to let her see that it was just a place, nothing more. And I'd disagreed, but only once out loud because her jaw had set into that stubborn line of insistence I knew so well.

Over the past months I'd watched helplessly as the angles in her face grew more pronounced, the shadows under her eyes darkened and the defeat in her voice became more prominent. And I knew being over there was doing the opposite of what she'd thought it would. But there was no pleasure in my being right this time. The only thing I'd had to hold on to was that when she came home, she could begin to heal again, away from at least one stress. Another step closer to her completing the contract that exchanged med school for seven years of service still tying her to the military. In less than two years she'd be done.

Jana stared at the pizza box then pushed it aside. "How's work?"

The question drew me away from my introspection. "The wrong side of hectic." I didn't mind. Being busy helped keep my mind away from the loneliness.

"Anything exciting happening?"

"The usual gunshots, stabbings and car accidents. Oh, actually no, I did have something interesting today. An MVA where the steering wheel broke and the impact threw the driver forward onto the column. It was still embedded in—"

"No! I don't want to know." Both her hands came up palms out, fingers splayed wide in the biggest STOP gesture she could make. "I'm sorry I asked."

I smiled into my champagne. "Almost got it past you." Jana hated gore and it had become a game to see how much detail she'd listen to before cutting me off. I also hoped that telling her some of the realities of the people passing through my trauma unit might scare her into moderating her driving a little—she'd look right at home on an Indy 500 track—but after all this time, it seemed a lost cause.

The MVA *was* an interesting case. It'd taken me and my team hours to remove the shaft then repair the damage, and I'd thought how much I would have liked Sabine's steady hands working alongside mine. We often spoke about our cases during this deployment, and if I'd wanted to I could pretend it was just like when we actually worked together. Almost…because being without her was a constant dull ache that no amount of make-believe would ever dispel.

After Jana and I finished dinner and cleaned up, we relocated to the den to watch mindless television and talk about mindless things. The date she had tomorrow night, Sabine's homecoming, whether Jana really needed a dog. Most of the bottle ended up in my glass and when nine o'clock rolled around, Jana stretched, her toes pointed like a dancer. Her nails were still the delicate pink from our day at the spa last week. "I'd better get home."

"Not staying?" She had a room here in case of emergencies. Like too much wine.

"Ugh, no. I wish I could, but I need to file a brief tomorrow and if I stay here we're going to open that expensive bottle of scotch you're saving for Sabbie." Jana sprung to her feet and wasted no time putting her heels back on—they really were very nice—and gathering her coat, handbag and briefcase in a whirlwind.

"You know all you need to do is come around, and you can share it. Maybe we can open it up this weekend. The three of us." The thought made my stomach flutter with excitement. We were so close to normality.

"Mhmm, sounds good." Jana flicked the collar of her coat up. "I guess she'll call me when she's settled."

"I'm sure she will." Probably before she'd settled if I knew Sabine. I wouldn't be surprised if she asked me to stop at her sister's office in the city on the way home from the base. The thought of being in a car, doing something as mundane as driving with my girlfriend sent another surge of excitement through me.

"I can't wait to see her," Jana said quietly, pulling open the door.

"Me either…" In the open doorway, I embraced her tightly. "Thanks for coming over. Drive safely."

"Will do. I'll talk to you guys really soon!" Jana released me with a cheerful, "Love you."

"Love you too."

She squeezed my shoulders then strode to the brand-new silver Mercedes she'd only had a month, parked in the driveway. Clearly, messy divorces did pay well. When she'd reversed out and driven away at her usual terrifyingly excessive speed, I went back inside to tidy up.

I ran a cloth over the counter, lingering and smiling to myself as my thoughts flickered briefly to the first night I'd been here, two years ago. Before that, for over eighteen years, I'd worked within an institution that made me suppress a part of myself and I'd always felt pride in my discretion and incredible willpower. Then the first time we'd operated together, Sabine had torn it all down with a lame joke and a sheepish, helpless look.

She'd slowly stripped away every bit of self-control I had until I'd broken down, acted against protocol and come to this house during recreation leave. When I'd knocked on Sabine's door it wasn't as her superior officer, but as a woman wanting a lover. We'd danced around the inevitable until I'd shed my clothes, hopped onto this very counter, opened my legs to her and begged. We'd devoured each other for most of the night and the next day, and every day we'd been together since only strengthened my conviction that I'd done the right thing for us.

After one last check to make sure the house was locked up, I turned out the lights and climbed upstairs. The champagne had dulled me to a pleasant sort of inebriation and I wondered if I might actually fall asleep in a reasonable amount of time, rather than lying awake thinking of everything I had to do the next day. It was wishful thinking. I'd always been prone to insomnia—a consequence of being on call—but with Sabine away it had increased. I'd been subsisting on around four hours a night, supplemented with naps in on-call rooms.

I pulled on one of Sabine's old tees and climbed under the covers. After an hour, I was still running through mental lists. Finish cleaning the house, grocery shopping, brush the cat and make the bowtie I was going to sneak onto him, plan meals. The other side of my insomnia was because I hadn't heard from her in a few days. I knew firsthand how hectic the last days of deployment were but still, I worried.

Rationally, I knew that if something had happened, we'd have been notified. I'd made that exact call to her parents and my stomach still churned whenever I thought about it. Even more rationally, I knew that the chance of Sabine, a member of AMEDD, the Army Medical Department, being involved in anything dangerous was unlikely. She'd already defied probability once. Twice was unthinkable.

I closed my eyes and pictured the moment when Sabine would be back in our house. A pleasant warmth bloomed in my chest, spreading through my body and bringing a comforting lightness. I relished the thought of just being able to *breathe* again. Her return wasn't even about the physical side of her being here, though I missed intimacy more with every passing day.

I couldn't wait to see her face, to reacquaint myself with her features and learn those new things that would have changed, which would be almost imperceptible to anyone else. To watch her long eyelashes cast shadows over those glorious cheekbones, and the freckles spreading to the straight bridge of her nose. After so much time where we couldn't acknowledge what we wanted, and having spent so little time together, I still marveled at the physicality of her. Everything symmetrical and proportionate. Knowing Sabine and her demand for self-perfection, she'd probably spent her time as a fetus forcing her body to grow with straight angles and complementary features.

I couldn't help reveling in her lithe, strong body. To let myself be lost in eyes so dark they were almost black. To enjoy the touch of her hands, a little larger than mine and always punctuating the air when she spoke. I could spend hours kissing full lips, so frequently lifted in a smile or a grin, and listening to her deliciously husky voice. I never tired of running my tongue over her small breasts or the tightly muscled planes of her body.

If I loved the physical, then I worshipped her intellectual and emotional aspects, all that simultaneously pleased yet confounded me. I would spend my life studying her, trying to work out the intricacies that made her *her*, and I'd never grow tired of it. She could be so serious and strict, and then turn around and laugh or joke about something most people wouldn't find funny. Sabine held herself to impossible standards, but forgave almost every shortcoming in those she held close. She was a perfectionist in every aspect of her life and I loved her more than I could ever put into words.

I loved the way she'd appear seemingly out of nowhere to ask me something or just tell me of something funny she'd just seen. Her intricate stacking of the dishwasher and how she'd give me that look when I stacked it *wrongly*. The way she always parked her car against the garage wall with millimeters to spare so I'd have plenty of room for mine. Her one-sided conversations with the cat. Her laughter. I opened my eyes again, imagining that sound. Without it, the house seemed empty and stale.

At FOB Invicta Military Hospital in Afghanistan, despite us living and working in the worst of circumstances, I'd rarely had a day without hearing her laugh or make a joke—always dry and quick-witted. I would hear her distinctive voice and laughter bouncing through the barracks or hospital as I sat in my office, and the sound would have me stop what I was doing to listen until she was out of earshot. And I'd wish that I knew what had fueled her mirth, or even more pathetically, I would wish it was me making her laugh.

A low throb in my depths brought me back to the present and I considered sliding a hand under the sheet. But I didn't want that impersonal solo release, not when she'd be home so soon. I pushed my remembrances aside and shifted my focus to tomorrow. Clean the house, change the sheets, buy groceries, mow the lawn, choose lingerie…

When I woke, I couldn't figure out what had roused me, but after lying quietly for half a minute, the reason became terrifyingly clear. In the still night came the unmistakable sound of movement downstairs. Soft, steady footsteps made their way up the stairs and along the hallway. I fumbled on the bedside table for my glasses and reached for my phone, thumb playing over the screen to unlock it. 11:16 p.m.

The gun, locked in our closet safe, was no more than ten steps away but it might as well have been ten miles. We had been a gun-free household, but Sabine insisted that while she was gone I should have a handgun for protection. Given her overall anxiety, I acquiesced. After my time in the military I was more than comfortable with firearms. D.C. was much safer than it used to be, and I never actually expected to have to use one in this capacity.

I flung the covers aside, slid stealthily from the bed and started backing quietly toward the closet. The footsteps paused, then the partially-open bedroom door cracked open further. Despite my panic, and my thumb readying to dial 9-1-1, I couldn't help myself, whispering hopefully, "Jana? Is that you?"

The door opened further and a dull thud of something being dropped on the wooden floor echoed through the room. "Almost, but not quite."

I would have known that voice anywhere. In my dreams or awake. Under water, from across a desert or crowded room. Most importantly, I knew it from where it spoke fifteen feet away. The light flicked on, illuminating the best thing in my life.

She was dressed in her ACU, and though she would have been traveling for at least twenty-four hours the combat uniform was immaculate. Her smile was both cocky and shy, and her dark eyes studied me with intensity. She rubbed the back of her neck, then raised her hand in an uncertain gesture. "Hey, honey. I'm home."

It took only two seconds to cross the room and the moment I was in reach, Sabine grabbed me and pulled me against her body. I let out a choked sob, wrapping my arms tightly around her waist as she held me. God how I'd missed her hugs. She loved hugging, and hugged hard and with her whole body, like she was trying to transfer love through osmosis. I buried my face in her neck, unable to stop the tremor in my arms. Her grip eased fractionally before she bent her head to kiss me.

She tasted like her spearmint gum, smelled exactly the way I remembered and felt like the safest place I'd ever been. I couldn't hold her close enough, couldn't touch enough of her and couldn't quite believe she was really here. "Why didn't you tell me you were back today?" I asked through my tears.

She pulled away slightly, wiped the moisture from under my eyes and grinned a trademark Sabine grin—a little crooked, and so bright it was like the world had been in shadow before. "I wanted to surprise you. I'm sorry it's late and you're already in bed." Her normally husky voice was even rougher with an edge of gravel, breaking on words the way it always did when she was tired.

I laughed through my tears. Of all the things to apologize for. With my hands running up and down her arms, I soothed her. "It's okay, sweetheart."

"And I'm gross. I haven't showered since I left Afghanistan, and I was going to get flowers, but I couldn't find the right ones." She was over-explaining, trying to justify why she wasn't here at the time or in the way she'd wanted. It was *so Sabine*, trying explain what she deemed a lack of perfection and being blinded by the fact that all I cared about was that she was here. "And I—"

"Darling, I don't care. I don't care if you haven't showered or brushed your teeth or hair or whatever. I love you, and I am so happy you're here." I took her face in my hands and kissed her again.

Sabine reached up to grasp my wrists gently, the way she always did when I held her face and kissed her. This simple familiar action brought a fresh round of tears. Kissing her felt like that first sweet intake of breath after leaping into a pool. As she held me, kissed me softly, I realized how relieved I was at her sudden appearance. If I'd had time to think and prepare all day tomorrow and the next morning, I would have been nervous about how to interact with her. About what to say, what to do. This was pure instinct.

Her forehead rested against mine, her voice thick with emotion. "Bec, I have spent the past ten months thinking of what I would say to you when this moment finally happened and now I can't fucking remember any of it." Sabine shrugged helplessly and her voice wavered. "Except that I love you. And I've missed you so much."

"Me too," I managed to say around the hard lump in my throat.

"Look at me." Sabine lifted my chin with a forefinger, her eyes shining with unshed tears. "I love you," she said again. Then her lips were on my neck and my cheek before they found my mouth again. We kissed like kissing was sustenance. We kissed like being together was the only thing keeping us alive. Now that she was home, and in my arms—it was.

CHAPTER THREE

Sabine

The blaring alarm jolted me from deep sleep. Incoming casualty alert! Adrenaline tightened my stomach, the anticipation of hours of surgery displacing my lingering just-woken grogginess. At any moment, a message would blast across the base calling the FOB personnel to attention.

But it never came.

Grasping the sheets in tight fists I sat up, battling my confusion. The bed was too big, the sheets too soft and the duvet thick and warm. And I was naked. I cast a panicked gaze around the sunlit room until my eyes fell upon the dresser with photographs lined up neatly atop it. My sister and parents. That photo I loved of Bec and me at my cousin's wedding last summer. Vacations in California and Canada. Titus in cute cat poses.

Home. You're home, Sabine.

The car alarm down the street shut off abruptly, but the discomfort of waking up in a strange place remained. I gave myself a mental wrist slap. The bed you share with your girlfriend is not a strange place. An exploratory hand to my right told me the bed was empty of said girlfriend. Unsurprising at…shit, almost nine thirty in the morning.

I rolled over and buried my face in Bec's pillow, breathing in her scent. Almost immediately my discomfort dissipated. All those months away, I thought I'd remembered the way she smelled, looked and sounded in the flesh. But memories were nothing compared to the real thing, to seeing her and touching her. Kissing her.

Last night came rushing back. After I'd finally come in a little after eleven, I'd taken a long, soothing shower before Bec took me to bed. Hot, frantic foreplay had promised even hotter sex but for the first time ever, I'd felt disconnected from it. Disconnected from *her*.

I'd wanted her so much, and my body responded with exactly the same excitement it always did, yet something in my brain kept glitching. I just couldn't get past how scared I was. Scared she'd find my scant, hard post-deployment body unattractive, scared she hadn't missed me that way and was just humoring me. Scared that I wouldn't be able to climax because I was so worried about everything. Just…scared.

I'd never had this issue coming home before. After my first deployment when I was still with my ex, we'd barely made it through the door before clothing was removed and hands and lips were on skin. But that relationship was so different to the one I had with Bec, so surely it wasn't unreasonable to expect this homecoming to be different too? Surely there wasn't anything wrong with *us*. It had to be me, my issue, because Bec seemed the same as always.

I wondered if she'd known there was something not quite right. With my face still in her pillow I replayed last night, lingering on each look and touch, the needy words whispered with urgency, Bec sliding down my body to—

Wait.

Bec sliding down me to…to…

I drew a complete blank.

Oh shit. I hadn't, had I? I sprung from bed, hastily pulled on clothes, snagged my Uggs from my still-unpacked kit bag and rushed downstairs. "Bec?"

The cat regarded me warily, sprinting down the hallway the moment I got close. No big deal, Titus. I'm only the one who rescued you from the shelter, you ungrateful shithead. The kitchen and dining room looked much the same as they had when I'd left, except now we had a different fruit bowl and complicated-looking toaster. New photos on the fridge, mostly ones Mitch had taken of me in scrubs or uniform *over there*. Clean dishes in the drainer and the half-full coffee pot on its warmer told me she was here. Somewhere.

"Bec?" I tried again, a little louder this time.

She emerged from the den and I felt the familiar quickening of my heartbeat that happened when I saw her for the first time each day. The emotion intensified, filling my chest until I thought I might choke on my love for her. Bec smiled, the same smile she'd given me when she'd come home to me after she'd quit the Army for good. She smiled like seeing me was the best thing in the world.

Bec crossed quickly to me, grasping my soft cotton tee and stretching up for a quick kiss. "Morning, sweetheart. Sorry I didn't wake you. How did you sleep?" She didn't take her hands off me, rather slid them under my shirt to rest against the bare skin on my hips.

I held on to her waist with one hand. "Okay." With my other hand, I grasped the top of my shoulder, massaging the tight, sore muscle. A day and a half of travel and waiting around in cramped spaces was catching up to me. "Except...I totally passed out while we were making love, didn't I?"

Bec's dimples came out when she buried her teeth in her lower lip. "Mhmm," she confirmed, eyes sparkling with mirth. God, I'd almost forgotten how vivid those eyes were, nothing like in our video calls or the photos on my laptop. She'd also had a few inches taken off her hair and it fell midway down her neck instead of to her shoulders, the blond a little lighter and the curl tighter.

You fucking idiot, Sabine, falling asleep on this beautiful woman in the middle of our first intimacy in far too long. Despite my weird not-quite-there feeling that Bec didn't need to know about, she deserved more. At the very least she deserved my *participation.* If I hadn't been such a mental fuckup, I wouldn't have let myself just…check out like that. I pulled my hand from my shoulder. "Bec, I'm so sorry. I had all these plans for me coming home and I've screwed up all of them."

Bec recoiled slightly, frowning. "Darling, come on. You've got to be exhausted, it's fine, really." She twisted me from side to side as if trying to shake me out of a bad mood. "And besides, it was kind of funny. Oh God, oh yes, right there bab— Snore." Her grin was one of genuine amusement, not something just to placate me.

"I'm mortified," I mumbled.

"I know you are." Bec stretched up, wound her arms around my neck and brushed her nose against mine. "But we've got plenty of time to make love. Right now, I want to cook you breakfast and talk and just be with you." Her arms slipped back to my waist, her head coming to rest against my shoulder.

"Sounds great." When I hugged her, Bec made a quiet sound, the same one she always did when I held her. Like a low purr of contentment. How could I have forgotten it? She nuzzled herself under my chin and I dropped my face to her hair, breathing her in.

"There's not much food in the house. I meant to go to the store today to be ready for you tomorrow," Bec said against my tee. She meant it as an explanation and it was completely without malice or judgment, but I still felt a pang of contrition.

Silently, I chastised myself. Should have told her I was coming back. Shouldn't have just sprung it on her. "Whatever's here is great, honey."

"Pancakes?"

"Sounds perfect. Thanks."

Bec drew back, her hands moving to my stomach. Slowly, she stroked my skin, as though relearning how my body felt. One hand stayed on my waist, the other cupped my cheek as she kissed the edge of my mouth. The press of her lips was brief and chaste then she stepped away and backed toward the kitchen, pulling me along with her.

Bec poured coffee and added exactly the right amount of milk before passing the mug over with a smile. When I tried to help, I was swatted away playfully and shooed back toward the table. But I didn't want to sit and watch her waiting on me. I wanted to get in there the way I always did, sharing cooking and then cleaning up afterward. Or to press myself against her back with my arms around her waist while she stirred something on the stovetop. I settled for watching from the other side of the counter while she started pancakes from scratch.

Bec unscrewed the lid from the flour jar. "How many do you want?"

"Maybe two?"

She added a couple of scoops of protein powder to the batter then resumed her careful mixing. I made myself set aside my discomfort and accept that she was doing that because she cared, not because she didn't like how I looked. Even before we were together, when she was my boss, I'd known Bec was motivated by concern and a genuine need to help people. She did things like add weight-gain powder to my breakfast because losing eleven pounds on a ten-month deployment is not healthy.

I watched the play of muscles in her forearms as she stirred, and my gaze inevitably drifted to her face and the concentration crease between her eyes. I'd always loved that expression, the one she wore during surgery or signing reports or getting rid of lumps in pancake batter. Bec looked up, saw me watching her and smiled. "What?"

"Nothing. Just…happy to be home, here with you." Bracing my hands on the countertop, I hoisted myself up and with feet dangling off the floor, leaned over to kiss her.

The bowl clattered as she lowered it to the counter without breaking the kiss. Our tongues met with gentle reacquaintance, the kiss soft and unhurried until she let out a low groan. Bec spoke quietly against my lips, "Are you going to climb all the way over here and finish what you just started?"

"Maybe." I pulled back slightly, swallowed against my suddenly dry mouth and glanced over Bec's shoulder. "Looks like the butter in that frying pan is about to start smoking."

She regarded me for a moment, then picked up the bowl and stepped over to the stove. Bec raised the bowl, swirling it slightly as she poured batter. She leaned over to grab a spatula from the hooks on the side of the cupboard. "Peanut butter and banana?"

"Sounds great." I slid around the counter to fetch ingredients but Bec brandished the spatula like a sword.

"Stay," she said playfully. "Let me take care of you?"

I nodded my assent and leaned against the counter while she finished the pancakes—overcooked to almost burnt, just how I liked—then smeared peanut butter and sliced a banana over them. "Syrup?"

"Yes please." I could have cringed at the polite deference in my voice. This was so damned awkward, almost like the morning after a one-night stand.

Bec gathered cutlery, carried my breakfast to the table and set it down, placing the knife and fork on either side of the plate. The wrong way around. I frowned. She'd *always* set the table back to front for me because I'm a lefty. After a beat, Bec shook her head, a low chuckle slipping out as she swapped the knife and fork. And I wondered who'd been sitting in my chair.

I dismissed the intrusive and insulting thought and made myself smile. "Thank you, honey. This smells fantastic."

Bec sat opposite me and drank coffee while I ate. She didn't stare exactly, but every now and then I felt her calm observance. The silence between us lengthened into the uncomfortable, strained kind. "This coffee seems different," I said, just to break the quiet.

"Jana's had a few dates with a guy who owns a roasting company. He gave her a bunch of free bags." Bec's fair blond eyebrows rose. "You don't like it?"

"No, I do." I set down my fork. This stilted, polite exchange was so absurd that I couldn't help but laugh. "This is weird, right? It's not just me?"

The lines around her eyes appeared a moment before her dimples. "It is weird."

"Okay, good. Well...not good." I exhaled some of the tension from my body and pulled out the chair to my right. "For starters, why don't you come sit here."

Bec slipped around and sat beside me, shuffling the chair so she was inches away. "Like this?"

"Much better."

The mood eased a little when she kissed me, and then further when she moved her hand to rest on my thigh. We talked, we snuck kisses, she stole a piece of pancake from me and she never once uttered my most hated question: *How are you doing?*

We cleaned up together and the moment her hands were free, she pressed herself to me in another tight hug. "I'm so glad you're back, darling."

"Me too." I kissed her temple, then down her neck until my face was nestled against her shoulder. Her shirt smelled different. "New laundry detergent?" I mumbled. Eucalyptus now, and the change made me unexpectedly uneasy. Something simple, but a decision made without me. I shoved the thought aside to sit with all my other absurd ones.

"Yes."

I pulled back. "It's nice. You changed your hair too, I really like it." Studying her, I allowed all the tiny details that become fuzzy after so long away to come into focus. "All those months with nothing but photos and video calls, I feel like I was blind. You're so beautiful, Bec."

She smiled, obviously pleased. She'd always been better than me at taking compliments. "Thank you." Bec thumbed the edge of my mouth. "What do you want to do today?"

"Whatever. What did you have planned?"

"Housework, grocery shopping, getting ready for you to come home. When do you have to go back for processing?"

"Monday. They confirmed it'll only be a week." I hated that I was almost but not quite over the deployment yet. Instead of being able to take some time off work, we had to attend briefings, debriefings, screenings, evaluations and all that crap before they let us take vacation time. At least it was short, and we wouldn't be sequestered on base for the duration like some combat units.

"Not so bad. We have four whole days together then. I was talking to some friends last week, and they said the new medical center is great, but traffic is awful during peak times and staff parking even worse."

"Good to know, thanks." I knew what she was implying. That I should take the bus or Metro instead of driving. Not an option. Not these days. Besides, my new duty station was only six miles from my previous one.

"I'm sure you'll figure it out." Without warning, her expression changed to mild panic. "Shit."

"What?"

"I just remembered I've got our final football game tonight. I thought it'd be okay because you weren't due back until tomorrow." The crease between her eyebrows appeared momentarily. "It'll be fine. I'll call Gayle and let them know I can't make it. I've skipped a few games this season because of work, they'll be able to find a sub."

"Babe, no, don't cancel. You've been busting your ass all season and the team needs you." Bec had missed our weekly flag football games so much she'd joined an all-women's league back here in D.C. "Know what? I'll come watch and cheer you to a resounding victory. Actually, it'll be great to watch you from the sidelines rather than sneakily checking you out between plays while I'm on the field."

Bec feigned shock. "Checking me out, you pervert! For that, you can sub in for us when we're losing."

"I'm a bit rusty," I deadpanned.

Her laugh was low and amused. "Oh, sure. It's been what…a week since you last played?"

"Not even." I grinned facetiously. "We had a game the morning we left."

"Whose team won?"

"Mitch's, but he cheated. Asshole."

She laughed. "God I've missed you. Are you sure? I kind of imagined we'd just lock ourselves away for a while after you got back."

"Well…we can do that if you'd like." An uneasy twinge in my chest made me want to frown and I forced myself to tease and be light. "You'd probably be sick of me and have cabin fever after a few days."

Bec craned her neck to look up at me in the way that was so achingly familiar. "Hardly. I'll never be sick of you, Sabine. Are you glad to be home?" The question was tentative and it made me realize I hadn't shown much enthusiasm since arriving last night.

"More than glad." I grinned. "But ask me again once I've listened to three hours of Mom complaining that I didn't call her as much this deployment as I did the last." Because once a week plus two or three emails apparently isn't good enough.

"Good, because *I'm* glad you're home." Her kiss started gently but the way she teased my lips apart with her tongue, and the scratching of her nails on my back left me with no doubt as to what she wanted. She pulled back slightly. "Do you want to come take a shower with me?"

"I...thought I might—" I swallowed, ran my tongue over my teeth and tried desperately to not look like I was stalling. Bec tilted her head, her eyes both gentle and appraising. She knew. No matter how hard I tried to hide, she always knew.

"You look a little tired, sweetheart," Bec said eventually. "Are you sure you slept okay?"

Maybe I did look tired, but I wasn't too tired to make love to my girlfriend for the first time in ten months. Especially after my failed attempt last night. I wanted her so badly, but there was still a stupid persistent *nope* in my brain. It was something that kept short-circuiting that final thing that'd allow me to let go and just...fuck her.

We'd always fit together that way, frequently unable to make it into the bedroom, or even the house before we were tearing one another's clothes off. So many times I'd taken her in the garage, on the hood of a car, unable to wait a moment longer to taste her, to hear those gasps of pleasure. Now, all I felt was an anxiety that I couldn't pinpoint. And she was giving me an out and telling me in not so many words that it was *okay*.

"Mmm, I slept fine." In between the familiar nightmares that is. I unclamped my teeth from the ragged skin inside my cheek. "I, um, just need to call Jana and let her know I'm back."

"Of course. I'll leave you to it." She kissed me again and left the kitchen, heading back toward the den.

Upstairs, kneeling on the bedroom floor, I fumbled in my backpack for my phone charger. Instead of hard plastic, my fingers brushed against soft velvet. I pulled the small box out and whispered, "I had such great plans for you last night."

Talking to an inanimate object. Nice one, Sabine. Quickly, I opened the safe in our closet and locked the small box away, hidden behind Bec's gun, the magazine sitting on top of a box of ammunition and another velvet box containing the medal that signified one of the worst days of my life.

I plugged my phone into the socket beside my nightstand, sank down to sit on the floor and called my sister. She answered after a few rings. "Jana Fleischer."

The pure sound of her voice, untainted by poor-quality satellite and video calls, made my eyes prickle. "Jannie, it's me."

"Sabs! Hang on." A toilet flushed, and a stall door banged open. Over the sound of running water, my ever-charming sister asked, "Where are you? Are you guys in Qatar already? When're you landing? Could you please pass me some paper towel, thanks!"

Clearly the last statement was meant for someone in the ladies' room, not me. "I'll be there around eight thirty tonight."

"You're early, that's fucking incredible! Bec's still coming to get you right?" A door creaked open.

"Nah. I'll drop by your place at eight thirty, like I just said."

"You're landing at eight thirty?" Quick footsteps of heels on the polished wooden floors of her office accompanied her words.

Was I speaking a different language? "I'm in my bedroom in D.C. right now," I enunciated with exaggerated slowness. "We landed yesterday. Bec and I will be at your place tonight, at eight thirty, after her football game."

My sister squealed. Loudly. In my ear. Muffled apologies followed, presumably to the inhabitants of her office who just got an earful. "You sneaky bitch. Bring dinner if you're coming around. I'll cancel my date. I love you." And then she hung up.

Smiling at my sister's outburst, I set my phone on the side table to continue charging. Some things never changed and I was eternally grateful for that. I needed that stability, now more than ever. Staring at my hands, I traced one of the faint shrapnel scars on the back of my right wrist. I could only hope that deep inside where it mattered, I was as unchanged as everyone else in my life.

* * *

I drove Bec's Audi while she directed me to the fields where they played football every Thursday evening. Moments like this—letting me drive her treasured convertible—were when I felt an extra swell of love. And relief. Bec adored driving, but she handed me her keys as a matter of routine and settled comfortably in the passenger seat.

After the first time I'd asked if I could drive and explained why, she'd accepted it without comment. Since The Incident, the lack of control as a passenger was uncomfortable to the point of unbearable, and being in the backseat was out of the question. Whenever I'd had to get in a vehicle during the deployment, I'd puked. I only managed yesterday morning without a freak-out because of Mitch, Amy and diazepam.

There was a faint whistling sound near my ear, as if the car's top wasn't fully locked into position and wind was sneaking in somehow. I ran a forefinger along the seam between the window and the soft-top, trying to find the spot.

Bec leaned closer, head cocked, looking at my hand. "What's wrong?"

"I hear something," I said, still probing with my fingertips. Nothing felt out of place, but the sound was definitely there.

She leaned over further. "I don't hear it."

"Mmm." Suddenly self-conscious, I withdrew my hand. "Have you played this team before?" I asked, more for something to say to shift the focus away from me and my apparent auditory issues.

"Twice. We've won and lost one each. They're good but their defense is weak." Bec twisted sideways to grin at me. "Easy to slip through."

"Well, when you're as slippery as you are…" I took my right hand off the wheel and let it rest on my thigh, palm up.

Bec took my invitation, sliding her hand onto mine and lacing our fingers together. "Have I told you recently how much I love you and how excited I am that you're home?"

I pretended to mull it over. "Maybe once or twice."

"Mmm, I need to do better then."

"Maybe you do," I teased. I made my two-minute sweep of my surroundings, knowing even as I did it that it was totally unnecessary. There are no insurgents about to shoot at the car, Sabine. While deployed, my job as surgeon had me behind the wire in the relative safety of an FOB hospital, not on patrol in *real* danger. So why did I need to be so vigilant? I just couldn't help myself. Stupid Incident.

Bec pointed with her free hand. "Turn up here."

I pulled in and parked where she indicated, and while Bec retrieved her gear from the trunk I examined the roof. The whistling was real. I'd heard it. I wasn't imagining things. But the soft top seemed fine, not warped or bulging. Still, I'd arrange to have the car checked out.

"Sabine? Are you ready?"

"Yep. Let me take that." I shouldered her gym bag and walked with her across the gravel parking lot toward the fields. There were three, and on each, groups of women had massed— some running slow laps around the outside, and others talking or stretching. The flood lights were coming to strength, the low buzz an uncomfortable background noise that made my teeth feel strange.

Bec led me to a group of women in bright yellow and red striped jerseys the same as hers, and I stood awkwardly while they greeted one another. Most of them looked my way, but none acknowledged me with anything more than an appraising glance. I stood slightly to the side and behind Bec, suddenly aware of how out of place I was.

This was another thing that'd crept up on me, a discomfort in my own skin. I felt like my body didn't belong to me and I didn't know what to do with my hands. They felt strange, as if they should be holding surgical instruments, or a weapon, or doing something productive the way they usually were. I tried putting them in my pockets, then crossing my arms and tucking my hands into my armpits. Eventually I just let them hang by my sides, wooden and useless.

Bec tugged me forward and I smiled politely as she introduced me to the group of six women, whose names I knew I'd never remember. My girlfriend finished with a proud, "She only came home last night."

Baby Butch…uh, Charlie, stuck her hand out and as she shook mine vigorously, said, "Well! We were starting to think Becky made you up to stop Gayle from asking her out every week."

Becky? Nobody called Rebecca that. I forced another smile. "Actually I'm just an actress she hired." Nice one, Sabine. Put a dollar in your *think before you blurt stupid shit* jar. Current balance? Somewhere in the millions.

Bec laughed, the way she always did when I said something fatuous, and after a moment the other women joined in. They probably thought I was mentally deficient. Stocky Brunette turned to Bec and said, "So she's been home for less than twenty-four hours and you dragged her out to watch your sorry ass, Granny? Thought you wouldn't leave the bedroom for a week."

I ignored the suggestive comment and bristled at the nickname Granny. The rest of the team were about my age or younger, but Bec's forty-five was nowhere near *Granny*. Bec seemed completely unconcerned by the comment and I told myself I was being sensitive and overbearing. Set it aside, Sabine, it's not important.

Blond Beanpole made no effort to hide her ogling. I bristled again when she drawled, "Christ have I been looking in the wrong places. I'm gonna get me an Army girl."

Even if I'd thought of a response, I wouldn't have been able to get it out around the lump of annoyance in my throat. Bec's soothing hand found my back, rubbing soft circles through my shirt. "If you ask nicely, Gayle, Sabine might be able to introduce you to a friend." She drew me close and stretched up to kiss me, but I tilted my face away from her. And immediately realized my mistake.

Though she didn't say anything, I could see her surprise and the group went suddenly silent. My ears heated, and I forced myself to look up, to acknowledge the other women and what I'd just done. Squeezing Bec's hand, begging her to understand my reaction, I explained, "Sorry. I keep forgetting Don't Ask, Don't Tell is over now. It's…just a force of habit."

The official abolition of DADT was barely three weeks ago, and obviously this was the first time we'd been out together since. In public Bec and I had never been physically affectionate and rarely touched, because you never knew who might see. But now there was no reason for that. We were free. And I suddenly felt the lightness of it like someone releasing a lead weight from around my ankle.

I turned away from the group and their murmurs of acceptance, and took Bec's face in my hands. Her skin was warm, soft and she held eye contact with me. Her expression was unreadable, but when I dipped my head and kissed her I didn't need any help deciphering what she felt. I turned us slightly so my back was to the group, shielding her from their view, kissing her in a way that was not polite in company. And I didn't care. Her hands came to my waist and she stretched up, pressing herself to me.

Someone cleared their throat and Bec smiled against my lips before she pulled away. I stole another quick kiss and took her hand. Leaning down, I whispered in her ear, "Time to break those habits."

CHAPTER FOUR

Rebecca

Sabine woke me with a gentle shake and a not-so-gentle kiss that immediately chased away my sleepiness. I shoved the duvet aside and reached up to pull her back to bed but she carefully disengaged my arms from around her neck. Then I realized it was barely light and she was already dressed. She touched the tip of my nose with her forefinger. "Don't get up, I'm just going out for a run. Didn't want you to wake up and worry."

"How long will you be?"

"An hour, tops."

I wanted to tell her maybe she didn't need to go for a run, that she should climb back under the covers with me and go back to sleep. She just looked so tired, which was understandable given her long flight and the fact we hadn't arrived home from Jana's until well after midnight. But this tiredness seemed to go beyond jetlag and staying out late. Her hollow cheeks were even worse in person than they'd appeared during our video calls, and the ropey muscularity of her body had taken on a worrisome, almost unhealthy leanness. But she wasn't running for fitness—she needed to quiet her gremlins.

So I swallowed my words and used my fingertips to stroke a line from her temple to her chin. "Okay, I'll wait until you get back to start breakfast."

"Sounds great." Sabine turned her head to kiss my palm then loped out of the bedroom, leaving me to stare after her. I tried unsuccessfully to tamp down my worry. Stress and anxiety and guilt made her this way. It made her drive herself into the ground, both physically and emotionally, and nothing short of collapse or someone forcing her to rest would make her stop. That someone couldn't be me, not anymore.

I stretched under the sheet, groaning at the twinge in my hamstrings and the tightness of my lower back. I'd pushed myself harder than ever during the game the night before, and though we'd come away with a win to end the season, I was tired and stiff. And starting to feel like people were right when they said getting old sucked.

In five years I would be on the other side of fifty, and Sabine would be almost forty-three. Regardless of her age, she'd probably never lose that childish, irreverent streak I loved so much. The one that even PTSD hadn't squashed. The one she clung to even as her internal struggles threatened to break her.

My hot rage burned at whoever was responsible for sending her back to a combat zone. There were so many other options, yet some desk general had deemed her fit for service in a place she shouldn't have been. I knew it wasn't unusual, men and women with PTSD were sent on active deployment all the time. In part, it explained the high rate of mental illness experienced by returned service personnel. But they weren't my girlfriend.

My anger simmered to an uncomfortable feeling I'd been unable to push aside since she'd left here all those months ago. The feeling that maybe Sabine hadn't been entirely truthful with those who had determined her fitness. To be *unfit* was to fail in Sabine's eyes and she would hide any indication of her mental struggle as much as she could.

She returned after forty-five minutes and joined me in the kitchen where I was measuring coffee into the machine. In her arms was Titus who had finally relinquished his snippy aloofness at her lengthy abandonment of him. Sabine kissed the top of his head and murmured something I didn't quite catch but sounded a lot like cooing endearments.

I couldn't help smiling. "Admit it, sweetheart. You missed the cat more than you missed me."

"Well…" she drew the word out, smiling widely.

As I swatted at her she laughed, stepping deftly to the side. I started the coffee machine and turned around, lifting my hands behind me to rest against the edge of the countertop. "Sabine? About last night, at the game in front of everyone? I'm sorry, I just got excited. I wasn't thinking."

"No, Bec, *I'm* sorry. It's just ingrained after so many years." She crouched down and poured the cat out of her arms.

"I know." I'd separated from the Army seven weeks after her accident, which had negated any chain of command issues as we began our relationship properly. But despite that, we weren't openly affectionate in public because she was still on active duty, and someone might file a report against her for homosexual conduct.

"But that's all over and done with, so expect to be constantly grabbed and kissed senseless in public."

The thought sent a delicious tingle through my belly. "I look forward to it."

She stalked toward me, her full lips lifted in a lazy grin. "Maybe we need to practice, just to make sure we've got the mechanics down for when someone's looking." Sabine's hot, still-sweaty body curved into mine, pressing me against the refrigerator.

"Maybe," I managed to choke out around my sudden arousal. This was her second day home, we still hadn't had sex, and the anticipation was beginning to wear me down. After her first few gentle refusals I'd stopped trying to instigate it, fully aware that she would come to me when she was ready.

Sabine leaned down, her eyes locked with mine as she came ever closer. But she didn't kiss me. Rather, she lingered with her lips so close that I felt her breath whispering across mine. A thigh gently insinuated itself between my legs and pressed upward until I gasped sharply. Her hand snaked around my waist and pulled me even tighter against her.

She kissed her way along my jaw and down my neck, gently moving my top aside with light fingers to expose skin so she could continue her journey of kisses along my collarbone.

Every time I moved to bring our lips together, she'd carefully angle away, her lips finding another spot to kiss that wasn't my mouth. Her thigh kept up its pressure until I gave in to the sensation and ground down on her. An unconscious moan slipped from my mouth and I felt, rather than heard her quick intake of breath.

When Sabine was in the mood to tease, she was masterful. I'd be dangled over the precipice, then pulled back over and over until I felt I might come apart. Only when I finally gave in and begged her to let me come would she carry me to an exquisite climax. And then dive in to give me another. But she'd never withheld her lips from mine, never denied me kisses, and by doing so now she made me desperate for them.

The anticipation had my nerves firing, imagining what would come after, where she would hold me against the counter or pull me to the floor and take me. Again, I tried to kiss her, but Sabine moved away so my lips landed at the edge of her mouth, and I could feel the smirk at my failed attempt. I gripped a handful of her hair in a light fist. "Kiss me, please," I begged.

She made a low rumble, a sound that wasn't dismissal but certainly wasn't one of acquiescence. And still, her lips skimmed everywhere but near my mouth.

"Kiss me," I demanded this time, my free hand coming to the back of her neck. When I pulled, she held firm, the muscle in her neck tight with resistance.

"Tell me how much you want it, baby," she whispered. "Tell me what you want to do to me...what you want me to do to you."

I was so needy and not too proud to do what she'd asked. "God, you tease," I breathed. "I want you to kiss me. I want to get to my knees and lick you until you come in my mouth. I want you to bend me over the counter and fu—"

She cut me off with a deep, open-mouthed kiss. Just as I'd asked. My hands went under her shirt, nails scratching lightly across her back, and when I stroked her tongue with mine the thigh between my legs jerked. The movement switched the tempo of my arousal from a pleasant moderato to a hard-to-ignore allegro. I grasped the bottom of her tee and pulled it up over her stomach, fingers skimming her belly before dipping to the waistband of her running pants and slipping inside.

Before I found what I wanted, Sabine pulled away, her breathing quick and shallow and her dark eyes stormy. I followed, leaning forward to reclaim her lips but she moved back again, just a fraction, and I read her reaction immediately. It was a stop sign, loud and clear. I felt that part of her wanted this as much as I did but she still wasn't ready, mentally or emotionally or whatever it was she needed. The disappointment was so acute my hand came to my breasts as though I could actually push the feeling aside.

After so long without her, I ached for her touch, but I couldn't force it. The passivity went against my every instinct, but I knew why she was withdrawn and I also knew she would initiate intimacy when she was comfortable. After her accident she'd been exactly the same—frightened she wasn't ready and pulling away whenever things became heated. Then one day, her barriers had fallen and she'd come to me.

Knowing what I had to do, what she needed, didn't make it any easier to accept. Sex was one of our languages and I'd felt like something had been missing in all our communication over the months apart. Even though I knew she was struggling and it wasn't her fault and it wasn't permanent, I still felt cheated. And I was disgusted with myself for feeling that way, for selfishly wanting even when I knew she was pulling away.

Sabine buried her face in my hair. "I'm so sorry, Bec." Her voice was tight, the apology almost strangled. "I'm trying."

My hands soothed along with my words. "I know, sweetheart and it's okay, really." I stretched up and kissed her softly. "Why don't you go shower and I'll have breakfast ready when you come back."

After I heard her light steps along the hallway upstairs, I began to dig out things for breakfast. Underneath the layer of post-deployment awkwardness, I could feel her there, just waiting to thaw a little. This dynamic was different, strange and not one I'd ever had with her, not even when I was her boss. I rested my thighs against the cabinets, palms flat on the countertop and tried to calm myself down.

* * *

After lingering over breakfast, we decided on a visit to the Constitution Gardens and Memorials. Sabine wanted grass and trees and water, somewhere that was as far from the stark, rugged beauty of Afghanistan as she could be. I would have done anything she'd asked, as long as I could be with her.

Because she insisted on driving instead of taking Metro, heavy traffic stretched the trip by an extra fifteen minutes. Then it took almost twenty minutes of looping around the streets before she found a parking space. Her jaw was rigid with tension and it was easy to see her annoyance was based on nothing more than the fact her *issue* had caused a mild inconvenience.

I slipped my hand into hers and by the time we made our way toward the Vietnam Veterans Memorial, she'd settled again and was back to chattering inanely. We spent ten minutes paying our respects to those who'd lost their lives during the Vietnam War—including two uncles she'd never met—and continued along the path, still holding hands. The feeling of being joined to her was so sweet I felt like I might cry. We took our time, stopping at the Lincoln Memorial before strolling alongside the Reflecting Pool toward the World War II Memorial.

Being a Friday rather than a weekend, the crowd was fairly light, which meant we could move around easily. Sabine squeezed my hand before gently disengaging herself. When I committed to moving left around the circular structure, she wandered off to the right. This was the second time we'd visited together and Sabine had done the same thing then too, as though she needed solitude to work through her thoughts.

She came from a military line—her father was a sergeant in Vietnam and his two brothers killed in action. Her grandfather and great grandfather fought in both world wars. For Germany. Sabine was intensely proud of her German heritage, but I knew she had mixed feelings about her grandfather, a conscripted and unwilling infantryman who left his mother country for America the moment he could after WWII. The first time she'd explained her family history, she'd told me tearfully and emphatically, "He wasn't a fucking Nazi, Bec. They *made* him fight against America."

Standing in front of the Freedom Wall, I stared at the thousands of gold stars representing over four hundred thousand Americans who lost their lives in the Second World War. A hand brushed fleetingly over my back and I jerked in surprise.

"It's kinda quiet today," Sabine murmured.

Nodding my agreement, I turned to face her. "Are you ready to keep going?"

"Mhmm."

I pulled out my camera and hung it around my neck, and Sabine was patient while I photographed birds and snuck candid shots of her. We looped around the back of the pond and she paused to tug off her shoes so she could be barefoot in the grass under the grove of maples. I lowered myself to sit in the shadow of a tree, with my legs outstretched. Dimly, I registered people moving on the paths around us, but my attention was riveted to her.

Sabine had always moved like a jungle cat—lithe, graceful and confident. But now her gait was that of someone who couldn't stop moving, with long, quick strides constantly changing direction. She did handstands, walking along on her hands before springing into a series of backflips then rushing off again the moment she'd landed. She'd given up gymnastics as a child but when she was coiled up like this, it was as though she couldn't help herself.

I left her alone, and simply enjoyed watching the way she moved and how she'd turn back in my direction every few minutes as though reassuring herself I was still there. I reasoned that she needed to remember, to reconnect with her life here so she could leave the deployment behind. At the same time, I wondered how long it would take her to equilibrate so our lives could return to some semblance of normality.

After fifteen minutes of frolicking, Sabine came back and stood astride my legs. She bent at the waist, leaning down to kiss me. "What do you want to do about dinner?" Sabine stole another kiss, lingering against my lips. She'd become overly demonstrative, as though making up for all those years we couldn't be.

I let the camera dangle around my neck and rested back on my hands so I could look up at her. "We can do whatever you want. We can cook, we can stay out and get something in the city or order in."

She nodded thoughtfully, knelt beside me and began to wind strands of my hair around her fingers. "Will you make dinner?"

"Of course. What would you like?"

Sabine hopped up again and began to pace around in front of me. "Your chicken puttanesca."

"Sure, I can do that." It was the first thing I'd ever cooked for her, and though Sabine usually had something nice to say about my cooking, she'd never given any indication she was overly enamored whenever I'd made that dish again. I shielded my eyes against the low afternoon sun. "I'll have to pick up a few things on the way home."

"That's fine." She suddenly stopped her pacing, gave me a devilish look and reached into her pocket.

That expression made me suspicious, because it usually heralded mischief. "What are you doing?"

"Nothing." Sabine fished out her phone and held it up to face me. I heard the camera shutter clicking repeatedly. "You look so beautiful with the sun in your hair, that's all." She walked behind me and dropped onto the grass, sliding forward so she was pressed against my back with her legs along the outside of mine.

I rested against her, letting my head fall against her cheek. Despite the cool breeze, she was hot from her gymnastic display, arms damp with sweat as they came around to encircle my waist. Sabine fidgeted, tapping my thighs with her fingertips before she brought her phone around in front of us, arm out to take a photo. I groaned. She knew I disliked selfies, unable to figure out the point of them.

"Photo time, Bec." She chuckled, her fingers now playing lightly over my ribs as I squirmed to get away from her threat of tickling.

"Why? Come on, that's not fair," I complained, but I was already laughing.

"Just one, babe. Please?" She was kissing my neck and tickling me, attacking me from all directions, trying to get me to submit. I stopped moving, hoping that playing dead would stop her. It didn't. "Got you," she whispered in my ear. Her hands came around the front again and she adjusted the phone angle, lifting it just above us. I smiled, and the camera sounded again a few times, finishing as she planted her lips on my cheek.

"That's more than one."

She laughed and wrapped her arms around my torso again, pulling me back against her. Her knees were bent, heels on the ground and she pressed her thighs inward to hold me in place. "I'm going to change all my social media settings to public and post a billion photos of us."

"Only a billion? Clearly you don't love me as much as I thought you did," I deadpanned.

"Geez. Tough crowd. Three billion then."

We laughed together, her arms tightening around me. I placed mine over the top and let everything else fall away until it was just Sabine and me finally together with nothing else in the way. Quietly we watched birds pick worms from the grass and laughed at a toddler trying and failing to throw handfuls of grain for ducks, then panicking as the ducks swarmed around his feet.

"Do you ever miss it?" Sabine asked out of nowhere.

I twisted around to look at her. "Miss what exactly?"

"Being in the Army."

The Army. A career stretching eighteen years and eleven deployments, with countless people under my command. When my aunt died, I'd decided I was a lifer—I would be in the military for as long as I could. There was no family to worry about back home and the lack of a stable romantic relationship didn't bother me. I bounced around from medical centers stateside to the hospital in Germany, interspersed with deployments in Bosnia then Iraq and later Afghanistan.

I had casual relationships that lasted as long as my time at home and I was comfortable with the life, couldn't imaging changing it. Until I met Sabine when she reported at her first duty station, the old Walter Reed Medical Center, fifteen years into my career and just a few days into hers. She drew looks from people without realizing it, and she'd drawn mine almost from the start. The physical pull had been unexpected, unwanted and had brought about immediate panic because I'd never felt that kind of attraction to anyone I worked with. The fact I was her commanding officer only made it worse. The pull of her personality came soon after, and I wondered how the hell I was going to work alongside her without giving myself away.

Not once in my career had I *ever* thought about crossing those lines—the clear line between superior and subordinate, and the even clearer line of Don't Ask, Don't Tell. With her, I thought about it nearly every day and hated my weakness. I'd make excuses to be near her, seek her out for an opinion on a case. Yet even as I did that, I would keep us apart during surgery because I couldn't bear being so close to her and the unavoidable contact. Until the urge would overwhelm me and I would give in and assign her to my team.

I'd heard her video calling with someone back home, someone who was more than a friend and I was consumed by jealousy. Then came the breakup, and her breakdown, and I was disgusted by the small swell of hope that nestled alongside my concern for her. The change between us had happened so quickly that there was no time to think, only act on everything I'd been suppressing.

Would I change it if I could?

I leaned back and rested my head on her shoulder. Sabine's lips pressed lightly against my temple and I exhaled, relishing the closeness. I knew the answer to her question with as much certainty as I knew my own face. "Do I miss the Army? Sometimes I miss my friends and the camaraderie. I miss working with you. But I don't miss not *being* with you."

CHAPTER FIVE

Sabine

Bec and I spent the rest of the weekend doing mundane things like grocery shopping, housework and watching television cuddled together on the couch. The four days felt like nothing more than a cruel teasing promise of our vacation once I'd finished with all the post-deployment stuff. By Sunday evening there was still nowhere near the easiness I'd expected for our reunion, and I couldn't help wondering if the reason I felt so off was just that subconsciously I was still in a deployment mindset, waiting until I could *really* relax.

Before I could test my theory, I'd have to spend the week at work being subjected to boring crap like psych and physical fitness evals, questionnaires and debriefs. To break the tedium, someone would start a betting pool, away from the eyes and ears of our bosses. We'd bet on two things—how long we'd be stateside before deploying again, and also where we'd be sent. I was going to put my money on Landstuhl, Germany, in seven months and thirteen days. It would be my final deployment before I officially finished my contract. Worth putting down at least a hundred bucks.

Monday morning, I left early so I could hopefully beat traffic and find a parking space. I also wanted some time to familiarize myself with the grounds of my new duty station, though I'd already studied the map layout until I thought I'd go cross-eyed. I was the first person in the briefing room a little before 0800, and after a quick internal debate, settled five rows from the back in the fifth seat from the end. Thirty minutes until we began. May as well get a head start on a post-deployment questionnaire. Laptop resting on my knees, I logged in and brought up a health assessment form. Name, Social Security, DOB, Gender, Service Branch, Pay Grade, blah blah. I rushed through a few basic health questions until I got to the portion which was basically *How physically and mentally damaged are you?*

Ever feel like you were in danger of being killed? Yes or no? I moved the cursor between the two, knowing full well the only reason I'd felt that was because of the PTSD. Not a *real* fear. I chose no. Did you encounter dead bodies or people killed-slash-wounded? That was always a weird one, because seeing wounded people and unfortunately sometimes dead people is kind of my job. And dead people are usually the same as people killed. Yes. Did you receive care from combat stress? Yes…

I kept scrolling, clicking answers and filling in details when they asked me to *please explain*. At least this time I could answer *no* to the questions about rocket-propelled grenade, vehicular accident, fragment or bullet wound. Good for me. One hundred percent injury free, unless I wanted to count banging my knees against the end of my bed nearly every time I got up to pee in the middle of a sleep cycle.

Prescription medications? Zoloft, Valium. Have I been bothered by…no, no, no. Menstrual cramps—bothered a lot, please convene a committee to work on that. Noises in head or ears? Yes, some intermittent tinnitus. Becoming easily annoyed or irritable? I, well…a little, sometimes when things weren't set up right in the OR. I blew out a breath. Pretty much all of my *yes* answers related directly to The Incident. Great.

My coworkers were filtering in, and unlike me, seemed to take seats with no thought. Their noisy chatter filled the space and I distractedly returned greetings as I rushed through the rest of the questions. I closed the laptop and set it on the floor just as Amy dropped into the chair beside me. She stretched out her long legs until her feet disappeared under the chair in front. "I'm so fucking glad to be back at work," she mumbled. "Four days and Ethan is already driving me insane."

I turned sideways, slinging my elbow over the back of the chair. "What's up?"

"Usual post-deployment shit. Won't go to bed then won't stay in bed. Won't eat dinner. Won't do his chores. Won't listen to Rick or me. Talking back." Amy rolled her neck, letting out a long breath. "He should settle down in another few weeks but I'm about ready to throttle him."

"Shit."

"Shit indeed. As in, he's being a little shit. Anyways, screw talking about kids. This is my time away from the insanity." She grimaced and grabbed my arm tightly. "God that sounds awful. You know I missed them, Sabs, God I did and I love them so much but it's such an adjustment coming back to that crap. Though at least this time Rick and I are on the same page about how to deal with the misbehaving kid."

Shuffling back in the chair, I crossed my legs. Obviously I didn't have a child acting out back at home, but coming back to a lover and your family had its own challenges. I let out a breath. "You'd think we'd have it all figured out by now."

Amy snorted a laugh. "As if." She side-eyed me. "Things okay with you and Keane?"

"Yeah, you know, kind of awkward but I think it'll start getting better now."

"Everything good in the bedroom?" One of the things I adored about Amy was her utter lack of filters. If she wanted to know something, she asked and if she had something to say, she said it. Her intentions were so uncomplicated that I could never be upset with her, and she was right—a healthy sex life was… healthy.

I smoothed my palm over my thigh. "I uh, we haven't." After a beat, I looked up. "I just don't feel right, you know? Like I *want* to, but…"

Amy bumped me with her shoulder. "Totally normal, love. Ugh, after last deployment I didn't even want Rick to touch me. It was like coming home to a stranger and I was so fucking grossed out. This time he was treating me like a virgin until eventually I just had to tell him to get over it and do it because his pussyfooting around was freaking me out. Being away screws with your head."

"Don't I know it," I mumbled.

"What'd I miss?" Mitch asked breathlessly, climbing over to settle on my other side and elbowing me in the process. I couldn't tell if it was accidental or intentional. Probably the latter.

"Nothing," Amy and I answered simultaneously as Lieutenant Colonel Henry Collings, the CO who'd taken over Bec's job, strode with his usual briskness into the room.

The room quieted as Collings placed a stack of folders on the desk. He turned on the projector. "Morning, team! I hope you enjoyed your time over the weekend with family and friends." Collings was no Lieutenant Colonel Rebecca Keane, but he was still a capable and compassionate leader. I liked him well enough, but I couldn't deny that I missed the warm, safe feeling I'd always associated with having Bec around. Even before we'd been involved, she'd just made things easier.

After a chorus of *Good morning, Colonel* and *Yes, sir!* he smiled and raised both hands. "Right, let's get on with it so I can send you all off for some much-needed leave, and I can head on up to North Dakota for some fishing."

A low chorus of laughter echoed through the room. I opened my new notebook, clicked my pen and stared intently at my boss. Let's get on with it indeed.

* * *

After lunch, on my way to my psych session, I snuck into a bathroom to check my uniform. Only after I'd spent one full minute making sure it was smooth and sitting symmetrically did I start toward the Behavioral Health services building. Almost unconsciously, I began to count my steps away from the building I'd just exited.

One. Two. Three…

Shit. No, no, no, don't do that. But I'd already started and couldn't stop now. Each footfall sounded dully on the concrete, the rhythm perfect. But I didn't feel better for the regularity, I felt like shit because I couldn't help myself and the insistent counting.

…two hundred forty-one, two hundred forty-two, two hundred fort—

Wait. I planted my feet, staring at the building in front of me. The bottom of the concrete stairs seemed roughly five feet away which would be about five steps plus the five going up to the door. Two hundred and fifty-three. That won't do. If I did two huge strides before the stairs I could make it two-fifty.

Two-fifty is an even number, a multiple of five, and also one quarter of one thousand. Or…if I did three slightly big strides before taking the five stairs it would make two fifty-one which is a prime number and that's awesome. Two fifty-seven is also a prime number. No, that's too many steps before the stairs, I couldn't do that without looking really weird.

I slid my tongue over suddenly dry lips, my posture rigid as I stared at the building, trying to rationalize with myself. The longer I waited, the greater the gnawing in my gut, but I just didn't know what to do. Make a choice, Sabine. It's not a goddamned life or death situation. What the fuck is wrong with you?

The door swung open and an unfamiliar lieutenant jogged down the stairs, took few purposeful strides, then came to an abrupt stop when he saw me. He greeted me with a salute. "Good afternoon, Captain."

My right hand automatically found my brow. "Good afternoon."

"Taking a few minutes to enjoy the sun, ma'am?" he asked politely.

I made myself smile. "Yes, indeed. Beautiful day." My toes curled inside my boots and I lifted up on the balls of my feet as though I might stretch the tension from my body.

"It sure is. If you'll excuse me, Captain, I have papers to deliver. I hope you continue to have a pleasant day, ma'am." He snapped another salute, waited until I'd returned it and dismissed him with a nod, then strode off again.

I returned to my dilemma. After half a minute, I decided on two hundred and fifty. Yes, that's a good idea, the number with the most going for it. No, wait. What if that's the wrong choice? Why not just walk into the building like a regular person? But then all the counting would be in vain. I closed my eyes and inhaled slowly, trying to stop the thoughts tumbling around my head. Pinching the skin on the inside of my wrist, I chanted under my breath, "Bec, kittens, skiing, Bec in a bikini, grass."

Just move, Sabine. I took two regular steps forward, intending to just walk into the building—step count be damned. Intending to, until a wave of anxiety hit and I had to stop. Right on cue, pain lanced through my ribs under my right armpit, almost bending me in half. Stand up. Someone's going to notice. Just walk. I sucked in a couple of quick breaths and forced my feet to move.

Two hundred and fifty.

By the time I'd found the correct floor, checked in and taken a seat in the small institutional waiting room the anxiety had eased to an ignorable level. I nodded politely to the other six waiting who all looked as uncomfortable as I felt. A quick glance at my form listed Lieutenant Colonel Andrew Pace as my appointed shrink.

Sitting ramrod straight with my hands curled into loose fists on my knees, I stared at the posters and mental health checklists on the walls. Same shit I'd been seeing since I'd first begun my therapy career. Stuff about PTSD, the importance of self-care, the onus is on you to report any mental health concerns, etcetera.

"Captain Fleischer?" came the call in a calm tenor with a slightly twangy Midwest accent.

I jumped up, brushed myself off and strode down the corridor. The guy in the doorway stared at me over the top of his bifocals, his pale blue eyes at once gentle and appraising. He was about my height, stocky with unruly brown hair just turning gray at the temples. He reached a hand toward me. "I'm Andrew Pace."

I shook it. "Good afternoon, Colonel."

Pace stepped aside to let me pass. "Come on in." He closed the door then gestured to one of the seats against the far wall. "Please sit down. How are you?"

Oh, just fine, all things considered. Like the fact I stood in front of this building arguing with myself about how many steps I should take in order to get inside. I pasted a smile on my lips. "I'm well thank you, sir." I sat where he'd indicated and folded my hands in my lap. On the desk to my right lay a file with my name on it. Clearly doing your homework, LTC Pace.

The chair beside me creaked when he lowered himself into it. "Wonderful. And how are you finding being home from deployment?" He settled the regulation shrink notepad on the arm of the chair, a pen held lightly in his hand.

Straight into it. Typical. "It's an adjustment as always, sir. It's only been a few days, but I believe I'm coping well."

Scribble. "Good. Were there any specific incidents during your deployment that you'd like to discuss?"

"No, sir." Nothing specific, just one great big, ten-month long spell of discomfort really.

"You were seeing a combat stress professional while deployed, is that correct?"

"Yes, sir. Therapy during my deployment certainly helped me continue working through the PTSD." There was no point in hiding it, he would know all about The Incident and the treatment I'd had afterward—both physical and psychological.

Pace raised a brown eyebrow. They were like hairy caterpillars moving across his forehead. "Do you feel the PTSD is affecting you negatively on a day-to-day basis?"

"No, sir. It's been two years and I feel it's mostly under control." Please don't ask about it again, let's move on, I don't want to talk about it.

He made a few more notes. "Any anxiety? Loss of sleep, appetite or sexual desire?"

I nodded and tried to look sheepish, like I was admitting to something embarrassing rather than something debilitating. "A little anxiety, and I have nightmares occasionally." Like every few nights. "Aside from that, no problems with sleep or appetite." I deliberately ignored his question about sexual desire. I hadn't lost any of that, it was something else, something I couldn't nail down that was keeping me from being intimate with my girlfriend.

"Your nightmares. Are they about the event 'specifically, or random fears?"

I straightened in the chair. "Mostly about the event itself, and events directly after." Waking up as I had done post-op when I'd been on a ventilator, but in my dream it wasn't the intubation keeping me from breathing of my own free will. It was Bec kneeling on my chest, hands over my mouth and nose, smothering me. And the only way to make it stop was to rip my hands from their restraints, until I was covered in blood and hurting even more, then hold her down and smother *her* to stop her trying again. I bounced my heels on the floor. Don't think about it. It's not real.

He took almost half a minute to scrawl a few lines. "Would it cause you extreme anxiety to discuss the accident with me?"

I shook my head. "It wouldn't give me pleasure, sir, but we can talk about it if you wish."

"That's fine, Captain. I've read the pertinent details."

I kept my face impassive. Why ask if you don't want— Ohhhh. It's a test. Well, I think you passed, Sabine. I mentally high-fived myself.

The pen didn't still as he fired off rapid questions. "Any changes in behavior that you've noticed? Loss of time? Compulsions or delusions? Hyper-vigilance? That sort of thing?"

Geez, sir, I don't know…does counting steps qualify as a compulsion?

Time to deploy a charming smile and a touch of bullshit. I grinned. "Not unless you count the sudden compulsion I now seem to have to watch awful reality television. All that boredom at home during my recovery seems to have ruined my tastes."

Pace returned my grin. "Your secret is safe with me, Sabine." He paused, studied me. "What about the other issues I just mentioned?"

Goddammit. I'd hoped he wouldn't loop back around. I paused, nodded, then offered him something that was easier to admit, something pretty much everyone who knew me was aware of. "Sometimes I feel weird about being in a car. I have to drive, or at least be in the front passenger seat and I have to keep…checking that nothing's amiss." And there's the vigilance you were asking about, sir.

He nodded. "Does it ever become so overwhelming, or cause you such anxiety that you have to cease what you're doing?"

"No, sir," I answered truthfully.

"What about being in military transports? Any flashbacks to your trauma?"

Fuck. "The transports during my deployment were a little more difficult, but I got through them. And no, not flashbacks as such, but there was anxiety, sir." I moved my lower jaw back and forth, hoping to ease some of the tension. "And sometimes I had additional physical responses. Shaking, vomiting, that sort of thing."

An eyebrow rose. A hand wrote frantically. "What were your coping mechanisms when this happened?"

"Reminding myself that it's not real, that I'm safe and I'm in control. Using my distraction techniques like my five senses lists, or my five comfortable things. Asking my friends to support me." And a whole lot of being really fucking anxious and uncomfortable until I could get myself calmed down.

"Were these techniques successful in bringing you back to the present?"

"Mhmm. Yes, sir." Also not a lie. They *did* work…eventually.

"Good, okay then. Tell me about your support network."

"My parents are in Ohio and I speak with them a few times a week. My sister lives nearby, we're very close and I see her frequently when I'm stateside. And my—" Say it, Sabine, you can say it now. "My *girlfriend* is intimately familiar with the workings of the Army and the stresses of my particular job."

Pace set his pen down and peered at me. Were we off the record? "You served under Don't Ask, Don't Tell, yes?"

"Yes, Colonel." Served and suffered.

"How are you finding things now that the repeal has passed?"

"Well it's only just happened, sir, but I haven't noticed any changes in how my coworkers act around me, or vice versa." Nor had I ever expected to. I cleared my throat. "I'd like to say that for me personally, it feels like I've managed to choke up a massive stone I've been carrying around in my gut for years."

"What do you mean, Sabine? Explain it to me." It wasn't an order, but a gentle invitation.

"I…my previous relationship broke down while I was on the deployment before this one, Colonel, but I couldn't tell anyone. Because that would have broken the rules. And it affected me greatly, affected how I did my job, because all those toxic thoughts had nowhere to go and they kind of built up until it was overwhelming." Almost unconsciously I shook my head, trying to shove the past away, because it didn't matter anymore. "Now, not having to skirt around using *she* or *her*, not having to worry constantly about someone finding out, and being able to tell you that my significant other is a woman rather than lying or brushing aside part of who I am? It's an enormous relief for me. Hiding such a big part of your life like that takes up a great deal of emotional energy, sir."

"I can understand that, and I must say I'm pleased to hear it seems the repeal is having a positive effect as intended." Pace picked up his pen again. "Now, you've been taking medication for PTSD?"

"Yes, sir. I was prescribed sertraline, and also diazepam for use as needed." Prescriptions. Medications. Uselessness.

He scribbled, murmuring, "Zoloft and Valium. Understandable. Does the medication help?"

"Yes, sir."

"What dosage are you taking now?"

"Five to ten milligrams of Valium as required." After a pause, I admitted, "I'm no longer taking Zoloft."

"Why not, Captain?"

An uncomfortable twinge settled in my neck. I could feel myself being maneuvered and there was nothing I could do about it. "Because I didn't feel I needed it."

"Did you cease on the advice of a medical professional, or discuss it with your behavioral health contact while deployed?"

I am a medical professional. Semantics. "No, sir. I didn't," I said quietly. There was no way to make him understand that every time I swallowed my pills I felt like I was swallowing the events of that day and keeping them inside my body.

He took his time writing a few lines of notes. "When and why do you take Valium?"

"Whenever I need it, Colonel, for my anxiety."

"Anxiety." His hand stilled, and he repeated his earlier question. "Do you feel PTSD is having a direct, negative impact on your day-to-day life, Sabine?"

There it was. He'd tripped me and done it masterfully. Well done, sir! Clearly you've done this before. Pace studied me, and the expression reminded me of the way Bec sometimes looked at me, calm and measured. It was a look designed to make you talk, one that held no judgment or accusation. It was a look that had always made me spill my metaphorical guts.

I exhaled lightly, trying to keep it from sounding too much like a sigh. In a quiet voice, I admitted, "Yes, sir. Sometimes I do feel that PTSD is having a negative impact on my daily life."

His expression was gentle and neutral, and when he spoke, the tone was inviting. "Okay then, why don't you tell me about it so we can work on helping you with that."

* * *

After a teasing back and forth because she was still in *Taking Care of Sabine* mode and didn't want me doing anything, Bec started on dinner alone and I trudged upstairs to unpack all my deployment gear. Colonel Pace had been surprised that my bags had remained untouched, and hinted that he thought it a good idea to put my things away so I could begin to set the deployment behind me as well. He was right, but I'd been avoiding it, not wanting to think about my time apart from Bec and the associated anxieties.

I emptied my bag and made piles for laundry and storage. I'd been through this routine a number of times and it was second nature. Some of the stuff, like my portable coffee maker, camera, headlamp and hard drive full of movies and television shows wasn't required until my next deployment and would be put in the spare room closet alongside Bec's old gear and uniforms. The rest was everyday work uniforms, toiletries and the like that I'd need.

Kneeling over the pile of clothing, I counted my ten T-shirts and began to refold and stack them neatly into the laundry basket. The pile grew to six shirts. I pulled one down and stacked others on top to make two piles of five. Better. The rest of my clothes were also made into neat, even piles and when I couldn't evenly split my five long-sleeved thermal tops, I folded the fifth carefully and laid it over the others.

What the hell are you doing, Sabine? Why are you folding shirts that are going to be tossed into the washer? I wanted to tousle them into a rough mess but just couldn't make myself do it. I shoved the basket aside and got to work on my backpack.

In the front pocket was one of my most treasured possessions, a German-language copy of Kafka's *Die Verwandlung*—*The Metamorphosis*. Oma had gifted it to me for my fifteenth birthday and I'd read it more times than I could count. I'd taken it on all my deployments, carried it with me on vacation to Australia, South America, Europe and Asia, and it lived permanently on my bedside table rather than on the bookshelf.

When she was just my boss, Bec had caught me reading it on a few occasions and her expression was always the same. Amusement and what I'd fancied back then as a touch of admiration. Not long after she moved in, she'd found me reading in one of the few comfortable positions I could find for lounging while my injuries were healing—lying upside down on the couch with my back flat on the seat and my legs slung over the rear of the couch.

She'd sat on the floor near my head so I didn't have to move and asked me why I was always reading that same book, and what it was about. And I'd explained to her the story of Gregor, a man who is suddenly and inexplicably transformed into a strange and grotesque insect-like creature. Bec had nodded while I told her how disgusted and hateful his family were, and how annoyed his sister was at being saddled with the burden of this incommunicative monster.

I'd grown more and more excited as I explained—telling her it made more sense in German than English—and she'd watched me with her amused smile firmly in place. What was it about *this* particular book that drew me to it? I'd faltered then, unable to tell her exactly why. It was just something I'd had for so many years, something that was intrinsically connected to who I was. Bec had kissed me softly, then laid her head back on my shoulder while I kept reading, her warm breath caressing my cheek.

The book was worn now, the hardcover cracked diagonally across the top corner and the binding so pliable that the pages felt loose. I opened to a random stained and tattered page, noting with unease that Kafka's masterpiece suddenly seemed to be sitting a little too close to home. Discomfort constricted my breathing as I realized that I was not unlike Gregor. I'd changed completely from the person I was two years ago, undergone my own metamorphosis and certainly not for the better.

I swallowed hard, running my fingers over the text I knew so well.

...Gregor would have realized a long time ago that the coexistence of people with a hideous animal isn't possible, and he would have voluntarily left them...

I slammed the book closed and crossed the bedroom quickly to place it on the shelf. After a moment I pulled it back out and turned it around so the spine was facing away from me. I didn't want to look at the title. Didn't want to be reminded that in the end poor broken, misunderstood Gregor lies on the floor of his room, and out of love for his family, just…dies, so they no longer have the burden of caring for him.

Deadweight. Encumbrance. Strain.

No. I didn't want that, not the way Kafka wrote it, that wasn't me. Despite everything that'd happened, I'd never wanted to check out permanently. But…maybe it would have been better for everyone if I'd moved somewhere else and relieved them of all my problems. The constant emotional and physical needs directly after The Incident, the months of recovery, the PTSD that might eventually dim but would likely never fully go out. Bec, my family, all their lives put on hold for me and what was I doing? Wasting my life wallowing in self-pity.

Fucking stop it. Stop. It. For the second time that day, I pinched the skin of my wrist to reset the negative thought. Kittens, beach, skiing, sunset over the mountains in Afghanistan, Bec.

Bec…

Bec, I think I'm losing myself. No, not losing. Lost. I think I've lost something, and I don't know what it is and I don't know how to get it back. I don't know why I feel so uncomfortable when I think of you making love to me. I need you to help me, but I don't want you to have to help me. My throat was tight with the effort not to cry and I had an overwhelming desire to be near her. To be comforted by knowing that she was there and she loved me.

I rushed out of our room and along the hall. "Rebecca?"

"Still in the kitchen, sweetheart," she called. I forced myself to slow down, to stroll instead of run down the stairs and into the kitchen. Bec glanced up, set down the knife and wiped her hands on a dishtowel. "What's up?"

The words I wanted to say died in my throat. "Nothing," I said and snatched a piece of carrot. "Just need a break from unpacking."

"Understandable." She eyed me speculatively. "Who did you see today?"

"LTC Andrew Pace."

Bec's expression softened. "Oh, that's great. I know him, he's very capable and also just a really good guy." With a grin she added, "Except for an incident involving moonshine he procured while we were in the Balkans in ninety-six. I still don't think my liver's recovered."

I smiled at her anecdote and felt lighter with the knowledge that Bec knew and apparently trusted my new shrink. In a professional capacity at least. "Yeah, I like him." I chewed the inside of my cheek, then made a conscious effort to stop. "I told him, Bec."

"Told him what, darling?"

"That I had a girlfriend, and it felt so fucking good to get that word out at work. *Girlfriend.*"

"Sabine, that's wonderful." Bec's smile came out like the sun from behind a cloud. "I can imagine how much of a relief that must have been." She grasped my hands. "What else did you talk about?"

"Just…the usual stuff. I—" The words I wanted wouldn't come out. I'm struggling, Bec. I need help. I need *you*. Say something, Sabine, say anything. "…have you seen that big plastic box I keep my deployment gear in?"

She tilted her head, her eyes gentle but with a definite question lingering in them. After a beat she said, "It's in the spare room, where it always is. I saw it last week."

"Okay. Thanks. I guess I'll get back to it." I kissed her and backed away, having said nothing of what I'd actually wanted to. You are such a coward, Sabine.

CHAPTER SIX

Rebecca

It was well past lunch and I hadn't had a text message from Sabine all day. Though I wasn't worried, it was definitely odd. During the past four days, she'd texted me at every break—mostly complaining about how busy and boring it all was, asking about my day, what we were doing for dinner, then signing off with a flurry of x's and o's.

The elevator doors slid open, and as I stepped out, someone crossed my path and I had to pull up short to avoid a collision. My abrupt stop caused a pileup, and one of the students with whom I'd shared the elevator bumped hard into my back, sending me flying forward into the person I'd been trying to avoid. Vanessa Moore, a fair and delicately-featured neurosurgeon about my age grabbed my arms to steady me as the student apologized profusely on her way to catch up with the other sleep-deprived bodies.

Vanessa smiled broadly and her contralto voice was amused when she said, "Rebecca Keane. I was just thinking I wanted to talk to you today and here you are." She gently steered me out of the way of a gurney being pushed hastily down the hall. "Maybe I should think about world peace and hey presto, it'll happen!"

Laughing, I straightened my top. Vanessa had consulted on quite a few cases for me and I'd always found her competent, friendly and charming. "How are you? And how can I help?"

"Busy, as usual. Too many things to do, not enough time. I wanted to talk to you about my son, actually. I wonder if I could ask you something?" Vanessa dipped her head to catch my eye. She was about an inch taller than Sabine, perhaps five-nine and with curves to rival Monroe's. Lightly made up, blond hair still perfectly in place despite the hours she'd have been on shift, she even managed to make scrubs look elegant.

"Of course. Is everything all right?"

"Can we walk and talk? I'm on my way to a post-op." At my nod of assent, she continued, "I heard a rumor you were in the Army."

Right away, I knew where this conversation was headed. "It's not a rumor," I said, stretching my legs to keep up as we strode down the hall. "I served for almost two decades. I've been out for two years."

She glanced sideways at me. "And you enjoyed it?"

"Very much so. It's not without challenges, but it's extremely rewarding." I looked up at her and smiled. "Let me guess. Your son has a desire to join one of the Armed Forces."

She pulled a face. "Got it in one."

"What exactly would you like to talk about? Are you unhappy with his decision?"

"Unhappy, proud, terrified, elated." Vanessa shrugged, smiling sheepishly. "The usual mom emotions whenever they say they're going to do something life-changing or dangerous."

"I can imagine that must be a difficult part of parenting."

Both her eyebrows rose. "You don't have kids?"

"No, I've never felt inclined." Thankfully, neither did Sabine. Gently, I directed the conversation back. "Are you worried he won't be able to cope, or are you worried he'll love it?"

"Honestly? A little of both. Rebecca, he's an idealist and I want him to get some feedback from someone who knows how things work, without being bombarded by all the serving and sacrificing-for-your-country rhetoric."

"Of course, I—" My phone vibrated with a text alert. "Excuse me." I glanced at the message. Not Sabine, but Jana asking if we wanted more bags of coffee. Pushing my disappointment and concern aside, I dropped the phone back into my pocket. "My experience was limited by the parameters of my job. There's enough horror behind the wire, but I was never *out there* fighting." I cleared my throat. "Still, we had some uncomfortably close calls." Surgical units were targets, and over the years there had been a number of attacks where I'd been stationed.

"I'm just worried he hasn't thought it through," Vanessa admitted.

"It's a great honor to do your duty for your country, but it isn't for everyone. And there's no shame in that. The military is an institution, a lifestyle, a family and it can be your best friend or your worst enemy. But it teaches you things you never forget, and skills you will always use."

"That part, I like," she mused. "It's the danger part that worries me."

"Understandable. I'd be more than happy to talk to him and give him an overview of how it works, and what he might expect."

She grasped my forearm, pulling me to a stop. "Would you? I'd be incredibly grateful. I'll speak with him and get back to you? Perhaps we could take you to dinner for your trouble."

"Absolutely. I'd like that." After a pause, I added, "What exactly are you hoping I'll say? Do you want him discouraged, or…" I let the question hang.

She seemed surprised I'd even suggested it. "Oh no, of course not. I'd never do that. It's his life but I just want him as informed as possible about what he's getting into."

"Well, I can certainly do that."

We'd reached the doors of the trauma ICU and she turned to face me, one hand on the swinging door. "Can I ask what level you were when you left?"

"My rank? Lieutenant Colonel. Another few years and I'd likely have made Colonel."

Two perfectly-shaped eyebrows arched skyward. "That's fairly high? A leadership type role?"

I made a noncommittal gesture. "Somewhere in the middle. And yes, it is."

"You must really love administration."

"Actually, I do." There was something deeply satisfying about doing the work needed to keep the machine running. Add to that the mother-hen streak that made me want to nurture and support those under me and I was in my element when balancing surgery with leading a group.

"Mmm, better you than me. Running a level-one trauma department is my idea of hell. I don't know how you do it." She paused, then asked quietly, "If the Army is all these wonderful things, why did you leave?"

Tilting my head, I said honestly, "I came to realize that some things are more important to me than a job."

She smiled knowingly and pushed through the door. I stood still for half a minute, mentally setting aside everything but the current necessities. I'd honed the technique early in my Army life, finding it the best way to deal with stress. Despite my best attempt to clear my mind, thoughts of Sabine snuck in. She'd always existed alongside everything else. She was the one thing in my life that refused to be sidelined.

I checked my phone one more time, knowing even as I did it that there would be nothing. Unable to help myself, I thumbed a quick text.

Hope everything's going okay. Love you, see you at home.

* * *

By the time I'd finished work almost four hours later, Sabine had responded to my text with a brief apology and explanation that she'd been caught up. With what, she didn't say. I arrived home just before she did and was immediately conscious of how off balance she was. And I knew the reason. She was uncomfortable and trying to push the feeling aside. My assumption was that her discomfort had something to do with whatever had kept her busy at work.

She was practically attached to me—following me around the house, even sitting on the closed toilet lid while I showered. And she *talked*. Endlessly. It wasn't a real conversation, mostly just her rambling. I agreed with her statements, answered her questions and prompted here and there for no other reason than I wanted to listen to her wonderful stream of thought. And...because the more she talked, the more likely it would be that she'd eventually arrive at whatever was bothering her.

Her inane chattering continued through dinner, as we cleaned up and then when we settled on the couch. "What do you want to watch?" I asked as I stretched across her for the remote.

Sabine shrugged. "Nothing heavy, I'm kind of brain dead after seeing Pace again today."

Ah. Clue number one. "How about a movie? Trashy reality show?"

She paused, the silence sitting heavily between us until eventually, she shook her head, slow and certain. "Neither."

I set the remote on our heavy wooden coffee table. "Okay, well what do you want, darling?"

She smiled, then it flickered like a dying light bulb. Her expression told me she was having an internal debate and for a moment I wondered what about, and which side was winning. After a deep inhalation she said quietly, "I just...want you, Bec." Sabine grasped my forearm to pull me close, then tugged my thigh, until I was so off balance I had no choice but to straddle her.

Finally, after hours of talking, she was quiet. Her hands slid down over my ass, pulling me forward, and I could feel her heart beating against my breasts, her pulse quick but steady. My stomach fluttered, and my own pulse made itself known in my groin, deep and needy. Celibate for close to a year, teased for days, I was about ready to burst. The way she kept rocking me back and forth in her lap wasn't helping.

Sabine studied me in that way she had when she didn't know how to put words to thoughts. Then she whispered, "I'm sorry, I'm just so confused."

It was increasingly hard to concentrate, the way each movement pressed me against her, and I wondered if she even realized she was doing it. I forced the sensation away long enough to ask, "About what, Sabine?"

"About *this*. Us. Sex." In the dim light, her eyes were so dark the pupils were barely visible. "I want to make love with you, but I'm scared. Something feels weird."

"I thought so," I murmured. Clamping my knees around her hips made her cease her tantalizing movement. "About what exactly? Will you talk to me?"

It took her a little while to answer, and I gently stroked the back of her neck until she admitted, "I'm scared you might feel differently about me." After a long breath she added, "And I'm scared of hurting you."

The relief of having her respond without evasion, of having her look inside herself and offer me something about her *feelings* was so acute that I had to blink away tears. I took her face in my hands, forced her to focus on me. "I feel exactly the same way I always have about you, Sabine. I love you. You won't hurt me, how could you?"

She scrunched her eyes closed, as though hiding from her own admissions. "Because I want you so badly, and it's been so long that I might forget myself. I don't want to be too rough, Bec."

"Oh, darling, you won't ever do anything I don't want." I kissed her forehead, her closed eyelids. "And besides, what's wrong with a little rough sex? It's not like we've never done that before."

"Mmm," she agreed, but she didn't sound entirely convinced. Her eyes fluttered open.

"Do you remember our six-month anniversary? That little mountain place in Banff where we stayed inside and just made love for days. Those toys you'd bought…" The memory sent a shudder down my spine. Maybe I shouldn't have pushed her by dredging up memories of previous lovemaking, but I was selfish and greedy for her. I couldn't help myself. I'd never been able to help myself when it came to Sabine.

The change came over her immediately. She swallowed hard, her hands tightening on my ass. The coiling in her muscles, the unconscious way she pulled me closer and lifted her hips to meet me were achingly familiar. I kissed her lightly, teasing my tongue along her lower lip. "And that time we were driving home from the movies and you touched me the whole way? Then you stopped in the corner of that empty parking lot and dragged me onto your lap, pulled my dress up and took me hard and deep until I came all over your hand."

Trying to excite her with memories had me even more excited and I let myself go, relaxing my knees and rocking forward to press against her again, enjoying the jolt of pleasure it sent through my body. Licking her neck, I tasted the sheen of sweat misting her skin and couldn't help but think of other tastes. I bit her lightly. "I want all of it, baby, just the way I always have."

Her breath caught. Without a word, Sabine twisted us sideways, dropped me down onto the couch and lay on top of me. I arched my body up, trying to make contact with as much of her as I could, loving the familiar weight of her. Sabine's mouth was hard against my lips, almost bruising and I let her in, stroking her tongue with mine, welcoming the desire and urgency in her kiss. After the lightest nip at my lower lip, she kissed her way down my neck, licking and sucking until she reached my collarbone. She sucked the skin just above my breast, groaning that low needy sound which made my pulse quicken further.

Sabine lifted herself off me, kneeling up enough that she could yank off her tee. She pulled at the string of my sweats, tugging them down and tossing them aside. My underwear followed quickly. We were both clumsy, fingers catching in fabric and on buttons as we tried to remove the barriers keeping our skin apart. I sat up, removing my shirt while she wiggled out of her jeans.

I slipped both hands around the back of her neck. "Come here," I murmured, pulling her down to me again. Our legs intertwined with thighs pressed hard against each other's sex, and when I lifted my leg, increasing pressure, she began to slide up and down. As she rocked against me, I could feel the evidence of her arousal, knowing my own would be just as evident on her skin. The butterflies in my stomach went crazy.

She groaned again when I grabbed her ass and locked my leg around hers, pulling her closer and holding her in place against me. My nails raked along her back, and I knew she would have scratches when I was done with her. When she was frantic like this, she always wanted a little pain. I pulled away to suck at her neck and bite her shoulder just hard enough that I felt the muscle tense, and then I soothed the bite with my tongue.

Sabine's hand slid down, lingering on my breast to pinch my nipple before it trailed over my belly and slipped between us. I couldn't help but bite her again when her fingers made contact then skittered away again. "Sabine, please." I was almost incoherent with need. "Right there, baby, please."

"You're so hot. So wet," she breathed, teasing me with the lightest, laziest circles over my clit. "Maybe we should go up to bed…"

Writhing underneath her fingers, I bucked against her to get more friction, something, anything. But she began to pull away. Some distant part of me recognized that she was doing it to tease and build my climax, rather than because she was afraid of what might happen. But the reason didn't matter, not now, not after so long. I needed her knowing, certain touch, and I needed it right now.

I grabbed her shoulders, trying to keep her close and she went still, holding her weight off me. My fingers fluttered over her shoulders, up her neck. "No, please don't stop touching me. I've missed you so much." My leg clamped harder around the back of her thigh, both of my hands tangled in her hair. I was almost sobbing with frustration. "Don't tease me, not now. I need you so badly, I can't stand it." I was so far gone that I knew if she stopped, if she pulled away now, I would have to finish myself off. She would hate that…and so would I.

Abruptly, Sabine rolled off me, her momentum breaking the grip of my legs around hers. She dropped to her knees on the floor beside the couch. Hands grabbed my thighs and she yanked me forward so my legs fell off the couch. She was just those few inches taller than me and strong enough to shift me around. And I loved it. I loved her gentle dominance, the concentrated fierceness in her eyes when she quietly ordered me to open my legs and show her how much I wanted her to fuck me.

She touched the inside of my thighs, pushing my legs further apart. Her hands curled into loose fists against the top of my thighs and then opened again, as though she'd been hit with a sudden wave of indecision. "What do you want me to do, Bec?" she murmured, the slightest hint of hesitation still lacing her words.

I grasped the armrest with one hand, my other reaching for her. I wanted to tell her something crude to push away any lingering uncertainty and fuel her desire—that I wanted her to tongue fuck me, to finger me deep and hard, to take me from behind until I came around her tongue and fingers. Instead, my voice cracked when I told her, "I just want you to love me."

"I do love you," she whispered. "More than I could ever find words to tell you."

"Then show me," I urged. "Please."

Sabine wasted no time, leaning forward to press her hipbone against my aching center. She pulled my leg up and hitched it around her waist, tilting me back to open me wide before her fingers found me again. But she didn't take me. She teased and stroked, slicking fingers through my wetness to linger near my clit before they danced away.

When I tried to reach between us to thumb her small, tight nipple, she moved backward out of my reach. "Nuh-uh. I won't be able to concentrate if you touch me." Light kisses peppered my collarbone, my breasts. "I need this, Bec. Please just let me have you first."

I nodded, swallowing thickly. Craning my neck, I watched Sabine's tongue sweeping across my hard nipples, sucking and biting before moving down...down...down. I tugged softly on her hair as her tongue slid over my hipbone and down my thigh, tantalizingly close but still so far away. A deep, unconscious groan fell from my lips as her fingers slid into my heat.

Sabine withdrew and I groaned again, this time with frustration, clutching her wrist until she entered me again, curling her fingers forward. The fluttering pulse became a deep, insistent throb. She said something I couldn't quite make out but the tone was one I recognized as self-chastisement, and in current context it made no sense. But when I opened my mouth to ask, she silenced me with a deep kiss and a deeper thrust.

She sucked my neck, a tiny center of pain to enhance each of her deep, measured strokes. With each one I rose up to meet her, my moans loud and unashamed as Sabine fucked me, pressing me back into the couch with her sweat-slick body against mine. It was *so good*, I almost felt I was coming apart. My limbs felt molten, my breasts full and heavy and I had to take them in my hands, kneading and stroking.

Sabine lifted herself slightly, and gently pushed one of my hands away to pinch my nipple. She dropped her head to the other breast and sucked my finger before her mouth closed around the other nipple. She bit and licked and I began to build, the heat scorching until I knew release was imminent. The moment I cried out, her thrusting ceased until I came down again without climaxing. I knew what she was doing, but it didn't make it any less frustrating and I couldn't help the strangled grunt that spilled from my lips.

Her hands and mouth stilled. "Bec?"

I opened my eyes, trying to focus through eyes hazy with pleasure and anticipation. I had to gasp and swallow before I could answer with a simple, "Yes?"

Those magic fingers began to dance inside me again. "I *am* going to show you how much I love you. How much I've missed you. How much I need you." She dropped her head, licked her way down my stomach to my parted thighs, and took me in her mouth.

CHAPTER SEVEN

Sabine

I rolled a pair of jeans into a tight tube and placed them in my suitcase, perfectly parallel to the side. As I reached for the second pair, Bec's voice floated up the stairs. "Sabine? Gavin's Skyping you."

"Can you answer it please?" As I jogged down the stairs, I could hear her talking and laughing with my friend before saying her goodbye. I jumped over the final two stairs and rushed toward the den.

Bec passed me in the doorway. "I'll be in the garden." She kissed me in passing, continued on her way, and I heard the soft click as she closed the back door. Whenever I had a call with Gavin, she always took herself somewhere she wouldn't hear our conversation. I'd always assumed this separation was Bec's way of letting me have what amounted to a therapy session without fear of having to filter myself. Every time she did that for me, the part of me that was full of love for her filled even more.

Gavin Elliot had contacted me in the months following my discharge from the Army Medical Center, and I'd almost ignored that first email message from an unknown sender. Until the subject "Transport Blue" and the last name Elliot triggered a memory.

Transport Blue, do you copy? Looks like you have hajji en route… My hands had shaken as I'd read the greeting. Hey Doc.

We'd been in regular email and video-call contact ever since, bonded in the way of two people who have shared something horrific. I hadn't known him before that day—Gavin was just a guy enlisted to give me a ride in a Humvee to and from somewhere I technically shouldn't have been. But after The Incident, he became one of my closest friends. One of the few people I could be completely honest with, and he with me.

I settled on the couch and pulled the laptop onto my knees. "Hey!"

His gray eyes were bright, and he looked cheerful and healthy as usual. "Doc! How're you doing?" Despite my telling him to call me Sabine, he still referred to me as *Doc*, or in his rawer moments *Captain*. Just like he had that day. Aside from that, there was no *ma'am* or proper protocol here. Here, over the Internet, we were just two people talking about a shared experience. Gavin leaned forward. "And unless Rebecca made a trip back to the desert to visit, I'll assume you're home."

"Sure am. Touched down stateside last Wednesday. Finished up our processing yesterday and now we've got two weeks leave."

"All right!" He pushed his fist to the webcam and I did the same for a virtual fist bump. Gavin was fourteen years younger than me, and his exuberance made me feel like a teenager again, helping to balance the inevitable somberness of our interactions. He'd been barely legal drinking age when it'd happened and had looked so much like a young boy I could hardly believe he was serving. Now he was twenty-three and still a boy, but with that awful look I saw in so many eyes. Including my own at times.

Haunted, wary, changed.

"So, any news?" I asked. We always started with the general life stuff before moving on to our inevitable informal therapy sessions. In addition to mandatory therapy while stateside and combat stress appointments while deployed, I'd tried PTSD support groups. But they were claustrophobic and anxiety-inducing rather than helpful. Supplementing Army shrink sessions with Gavin worked well. Or as well as any therapy could for me.

He rubbed his chin, slowly and with mock thoughtfulness. "Well, nothin' much unless you count getting engaged!"

"What! Congratulations! Oh my God, I'm so happy for you." I made a *gimme* motion with both hands. "Come on, don't leave me hanging. Tell me about it. You proposed? Or did Hannah get in first?"

"All me, Doc." His grin was so wide I couldn't help but match it. Gavin leaned close to the webcam. "Okay, so I got the ring, this real pretty diamond I knew she wanted. Made a dinner reservation at the fanciest place, new haircut, closest shave, best suit, parade-shined my shoes, the works. And right before we left, I was just checkin' my hair in the mirror when I notice this almighty, disgusting zit on my temple, like I dunno…stress of the proposal or something. Hannah comes out, dressed up real nice and she smells so good and looked so damned beautiful. And she sees this thing on my face, grabs my head in one hand to stop me moving, grabs a couple of tissues from her handbag with the other, then pops it without askin' me, you know, the way women do."

"Mhmm." I put my hand over my mouth to stop laughing. He was so gleeful in his runaway retelling that it wouldn't have mattered if I'd burst into a fit of giggles, but I wanted to hear the rest of his story.

"I just thought that this is so comfortable, you know? Like her squeezing this gross thing on my face before we go out, this is how we're going to grow old. This is our life and we've had it all already, the good and the bad and the frightening and the disgusting, and isn't that what love is?" He shrugged, still smiling. "So I pulled the ring out of my jacket pocket right there, in the entryway, with her holding these gross zit tissues. Got down on one knee, and I just asked."

I couldn't help clapping. "I think that's the best proposal story I've ever heard. Nobody is ever going to top that. Ever."

"Yep, it's up there." His expression grew earnest. "You and Rebecca will come to the wedding, right? It won't be for another year or two 'til we can save up enough money to have a real nice one, and I know Alaska isn't super convenient and that's even assumin' the Army doesn't move me again, but it would mean a whole lot to us if you were there."

I didn't even have to think before answering, "Gavin, we wouldn't miss it for anything. I'd be honored to be there when you two get married and I know Bec will feel the same."

The corners of his eyes crinkled. "Awesome." Gavin propped his elbows on the desk and rested his chin on clenched fists. "So, how you been, Doc?" The banter was over. Shit.

I'd learned that if I hesitated, I would either clam up completely or be evasive, and that was almost as bad as not talking about it at all. Before I could let myself think, I answered, "Up and down. I was having compulsions again this week like I did on deployment. It's that damned control thing." I cleared my throat, still not fully able to push aside the default reticence I had toward talking about such things. "It's back to feeling like I have to do it or something bad will happen."

I sighed, recalling my meltdowns in Afghanistan. The position of my boots in my locker, the number of paces between the prep room and the theater, and the times I'd uncharacteristically snapped at a nurse for setting one of my clamps slightly out of line or having the tray at an odd angle relative to my body.

Gavin nodded once, the movement short and sharp. "Keeping it all squared away. I get it, and hell I got the same. Holy shit, and the constant vigilance still, like I'm paralyzed because I'm so terrified someone's coming for me and Hannah. Some nights I can't even sleep, just *have* to stay awake and make sure everything's okay." He drew in a long, unsteady breath, shaking his head as though shaking the thought out. "You told someone? About the compulsions things?"

"Mhmm, I mentioned it to the shrink this week." In a roundabout, not-fully-elaborated kinda way. "Are you and Hannah still communicating?"

"Yeah, and she's so good at bringing me down from it now. Usually just by being there, you know?" He scratched his jaw. "How're the dreams?"

"Down to twice a week or so."

"What am I doing in them?" It was a bit of a joke from our partners that we dreamt about another person more than them. Hannah even called me *Gavin's Other Woman*.

"Same as always. The radio call, then you ask if I've got my gear on and my rifle ready, and I think that's what trips me up and paralyzes me in the dream, because you didn't ask that."

"No," Gavin agreed quietly. "I didn't."

It was Richards, his platoon mate and friend who'd asked me "Are you dressed, Captain?" just moments before he was killed. He was checking up on me, making sure I was okay and prepared for what might happen because I'm not a field soldier. I'm a surgeon and I shouldn't have been there.

I would never be able to shake the embarrassment of a soldier who ranked underneath me having to make sure I remembered what to do in a combat situation. Nor could I get rid of the ugly bitterness inside, *survivor's guilt* they all called it, which was about right. There was nowhere to direct the feeling except back at myself because I'd pushed my commanding officer, Bec, to let me go even when I knew I shouldn't have even asked.

But I did ask. Because everything with me and Bec had been so confusing, with no workable solutions in sight, and I needed some time away from the FOB. From her. So I'd asked her to let me go away for a day to perform a routine medical procedure on a bunch of soldiers at a neighboring Army installation just so I could think and *breathe*. And it'd worked as I'd thought it would. Until The Incident.

I pinched my thigh hard, the pain resetting my thoughts as I'd hoped. "Then I see the light, and I know what's coming and I just know there's fuck all I can do about it." Either I'd wake in a gasping, sweaty panic or the dream would bleed into another and I'd spend the night fighting unwinnable battles in my sleep.

"Yeah…" He closed his eyes, his lips moving as he silently counted to ten. Then he opened them again. "Stupid thing is we know I never saw it. Never saw them. But I see them in the dreams." A flash of panic clouded his eyes. It'd taken almost eight months into our conversations before he'd stopped constantly apologizing for all he thought he didn't do, or that he thought he could have done better or differently. But he still had moments of intense self-doubt and loathing. As did I.

"I know you didn't, hon. Neither did I."

Both his hands came up helplessly. "You know, just a little faster, or a swerve or somethin'…"

I kept silent. There was nothing I could say, these were simply thoughts that needed to be worked through out loud.

"…but then it could have been me or you and not Richards." Gavin let out a choked exhalation, and quickly dashed his palms under his eyes. "How do you make a choice like that?"

My throat felt so tight, I didn't think I could answer. But I had to. For him and for me. I had to remind him of something we'd said so many times already. "You don't. Someone else made it for you. For us."

"I know," he agreed quietly, his voice still edged with tears. "I think sometimes the what-ifs are the hardest."

I nodded. What if I hadn't selfishly wanted to get away and pushed Bec to let me go do a job that a nurse usually did…what if I'd been sitting a couple of feet to my right…what if we'd left a minute later or earlier? What if I'd never joined the Army in the first place?

Gavin and I sat separated by thousands of miles, but staring at him on my laptop screen, it felt as though he was with me. His head was slightly bowed but he still felt present, and the comfort of it was immeasurable. This quiet reflection was another of our themes and after all our time together, we'd become adept at knowing when to break the silence.

"How's the physical stuff?" I asked when I sensed the small change come over him. "Any pain?"

Gavin huffed an exaggerated sigh, a smile breaking through his somberness. "Just like you Med Corp, always pushin' us to tell you where it hurts."

I gave him an answering smile. "Bite me."

He laughed. "Hip aches a bit in the rain but other than that it's fine. How about you?"

"Okay. Been getting a few nerve twinges in my thigh where the shrapnel was." I couldn't help but look around, even though I knew Bec was outside gardening and wouldn't be able to hear my quiet admission. "And this weird…well, it's fake pain. Psychosomatic. Under my armpit where I was shot."

His expression grew serious as again, he asked one of his favorite questions, "Telling the shrink? And your doctor?"

"Mmmmmmmm." My evasive answer ran up and down through about three octaves.

"Doc," Gavin sighed. "Come on. If I gotta talk about all my nitty gritty stuff then you do too."

"Yeah I know. I will, I promise." At some stage, when I didn't feel like I'd choke on the words. I made an expert deflection, not entirely selfish because it *was* pertinent to our friend-therapy. "Have you got your deployment orders yet? Wasn't there a rumor they were coming soon?"

"Word is within three months." It would be the first time his platoon would deploy since he'd been wounded two years earlier, and he'd be out running patrols in the thick of things, not like me who worked behind walls. Afraid. Hiding. Safe. Or, safer.

"How're you feeling about it?"

"Same as always but with this little voice in my head now." He peered at me, eyes a little brighter. "And yeah, I actually told the shrink."

"Smartass," I said, but I was smiling.

"Yeah yeah." He paused, a long sigh escaping. "Once is bad luck, right? Twice is near impossible. Or that's what I keep telling myself."

"That's what they say." It sounded like a platitude, and I hated myself for it. But what could I say? Yeah the odds are in your favor, but it could still happen, again, because nothing is guaranteed over there.

He glanced off to the side, nodding once before turning back to me. "Okay. Sorry, Doc, I gotta go. Hannah's waving at me to stop talking and have breakfast. I'll see you in a few weeks, same time, same place?"

"You know it. Take care of yourself, hon."

"You too, Doc."

"Give Hannah my congratulations. Or my regrets," I added playfully.

He laughed and the video went black.

I thumbed dust from the plastic ridge edging the screen and stared at the background picture of Bec and me at Universal Studios, taken a few months after I finished my medical leave. Something that somehow snuck by all our *getting to know you* was her love of adrenaline rides—the scarier and more vomit-inducing, the better she loved it. My concession was joining her on the less thrilling ones, the kiddie-coasters as she so teasingly called them.

Bec still had all these little bits of herself that she kept giving me and each one was another piece in the jigsaw puzzle of our new, shared life. I'd never had this sort of connection with anyone before, never felt so balanced by another person. It wasn't that I felt incomplete by myself, but more that with Bec I was somehow made whole. Like she filled all those holes that'd opened up inside me with pieces of herself to keep me together. It was her love that pushed the darkness aside.

Gavin was right. Love was the easy and the hard, all the scary and disgusting things and the sweet and gentle and kind. Bec and I had had all of that good and bad stuff, and we were still together. Still in love. I needed that if I was ever going to move past this crud in my head. Needed her. I closed the laptop and ran up the stairs two at a time, rushing along the hallway to our bedroom.

I unlocked the safe, shoving everything out of the way until I found the box I wanted. I cracked it open and stared for what felt like the hundredth time since I'd bought it. I could see it on her finger. Imagine her response, hopefully the one I wanted. But I couldn't quite picture myself asking her. That disparaging voice came back again to tell me I wasn't good enough for her. I wasn't worthy of her when I was as ruined as I was, like a rotten piece of fruit.

Rotten apple actually summed it up pretty well. Looked all right, so long as you didn't touch it or take a look inside. Be quiet, Sabine. You're never going to give her this ring if you don't suck it up and get your shit together. It's easy. Just say… Bec, I love you so much I can't even think of what to say. Nice one, that's totally romantic and memorable. Bec, I want us to spend the rest of our lives together? I love you. Marry me? Great, very convincing.

I hid the box again and locked it away. My footsteps were light as I made my way back downstairs and through the kitchen. I quietly opened the screen door and leaned against the doorframe, staring into our backyard. Bec kneeled on the grass beside the vegetable garden, stretching over to reach a weed. Her broad-brimmed sunhat, those dorky gardening gloves and slip-on shoes all made a picture of perfection.

I relished these mundane domestic moments. I loved knowing that before me, before us, she would have done the same thing—on a smaller scale in the planter boxes on the tiny balcony of her studio apartment. Gradually, the gardens here had been transformed under her green thumb. Less than a month after she moved in, the hedge I despised along the side fences had been pulled out and replaced by flower beds. Her rosebushes filled our front gardens and while they were blooming I'd often sneak out and smell the blooms. I'd never cared much for the garden before but I loved everything she'd done. Because it was hers and she'd made it ours.

When my shadow fell over the tomato plants she was attending, Bec twisted around, her greeting a soft, "Hello, darling." As well as making herself scarce, Bec never asked about my contact with Gavin. I think for her it sat in that strange area of a call between friends, and therapeutic.

"Hey." I knelt beside her and rubbed a smear of dirt from the side of her jaw, kissing the spot when I was done. "Gavin and Hannah are engaged."

Bec straightened, the smile of delight bringing out her dimples. "Really? That's fantastic news! I'll pick up a card to send them. When's the wedding?"

"A year or two. We're invited."

"Sounds lovely. Did you get any more packing done?"

"No, but I just need to toss a few more things in and I'm set." Toss…carefully place in exactly the right spot in the suitcase. Same thing.

Bec arched her back, groaning faintly. "I suppose I should pack too. In a bit. Are you hungry?"

"Not yet. Soon though." I ran my fingers through the inch-high grass beside my knee, relishing the softness of it. "I think I'll mow the lawn."

"Why don't I start some lunch then and it'll be done when you are?" She pulled off her gloves and stood, offering me her hand.

I took it to pull myself to my feet. "Sounds great. Thanks."

Bec studied my face, her expression relaxed and thoughtful. Slowly, and with what seemed like unnecessary caution, she brought her hand up to caress my cheek. A moment later, her lips touched my mouth, then without saying anything else, Bec gathered up her gardening things and walked away.

I watched her making her way across the yard and into the house. Checked her out was more like it. Though she was still fit, with her flag football and jogging a few times a week, she'd lost some of the hard muscle from her military days. Bec had always been so *female*, with full breasts and curves that made my stomach flutter and my mouth go dry. Now she'd softened, just a little, and become even more delicious. And I loved it. Loved the contrast to my lean greyhound body.

Heat built in my belly when I recalled the night before when I'd reacquainted myself with every delicious inch of her. I let the desire take over, until the other thing rose up, the thing I recognized as self-admonishment. Beautiful, sexy, sensuous girlfriend and I'd been too scared to make love to her. Made her wait even longer. Only done it once. Hadn't really let her touch me. Shut upppp, Sabine.

I set hearing protection over my ears, yanked the starter cord on the mower and had a sudden moment of panic where I couldn't decide if I wanted to mow in lines or concentric shapes. I stared at the grass and imagined each outcome. What does it matter? The grass doesn't give a shit and nobody is going to know how you mowed it.

I pushed the mower right across the middle of the lawn. There, who cares. Still, the uncomfortable tightness at the back of my neck didn't ease until I'd erased the line with a perfectly aligned back and forth pattern. Once I'd finished with the back and started to make my way to mow the front lawn, Bec waved at me from the deck.

I cut the mower and pulled the earmuffs off, leaving them looped around my neck. "Sorry, what was that?"

Her expression told me she'd been trying to get my attention for a while. Grinning, she bounced down the stairs toward me. "You and your safety gear." Something she always teased me about—the fact I couldn't do any chores without donning some sort of ear and eye protection.

"I like my eyesight, thank you. And I want to make sure I can still hear you nagging me when I'm ninety."

The corners of her mouth edged downward. "I don't really nag, do I?"

"No, honey," I said automatically, because that was the only correct answer.

She bit her lower lip but the crease in her cheek gave her amusement away. "Hmm. And ninety?"

Her question made me pause. "Well...yes." The concept of Us was something I'd always assumed, that this was the last relationship we'd each have, together until the end. But we'd never explicitly discussed it. We'd mentioned marriage in an abstract way about a year ago when discussing our shared bank account, but other than that it remained unspoken.

A sudden panicked and irrational thought came to the forefront. Maybe this was a temporary thing for her, something to tide her over until someone more suitable came along. Someone less weird and less stricken by invisible ailments. Someone whole. Suddenly, all I could think about was that box in the safe. So stupid, Sabine. As if you're even worthy of asking her for *that* right now.

She kissed me lightly, her thumb caressing my cheek. "I'll be ninety-eight, darling. And if I'm still nagging you by then, you should be grateful." Bec reached around and patted my butt. "Can I *nag* you to come inside for lunch?"

The thudding of my frightened heart eased. "Sure. I'll be in as soon as I've finished the front." And spent five minutes trying to decide exactly which way was the right way to mow.

CHAPTER EIGHT

Rebecca

We flew into Ohio just after ten thirty in the morning, renting a car for the hour and a half drive to Sabine's parents' house. Sabine only grumbled a little when I insisted she pull over at a roadside flower stall so I could purchase a mixed bouquet for her mother, Carolyn.

"You know she doesn't expect that, Bec," Sabine told me once I'd carefully propped the flowers on the backseat, wedged between the door and her messenger bag.

"I know, but it's polite. And just how I am," I added with a smile.

Sabine leaned over to kiss me. "I love how you are, and so do my parents." She buckled her seatbelt, then glanced down as she always did to check I was belted in too before driving on.

Her parents were out the front door before we'd managed to get out of the car. After tight, tearful hugs all around and a gleeful acceptance of my flowers, Sabine and I were sent straight up to her old room with instructions to come back down as quickly as we could. Her parents hadn't seen her in close to eleven months and clearly didn't want to waste a moment with tedious things like unpacking and settling in. Sabine's expression said it all, and once we were alone upstairs, I erased the thin set of her lips with a soft kiss.

The bedroom was a shrine of sorts, her mother insisting on keeping it as a testament to Sabine's childhood. Jana's room was the same, and this sweet maternal love for her adult daughters made something inside me swell with even more adoration for Carolyn. Trophies and ribbons sat on shelves and hung on special racks, photos in frames dotted the walls and top of the dresser, and a vase of fresh flowers rested on the windowsill. The small double bed was neatly made, with a raggedy teddy bear sitting up in the center of the spread. With a huff of exasperation, Sabine quickly snatched up her childhood toy and put it on the dresser.

Good thing we slept so closely together or it would be an uncomfortable week. During our first visit, we'd stayed in a hotel so Sabine could have more space to sleep with her healing wounds and so she didn't have to negotiate so many stairs. Each time we'd come since, she had tried to insist we book a hotel, but that notion was always squashed flat by her mother. To stay in a hotel unnecessarily was out of the question, and to stay in the guest room even more unthinkable—this was Sabine's room and that was that.

Despite what her mom had said, Sabine insisted on unpacking both our suitcases, and as she hung clothes in the closet and folded them in drawers, I studied the photographs I so loved. Gap-toothed Sabine holding a puppy. Sabine with braces and an academic award and wearing one of the biggest smiles I'd seen. Sabine riding, and leaning down to pat her horse as a ribbon was fastened around its neck. Sabine with her sister on the beach. Sabine giving the valedictorian speech in high school.

I picked up one of the whole family wearing garish Christmas sweaters, a Fleischer tradition I'd discovered when one had been given to me with the joking instruction I was to wear it, *or else*. "Why do you keep these photos here instead of at home?"

She paused with one of my casual tees in her hands. "Mom likes them, and I guess I've just never gotten around to having copies made."

"Mmm. Speaking of, your mom's going to be fretting downstairs. Why don't we unpack later?"

Her grip on the garment tightened. "I just want to get it all organized, Bec. She'll be fine for a few minutes." She carefully folded the tee into the drawer of an old mahogany dresser.

I loved that dresser, this room, the whole house. I turned away from her and stared out the window, looking down onto the huge backyard which bordered pastures as far as I could see. Set on just over twenty acres, the old farmhouse—renovated in the years following Gerhardt and Carolyn's marriage—was full of polished wood and glorious stonework. A beautiful old barn sat on the hill closest to the house, and wooden shelters lay scattered over the gently undulating country. The fields which used to hold Sabine and Jana's horses now housed a herd of cattle that as far as I knew did nothing but produce adorable calves which Gerhardt sold only to friends who wouldn't eat them.

Sabine's father appeared imposing—tall and rugged, and often with an expression that made him seem aloof. But I'd learned it was just him absorbing the goings-on in his watchful way, and that he was a kind, gentle man at heart. When I'd first met him, I'd been worried about how he would receive me, so I'd smiled politely, offered my hand and called him *sir*.

Given the Fleischer family history and his own service, Gerhardt was a stickler for military protocol. And I'd broken one of the fundamental rules—do not become involved with those under your command. He'd laughed, bright blue eyes creasing, then hugged me, thanked me for bringing his daughter home and told me to call him Gerhardt. Ever since Sabine had mentioned I had an interest in military tactics and weaponry, he would pull me aside every chance he got, stick a drink in my hand and we would talk until Sabine or her mother told us enough was enough.

Carolyn was as sweet and kind as Gerhardt and was fiercely protective of her family. Within moments of our first introduction, she too had pulled me in for a hug, crying and thanking me over and over for taking care of Sabine, and telling me I was part of the family now until I was crying too. I always felt stupid thinking it, but they really were just like an adoptive family. There had never been any awkwardness, and I still felt as though I'd stumbled into something wonderful.

Sabine closed the drawer decisively, the sound of wood on wood echoing sharply in the enclosed space. "You ready?"

"Yes." I held out my hand.

She took it and pulled me close, burying her face in my hair and I felt the deep breath she took before she kissed my temple. She'd been quiet and reflective ever since we'd left home. Just something that needed time and some rest to fix.

Hand in hand we made our way downstairs, and the first thing I noticed was the wall opposite the bottom of the stairs held photographs of us that hadn't been there on my last visit. Alongside the photo of Sabine receiving her Purple Heart hung one of us standing together out in the field that bordered the backyard. It must have been taken when we were here last summer.

I stopped in front of it and stared. Sabine wore a cobalt sundress, one tanned arm slung casually over the wooden fence railing behind her, the other wrapped around my shoulder. I was leaning into her, smiling down at the grass, and Sabine was grinning at me. I remembered the funny thing she'd just said, but I didn't remember the photograph being taken.

"I love that one of you two," murmured Carolyn from behind us.

She walked away to place the platter of snacks in the other room, and I tugged Sabine so we could follow. But Sabine slipped her hand from mine and remained standing where she was, absorbed in the photo. Tension radiated from her like heat waves, the emotion odd given our current surroundings and circumstance. When she spoke, the words came out as a hoarse whisper. "We look really happy."

"Yes, we do."

Sabine turned to me. "Are you still happy, Bec?" she asked, her tone quietly intense.

The question was so unexpected, I was momentarily stunned. After a quick glance to make sure her parents were out of earshot, I said forcefully, "Yes, I am."

"Good," she breathed. "That's all I really want." Before I could ask a reciprocal question, or get her to elaborate, Sabine pulled me toward the den and I could do nothing but follow mutely.

I could find no room to mull over her question because the family conversation began the moment we entered the room. Gerhardt poured wine and Carolyn distributed food, both of them waving aside my offers of help. Sabine's wide-eyed look told me I was wasting my time asking. I accepted a plate and relegated our odd exchange to a mental compartment where I could examine it later.

As was customary at any Fleischer gathering, the conversation went around and around a variety of topics, never slipping into a lull. We spoke of Sabine's deployment, my job, the addition of a new shelter for the cattle, Franz the new bull and how he'd sired the highest number of calves ever, Carolyn's ongoing feud with the neighbor who'd stolen her cake container after a bake sale held to benefit the local women's group, the fact both Sabine and I would probably be working and wouldn't be able to make the family Thanksgiving next month.

Sabine relaxed, leaning into me with her thigh pressed against mine until I could feel the tension had all but left her. She pulled my hand into her lap and didn't let it go, leaving us both to juggle wine and food one-handed. Randomly, she'd squeeze my hand and I couldn't tell if it was a reassurance or if she was trying to telegraph something. Every now and then, either she or Carolyn would get up to check the progress of our late lunch, top up glasses or the platters.

After the second bottle of wine was half empty, Gerhardt stood and walked to the window. "Come take a walk with me,

Rebecca. I need to check the water and I'll toss out some hay for Franz and the ladies."

I nodded lazily, a little dulled by a few glasses of wine before two p.m. "Sure."

Carolyn peeked around from the kitchen. "Lunch will be ready in half an hour, Gerhardt. Don't lose track of time out there, and for heaven's sake don't make poor Rebecca listen to you talking about herd health."

He waved dismissively, left the room and I could hear his chuckle echoing from the hallway. Sabine's face appeared beside her mother's. She rolled her eyes expansively then padded over to steal a kiss. Hugging me, she whispered in my ear, "Help. I might commit matricide if I have to listen to another word about how all her friends have grandchildren and she doesn't."

I laughed and squeezed her tight, grateful that she'd settled back into what seemed her usual self. "I'm sorry, darling, but I can't help you with that one."

"You're cruel." Sabine kissed my neck, warm lips lingering against my skin. "I'll be right here. Biting my damned tongue," she added under her breath as she turned to trudge back to the kitchen.

I slipped into my coat and waited by the back door, looking across the upward-sloping backyard and into the field beyond. Gerhardt appeared with tumblers each containing half an inch of amber liquid, one of which he handed to me. "Brandy. Fuel for the walk." He grinned Sabine's grin and held the door open.

"Thank you." I tucked my free hand into my pocket as we walked across the large back lawn toward the pastures. The grass was showing signs of the cooler weather, the tips just turning brown and crunching underfoot. Gerhardt opened the gate and we headed up toward the barn, my lungs grateful for the cool, clean air. I took an appreciative sip of my drink, the spirit settling warmly in my belly.

Sabine's father stopped and spun as if getting his bearings, looking left and right. "Herd must be over the hill." He put two fingers in his mouth and whistled, then turned intelligent blue eyes toward me. "Did Sabine ever tell you about the time she dislocated her shoulder?"

This sudden turnabout threw me off, and I waited a long moment before answering, "No, she didn't."

"She would have been around sixteen and mad on English horseback riding. Been competing in dressage mostly for years, real fancy sort of stuff, training hard and having lessons all the time. Carolyn and I didn't know a damned thing about horses, but we drove Sabine to shows nearly every weekend until we thought she could handle the trailer herself." He paused, sipped his drink and kept walking. "Well, she had her second horse, we bought him already trained up to high level and she was doing pretty good on him. Winning a lot of classes." Gerhardt glanced at me as if to see I was still following his story.

I nodded. "She's told me about a little about her horses." I knew both Sabine and Jana rode until Sabine left for college—Sabine competitively, and Jana casually and only because she wanted to do everything her older sister did.

"Mmm. Well, the day before she had this big competition to qualify for the state championships, she went out with some friends for a ride on the trails, just for something fun to take a break from training. The damned horse tossed her and she dislocated her shoulder."

I cringed. "Ouch."

He paused to check the levels in the large circular water troughs that were concreted into the ground outside the barn. "I'm not sure what happened exactly, but I think she convinced one of her friends to put it back into place, probably talked them through the whole thing. She made Jana wash the horse and braid its mane ready to compete the next day and she never said a word to me or her mother."

I ran my thumb around the smooth rim of the cut-crystal glass. "She didn't go to the emergency room?" She would have been driving by then and could have taken herself if she'd been hiding it.

"No. I found out later she got some sticky bandage from her horse first aid kit and had Jana tape her shoulder up, probably got the technique from one of the medical textbooks she'd saved her allowance for. She used to make us take her to the secondhand college bookstore, spent every dime on books."

I couldn't help smiling. "I think she still has some of those textbooks."

"I'm not surprised. She's always been sentimental about her special things." He turned back to the barn, lips twisted into a smile of his own.

Though I was certain I knew the answer, I asked anyway, "She rode in the competition, didn't she?"

"She did and she won both of her classes. Two blue ribbons, and qualified for the championships. Jana came along that day and got the horse's saddle on and all that. Course we didn't know that Sabine was hurt, and we thought Jana was just being nice and was excited to see her sister ride. Turns out Sabine swapped two weeks of math homework for her sister's help, and her silence."

I was incredulous, but at the same time not overly surprised. "What about the pain?" If her friend had managed to reduce the dislocation without incident then the pain should have been manageable without a prescription. But still.

Gerhardt laughed. "I believe she took enough ibuprofen to kill a small elephant." He pointed off to his left. The herd of black and white cows along with the massive Franz were beginning to make their way to the barn from the small valley to the west. I had a feeling Gerhardt came up here often and fed them just for the hell of it.

"How did you find out she'd hurt herself?" I swallowed another mouthful of my drink, wondering why she hadn't ever told me this story, and more to the point, why her father was telling me now.

"After she received her ribbons, she was riding back to the trailer and passed out, fell off all over again and Jana spilled the beans. Then when we took Sabine to the ER she sat there, all uppity and telling the doctor exactly what kind of dislocation it was and how she'd treated it." Gerhardt laughed and slid the wide door of the barn open. "Of course, she was absolutely right.

I wanted to throttle her for being so arrogant and stupid about it, and hug her for being so damned clever. Hold on a minute."

He walked inside and momentarily, fluorescent lights buzzed and flickered before illuminating the barn. It was a roomy wooden structure with a rough concrete floor, a laneway with two stables on each side, and toward the back stood a room and an open bay which was piled almost to the roof with stacks of fodder.

I'd been in here once before, in the dark, during my second visit to Ohio. After we'd taken a walk, Sabine had brought me up here, insisting there was something she wanted me to see. She'd dragged me just inside the door, pushed me gently against the wall and dropped to her knees in front of me. Surprisingly, the memory of our frantic coupling stirred nothing in me now except sadness when I compared it to how detached she'd been the other night when making love to me.

Gerhardt set his glass on a ledge. "Take a look around. I'll just toss some feed out."

I sipped my drink and walked slowly across the laneway to peer over one of the half-doors, resting my forearms on the wood. The floor was bare of bedding, cobwebs adorning the corners of the stall. I could easily picture Sabine in there, grooming a horse or cleaning up the stable and probably chattering to herself or the horse the whole time.

Gerhardt came back after a few minutes, brushing hay off his pants. "There, that should keep them happy." He picked up his glass and leaned against the stable door. "I'm sure you've seen all the ribbons and trophies in her room."

"Yes, I have." Strangely, none of her childhood awards were at home.

He gestured to the stable beside him and I walked over to take a closer look. A tarnished brass nameplate on the half-door proclaimed that the stall had belonged to MONTE. Gerhardt pointed to the mesh that made up the top half of the stable where two dirty, faded ribbons were woven through the bars. They were embroidered with NODA 1990.

"If she keeps all her ribbons and trophies in her old bedroom, displayed so proudly, why do you think those two are there?"

His eyes were shrewd and before I could answer, he continued, "That Purple Heart of hers is hidden in the darkest corner of your closet, isn't it?"

His question was uncannily accurate. I raised an eyebrow. "Yes. How did you know?"

Gerhardt shrugged, a careless sort of gesture as though it would explain everything. "I know my daughters, Rebecca, but Sabine and I are two peas in a pod. She can't stand to have that medal out and on display because of how it happened." He jerked his chin at the fabric threaded through the mesh. "Same as those. She wasn't at her best, or she could have done more. She doesn't want the…proceeds of those achievements with her other *good* things. She doesn't think she deserves it. You know what she said to me when we were leaving the hospital? She was mad that even though she won, her percentage points weren't as good as she wanted them to be because she was hurt and couldn't ride as well as she usually did. It's illogical to us. But not to Sabine."

I frowned, biting my suddenly trembling lower lip. What he said made absolute sense. Why hadn't I realized? Gerhardt hooked an elbow over the half-door and looked at me. "We raised both our girls the same way, to be good people, to do their best and work hard, but Sabine's always had some sort of extra drive. She'll flog herself to do everything perfectly, and she won't quit unless you take the whip off her and hide it somewhere she can't get at it." What he said was true—Sabine had no off button, she was like an out-of-control machine that needed its kill switch hit to make it stop.

"How is she?" he asked, sounding as though he was trying not to cry.

"She has PTSD," I said matter-of-factly. Saying the words aloud made my eyes prickle and I blinked hard to stop my own tears forming.

"Of course she does." Then he echoed a sentiment I'd heard before. "Don't we all, everyone who's been out there, have it to some degree?"

I raised both eyebrows. "I suppose you're right."

Gerhardt rested a weathered hand on my forearm. "Is she okay?"

I sipped my drink, trying to dampen my throat enough to tell him. The brandy burned and I relished it. "Most of the time she seems fine, like herself, but every now and then I can tell something is off. Something that feels like more than PTSD and I can't quite pin it down. She's been attending counseling." I didn't mention that while deployed she'd stopped taking the medication.

"What about you?"

"Me?"

"How are you after everything that happened? Are you talking to anyone?"

His question was so unexpected that it took me a few moments to respond. I felt like a deer caught in the headlights. "Yes, I have been." My answer was truthful. But the truth was also that with work and the emotional fatigue that'd settled over me during Sabine's deployment, my therapy had dwindled to once a month and then even less. I fought off tears.

Gerhardt rested a comforting paternal hand on my shoulder. "Good." He sighed. "She's always hidden her pain, Rebecca. Physical and emotional. I've never been able to figure out if it's because she can't stand the thought of being *less than* or something. Or if she's scared that we'll be angry at her for some reason, or if she's hiding it so we don't get upset. Drives me and her mother nuts, but it's just the way she is."

"She's doing better," I insisted hoarsely. "She's trying so hard, she really is, but it's going to take some time." I was desperate for him to understand that I wasn't just ignoring his daughter's struggles. That I wasn't ignoring *our* struggles, because Sabine and I were inextricably intertwined.

"I know. And she's trying for you." After a beat, he frowned. "But...do you think she could be trying *too* hard?"

"What do you mean?"

"I think sometimes she gets too focused on one thing, to the detriment of everything else." He shrugged. "Maybe I don't know what the hell I'm talking about, but I'm just worried she's pushing so hard to get to this place she wants to be, and it's doing her harm rather than good. She doesn't know any other way except to barrel right through whatever's in her path. And sometimes that just doesn't work."

The tears that were just prickling before now spilled to my cheeks. Gerhardt fished a handkerchief from his pocket. "Clean, I promise," he said with a slight smile. He held my drink while I wiped my eyes and blew my nose.

"I'm sure she's told you this but I know she never wanted to be in the military. She did it for me, and her opa, because she's so set on doing the *right* thing." He let out a long breath. "She took it upon herself because she knew there was no way Jana would join up. Sabine has such a strong idea of the way she thinks things should be."

"I know," I murmured. After another brief nose blow, I glanced at him. There was nothing I could say because I understood the motive behind her behavior. My thoughts looped back to what he'd said about taking away the source of Sabine's torment.

As if he knew exactly what I was thinking, Gerhardt took my hand and gently squeezed. "Do you understand what I'm saying, Rebecca? You need to take away the thing that's making her push herself so hard. She needs to slow down and just breathe for once. It has to be you because Lord knows she won't listen to us."

There was nothing I could do but nod tearily and offer a helpless, "Mhmm."

"I'm sure you'll both work it out. She'll get there, especially with you helping her. She's lucky to have you, Rebecca. We're all lucky to have you." He wrapped an arm around my shoulders and hugged me to his side. "Come on, let's get back before Carolyn has an apoplexy about us being late for lunch."

We made our way out of the barn, and down toward the house. As I carefully negotiated the slope, I mulled over what Gerhardt had said, and the more I thought, the closer I came to an uneasy realization. I looked up at him, but I couldn't get the words out. Because…what if that thing is me? What if the problem is us?

Again, I thought of our intimacy the other night, and couldn't help the uncomfortable sensation worming through my body that she hadn't really wanted it, but had only gone along because she knew how much I'd missed making love with her. What if Sabine was trying so hard to be what she thought I wanted, that she would hurt herself to get past her pain instead of working through it safely?

And if that was the problem, how the hell could I even begin to fix it? I had absolutely no idea what I was going to do.

CHAPTER NINE

Sabine

Just before we'd left Ohio to come home, Amy texted announcing an emergency barbeque the following day, Saturday—attendance mandatory because pretty much everyone else they knew was busy at such short notice. The reason? Her "darling husband thought it was a good idea to buy half a dead cow from a friend" and they needed help eating it. I replied that we'd be there, asked what to bring and was told promptly and in typical Amy style, *Huge fucking appetite. Amazing potato salad.*

We took my car, the backseat packed with Bec's potato salad, her ubiquitous flowers and a cooler with nonalcoholic drinks for me as well as a few wine bottles that clinked together the whole drive. The constant clanging made me want to grind my teeth, and it was all I could do to not pull over and throw the bottles out of the car. Amy lived about thirty minutes from our place, in one of the quiet, family-friendly suburbs in Maryland. Thirty. Clinking. Minutes.

Midway through my fumbling over their wooden side gate for the latch, Amy flung the gate open and pulled me into a tight hug. "Ohhh, it feels like I haven't seen you in ages," she said, keeping me in a rib-crushing embrace.

Laughing, I returned her hug one-armed and with the other held the salad aloft. "It's only been a week, Ames." Never mind the fact I'd see her back at work next Monday.

"Exactly. An eternity." She let me go to acknowledge Rebecca. "Colonel Ke— ma'aahhh, um…" Amy glanced at me, her panicked confusion hilarious. Since Bec's retirement, we'd had a handful of social occasions, but Amy just could not settle on what to call her former boss.

Bec laughed, stepping forward to clasp Amy's hand. "Just Rebecca. How are you, Amy? It's wonderful to see you, it's been far too long." She offered the flowers and picked up the cooler from where I'd set it on the stone path. "I'll take this through into the yard."

Once we were alone, I prodded Amy. "Seriously. Don't you think it's about time you got over calling her *Colonel*?" I bit the inside of my lip, but my smile broke free anyway.

Amy leaned close to whisper in my ear, "Well, I suppose it's easy to forget you used to have to call her *ma'am* when she's lying underneath you, and you've got your fi—"

"All right! Here's the potato salad, as requested." I shoved the bowl at her. "So, instead of boiling, Bec roasts the potatoes first."

"Nice sidestep." She snorted, patted my shoulder and pulled me forward. "Come on. Everyone's here."

We walked through to the undercover barbecue area in the back of Amy's large, neatly mown backyard. After hugs from Mike, Mitch and Rick, and a shy handshake from Amy's seven-year-old son, Ethan, I poured Bec a glass of wine and left her talking to the boys while Amy and I went inside to deal with the salads.

"Shoes, sorry," she said at the back door. "Rick had the floors done as *gift* for me while I was away. Like…give me a pair of earrings or something, not polished hardwood."

Laughing, I took off my shoes. "Isn't it the thought?"

She hmmphed and quickly arranged Bec's flowers in a vase, put the potato salad in the fridge and extracted wine. "Do you want a drink?" she asked, holding the bottle of white aloft.

"I'm good with water for now, thanks." In another lifetime, I'd have caught a cab to a social event and had a few drinks. Or swapped driver duties with someone. Now all I could think about was how I *was* the driver on duty most of the time and it was all my own choice. Another thing for the stupid brain shit list.

Amy poured herself a glass, swallowed a huge mouthful then topped herself up. "So. Any news?"

"Nope." I shrugged, trailing a fingertip over the black granite countertop. "All the same. All good."

"Good. Me too. So we're all caught up." She grinned, pointing to the cabinet opposite me. "Can you please grab the ugly glass salad bowl from in there?"

I set about fetching what she wanted while she yanked things from the refrigerator with typical efficiency. From outside I heard Mitch's exuberant shouts, and Ethan's answering cries. Amy stared out the kitchen window, a faint smile lifting the edges of her mouth. "Boys."

"Mmmm," I agreed, rinsing a head of lettuce and shaking it dry. The water splattered over the sink and backdrop, droplets marring the surface. I wiped them away as quickly as I could. Amy and I worked together silently, chopping and mixing, and I took my time, making sure my carrot was sliced into perfectly matched sticks.

"Sabs?"

"Mmm?"

Amy's expression was oddly contemplative. "Seriously. What's up?"

Apparently I couldn't even make salad without looking weird. I set down the knife, wanting desperately to brush her question aside with a *nothing is wrong*. Instead, I said, "I…don't really know, and that's the problem." After a shrug I added, "Have you ever just felt wrong, Ames, but not known exactly why?"

Amy nodded once, then moved away, opened her pantry and reached up to the top shelf. Unwrapping something as she came toward me she said, "Sometimes. I think we all have." She held up a peanut butter cup. "Open."

She popped it in my mouth then unwrapped another for herself. It was just like the pair of us during deployments—her telling me to open wide first thing in the morning as we rushed toward the prep rooms, then stuffing a bit of protein bar or muffin in my mouth so I'd have something in my stomach for the hours of surgery ahead. Later in the day, I was certain to find a piece of candy or semi-melted chocolate she'd stashed in one of my pockets.

Amy pushed another PB cup into the front pocket of my jeans where I'd likely forget about it until I did laundry. "Are you…feeling okay?"

I ran my tongue around my teeth to snag the last bits of chocolate. I knew what she was really asking, and after all we'd shared, she deserved an answer. She'd stuck with me when I fell apart after my ex dumped me from thousands of miles away. Then after The Incident, during my recovery, and this past deployment when I'd freak out at random times about random things. Or when I'd wake drenched in sweat from a nightmare, and she'd helped me strip and remake my bed in the middle of the night without hesitation.

Amy was larger and louder than life, and always moving at top speed. But whenever I needed her to be, she became slow and gentle. I loved Mitch like a brother, but he always took my wellbeing as a personal mission and could be overbearing in his love and desire to *git it fixed*. Amy was different.

Eventually I answered, "Same I guess. Maybe a little worse sometimes? I don't get it. What's the problem? I'm home, Bec's wonderful, I'm alive. So why do I feel so fucking lost?"

"I don't know, love. Are you seeing someone?"

"Mhmm. I saw Pace a couple of times during processing week and I'll keep seeing him when we're back at work."

"I had my post-deployment interview with him, he's a nice guy. That's all you can do I guess. What about medication?"

The question was put across carefully, almost nonchalantly. Amy knew all about me stopping the prescribed meds and aside from a thin-lipped stare from across our small room when she'd realized, hadn't said anything.

"No. You know I just ha—" I reached for the heavy eight-inch chef's knife, but instead of grabbing the handle, I knocked it from the countertop. Instinctively, I pulled my hands away from the falling blade but before I could think about moving anything else, I felt the sharp bite on my sock-clad left foot. "Shit! Goddammit!"

"What?" she asked around a mouthful of cucumber.

"Dropped it on my fucking foot."

"Bad?"

"I don't know. I didn't exactly measure twice, cut once." I yanked my sock off to inspect the damage, noting the blood welling from what looked like an inch-long wound. Blood. Bleeding. Dying. I could do nothing but stare, my heart racing. Blood is made up of…

Shut up, Sabine.

Amy slipped around the counter with a dishtowel in hand and crouched in front of me, pressing the wadded cloth to the top of my foot. In the time it'd taken her to put pressure on the cut, the blood had run over the side of my foot and started a small puddle on Rick's nice gift floor. She glanced up. "Missed the dorsalis pedis artery. It'll stop bleeding soon."

"Mhmm." Bleeding. I scrunched my eyes closed and tried to ignore the stinging, my shaking legs, the strange sensation akin to weightlessness that was moving along my arms. "I…I—" Blood. My blood. It's made up of erythrocytes, leukocytes and thrombocytes. The average female has roughly four liters— No, be quiet.

"Sabs? Open your eyes and look at me."

I forced my eyes open, staring down into her familiar green ones. The weird feeling in my arms moved into my fingertips, the tingling like the worst pins and needles.

Amy stood and I could feel the pressure of her foot on top of mine, holding the cloth down. She put a hand on each of my shoulders. "Can you hear me?"

I nodded, though the rush of blood in my ears made her words sound distant and distorted.

"Good," she soothed, her fingers pressing into the top of my shoulders. "Can you feel that?"

I took a few moments, trying to isolate all the sensations in my body. Yes, I could feel her touching my shoulders and again, I nodded.

"Where are we?"

Shaky breath. Think. "We're…in your kitchen." The words were broken around my near-hyperventilation.

"Right. Exactly. And what are we doing?"

What had we been doing? Driving in a Humve— No. No. We're not doing that. It's… "We're making, uh salad."

"Yes we are. Why are we making salad?" Gently, she squeezed me, and when I didn't answer, Amy said calmly, "Breathe in, love. Just in and out. Why are we making salad?"

I did as she asked, trying to concentrate on drawing air into my body. When I felt it reach down into my lungs, I exhaled. "Because…I…Bec and me, we came here for a barbeque."

"That's it. And who else is here at my house in the suburbs of Maryland, in the States?"

"Uh…it's me and Bec. You, Rick, Ethan. Mitch and Mike."

"That's right." Her fingers made circles, massaging the tense muscle of my shoulders. "You're here with Rebecca and your friends and you're safe."

I nodded.

"Tell me where you are."

"I'm in the States in your kitchen. Bec is outside and you're here and so are my other friends." A deep trembling breath. "I'm safe."

"Yes you are." Both her hands moved up to my face. "You are safe." She blinked rapidly and repeated, "You are safe."

I reached up and grabbed her elbow, grounding myself further in the feel of her soft woolen sweater. "I'm so sorry," I whispered. "I just need a minute."

Her thumbs stroked my cheeks. "Take what you need, love. I'm right here. Do you want me to get Rebecca?"

I shook my head. I couldn't run like a baby to Bec every time I had a freak-out or felt bad. She had enough of my shit to deal with. "I'll be fine. Thanks." We stood quietly for a few minutes until the shaking and nausea had subsided enough for me to think more clearly. I had a problem. A cut on my foot. Just a knife cut. Nothing else. "Okay…let's sort this thing out."

Amy studied me for a few seconds, and apparently satisfied I was no longer in danger of an imminent breakdown, eased her foot from mine. "Keep pressure on it, I'll be right back."

"Thanks for the first aid advice, Ames," I called after her, moving my right foot to press down on the small wound. Don't look down at it, it's not bad. Leaning against the counter, I drew in a couple more deep breaths and let each one out slowly.

In all my thirty-seven years, I'd never cut myself. Not with a knife, or a scalpel or even a utility blade. Never dropped a tool. Never hit my thumb with a hammer. Well done, Sabine. That's a D minus for blade competency. I pushed down harder, trying to press the sting away. I took stock of my body, of the lessening tingling in my fingers, the subsiding nausea. It's okay, you're okay. Bec outside, friends, a thick steak, clear fall day, a glass of Pinot when you get home.

Amy rushed back into the kitchen. "Haven't bled out yet?"

"Nope, but it's looking dicey." Jokes are good. Jokes are normal.

"Another pun like that and you're out on your ass," she said, but she was smiling.

I stared at the massive first aid kit in her hands. "Jesus. How often do you guys hurt yourselves?"

Amy snorted. "Blame my husband. You know he's into that doomsday prepping bullshit." She hoisted the kit onto her kitchen table. "Good thing he is. Screw wasting time at the ER when we can just deal with it here."

"It might only need a Band-Aid." I glanced out the window to make sure Bec wasn't about to come in. She was lingering near the grill, talking to Rick, while Mitch played with Ethan. Mike sat between the two groups with a beer in his hand, interacting easily with everyone.

"We'll see. Gimme a look," she said gleefully.

After thoroughly flushing the gash with saline, we agreed that the slice needed more than a Band-Aid. Amy pulled the box open and passed me a few things. I put a sterile drape on the chair beside me and carefully swabbed my foot with Betadine, teeth gritted the whole time.

Murmuring to herself, Amy kept rummaging through Rick's kit. "Oh for fuck's sake…what the hell is this?" She held up what looked like a roll of thin tape. "Don't bother asking your surgeon wife what's best, Rick, just buy some weird shit off the Internet. Who the fuck even makes Steri-Strips in a roll?" The fact Amy was now acting as she usually did helped soothe my panic.

"Is it even skin closure tape?" I asked dubiously.

She handed me a pair of scissors then pulled on gloves. "Looks like it. If it doesn't hold, I'll just use this glue and hope it isn't some cheap shit off the Internet too. Hand it over." I shuffled my foot closer and Amy adopted a faux-serious physician tone. "How's your general health? Any allergies? Tetanus up to date? Any communicable blood illness I should be aware of?"

"Not unless you count Hep A."

Amy paused, staring at me with an expression of mostly disbelief mixed with just a touch of amusement. "Um…"

I swatted at her. "It's a joke, you jerk." I had to joke about it or I'd cry about the fact I'd done something as stupid as drop a knife on my foot. Cry about the fact it'd triggered a freak-out. "Okay, let's get this done quickly before someone comes in and you have two more surgeons watching you work." I picked up the scissors, holding them in a position for her to grasp when she needed to cut the closure strips.

"They can fuck off. This cut is mine."

I stared out the window, noticing Mitch and Amy's son playing a vigorous game. It looked like Mitch, apparently a scary monster, was about to be thoroughly slain. He picked Ethan up and held him high above the ground before carefully and strategically bringing the boy close enough to make the final killing blow. Mitch's theatrical death scream carried into the house as he fell to his knees, gently lowered Ethan to the ground then flopped dramatically onto his back. After a few jerks and twitches he lay still.

Smiling fondly, Amy glanced out the window. "He's great with Ethan." She carefully drew the sides of the cut together and placed the first strip, smoothing the edges down.

"Mitch loves kids. He's always wanted to be a father."

"How about you?" Amy took the scissors from me, snipped the tape and gave them back. "You make an excellent theater nurse by the way."

"Thanks, and ugh, no thanks for kids. Aside from the whole not understanding children, I just…I think I'm too selfish. I like my life the way it is, with Bec." I tapped my temple with the butt of my palm, careful to keep the instrument pointed away from my face. "Plus with all the stuff up here, probably not a good idea."

"What about Bec?" A second strip joined the first.

"No. She likes kids, but she's not interested either." A frisson of alarm tightened the muscle of my neck. Something was nudging at my subconscious, but I couldn't quite grasp it. Conversations about children and not wanting them, then something else…Bec changing her mind? But the memory had a vague, dreamlike tinge at the edges of it.

"I hear ya. Ethan was an accident, never thought I'd have any." She grinned. "Now I can't imagine life without him, but back then I was definitely having a what the fuck am I going to do sort of panic. One more?"

It took a moment to realize she was asking about my foot, not if she should have another child. I checked her work and nodded, trying to shake off my strange thoughts. "Well, no accidents for us."

She laughed, loudly, ending with a snort. "Very true." After placing the last strip, she leaned in. "Right, we're done. May I draw your attention to this goddamned work of art."

"Magnificent," I agreed.

"Only the best for you," she said as she quickly dressed my foot. While we packed up the first aid kit and assorted trash and wrappers, Amy spoke quietly, "Seriously, Sabs. You know I'm here to talk or whatever. Remember that."

"I know." She'd proven that time and time again, including less than fifteen minutes ago. "It's just…everyone's so fucking great. So helpful and so wonderful. And sometimes it makes me feel worse." They were all there, ready and eager to listen and help. But what if I didn't even know what to say? What if I didn't know what sort of help I needed?

"What do you mean?"

"What am I giving back? I feel like I'm all take and no give at the moment." I heaved a long sigh. It'd felt that way for a while now. "I've already asked everyone for so much. I'm not sure I can keep asking again."

"Friendships and relationships aren't about keeping score, Sabs," Amy said, and the serious tone felt odd coming from her.

"I know that, but it's just…what's the tipping point? At what point will it become too much? Surely someone's going to cave under the weight of all this shit in my head, and bail."

"No we won't," Amy said instantly. "Because we love you. But you have to let us in, tell us what's going on." She hugged me long and tight. "Give me a moment to get you some clean things and wash this floor."

I started to rise. "I can do it."

"No, love. You sit there. Won't take long."

After efficiently cleaning my mess from the floor and presenting me with socks and a pair of soft comfortable slippers, Amy picked up the salad—sans my abandoned carrot—and slipped out the back door. I collected the potato salad from the fridge and limping, followed her outside to where the rest of the group were milling about.

Amy flitted around, having simultaneous conversations about what kind of idiot buys that much meat and when will the grill be hot enough to start cooking, does everyone have enough to drink, and finally assuring Ethan that yes she'd seen him slaughter Mitch and to please not use words like slaughter.

Bec shielded her eyes and flashed me a smile. Her gaze shifted to my feet before returning to my face, her eyebrows lifted in silent question. I should have known she wouldn't miss the fact I was limping, and also wearing Amy's slippers. I smiled and shook my head to indicate everything was fine, and after a beat, Bec nodded in acquiescence before returning to what sounded like a conversation about peak oil with Rick. She was doing a very good job of seeming interested.

Mike looked up at me, grinning lazily. I stopped beside him, staring out at Mitch, who was still lying prone on the ground while Ethan jumped around him apparently trying to figure out what to do with the slain beast. "I kind of wonder which one of them is the kid," Mike said.

"I don't."

The Monster miraculously revived, hopping to his knees. "You wanna play, Sabs? Soon we'll be lookin' for a princess to rescue."

"Can I do it sitting right here?"

Mike laughed and leaned his head against my hip. "That's pretty much what I said." He turned to smile sweetly at his boyfriend, who'd adopted a wounded, pouting expression.

"Y'all are no fun," Mitch grumbled. "C'mon, Ethan. Let's go find some beetles to drop down their shirts."

I mussed Mike's hair before settling on the deck chair beside him. One of the many things I liked about him was that he was content to sit and watch, didn't feel the need to fill in silences. His quiet mood suited mine perfectly. I propped my feet up and watched Bec talking with Amy's husband.

Smiling, my girlfriend raised her wineglass to me then turned back to her conversation.

We arrived back home a little after six, still so replete from the late lunch that we agreed to skip dinner. After a shower, I awkwardly toed the scale from under the bathroom counter, the sharp sliding sound along the bathroom tiles announcing what I was doing. Before I could think about whether or not I'd *improved*, I stepped on, glanced at the number then hopped off again.

Bec came into the bathroom just as I was pushing the scale back into its hiding place. There was no way she wouldn't have caught what I was doing, but she didn't ask. She stretched up, kissed my cheek and asked, "Did you have a nice day?"

"Mhmm." I stared at the floor, not wanting to look at her. But talking without eye contact felt wrong, so I forced my eyes up, found hers in the mirror and said, "Almost a pound and a half up since I came home. Though it could just be from Mom's overfeeding and all the food today."

"That's great, Sabine." Her hands came around my waist from behind and she pressed herself to my back. Her breath tickled my neck. "You know…it's not about how you look, darling. I just want you to be healthy. That's all."

"I know." I put my arms over hers, pulling her closer. After a pause I added, "Thank you."

Bec rested her chin on my shoulder. "How's your foot?" She'd asked what happened the moment we'd settled in the car, and seemed satisfied with my answer, if not a little put out I hadn't called for her to come and help. But I couldn't figure out how to explain that I couldn't stand the thought of her fixing my small injury when she'd already fixed the major ones inside me.

"Fine. Throbs a little and kinda hurts to walk, but I'll take some Tylenol."

"Good." Bec pressed a few soft kisses to the side of my neck, her breath whispering over my skin. "I'm exhausted, I think I'm going to read in bed for a while."

"Okay. I might watch some TV. I'm so full I feel like I need to be recumbent on the couch for a week."

"Then I'll see you when you come back up." She slipped out of the bathroom and left me alone.

I stared at my face in the mirror, trying to find something different on the outside to match all that was different on the inside. Nothing. Same face. Just a changed person. I flicked the light off, smiled at Bec on my way past and hopped my way downstairs.

Sprawled on the couch, I trawled through channels, unable to stick with anything and only half-watching the screen. I'd been hoping some brainless viewing would help relax my mind, but it felt like it was having the opposite effect. And I couldn't go up to bed, not feeling so unsettled.

After almost three hours Bec came into the den with her robe belted loosely around her waist. "Lonely up there without you," she explained with a smile, sitting at the other end of the couch. She swung her legs up and placed her feet in my lap. Her toenails were her usual fire-engine red, just like that first night we'd spent together.

"Kinda lonely down here too," I said as I started massaging the balls of her feet.

A groan slid from her mouth. "God your hands are magic."

As I massaged, my unease ebbed and flowed. Having Bec with me helped my anxiety, but then I'd think of all the issues I was having at the moment, and how I couldn't do anything about it and the panic would rise again. We sat quietly for a time, her head thrown back onto the arm of the couch, a contented smile on her face as I kneaded her feet and calves.

Eventually my discomfort grew so overwhelming that I couldn't stand it. I had to verbalize it, to get it out before it strangled me. Quietly I said, "I think there's something wrong with me, Bec."

"What do you mean, sweetheart?" Bec lifted her head, giving me her full attention. Carefully, she withdrew her feet from my lap and sat up.

"I just…I'm back and we're together and don't have to hide anymore. I'm so happy and I love you so much."

"Me too, Sabine," she said softly, reaching forward to cup my cheek.

"Then why do I feel so lost?" Gently I brushed her hand aside, but not before I'd kissed her palm. I lifted my left foot so it was in view. "Like this? How did that happen? I've never cut myself, ever. How am I supposed to work if I can't even handle a kitchen knife without dropping it?"

"I hardly think a kitchen accident is an indicator of surgical incompetence," Bec said carefully. "I've nicked my finger in the kitchen a few times and dropped plenty of mugs and plates."

"I know," I mumbled. But Bec wasn't me. I just didn't do things like that. Make mistakes. I stood up and began to pace, limping my way across the carpet, loathing the way my body felt—coiled and tight like if I didn't move I'd scream. "I feel like…like I can't sort my thoughts into their proper order."

"Is this a new thing?" she asked, tracking my progress back and forth across the floor.

"Yes. No. I don't know. It seems like it's gotten worse, maybe in the past few months or so." Suddenly, I had that uncomfortable and thankfully infrequent since childhood sensation that I was about to stammer. My body was tense, my tongue tight and uncomfortable. I glanced away and after a few deep breaths felt disciplined enough to make eye contact again and say slowly, "You know the day I came home?"

"Yes. What about it?"

I realized what I was about to admit and had to move again, away from her sure disappointment. "We were done by eleven a.m." Still pacing, I watched her and waited for her to make the connection. The drive home would have taken less than an hour, yet I'd taken almost twelve hours to find my way home to her.

Her eyebrows drew together, her gaze on the wall behind me for a moment before she brought her focus back to my face. "Oh," she said quietly. "Why? If you'd told me, then I would have called someone to take the rest of my shift and come home to you. Why would you stay away?" The hurt in her voice was unmistakable, as was the gentle rebuke.

"I just…" My explanation came out in a quick tangle of words. "I was totally about to rush straight here, ready for when you got home. Or I was going to come by work and really surprise you. But when I stopped and thought about it, about seeing you and touching you I panicked." I slowed my steps, in the hope it might calm my frantic heartbeat. "Fuck, I wanted to see you, Bec. I wanted it so much the desperation was practically choking me. But every time I thought about stepping back through that doorway, *our* doorway, I just froze inside."

"Why do you think that was?" She reached out a hand and snagged my arm as I walked past.

Even as she touched me, I felt the distance between us as if it were miles. I let myself be tugged gently down to sit on the couch beside her. "I'm not sure. Just stupid fears. What if I'd changed so much during deployment you didn't like what you saw anymore?"

"That would never happen, darling." Bec lifted my hands, studying them as though she'd never seen them before. "Where did you go then if you weren't here?"

I shrugged. "Just around. I saw a movie, did some shopping, ate a few burgers, had a couple of beers. Then I grabbed a cab and came home around eight and I stood on the street, against that oak, and watched you and Jana in the kitchen tidying up after dinner. And I had the strangest feeling, seeing you two so comfortable together, thinking that maybe you didn't need me. You were all doing fine without me. So I hid my gear beside the house and wandered around the streets for a few more hours until the feeling went away."

"Sabine…"

"Please, Bec, wait. Please listen." If I stopped now, I'd never start again. I closed my eyes, pulling one of my hands away to scrub over my face. "I just can't make it fit where it's supposed to. I have all these things all over the place like some crazy jigsaw puzzle with all the wrong pieces and I hate it. I don't know how to be this version of myself. And the only right pieces are yours but I still can't quite figure out where they go now."

"Oh, sweetheart, I know how hard that is for you but maybe it's not all supposed to fit neatly right now." Her expression was so gentle and understanding and so like Bec. "Coming home is hard and stressful at the best of times. With everything else that's happened, I don't think it's unreasonable that you feel this way."

"Mmm, true," I conceded. "The stupid fucking thing is eighty-seven percent of the time, I feel okay, like I'm handling it. And then something like today happens, or I'll have a random thought and it trips back to *that* day and I feel lost all over again." Brilliant, Sabine. Eighty-seven percent? Why not drag out a pie chart and display the exact breakdown of all your thoughts and feelings?

Bec's thumbs were sliding up and over the back of my hand she was still holding. "I don't think that's unusual, darling. You had an incredibly traumatic experience both physically and mentally, and the ramifications of that aren't just going to go away. As much as we would like them to."

"It's not fucking fair!" I spat out. The moment the words left my mouth I felt the flush of embarrassment on my ears. I was acting like a petulant little kid.

"No, it's not fair," she agreed, her tone even.

"I'm sorry." I squeezed her hand firmly, then panicked that I might have hurt her, and pulled mine free. "I'm so sick of feeling like I don't have any control over my own thoughts. I'm tired of feeling like I'm a completely different person. A person I don't particularly like. I'm tired of waking up every morning hoping it'll be different, but it's always just the same."

"Oh, sweetheart." Those two words were choked, barely audible. She sounded like she was about to cry. Well done, Fleischer.

I tried to sort through my jumbled thoughts to explain, to make her understand it wasn't her, but it was me. "Bec, I feel like we're just…" I moved my hands together, the left skimming over the top of the right without touching. "Missing each other. You know? Like we're so close, but we're not quite connecting. And I can't tell if it's the PTSD, or just this deployment or if…" I paused, drew a breath and the rest of my words came out in a hoarse whisper, "Maybe I'm so different now that you don't want me anymore."

Bec's hands came immediately to my face, cupping my cheeks. "Darling, listen to me. What's happening in here—" Her fingers gently massaged my temples, then a hand moved from my face to cover my left breast, right over my heart. "Hasn't changed what lives in here. Everything that makes you *you* is still here. Everything I love is still here. I love you when you're strong and brave, and I love you at times like now, when you trust me enough to let me see you vulnerable."

I drew in a shuddering breath. "I'm so sorry, Bec. I've changed so much from the person you thought you'd be spending your life with. You gave up your career for me and I feel like I made you a promise I haven't kept."

"Bullshit!" she said with surprising vehemence. "I didn't give up my career, I left the *Army*, Sabine and I did that because I need to be with you. I did that for me. I did that for us and I've never regretted it. I'm still a trauma surgeon and I still love my job." Her eyes closed for a few seconds, and when she opened them and spoke again, her anger had diffused. "And yes, you've changed. But so have I. Every day something about us is different and every day, the love I have for you grows."

"Are you sure?" I whispered, aware of how pathetic and childlike it sounded.

"Yes. Love is adaptable, but mine for you has never faltered." Her forceful words were tempered by her thumbs sliding gently over my cheekbones, my eyebrows, my mouth. "I love you so much and I just want to help you. Please tell me how," she begged.

I didn't think she could help, not really, not by actively *doing* anything. But maybe I didn't need that, maybe I just needed her. I wiped away my tears with my sleeve, then took her hands again. "Please, stay with me? I think you're the only thing that will make sense when nothing else does."

She kissed me, just the softest brush of our lips, but it spoke of a deep, soothing connection. Resting her forehead against mine, Bec promised, "You know I will. I'm not leaving, Sabine."

CHAPTER TEN

Rebecca

The week after our visit to Ohio passed in a blur of domesticity—daily walks or outings and relaxing at home—just *being* together until the day we both had to return to work came up far too quickly. I spent the whole morning in surgery then after lunch, hid in my office trying to lower my pile of paperwork before afternoon rounds.

The day was shaping up to be one I wanted to forget. Barely two hours into my shift, I'd had a patient death, then for the rest of the morning worked on a teenage girl who'd been thrown through the windshield of a car in which she was joyriding. I could do little for her massive brain injury.

Something else popped up whenever I tried to push it aside. My eyes strayed to the dress I'd hung behind my office door ready for tonight, and the feeling became uncomfortably clear.

Guilt.

I felt guilty because I was going out to dinner with a coworker when I should have been home with my partner. My partner who was clearly struggling. My partner who today, had started her first full day back at work, in a new place at the freshly integrated U.S. Military Medical Center. My partner who'd admitted that she didn't feel like herself, didn't feel like she fit into our life. She hadn't said anything further since our emotional discussion last Saturday night, acting typically like nothing was amiss. The silence was telling.

Sabine was afraid and she was avoiding.

Chasing her would only make it worse, so I'd resigned myself to waiting until she was ready to come to me again. The fact I could be waiting a while settled like a lead weight. All I wanted to do was go home after a long and awful workday and curl up on the couch with her. To have her head pillowed against my breasts, both soothing and being soothed.

My pager beeped, interrupting my melancholy. I saved my report and rushed out of my office toward the bank of elevators fifty feet away at the end of the corridor.

Dr. James Felton, one of my newer trauma residents, was sweating. Thin rivulets ran from his temples to his stubbled cheeks and every now and then he would drop his jaw to his shoulder to blot the sweat away. By the look of him, he hadn't slept, showered or probably even eaten in a while. That was trauma surgery.

I pointed absently to the CT images, but my focus remained on him. "What do you think, James?"

Bloodshot hazel eyes moved back and forth over the monitor. "Penetrating ballistic trauma to…small bowel, other organs appear uncompromised?"

My poker face was in place but inside I was smiling. "Best course of treatment?"

James paused, eyes now moving between me and the scans at tennis-spectator rate. "The patient is hemodynamically stable…" He still didn't sound particularly convinced. "Laparoscopic extraction and repair?"

A resident who didn't want to go in scalpels flying. Interesting. I tilted my head as I posed the question, "Why laparoscopy?"

"It's a small caliber ballistic trauma with only minimal damage?" He swallowed and licked his lips, the movement furtive like he was trying not to give away how dry his mouth was. "In my opinion, laparotomy isn't indicated here. I think it's overkill to open him right up, Doctor Keane, and this less invasive treatment plan would give the patient a shorter recovery period. We could always move to a full laparotomy if we can't find the bullet." It was the first thing he'd said that hadn't been phrased as a question.

I stared at him. "You're sure?"

"Yes." Another glance at the scans, then a more confident, "Yes I am."

"Excellent, so am I."

James followed me to the sinks and as he pulled a mask down from the boxes affixed to the wall, I glanced over at him. Despite his relief after my confirmation of his treatment plan, his jaw was now rigid, tension radiating from his body. In the few months I'd known him I'd discovered he was a quiet young man, a little nervous but seemed focused enough and had the skill to back it up. I started my scrub.

Laparoscopic procedures weren't an everyday occurrence for us in trauma and each time I did one, I thought about Sabine and me removing a gallbladder in Afghanistan while artillery fire was dropping nearby. I'd sought her out to assist me, knowing it was a flimsy excuse to spend more time with her. She was adorably clumsy with the unfamiliar scopes, and when she'd finished, Sabine had glanced up, her eyes bright and creased with the smile that lay hidden behind her mask. I'd wanted to grab her right there and kiss her.

While we'd scrubbed out, nearby shelling shook the floor and Sabine's tension was evident as she stared at her feet. I'd wanted to draw her out, to relax her and see that smile I adored—so I'd teased that if she could do that procedure in a shaky OR, she could do it anywhere, and that she should put the skill on her résumé.

Sabine had looked up at me, a slow smile forming on her lips as she'd responded, almost cheekily, "May I use you as a reference for this particular skill listing, ma'am?"

I'd almost shuddered at the way she'd said *ma'am* in a slow, unconsciously seductive drawl. It was then that I knew I had to do something about the way I felt about her. So I made a promise to myself that I had to move past my attraction because it was becoming overwhelming. Then less than a month later, I'd done the complete opposite.

Felton cleared his throat again. Fatigue or nerves or doubt were starting to creep up. Still scrubbing, I turned toward him, my hip bumping against the edge of the sink. "You know, I once did a laparoscopic cholecystectomy in Afghanistan while troops were engaged in battle nearby. The floor was vibrating every few minutes and the instruments were rattling on the tray." I laughed softly. "It's quite interesting to operate in a theater that's shaking, worrying about artillery fire coming through the roof."

He looked over at me, eyebrows raised. "I imagine that would be quite difficult, Doctor Keane. I didn't know you were in the military."

I smiled at him, hoping he would see it in my eyes while I was hidden behind a surgical mask. "Yes, for eighteen years. I promise that all of this gets easier."

He remained silent, staring down at his hands as he scrubbed. I nudged the faucet to shut off the water and sniffed to clear the scent of chlorhexidine scrub from my nose. "A little fear is a good thing. Without fear, you get careless. But if you let the fear take over it will overwhelm you." I dipped my head to catch his eye. "Do you understand what I'm saying?"

"Yes, Doctor Keane." Slowly, he raised his head. "…but what if the fear never goes away?"

"Then you have to decide if what you want is worth it, if it's worth the time and effort to find a way to work around your fear. If it is, then you do whatever you need to do." Even as I said the words I knew I wasn't really talking about a surgical career.

I was talking about Sabine. And me.

* * *

I completed rounds on autopilot. Talk, check, confirm with nurses, adjust, sign, next. At a quarter to seven, I began to feel a glimmer of hope that I might be done on time and the moment

I thought it, I chastised myself. Superstition dictated if you thought about finishing on time, something would pop up at the very last moment. For once, I was lucky.

When my shift had officially ended, I sent Vanessa a quick text to let her know I'd be on time for our reservation, then texted Sabine with a simple *I love you, won't be home too late.* Then I rushed to my office before anyone could grab me, signed myself out, turned my pager off and set it to charge.

The institutional locker room and showers at the hospital reminded me of being on deployment, except the water was always hot and full-pressured. After a blissful shower I changed into a simple black dress and heels, then wiped the mirror with the edge of my hand so I could quickly but carefully apply makeup. A quick brush through my hair with my fingers, and I was ready.

Vanessa waited by the automatic doors, elegantly dressed in wool slacks and a cashmere overcoat, with a hint of a royal blue silk blouse showing that brought out the intense color of her eyes. Her heels gave her another few inches on the four she already had on me. She grasped my arm, her touch light. "How lovely that we both managed to finish work at a civilized time."

I smiled up at her. "Isn't it? I almost feel like a regular person."

Vanessa laughed, and gestured to her left. "Shall we?" After a quick stop to stow bags in my car, we began walking along the sandstone hospital path toward the sidewalk, talking about our respective days. It was a lovely late October night, with a lingering half-hearted threat of rain and the cool air hinting at the colder weather to come.

The ten-minute walk to the restaurant passed in easy, companionable conversation. Though we were a little early, we were shown immediately to our seats, settled and handed a wine list and menus. Vanessa perused the former and quickly made her choice—a white Pinot Noir. I requested the same and when the waiter left, I gave Vanessa a rueful smile. "Goodness, I could dive into a bottle right now."

"One of those days?"

I smoothed my hand over the tablecloth. "Yes. First day back, and I've had two bad outcomes. Doesn't bode well for the rest of the week." For some reason, as a civilian doctor, I found it harder to cope with losses. Most of my patients were victims of circumstance, which bothered me far more than my former job. And my former job had bothered me a great deal at times.

Of course my mood was due to more than just work, but I wasn't sure if I should mention personal issues. While Vanessa and I were friends, I wouldn't have considered us close. Still, it would be nice to have a sympathetic ear. Someone who wasn't involved the way Jana was. After my quick internal debate, I added, "And…things at home are a little up and down right now."

She frowned. "I'm sorry to hear that. Is it something you'd like to talk about?"

Talking about PTSD resulting from a military incident when I was about to tell her son about the Army probably wasn't a great idea. Before I could answer, the waiter returned with the wine. I declined a taste and indicated he should just pour. To my surprise, Vanessa also waved away a sampling, the action surprising me because I'd had her pegged as someone who'd send a bottle back if it wasn't up to standard.

Once we were alone again, Vanessa raised her wineglass. "Well, here's to better outcomes for the rest of the week. And good things at home."

I lifted mine. "Indeed." The wine was fantastic, rich and smooth with a hint of fruit. The kind of white Sabine would enjoy. I smiled to myself and mentally amended my thought— the kind she'd enjoy if she could tear herself away from red meat and red wine.

Vanessa's question broke me from thoughts of the woman waiting for me at home. "So, which came first? Medicine or the military?"

"Medicine," I said instantly.

She nodded slowly, her gaze unerring. "Why trauma surgery?"

I set the wineglass down. "My parents died in an MVA when I was five and I formed a, well…morbid sort of fascination with the surgeons who'd worked on them. I wanted to be as noble as I imagined they were."

"And the military?"

I laughed. "That was less noble. Running away from a relationship."

Her unselfconscious laughter caught the attention of the couple at the table beside us. "I don't know, Rebecca. I think there's a certain nobility in not deluding yourself or another person about what you really want."

I tilted my head in acknowledgement. "Perhaps. At any rate, it felt like a good decision at the time. Until I realized I didn't want to run away any longer."

She leaned forward, her fingers briefly brushing the back of my wrist. "Honestly, I admire your making such a big career change in leaving the military. I'm not sure I could do something so life-altering."

I turned the wineglass in slow circles. "It took me six months or so to adjust but the core of the job is the same." I laughed softly and added, "Though I admit I'm still adjusting to not being called *Colonel* or *Ma'am*."

Her mouth quirked into a mischievous smile, but as she was about to speak, a tall, sandy-haired young man in a charcoal suit appeared to her right. He acknowledged me with a polite smile then turned to Vanessa who aborted whatever she was about to say, stood and stepped into his outstretched arms. "Nicholas!"

After they'd parted, he raised both hands placatingly. "Sorry, Mom. Traffic was awful."

Vanessa gestured to me. "Rebecca, I'd like to introduce my son, Nicholas Spears. Nick, this is Rebecca Keane."

I stood as Nick offered his hand. He had a plain, open face, his mother's eyes and her broad, easy smile. He didn't, however, have her last name. Interesting. "Hi, Rebecca, nice to meet you."

His grip was firm, something I appreciated having spent my life enduring limp, soft-gripped handshakes from men. "It's a pleasure to meet you too."

Nick held my chair first and then his mother's. Once we were seated again, he took his place opposite me, his expression expectant and interested. "Well. Shall we?"

The rest of the evening passed swiftly and enjoyably. Nick, like his mother, was charming and polite. He was also deferential but confident—he would fit in the military like a hand in a glove—and I knew after ten minutes of conversation that regardless of what I said he was going to join one of the services. Vanessa listened without trying to sway opinions and her only real interjection was to try and suggest that her son become an officer.

After coffee and dessert, Vanessa took the check with a quiet, "I insist, you've been so helpful."

Pleased, I acceded. "All right then. Thank you." As Vanessa settled the check, I fished a card from my purse. "If you want to talk some more, Nick, please contact me any time."

He took it, turning it over. "I think you've given me a wonderful overview, Rebecca. Thank you so much for being so candid."

"I'm pleased to have helped," I said, meaning it.

Vanessa returned and escorted me outside. We exchanged goodbyes with her son and began to make our way back toward the hospital. Vanessa looked up, buttoning her overcoat. "Goodness I hope we have early snow this year."

"Me too. I am definitely a winter person." As was Sabine who loved to pull on a jacket, scarf and her Ugg boots to sit on the deck with coffee and a book while snow fell on our backyard.

"Oh? So how did you cope working in the desert heat?"

"Not very well." I laughed. "But most of our time is indoors, so it's semi-bearable." I caught myself. "*Was* indoors."

We crossed the road and continued toward the hospital's staff parking lot. An ambulance was pulling away and we stopped to let it pass. Once we'd started walking again, Vanessa said, "I'd like to hear more about your time in the Army. More stories as opposed to dry facts and statistics."

I smiled up at her. "Well, I have a number of stories." Some of which I would never tell. Could never. I unlocked my car and set my handbag on the passenger seat.

"How about dinner in the next few weeks?"

Something felt odd and it was on the tip of my tongue to say something about Sabine, to remind Vanessa about my partner. That I have a partner. A partner I loved and was still very much in love with. Instead, I thought about my presumption that her invite was anything more than just friendly, and the possibility of conversation removed from my current home situation. Conversation that wasn't fraught and what often felt futile, trying to get Sabine to open up to me. Conversation I didn't need to moderate. I sometimes thought trying to moderate myself was pointless, because by nature Sabine was prone to take any discussion of her mental health as evidence of her being less than perfect.

So I nodded, and agreed, "Sure. I'd like that."

"Wonderful." Vanessa gently squeezed my arm. "Thank you, Rebecca. I can't tell you how much I appreciate you taking the time to talk to Nick. And I certainly learned something too."

"It was my pleasure." I paused. "What about your…husband? Does he have an opinion on Nicholas joining the military?"

"My *ex*-husband doesn't care about much except spending what he got in the divorce settlement and telling our son that my bisexuality is the reason we split. Thankfully Nick is smart enough to realize the truth is I simply wanted to divorce a cheating, emotionally abusive alcoholic."

My cheeks heated. "Ah. I'm sorry, I didn't mean to pry."

Vanessa laughed, reaching to grasp my forearm. "You didn't."

"All right then. Thank you for a lovely evening."

"You're welcome, and I had a great time." After gently squeezing my arm, she closed the door for me, waved through the window and waited until I'd driven off. I made it home before ten and hadn't even closed the door before Titus sprinted from out of nowhere, howling insistently at me.

"No way, buddy. I know your mom's fed you." Probably more than once, knowing Sabine. He wound around my legs, still making hopeful sounds, while I walked into the kitchen and set my bags and coat down. When I didn't feed him, he walked away with his tail aloft, in that cat version of *screw you* I'd come to know well.

I murmured to nobody, "Speaking of, where is your mom?" Her car was in the garage but most of the lights in the house were off, with the exception of the kitchen and upstairs hallway. I plugged my phone in to charge. "Sabine?" There was no answer.

It was too early for her to be in bed. Wandering through the lower level, I checked the gym room and office without success. In the dark den, the streetlights illuminated a blanket-covered lump stretched out on the couch. "Sweetheart?"

The lump shifted and then sat up quickly. "Hey," she mumbled. "What time is it?"

"Almost ten." I flicked on the light, immediately twisting the knob to dim it for her just-woken eyes.

Sabine stretched, groaning. "How lame. I can't believe I fell asleep on the couch." Blinking, she studied me and let out a low whistle, a grin lifting the edges of her mouth. "You haven't worn that dress in a while. God you look totally fuckable."

"Mmm, thank you." Bending down, I kissed her lightly in greeting. I couldn't help myself and leaned in for another longer, firmer kiss. My tongue traced lightly over her lower lip, tasting her vanilla lip balm. I could have easily taken her suggestive comment and run with it, but Sabine ended the kiss, pulling back to drop a soft peck on the tip of my nose. I settled on the arm of the couch, stretching down to pull my heels off. "How was work? Did you have any surgical cases? Did you see Andrew today?" Aware I was pushing, I left it at those three questions.

"Work was work, just one, and yeah I did." She pushed a hand through her dark hair, leaving it even more disheveled. "He suggested I try yoga because it's relaxation but with some sort of structure." She made air quotes.

"Yoga," I repeated, trying to conjure the mental image of Sabine, who could barely sit still watching a movie, doing yoga.

"Mhmm. I might take a look next week." Sabine frowned, her mouth twisting the way it always did when she was gnawing the inside of her cheek. I knew the expression and exactly what it meant—she was thinking, and she was worried. After a long pause, she admitted, "I feel a bit weird about learning something new." Her unspoken *what if I'm no good at it* hung between us. "But if he thinks it'll help, I guess I'll try?"

I was surprised that frenetic Sabine had actually taken the suggestion that yoga might help. Alongside my surprise was a little spark of hope that she was still working toward listening and taking advice to help herself. I smoothed strands of hair away from her face and tucked them behind her ears. "Plenty of people start yoga and all manner of things when they're adults. Think of how flexible you'll be."

"Bec, if I were any more flexible, you'd bend me in half." Sabine bounced her eyebrows comically, then scooted over, patting the couch beside her. "How was your dinner?"

"It was lovely." I shifted from the arm to the seat and settled close to her. "Nicholas is a nice boy. Man," I corrected myself. "Well-mannered, confident, just what they need in an officer, which Vanessa insists he becomes if he's committed to the Army as a career. He qualifies for Officer Candidate School so I assume he'll go that route."

She tucked Ugg-clad feet underneath herself. "Where'd you go?"

"That French restaurant close to the hospital."

"What did you order?"

"Mushroom tart, sea bass, shared cheese platter for dessert."

"No wine?"

"Just one glass. A very nice white Pinot Noir."

She rested her elbow on the back of the couch, gazing intently at me. "What would I have eaten if I was there?"

It was beginning to feel a little like an interrogation, but I played along, unsure if she was trying to insert herself into the event to remind me that she was my girlfriend, or if she was considering it as a place for us to have dinner. I pushed aside my fleeting thoughts about not mentioning Sabine to Vanessa, and responded, "Hmmm, beet salad starter, veal main and profiteroles for dessert."

She grinned. "That sounds awesome. Maybe we could go sometime?" Sabine drew in a deep breath, the rest of her words coming out in a rush. "And take a cab so we can both drink?"

"Of course, darling, I'd like that very much," I said evenly. Even just suggesting allowing someone else to drive us was another huge step. I wanted to tell her how proud I was, but to acknowledge it would only draw attention to something she saw as a failing. So I said nothing.

Sabine took some of my hair in her fingers, winding it around in a loop. "So, this friend of yours doesn't mind if her kid joins the military, but he has to be an officer?"

"That's about it."

She scoffed. "Can you imagine? Pushing your child to be an officer."

I smiled, well aware of the unspoken expectations of her own family and sure she hadn't even realized what she was saying. In response, I hmmed.

Sabine let go of my hair. "What would you do if your kid wanted to join the Army?"

"What do you mean?"

"Exactly what I asked," she said, seeming confused by me questioning her question.

"I don't think I can answer that. I've never thought about it because I don't want children. You know that." I'd never wanted children, not even when I was younger.

"Maybe something will change."

"Sabine, it's definitely not something I want to start *now*, not that I ever did. What makes you think I want a child all of a sudden?"

"Nothing, I just thought…something made me think… never mind." Sabine looked down at her splayed fingers. "Maybe I just dreamed it," she murmured absently.

A dream? Gently, I squeezed her thigh. "Is everything okay? Do you need to talk about anything?"

She shook her head no, but I didn't know if it was no, things aren't okay or no she didn't want to talk. I tilted my head, studying her. What was I missing? This was weird, erratic and completely out of character. Something clicked into place. Things had been tumultuous these past few years. She was thirty-seven, maybe she'd changed her mind about kids. It wouldn't be the strangest thing. I had to take a breath before I asked, "Do *you* want to have a baby?"

She almost choked in her haste to get the words out. "Oh, fuck no. No!"

Relief flooded over me. "Okay, all right. I thought I should ask." My mouth was dry as I asked another question, in as neutral a tone as I could muster. "Sabine, seriously, what's going on?"

Sabine's coal-dark eyes were wide. "Nothing. I just have this weird feeling, like we'd had this conversation where you told me you wouldn't mind having a baby if it was accidental. And I can't help but worry about the…accidental part of it."

"Sweetheart, no, I have *never* said that. That's craz—" I paused, rethought was I was about to say, and tried a different tack. "How could it possibly be accidental? We've talked about both of us not wanting children and my stance certainly hasn't changed. I'm certain you just dreamed it or something." I smiled at her, trying to soften my words and keep her relaxed. This was getting really bizarre.

"Okay." She seemed to accept what I was saying but her expression remained confused.

Confusion was right, but I had to know what was going on in her head. I tried to pick my way around the right words, but there was no other way to phrase it. "Honey, have you spoken to Andrew about this? It kind of sounds a little bit like a… delusion?" I readied myself for her to come out swinging.

Her jaw tightened, working back and forth. "No I haven't." She gave a long exasperated sigh. "I guess I'll tell him. On top of all the other shit I have to tell him," she added in a mumble.

"Sure, okay. Good."

We sat in the semi-dark, not speaking, just looking at one another with our fingers lightly entwined. Every now and then, Sabine absently pawed at the right side of her torso, under her armpit like she was pulling too-tight clothing away from her body. She looked strangely uncomfortable, as though she didn't like her own skin.

The silence stretched until it became strained and uncomfortable, and I couldn't help thinking of my earlier conversation with Vanessa. How it would feel to be with a woman without thinking through everything I wanted to say and worrying how it would be taken. To have just one day where *this* didn't intrude into our lives. As soon as I'd thought it, I felt the flush of shame.

I had no right to think such things, and the fact I had made me feel sick. Sabine was my partner and I belonged right here. With the woman I loved with every cell of my body. With the woman who was suffering because of my decision when I'd already made so many wrong decisions.

But it was just so damned hard at the moment. I just wanted us to be the way we were, before The Incident. But I knew that would never happen. I swallowed, shifting on the couch until my back hit the armrest. Suddenly, I was desperate for Sabine's touch. For the comfort of her body against mine. "Come here, cuddle with me."

She popped up onto her knees, and we shuffled until I was stretched full length on the couch, my head against the cushions. Sabine lowered herself to lie between my legs, her torso pressed to mine half-on and half-off me. With one arm tucked up between us, the other wrapped loosely around my waist, she carefully rested her head against my breasts.

Sabine exhaled, a long and contented release. I felt the relaxation mirrored in my own body, finally having made it to the place I'd wanted to be all day. I cupped the back of her head, fingers massaging her scalp, then moved my hand to stroke up and down her neck. Kneading gently, feeling the raised edges of one of her shrapnel scars under my fingertips, I kept up the rhythmic movement.

"Feels really good," she mumbled, her fist tightening on the fabric of my dress. "I love you, Bec."

"I love you too, darling." I closed my eyes and let my thoughts drift wherever they wanted, until they inevitably came back around to the thing that stood like a fence between us, and the only explanation I could come up with for her behavior. PTSD. Not an unconquerable obstacle, but an obstacle nonetheless, made more difficult by the fact that being forthright about such matters was unnatural for her.

With painful clarity I realized that Sabine was right the other night, when she'd said that we weren't connecting. It wasn't just physically—we'd only made love once since she came home, or rather she'd made love to me—but emotionally as well. I felt like we were drifting past one another and I didn't know how to stop it. I couldn't tether us together. She'd rail against being forced or constrained. All I could do was follow her, keep her in my sights and hope that with everything we were fighting against, I could keep up.

CHAPTER ELEVEN

Sabine

Halfway to the lunch room, I realized I hadn't counted my steps. Do I turn around? If I turn around should I count back to the locker room and then from the—

No. Don't be such an idiot. My stomach turned over, a portentous fluttering in my chest stealing my breath. Stop it. Nothing's going to happen, Sabine. It's just numbers in your head that have absolutely no bearing on anything. The muscle of my jaw ached, tension radiating and coalescing into a sharp pain at my temple. Clenching my fists, I strode up the hall and into the lunch room. Not counting. And not having anxiety about not counting, no sir, not me.

Mitch sat at a table in the middle of the bland institutional space, a thick sandwich in one hand, a book in the other. Fruit and another sandwich spilled from the cooler bag he'd dumped on the table. We'd both choked down far too many disgusting meals on deployment to want what was on offer at the hospital cafeterias, and like most of our coworkers, brought food from home. After collecting mine from the communal fridge and waving to people dotted around the room, I slid into the seat opposite him. "Hey."

Mitch set down his book. "Hey, darlin'. How're things?" He bit off an enormous hunk of sandwich and swallowed almost without chewing.

"Usual. Busy-ass morning and looking like a busy-ass afternoon." I pulled part of my lunch from the cooler bag and peeled the lid from my salad bowl. "You?"

"Same." Mitch stared, not even bothering to disguise his disgust. "And what the fuck is that? Mix'n match day at the rabbit food factory?" To him, salad was the thing that you pulled off burgers and threw away with the wrapper.

Moving things around to make sure my lunch was evenly mixed, I said, "There's chicken and cheese in there. And I have a Snickers for later." Plus a protein drink, two bananas, and a container of crackers and dip. Bec was going a little overboard, making my lunches before work when I was not only perfectly capable of doing it myself but actually had more time in the morning than her.

It seemed extra pointless that she was going to that much trouble, because as she'd know, I rarely had time to actually sit and finish a meal during a shift. So I usually snacked, ate whatever I could on the run and left the rest in the fridge for anyone who wanted it. Then I took my empty containers home like a Good Sabine.

His eyes lit up. "Sharesies?"

"Whatever. If you don't tell Bec I'm giving away calories."

"Deal." Mitch frowned, the last of his sandwich halfway to his mouth. "She won't really be mad, will she?"

"Not mad, no, because she won't know. But she's practically been force feeding me since I got back." And watching me eat, while trying not to be too obvious about it. It was adorably sweet but also made me uncomfortable because it added to my feeling that I was doing something wrong.

"She loves you and wants you to be healthy. Nothin' wrong with that. And she's right, darlin'." Despite his agreement that I needed to gain back a few pounds, a sneaky hand still came forward for my chocolate bar.

I suppressed a sigh. "I know. And I know she wants to talk more about it and I just can't. Every time I think about it, I just feel like screaming." I stuffed a forkful of salad in my mouth.

He didn't even need to ask what about, he just *knew*. "You told her how you're feelin'? Really told her?" Ever so kindly, he'd only taken half the Snickers, folded the wrapper back on itself and stuffed the remainder back in my lunch bag.

"Sort of." I shrugged. "I can't tell her everything because she'll just worry all the time, and it's bad enough now. I can't stand how she looks at me differently." Not to mention the odd way she'd looked at me the other night after she'd been out to dinner and I'd brought up the kids thing. The kids thing… Which according to Pace when I'd mentioned it to him that morning *was* nothing more than another fucked up fake thing in my brain. I couldn't even trust some of my own memories as being real anymore. Just another symptom to keep an eye on.

"How's that?" he asked quietly.

"Like I'm about to break. Or break down." I blew out a breath. "And it hurts."

"I know it does, angel."

"No, Mitch, I mean it really hurts. Like physically hurts." I lifted my right arm and jiggled my hand near my armpit— the area where I was shot. "It just fucking…aches, all the way through to my back whenever I think about the *why* of it all and how the hell I'm going to get the words out."

"What's the shrink say?"

I had actually told Pace about the pain, something that had both surprised and scared me. "Nothing I didn't already know. It's psychosomatic or some such bullshit. No physiological reason. All up here." I tapped my forefinger against my temple. Stupid brain.

His hand closed over mine. "You'll get there, darlin'. It's gonna take some time, but I know you'll be just fine."

"I don't want to be just fine, Mitch. I want to be *me* again." I pressed the lid back on my bowl, unsurprised that my hunger had evaporated.

"Oh, darlin', I'm so sorry." His expression softened and for a moment he seemed like he might cry.

"Me too. I'm just so sick of it all."

Before my friend could respond, Colonel Collings strode into the room, his gaze sweeping the space before settling on Mitch and me. "Ah! Fleischer, Boyd. Just who I've been looking for."

Mitch and I stood, speaking in unison. "Sir?"

"Come with me please." Collings turned on his heel and walked out of sight. Quickly, Mitch and I packed up the rest of our lunches and stuffed the bags into the fridge. A new worry overtook everything I'd been thinking about a few moments earlier, and I mentally raced through my last few days of surgeries and completed paperwork. Everything in order. Situation normal there at least.

Mitch glanced sideways at me. "What'd you do this time, darlin'? And why're you draggin' me down into the dirt with you?"

"Not a damned clue." I elbowed him hard in the ribs and we both raced after our CO. "How can we assist you, sir?" I asked when we drew level with Collings.

"Publicity stunt," he said tightly. "We've got a politician in our midst, Captains. You two are going to talk to him and have your photos taken, so smile real nice. Tell him about how wonderful it's been to merge the old Army and Naval Medical Centers into the new Walter Reed right here in Bethesda, how seamless the integration has been and how of course there's been no kinks in the last month. Talk about the new facilities and equipment, spin it out and hype it up. Don't make me look bad."

Fuuuuck. I knew where this whole thing would go and exactly what I'd end up discussing. "Yes, Colonel," I said smartly, brushing down my scrub top as we moved three abreast through the corridors toward the far end of the wing and a rarely-used ward.

The usual beds, chairs and medical equipment had been moved out of the way, leaving a single bed and a bank of monitors set up by the window. On the opposite side of the room, a table and some comfortable chairs had been moved in, and a smaller table with a coffee pot and pastries completed the picture of hospitality.

"Looks like a fuckin' movie set," Mitch said under his breath. "Are those machines even plugged in?"

I murmured my agreement. Mitch and I held back a few yards, standing at parade rest, as our CO went to a tall, pewter-haired guy over by the far wall. It took a few moments before I recognized him as Congressman Marcus Palmer. I supposed it could have been worse—at least he was a Democrat and had spoken up in support of LGBT rights.

Around the room, people were busy setting things up, or staring at phones or tablets. Next to a large white screen, a photographer fiddled with a light, clicking it through different brightness settings. What the hell had I just been roped into? Collings should have just asked Amy, who was practically a damned model anyway.

I fixed my gaze on the far wall, thinking of what I was going to tell Bec when I got home. Guess what, honey? I'm famous! Mom's going to be so proud. Cue her buying one hundred copies of this article and papering the neighborhood with my fifteen minutes of fame.

My boss laughed jovially, then both he and Palmer strode over. Palmer seemed taller and older than he looked in the media, but his brown eyes were clear and laser-sharp. Collings gestured to Mitch and me. "Congressman Palmer, this is Captain Mitchell Boyd and Captain Sabine Fleischer, both outstanding and seasoned front-line surgeons."

Palmer's smile was fixed in that way all politicians seemed to have perfected. "It is an honor to meet you both." He eyed Mitch, his expression turning to one of delight. "Well, look at you, son. You're so All-American you're practically made of apple pie!" He turned to me, and my inspection was a full up and down. "And with your pretty face, this is going to turn out a treat."

It was only by clamping my molars together that I managed not to snap back something about my *pretty face*. My smile probably looked more like a grimace, but I managed to push out, "Thank you, sir. I'm very pleased we could help out."

A brunette who couldn't be more than twenty-five, and who I could only presume to be an aide, leaned over and spoke into the Congressman's ear. Palmer eyed me, his expression changing to a mixture of respect, awe and sadness. It was an expression I knew. And loathed. My annoyance turned to mild discomfort and borderline alarm. Here we go. He's going to ask and you're going to have to tell him, Sabine.

"Captain…Fleischer was it?" When I nodded he continued, in a musing tone, "You were involved in an attack on one of our own a couple of years back, am I right?"

"Yes, sir, that's correct." Well done, Sabine. That was a very steady voice. You've got this.

He spoke to the brunette without lowering his voice. "Make sure you put that in the article. I want the readers to know this is a real hero."

I pressed my fingertips hard into my thighs. Bec, sunshine on my face, kittens, crunching leaves underfoot, Beethoven's Moonlight Sonata. "Sir, with all respect due, I'm not." Pointing to the doorway I added, "The men and women out there in those wards you walked past? Those are heroes, sir. I'm just a physician, I didn't…" After a steadying breath I finished, "Maybe I'm not the best person for this, sir."

Collings began to object to my objection, but Palmer raised a hand to quiet him. "Captain Fleischer, we're not here to diminish these folks' sacrifice, but having you, a surgeon who's not even a field soldier come out of something like that? That's good for Everyday Joe sitting in his living room."

I sensed that this whole thing was a lost battle. There was no point in reminding him of the man who didn't *come out of it*, or the other man who still carried physical and emotional scars as I did. I was an expert in false enthusiasm, so I straightened my shoulders, plastered yet another fake smile on my lips and chirped, "Well then, sir, I'm thrilled to do my part!"

"Good girl." He flashed a camera-ready smile of his own, clapped Mitch and me on the shoulder and pulled Collings over to the coffee urn. The aide gave us vague instructions on where to stand and wait for further instruction. Perfect. I was also an expert at standing and waiting. I turned slightly away and closed my eyes. Breathe in, count to five. Breathe out, count to five. Rinse and repeat. The exercise calmed some of the panic, but I still felt it like a living thing clawing at my insides. I thought of meeting Jana for coffee after work, of what I should pick up to take home for dinner, of the object in the safe at home. Bec, I love you, will you—

A hand touched my back, fingertips stroking gently down my spine, steady and supporting. "Sure you're okay with this, darlin'?"

I opened my eyes, fixating on familiar features. Mitch was here and it'd be okay. I shrugged. "Not really, but it's not like we have a choice."

"I'll cover you, if that's what you want."

"Thanks, Mitch but it's fine. I'm upset but I can handle it." I had to. I couldn't keep doing this. Couldn't keep turning in on myself every time I had to talk about it. This is good practice, Sabine. Do this and maybe you can talk to Bec. You need to sort this out or you're going to lose her.

The flustered aide appeared as though by teleportation. "Okay, we're just about set up, if you two would just go over there and Carla will take care of your hair and faces."

"My what and what?" Mitch asked disbelievingly.

"Oh it's nothing, just a little makeup to make sure there's no shine in the photos, that's all." She passed us each a bright red stethoscope. "Here."

Confused, I held it up. "But we already have our own? I've only got two ears, so…"

"Yes I know," she said in a tone that indicated exasperation at my questioning the *process*. "But this color has better contrast in pictures. Now, over there please." The aide gestured to two plastic chairs in the corner. I sat where directed, and Mitch stood at my side.

"This is turnin' into a goddamned circus," Mitch mumbled, swapping his ever-present black stethoscope around his neck for the red one.

I hmmed my agreement and swapped my stethoscope too, as a petite woman with amazing pink hair approached us with a small bag in her hand. This must be Carla of the hair and faces. Mitch's smile was broad, his voice cheery when he said, "I suggest you don't try to put any of that stuff on my face, ma'am. And I'm certain my hair's just fine." He scooted out of her reach, and beelined for the coffee and donuts.

Carla didn't seem at all offended, merely shrugged and turned back to me. I sat impassively in the chair, studying my hands while she did whatever she had to do. Then my five-hours-at-work-under-a-scrub-cap hair was pulled out and redone. I made an effort to be polite. "Maybe you could come over every morning and do that for me? I don't think it's ever been done so quickly or neatly."

"I could." She laughed. "But I'm not sure I could cope with doing the same hairstyle every day."

"It gets kind of boring, that's for sure." Or...comforting because of the sameness.

"I can imagine." Carla patted my shoulder. "You're all set."

"Thanks." I stood as a short, solidly muscular Hispanic woman was wheeled into the room—Lieutenant Anna Hernandez, a patient of mine, who surprisingly wore a hospital gown instead of her usual sweatpants. The gown gave a clear view of the stump of her left leg, neatly bandaged a few inches below the knee, and the supportive brace and bandaging on her damaged right leg. My mouth soured at the contrived display. For the pictures, right? They'd made her face up too, and I had to swallow convulsively lest I vomit.

Anna looked up at me, offering a smiling and polite, "Afternoon, Doc." A nurse wheeled her to the bed, positioning the chair close to the frame.

"You drew the short straw, Lieutenant?" I asked as cheerfully as I could manage.

"No, ma'am, I volunteered." The smile grew. "My partner's pregnant with our first baby, and this will be something cool to show them when they're older. Now I'll have met President Obama, Vice President Biden and two Congressmen. I'm hoping for the First Lady and Charlize Theron next." She held up both hands with fingers crossed, a goofy grin overwhelming her face.

Chuckling, I bent to lock the chair's brakes in place. I'd met her partner, Lauren, once during visiting hours but couldn't recall a baby bump. Excellent attention to detail, Sabine. For what felt like the tenth time today, I made myself smile. "Both worthy goals. And congratulations!" My smile grew unconsciously when I realized that even a few months ago, she couldn't have told me about such an exciting and personal part of her life. Catch you later, Don't Ask, Don't Tell and don't let the door hit you in the ass on your way out.

The nurse and I helped Anna onto the made-up bed and she maneuvered herself so she was sitting with her legs over the side, shuffling around so the gown covered everything important. I smoothed down the sheet. "Do you want to lie down?"

"No, ma'am. I think they want it visible." She gestured at her legs, seemingly without any discomfort or self-pity.

Of course they did. The flurry of activity around me intensified and I tried to block it out. Holding up my borrowed stethoscope, I said as brightly as I could, "Right, we should try to make this look convincing."

She laughed as I slid it into the gap at the back of her gown. A flash went off in my face and I flinched, my hand reflexively tightening on Anna's shoulder. My anxious nausea intensified, and I hoped with everything I had that I could hold on to my stomach. Breathe in, hold it for five. Breathe out. Just a camera. Anna looked up at me, her expression sympathetic, her smile both knowing and sad.

After a small nod to acknowledge our mutual discomfort at the camera flash, I pushed everything but the woman right in front of me from my mind. "So, do you and Lauren have any names picked out yet?"

* * *

The interview was invasive and discomforting. Instead of focusing solely on the work we did to bring people home to their families, the questions had turned to what it was like to have coworkers and friends operating on me, and my subsequent recovery and return to work. When it was over, I'd shaken hands with everyone, thanked them politely and rushed off—counting the whole way to the bathroom—to vomit.

I left work on time and took a half-hour detour to meet Jana. The parking gods smiled on me and after only fifteen minutes of swearing and pleading I found a spot a block away. Pulling my jacket collar up against the misting rain, I rushed along the sidewalk to my sister's favorite coffee shop. Head down, I ducked under an awning and at the last moment veered around a guy huddled on a step a few doors down from the café door. I stumbled, catching myself against the brick façade of the building and knocking over his damp piece of cardboard. "Shit. I'm so sorry."

"Don't worry about it," he replied amicably, fumbling for the sign which had fallen just outside of his reach. The man's eyes lingered on my uniform, then found mine and he added a polite, "Ma'am."

I leaned down to pick up the cardboard and propped it back up against the wall. My eyes strayed to the neat block lettering.

HOMELESS VETERAN WITH PTSD
ANY HELP APPRECIATED
GOD BLESS YOU

I swallowed hard, offered him a helpless smile and kept walking.

Jana was already seated at a table near the front window. I wound my way through the mostly empty tables toward her. My sister stood and tapped her watch, attempting a stern expression which was spoiled by her grin. Of course she'd enjoy this role-reversal. Aside from client meetings and being in court, Jana regarded being on time a crime.

"Fuck off. I don't work five minutes from here like you do," I said as we hugged tightly. "Why is it that we always meet somewhere super-convenient for you?"

"Because you always agree to it," she said with a charming, and fake, smile.

"Mmmph." This back and forth was nothing new, and I loved its familiarity. "What're you drinking today?" Jana was the most disloyal coffee person I knew and it never paid to assume.

"Hot Coffee Roaster wants me to try a ristretto. He says… it's as dark and flavorsome as I am."

"Wow. I'm sorry, we're still talking about coffee, right?" I said as I backed away.

Jana's laugh followed me to the counter. The server only blinked once when I asked for my sister's sexy coffee. After I'd ordered my not-as-sexy coffee, I added, "Actually could I also get one large takeout coffee and a burger, the biggest one you've got? And a….uh…cheese and salad on whole wheat, no mayo. And a couple of those muffins please, any kind is fine. Maybe all that extra stuff ready to go in twenty minutes?" The server blinked again slowly, then nodded when I handed over my card to pay and it seemed to register that the large order wasn't a joke.

The conversation between Jana and I went as it usually did—frantic and erratic, and with what felt like a hundred topics covered in a tiny amount of time. Jana declared her ristretto tasty, but too small and finished far too quickly. With a naughty grin she added that it wasn't unlike the man who'd suggested it. Time to take a moment of silence for yet another suitor fallen to my sister's unattainable list of attributes she wanted in a partner.

We made plans for dinner later that week, decided that like the trillion other times we'd discussed it she shouldn't lighten her hair, and confirmed that we were indeed throwing a surprise party for Mom's birthday in March. When Jana asked about my day, I brushed past her question with an evasive answer and looped the conversation back around to her soon-to-be-ex lover.

After almost twenty minutes of nonstop word blurting between my sister and me, a server arrived with the extra coffee and two paper bags. Jana stared, an eyebrow quirking. "Just a little hungry, Sabs?"

"No. Not for me." I glanced at my watch. "I should get going, I still have to pick up dinner on the way home."

She eyed me speculatively but said nothing more about the bags and tray in my hands. "Okay then. I have a pre-nup I need to pick apart and a bottle of red I want to finish."

"Your job is boring as shit, no wonder you need wine to get through it."

She gave me the same response to my teasing she'd given me ever since she'd learned how to poke her tongue out. This time it was accompanied by a middle finger. We gathered our things, I dumped some creamers and sugar into one of the paper bags and Jana held the door open for us. The rain had turned from light mist to annoying drizzle, so I huddled under her umbrella as we wandered back in the direction of my car. As we approached the veteran I'd spoken to earlier, I slowed. "Gimme a minute."

Jana stared at my tray and bags, then down to the guy who still sat curled up on the steps under the awning. She nodded and moved out of earshot, pressed against the building and angled slightly away with the umbrella tilted to afford us some privacy.

I crouched down in front of the vet, upset to realize the blanket was damp and he was shivering. "Hey," I said softly. "How're you doing?"

He straightened as best he could. "Not too bad thank you, ma'am." His gaze went to the patches signifying my rank and identifying me as Med Corps, and finally settled on the objects in my hands. I saw a flash of hope in his eyes before he schooled his expression to nonchalance. Shit, he was so young, probably only thirty if that. Younger than me and already used up and spat out on the side of the road.

With the cardboard coffee tray, I gestured to his sign. "When did you get out?"

"Twenty-oh-eight, Captain. Did three tours before my body and brain wouldn't let me do no more." Carefully, he pulled the blanket up and I saw the painfully familiar empty space where a lower limb should be.

By now, the reaction was automatic—a moment of anger and despair, then it was gone again, set aside so I could focus.

"It's not my place to tell you what to do but VA can help out, if you need it. Or you have other options aside from that."

"I tried, but I can't bear going in there, ma'am. All those broken people, it just makes me feel useless all over again."

"I understand," I murmured. It wasn't a platitude, I knew exactly how he felt, and that sentiment was part of the reason I stopped group therapy. Not wanting to dwell and perhaps trigger something for him—or me—I cleared my throat and forced my tone into brightness. "You're not a vegetarian, are you?"

He smiled. "Oh no, nothing like that, ma'am."

"Good." I offered the coffee tray and bags to him. "There's something for now and a few things for later in there. Creamer and sugar too if that's your thing."

The vet took the tray and bags cautiously, as though he expected me to snatch them back and yell *Psych!* at him. His voice was soft, incredulous when he said, "Thank you very much, Captain. I really appreciate your kindness."

"No worries." On a whim, I fished in my pocket and handed him all the cash I had in there. "Take care of yourself, okay?"

"I will, ma'am. Thank you very much." His fingers closed around the cash and he looked at me searchingly. His face contorted before he managed to regain control of his expression again. "You be sure to take care of yourself too, Doc."

I swallowed the hard lump in my throat, nodded and left him to his meal. Jana glanced up as I jogged over to her. She offered me shelter under the umbrella along with an unwanted piece of advice. "If you keep giving them handouts, Sabs, they're never going to get on their feet."

I almost choked on what had just come out of my sweet, generous, kind sister's mouth. Jana and I rarely fought and I couldn't believe that she'd say something so insensitive and narrow-minded. "Jannie, I love you but that's probably the stupidest fucking thing you've ever said."

She opened her mouth to protest but I cut her off. "That guy could have been me, you know. If it wasn't for you, Mom and Dad. Bec…" I shrugged, clenching my teeth hard to stop myself crying, but the words still came out cracked and broken. "It would have been so easy to just keep slipping until I was so far under I couldn't get back up again."

Jana pulled me to a stop a few feet from the curb. "Wait. Stop." She launched herself at me, the hug awkward around the umbrella, but still fierce. The rain fell on us as Jana held me, and I could feel the faint tremble in her body. "I'm so sorry, Sabbie. I didn't know." My sister sounded genuinely remorseful and more than a little upset. "I mean I knew, but I didn't *know*."

"I know."

"Why didn't you say anything?"

"You know why. Because I'm a fucking idiot when I have to talk about my feelings."

We parted, and I lifted the umbrella again to protect her good suit from the rain. She was crying, and her expression tore through me. "Are you okay?" Jana asked. "Like really okay?"

"Mostly, yeah." I made myself smile for my younger sister and carefully used my thumb to wipe under her eyes. "It's not as easy as just saying 'get over it'. You know how much I *hate* therapy and if I didn't think that working through my issues was the right thing to do for you guys then I wouldn't even be trying."

Trying.

Even as I said the word, I knew that I wasn't. Not really. It would be so easy to give up, because it was all so hard. I needed to do more, because the consequence of not trying was catastrophic. I'd seen where I could end up, huddled under a threadbare blanket in the rain.

"Is it helping?" she asked softly, fishing in her handbag for tissues.

"Some. But not as much as I'd like." Even after everything, I still couldn't fully let go and admit to everyone that something inside me didn't work properly anymore. And I hated myself for it.

"I don't know what to do," Jana said softly.

I threaded my arm through hers and pulled her close. "It's okay, Jannie. I think I might have finally figured it out myself."

It was up to me, and me alone.

I just had to work harder, try more, push myself and it'd all come back together. It had to.

CHAPTER TWELVE

Rebecca

The vibration of the garage door rumbling up announced Sabine was home. I reached for two wine glasses, debated, then set one back. If Sabine wanted a drink, she could be in control and choose it for herself. Control. So important to her, but even more so now. I poured a glass of Pinot and set the bottle on the counter. The first sip was soothing, the second even more so.

I heard Sabine drop her backpack at the base of the stairs, then greet the cat with a fond, "Titus! Hello, handsome. Did you have a nice day? Oh...okay, see you later then, precious boy." Footsteps made their way to the kitchen and she appeared with takeout bags in both hands.

I smiled, enjoying the easy pleasure which always accompanied her being near. "Hello, darling."

"Hey, babe." She leaned over to kiss me then placed our dinner on the counter. After a sneaky sip from my wineglass, Sabine began to empty her pockets, dropping the contents next to the Murano glass bowl which held our unopened mail. A needleless syringe, an unused Band-Aid, a packet of gum, the backing from a wound dressing and an interesting stone which she slid across to me. She'd always had this adorable habit of bringing me home little things she'd found during her day, like a cat bringing its owner a mouse as a gift.

I turned the smooth stone over, admiring the flecks of black and gray through it. It was warm from being in her pocket. "How was your day? Did you see Jana?"

"Mhmm. Looks like the coffee guy is history. Goodbye, free samples." Her smile was wide, her voice calm and even, but something seemed off. And she'd only answered one of my questions. I recognized the expression, her tone. She was upset and trying desperately to hide it.

Sabine turned away from me to fetch a wineglass. "I got sushi." She refreshed my drink and poured a glass for herself. "I was going to go to the deli but the line was too long."

"Sushi's great."

She drank a slow mouthful of wine, stared at the bottle then set it down again without topping up her glass. "Did you have a good day?"

"Busy. There was that school bus crash this morning." I pulled two plates down for us.

"Oh." She took off her uniform jacket and draped it neatly over a kitchen chair. Her stare was intense. "Are you okay?"

"Yes, darling. No fatalities, and they were all stable when I left." I ran my forefinger over the now-cool surface of her stone.

Sabine smiled wearily at me, a smile that didn't quite reach her eyes. "You are so clever." She sat at the table and began to unlace her boots, slender fingers pulling the laces with her typically efficient and careful movements.

She rubbed her thumb against the toe of her boot, as if trying to clean something off the tan suede, and I watched her for a moment, admiring the strength in her hands. God I loved those hands, capable of pulling me to dizzying heights one moment, then saving lives in another. "Not as clever as you, Magic Hands."

She made a little scoffing sound, but a slight smile tugged at her lips. Sabine was a surgeon, and as much as she tried to hide it, she had a surgeon's ego. She dropped her boots carelessly on the floor beside her then after a pause, almost as an afterthought, straightened them to sit parallel with the chair. "Actually I might take a shower before dinner."

"Sure." I turned away to unpack plastic containers of sushi and seaweed salad, placing them in the fridge for after her shower. "No chopsticks?" I asked, shaking the bags out.

"Pardon?"

"Chopsticks," I repeated.

"They should be in there. I asked for some. And extra wasabi for you."

"Oh…they must have misunderstood." I smiled. "Because neither of those things is in there."

Her beautiful mouth twisted into an ugly sneer. "Well, you know, I asked. What a bunch of fucking idiots."

The response was so uncharacteristically rude I couldn't think of a response. I turned away to hide my frown, opened the drawer and pulled out forks. "No harm, I'm sure it was just a mistake."

Sabine's hand closed over my wrist as I placed the forks on the table along with our plates. "Bec, I really did ask. I didn't forget, I swear."

I tilted my head, staring at her as though I could figure out why she was so worked up about this. "Sweetheart, I believe you. Seriously, it's not an issue. At all."

Sabine looked down at the table, her free hand flexing open and closed. She took a few deep breaths, then burst into tears. Clearly this was about more than chopsticks and wasabi. Despair stole my breath and I had to stop and force myself to inhale. I sat down and grasped her hands. "Hey, talk to me."

She leaned over and wrapped her arms around me, sobbing noisily against my shoulder. There was nothing I could do but hold her, stroking her hair and the back of her neck as I waited for her to calm down to a point where she could articulate. After a few minutes, she said a simple, quiet phrase through her tears. "I had a really fucking bad day today."

"Oh, darling, I'm so sorry." I rocked her gently, kissing her temple. "You're home now, you're safe. I promise."

My reassurance only seemed to make her crying worse and she clung tighter to me, her tears seeping through my blouse. I squeezed my eyes closed to stop my own tears and we held each other until her crying became erratic, hiccupping sobs. When her breathing had steadied a little, she pulled away from me and wiped under her eyes with her palms. I left her at the table and went to collect the roll of paper towels from next to the microwave.

Sabine unrolled a few pieces of towel, wiped her eyes and blew her nose. "I so did *not* want to cry." She flashed me a wonky smile. "I'm going to be famous, Bec. We had a visitor today, Congressman Marcus Palmer. Some publicity bullshit with photos and an interview too. Me, Mitch and one of my patients."

My gut began churning the moment she mentioned an interview. I had a suspicion about why they wanted her and what they would have wanted to talk about, but she answered my question before I could ask it. I placed my hand on her shoulder, gently stroking her neck with my thumb as she talked.

"I mean, it's obvious why me, right? They wanted something juicy to sell their bullshit of how well the machine is working over there if someone like me can come out of an attack like I did." She balled the paper towel in her fist and her shoulders shook as she drew in another unsteady breath. "Bec, it was *so* awful and all I wanted was to come and find you but I couldn't, because you're not there anymore and for just a moment, I forgot that. And then there was this guy in the city. A vet huddled under a stinking blanket in the rain. He was so young and cold, and he'd lost his leg over there, and now he's homeless and I just—" Sabine closed her eyes, more tears leaking down her cheeks. "I didn't know what to do."

There was so much torment that I didn't know where to start with helping her unpack it all. Massaging her shoulder, I prompted, "How did it make you feel?"

She coughed out a laugh. "Which part?"

"Why don't we start with the young man?" There was no point in asking her how being interviewed had made her feel. I already knew.

She looked up and her brimming eyes found mine. "So scared. That…could be me if I don't fix this." Her eyes widened and she tripped over the words in her haste to get them out. "It's not you, Bec, I swear. It's not something you've done or haven't done to make this better. It's me. And I need to change. I need to fix it. I need to get better or I think I might drown."

What could I say to that? Grief scratched at my insides like a caged beast. But I couldn't let it out. If I did, if I broke, then I didn't think she would be able to keep herself together. She needed me to be strong enough for both of us. A few deep breaths helped me find some words. "Darling, I know you're confused and upset, but it's going to be all right. I promise. I'm here, and we're going to work through this." I didn't know how many times I had to tell her, to show her, but if she needed it every day, every hour then that's what I would do.

The look she gave me was heartbreaking, as if she'd expected me to have an answer right then that would solve everything. But I had nothing because I too was so shattered by everything that had happened in the past few years. Too shattered by my guilt and having to atone. By being the pillar she needed. But now Sabine was home, it was wearing me down even more, right when I needed to be there for her.

She nodded, slowly. "Okay. I'm going to start right now. Bec, I hav—" She glanced at her ringing phone, her forehead furrowed. After a few rings, she snatched up the phone.

"Oma," Sabine explained. "I should probably take it." She cleared her throat and tapped the screen to answer. "*Oma, hallo! Wie geht es dir?*" Sabine spoke in her usual rapid-fire German, her voice miraculously steady. Her speaking voice was so naturally husky that her recent bout of tears was hardly noticeable, and I doubted her eighty-eight-year-old grandmother would realize anything was amiss.

I caught a few words as she left the room but most of it was unintelligible. The words were muted, the sound of her voice moving back and forth along the hall as she paced the way she always did on phone calls. I picked up my wineglass, but the deep red of the wine now seemed to taunt me.

Crossing the floor in a few swift strides, I tipped the Pinot into the sink and carefully placed the glass on the counter. Then I took a step back, another sideways, unable to find a way around my overwhelming sense of hopelessness. I gave in to it, leaned forward and rested my elbows on the kitchen counter with my face resting in my hands.

One simple decision. That's all it had been. It had seemed so innocuous at the time. A question asked by her and a favor given by me. And because of it our lives had been irrevocably turned about. The familiar guilt made me nauseated, and I drew my hands into tight fists as though I could force away the accompanying rush of gut-wrenching fear that appeared whenever I thought of that day. It was the same stomach-dropping feeling that had hit me when I'd heard her name on the incoming call. My colleague. My subordinate. My lover.

I knew she didn't blame me for what'd happened. She blamed herself. As though she could have cut and resewn the fabric of time to make it turn out differently. The blame I allocated myself was more than enough for both of us, but I would have shouldered hers too if she'd put it on me. I deserved it.

After the call informing me of what'd happened, it took twenty minutes for her to arrive. Right on sunset I'd stood with her friends and coworkers, watching the convoy of armored vehicles rushing through the checkpoint toward the hospital, knowing Sabine was in one of them. The rear vehicle dragged a ruined, uncooperative Humvee like a grotesque string of *Just Married* cans on a wedding car. I'd stared at the mangled vehicle and all I could think was that she'd been in that wreckage and somehow survived it. At least, up until that point.

Unconscious Sabine being carried in, her tanned face pale—unsurprising given the blood seeping through her field dressings. For the first time ever, I'd wanted to shed the weight of my leadership. But I had to carry those under my command while I tried to repair the damage to the beautiful body I'd loved less than a month before. Even if I'd been able to address my own needs, requesting someone else take the case was pointless because everyone at the FOB knew her. She was a professional conflict for us all.

The memories of that horrific day were always disjointed, which made reliving them even worse because I could find no clear path through the events. I could recall watching her as I'd scrubbed, her screams of pain bouncing off the walls of the OR while they prepped her. I could recall the way she kept moving in my peripheral vision, trying to catch people's eyes or talk, then choking on the blood in her trachea. And I could recall how I'd had to ignore it, had to shut it all away where it couldn't touch me.

There was nothing but blank space where recollection of her surgery should be. I knew the clinical details, but the memory of my hands inside her chest was lost and I was grateful for it. When they took her to recovery and I could finally breathe again, I'd had to get outside before I fell apart. I had to get some distance from her. I didn't shower after her surgery. Didn't even strip off my scrubs. Later, much later, instead of throwing them in the communal laundry hampers, I dropped them and my shoes into one of the medical burn pits.

They'd hidden the wrecked Humvee in a shed, waiting for orders on what to do with it. Inside the compound, it would become a shrine, a *Look what they did to our guys, and yeah we got 'em!* sort of morale boost.

When I approached the shed I heard all the loathsome macho revenge talk I hated, but I didn't begrudge them. Whatever they needed to do to get through their day was fine by me. But it felt wrong somehow because these weren't field soldiers chest-beating and talking smack to get them through their next terrifying mission. These were my Med Corps. At my approach, a dozen bodies straightened and came to attention.

In blood and sweat-soaked scrubs I could have laughed at the sight of them standing at attention before me. "At ease," I'd said, surprised by the steadiness in my voice. I was a master at holding my emotions, but I'd felt that tenuous grip slipping with each step I took away from the OR. I was so close to breaking. "Leave me, please. Wait outside if you must but I want this space cleared in thirty seconds."

A chorus of, "Yes, ma'am!" rang out and they filed silently from the shed, pulling the sliding shed door mostly closed.

In the enclosed space, I became aware of a mix of overwhelming odors. Blood and shit and vomit. Dried sweat and bile. The choking smell of dust. Diesel fuel. All of it mingled to create a nauseating conglomerate of horror. I'd picked up a flashlight someone had discarded near a deflated rear tire, and the click of its button echoed through the shed. The heavy metal tube shook in my hand.

The Humvee was upright, the driver's side door set on the concrete floor beside it. The metal was marred by large dents and bullet holes, the rear doors hanging open, two of four tires completely flat which made it sit lopsided like a drunk slumped in the gutter. I'd paced slowly around the vehicle, staring at every part of the mangled hulk.

Whatever had been launched at the Humvee had punched through the armor, leaving two gaping holes—one behind the driver's seat and the other through the bench seats opposite. I could have easily fit through either hole. My knees trembled so much I had to lean on the side of the vehicle and draw deep slow breaths, reminding myself that Sabine was alive. She would be okay. I mentally placed the fates of the other occupants where I set all the patients who'd passed through the FOB. Acknowledged, but not dwelt upon.

Where had she been sitting? The flashlight beam wavered over the interior as I tried to visualize where she would have settled herself. Though the entire interior was splattered with blood, the major pooling seemed concentrated in a few areas on the right side. Nowhere seemed like a position of safety. How the hell had she survived this? I'd never been particularly religious, but I leaned my head against the cold metal and I prayed my thanks to everyone and everything I thought might be listening for letting her come home.

Layered over the gratitude was that overwhelming sense of guilt, along with a feeling of almost sick satisfaction, like

I deserved this. I'd broken one of the most fundamental and unbreakable rules of the military, and this was my punishment, to have come so close to losing her.

Now I'd have to live with my own part in it for the rest of my life. I'd had to clap my hand over my mouth to stifle my choked sob, lest I was heard outside.

Then I had drawn in a deep breath, straightened my shoulders and strode out of the shed to my office. It was time to call Sabine's family back in the States and tell them she had been wounded in action, had had surgery and was currently classified as serious but stable.

I would forever remember the panic in Carolyn's voice as she'd screamed for Gerhardt to please *please* hurry up and come to the phone. And I could do nothing but convey the facts calmly and with the minimum of emotion. As I always did. The moment I'd hung up, I'd sunk to the floor, leaned against the desk and cried.

I'd led the team that fixed her broken body, but now it seemed I could do nothing for her precious, intricate mind. My helplessness was chipping away at me, one small piece at a time. I wondered idly how many more pieces I could lose before Sabine would notice.

I straightened as Sabine wandered back into the kitchen, gesturing expansively with her free hand. "*Nein, Oma. Ich habe leider keine Zeit fuer mehr Urlaub.*" She frowned. "*Weil ich, ich—*" Sabine's feet stopped as abruptly as her German, and when she spoke again it was in English and in a tremulous voice. "Because…because I just had a v-v-vay-cation."

The stammer alone would have caught my attention. She'd stammered as a child but had overcome it, and until a few years ago it hadn't happened since. Now, she sometimes stammered when she was upset—another side effect of The Incident and one I knew she was self-conscious about. Stammer aside, this sudden language switch was odd. She *never* did that. It was German or English, never augmented with words from the other.

Her eyes were wide, her expression one of horror. I moved toward her, fearing she'd suddenly received bad news but Sabine shook her head at me. She turned away and left the room again, words trailing behind her. "*Ich werde es versuchen. Ich verspreche.*" Her conversation was a little louder now, the words taking on a slightly clipped tone. After another few minutes she came back, the phone clutched in a white-knuckled hand.

"Is everything okay?" I asked inanely.

"I don't…what the hell was that?" Sabine tossed her phone onto the kitchen table and sank back down on to her chair. She blew through pursed lips for a few seconds, then muttered a quick stream of German as though running through a test list.

"What happened, sweetheart?"

"I don't know, it was like everything in my head was gone." Now her expression was blank, incredulous. "I've been bilingual since I first learned to talk, Bec. When I'm speaking German, I'm *thinking* in German but my mind was just…empty. I couldn't think of the words." Her eyes begged me to explain the unexplainable to her. "What the hell?"

I ran a soothing hand over her back, offering an unsatisfactory, perfunctory-sounding explanation. "You've had a difficult day, darling. I'm sure it's nothing more than stress." The muscles of her back were tight, and I drew my hand upward to massage the steel bands in her neck.

"I know, but that's *never* happened, Bec. Not even after the… thing, and that was stressful as hell." She buried her face in her hands, and the rest of her words were muffled. "I seriously feel like I'm losing my mind here."

"Why don't we schedule some tests? For exclusionary purposes only, just to give us a starting point," I added when she opened her mouth to give what I knew would be an indignant protest. She'd been checked for a traumatic brain injury during her recovery, and I really didn't think there was an actual physical reason for her issues. But it would give her the peace of mind to move forward and figure out what was going on.

Slowly she looked up, then nodded. "Will you come with me?"

"Of course."

Sabine inhaled slowly then let out another long breath. "*Ich liebe dich*," she said, then after a beat smiled awkwardly and added, "Just making sure I've still got it."

I smiled back. I knew that one. "I love you too."

She drew me closer, resting her head against my stomach. Her arms came tight around me. "I mean it, Bec." Sabine's voice was barely above a whisper when she pulled back. Her hands came under my blouse to stroke the bare skin on my back. "I love you. I need you."

The unspoken statement was in her eyes. A silent plea. "I know. Me too." I looped my arms around her neck, feathered my fingers in the hair behind her ears and answered the question she couldn't ask. "I already told you that I'm not leaving, Sabine. I promise." I would stay no matter what. No matter the cost. Because I loved her too much to leave.

She bit down on her lower lip, before asking out of the blue, "Have you drunk too much to drive?"

Frowning, I answered, "No. Just that half glass of wine."

Sabine stood so quickly I had to grab the chair to my right to stop myself being bowled over. She hurried toward the door, barefoot and only wearing her uniform pants and a T-shirt. Without slowing, she spun around, walking backward as she talked. "I want you to drive me somewhere. Anywhere, just make me sit in the passenger seat and fucking deal with it."

Before I could speak up to say maybe it wasn't a good idea to push right now with something that caused her such anxiety, Sabine insisted, "Now. *Please*, Bec. Before I change my mind. I need to start working on this *now*." Then she was out the door, leaving me with nothing to do but follow.

CHAPTER THIRTEEN

Sabine

Jana pushed the dishwasher closed with her foot and collected her wineglass from beside the stovetop. "Look, my point is why should I waste my time with boring guys, even if they tick most of the other boxes?"

I folded the dishtowel into a perfect rectangle and set it on my sister's kitchen counter, turning it until the cloth lay parallel to the edge. "Because you rarely give them enough time to show you if they actually *are* boring. What if they're just nervous? Shy? In awe of your beauty and charm?"

She smiled beatifically at me. "That might be true, Sabs. I am both beautiful and charming."

"And egotistical," I mumbled.

With her free hand, Jana picked up my perfectly placed dishtowel and snapped it at me. "I don't have time to find out what their problem is. I'm a busy woman, and they need to shit or get off the pot." She dropped the towel back to the counter and I had to resist picking it up and refolding it.

I turned away from the shapeless fabric mess and refocused on my sister. "That is like…the worst dating metaphor I have ever heard."

"It is pretty bad," Bec agreed from the couch where she was working on an after-dinner cognac.

Jana raised both hands, the wine in her glass sloshing. "Fine, yes, bad metaphor but that's not the point. Is it wrong to want an instant connection with someone? To be swept off my feet? To have marathon sex sessions instead of one-hit wonders?"

"Uhhh…no, but…" I looked helplessly to Bec.

She picked up the conversation where I'd faltered. "No, sweetie, but I think maybe sometimes you're a little picky." Only she could get away with saying something like that to my sister.

"Maybe…" Jana mused.

Bec laughed. "Maybe? Do you remember that guy you dated in April? The one who lasted a record seven dates?"

"What guy?" I looked between the two of them, waiting for someone to explain what I'd missed while I'd been in Afghanistan. "There was a guy who actually stood out?"

Bec made a *go on* gesture. Jana sighed, then explained, "He was a firefighter. Cute and really really fit, like muscles everywhere, but not too bulky, you know?"

"Mmmm, so your typical specimen of masculine perfection. What else?" I asked.

"Cute, funny, a gentleman of the door-and-chair-holding variety, similar taste as me in movies and music, not awful in bed."

"And why did you stop seeing him?" Bec prompted.

Jana looked like a kid who'd just been told to stand up in front of the class and read aloud a note they'd been caught passing to a friend. "Because he was a vegetarian. One of those scary ones who believes non-vegetarians are basically awful people who'll burn in animal-eating hell. And I thought you know, I really like steak and bacon, and it doesn't matter if he's sweet and funny and knows the meaning of multiple orgasms if he's going to scowl at me every time I eat a piece of an animal. Or worse, try to convert me."

Bec buried her face in her hands, shaking her head. After a strangled laugh she looked up again. "An *actual* hero, Sabine. He even rescued stray animals. And she ended it because of that."

I shrugged. Funnily enough, it wasn't the worst reason I'd heard. Jana once declined a second date with a guy because she didn't like the way he knotted his tie. Deep down, I thought it was less about pickiness and more about fear of rejection or of failed relationships.

Jana uncorked the wine and poured another half-glass for herself. "Hey, come on, Bec. It's not like you've got exceedingly high standards." She jerked her thumb at me. "You're still with her."

I raised a middle finger at my sister.

They both laughed and started up with sweet, good-natured teasing all directed at me. I laughed with them but at the back of my mind lingered an awful thought—why hadn't either of them told me about this guy while I was away? A small, innocuous thing but they both knew how important the seemingly unimportant is while you're deployed. Was I not worthy of being told about it? Did they forget about me? No, don't be an idiot. Just an oversight, Sabine, their lives didn't revolve around keeping you informed of every tiny thing while you were away.

Suddenly I wanted nothing more than to be safely at home, cuddled in bed with Bec. I'd let her drive us to Jana's, the sixteenth thing I'd done in the past five days that made me extremely uncomfortable, and the slight panic I'd felt at the start of the night was turning into something I was finding hard to suppress. As the night wore on the discomfort became layered with self-chastisement because I was at my sister's and should *not* feel uncomfortable. I should be feeling safe and happy, and enjoying dinner and the company of people I loved.

Just keep doing it, and it'll get easier. Right.

Adding to my anxiety was the decision I'd made yesterday to really push the limits of what I thought I could handle. To really ramp up my exposure therapy. Next Monday, after Bec finished her shift, I would take the bus from my work to meet her at her work. Lookit me! I can do things regular people do! Well, I can do it after over a week of planning ahead so I could psych myself up enough to follow through.

I snuck a peek at my watch. Almost nine thirty. Polite time for a getaway. "Right, speaking of multiple orgasms, I think it's time for us to head home."

Bec had stood the moment I said orgasms. Jana made a dramatic gesture. "Fine, go. Leave me here alone and on the verge of spinsterhood."

"Okay," I agreed, forcing a teasing cheer into my voice.

We exchanged hugs with my sister, and on the way to the door Bec slid her arm around my waist with her fingertips resting lightly on my hip. In the elevator, she leaned into me, her breath whispering over my neck. Soft kisses made their way to my ear before she murmured, "So, multiple orgasms…"

It had been an off-the-cuff comment, but when Bec's fingers slid up under my top I knew she hadn't taken it as such. She stroked along my spine to my ass, the sensation causing a shudder of pleasure to ripple down my back. I closed my eyes, relaxing into the touch until predictably, on the back of pleasure, came the panic.

The fingers stilled but stayed on my skin. I hadn't said anything, hadn't moved away or asked her to stop but she'd read me like a book. Bec had always been incredibly perceptive but seemed even more so with me these days. So much so I'd wondered if the near-constant stream of thoughts in my head were somehow coming out my mouth. The electronic numbers counted down three floors before she quietly asked, "Is it me?"

I turned slightly to the side so I could look into her eyes. "No! I swear it's not you. Not wanting you isn't the problem, Bec. I wish I didn't want you so badly because that would make this less distressing." Her thinking that I didn't want her that way, wasn't attracted to her, or that I didn't hunger to have my hands and mouth on her made my self-loathing well up again.

"What's making it so upsetting for you, sweetheart?" she asked, the hand resuming its stroking, but staying well north of my waist now.

I scrubbed a hand over my face. "Because…all the feelings are in there, but there's *something* sitting on top of them as well and I don't know what it is." Something that made me afraid to let her touch me that way. The elevator jerked to a halt and the doors slid open. "And I don't know how to figure it out."

The drive home was quiet, and as if by unspoken agreement, Bec and I went straight upstairs instead of heading into the den for some mindless television before sleep. We readied for bed quickly, the way we always did, sharing sink space and passing floss and face cream back and forth. Nice routine. Routine is good. Be quiet, Sabine.

Bec held the covers up for me to slide in, and once I was done wriggling into a comfortable position, she kissed me gently. "Night, darling." She snuggled close as she always did, body pressed tightly against mine and her head on my breasts, her hand rested on my stomach, its soft weight warm and comforting.

"Night…" I closed my eyes and ran my fingers lightly up and down her arm, hoping the soothing rhythm would help lull me to sleep. It didn't, neither did my usual foot squirming, and after forty-three minutes I still wasn't asleep. The more I tried to lie still, the more agitated I became. So I gave in and rolled over. Then rolled back. Covers off, back on again. One foot out. Where's the cat? Not here.

Stop being so ridiculous, Sabine.

I couldn't stay tossing in bed and risking waking Bec. But I didn't want to leave the room. Stealthily, I slid out of bed and crept over to the wingback chair in the corner of our bedroom. Bec's plush robe was slung over the back and I pulled it down to cover myself as I settled in the chair.

Over and over, my brain looped around with *what's wrong, what's wrong, what's wrong?* Then an answering repetition of *fix it, fix it, fix it!* I clenched my jaw hard, trying to force out the intrusion. There was nothing physically wrong with me. I'd had a barrage of tests and scans a few days ago, and as I'd expected, they had shown no lesions, tumors, scar tissue or other physiological cause. Perfect. All in my head, hiding in those tiny parts of my brain where no scan would ever find them. I desperately wanted something tangible that I could fix, but the cure was "Just keep plugging away at it and one day you might feel like yourself again." Exactly what I was not good at.

It was a few days until the full moon, and I could see Bec with its strong light stealing through the curtains. With my legs drawn up and my chin resting on my knees, I sat as still as I could and watched her, lying curled in fetal position the way she always slept. I should have been behind her, pressed tight, holding her with my cheek against her hair. But instead I watched her from across the room like a stalker. It was easier to say everything that was in my head when she wasn't looking at me with the expression that had always made me blurt out my secrets even when I'd sworn to myself I wouldn't.

Bec, I don't feel right. I don't like who I am anymore. I don't know what to do.

Perfect, Sabine. Why not just hang a sign around your neck saying *I'm damaged and not really getting better, feel free to bail on the relationship.* I scrunched my eyes closed. Stop it. I'd asked her so many times to stick with me and every single time, without hesitation, she'd given an affirming promise that she would. I believed her, trusted her, but deep down I still couldn't shake the fear that I really was too screwed up for her. It had to get better soon. Exposure therapy worked, right? Soon something would kick in for me and everything would be fine. It had to be.

The alternative was unthinkable.

The shape under the covers shifted, then rolled over to face my side of the bed. After a few moments, Bec sat up, looking about the room until her gaze fixed on me. "Sabine? Are you okay?" she said, the query sluggish with interrupted sleep. Bec reached over to turn on her bedside light, tilting her head away from the sudden brightness.

"Yeah. Just can't sleep."

A hand snaked out from under the duvet, fingers wiggling as they reached toward me. "Darling, come back to bed."

"I won't sleep and I don't want to keep you awake."

"Then we can talk if you want to. Please, come here."

I rose from the chair and crawled back into bed. Bec drew the duvet up over my shoulders, leaning forward to kiss my nose then my forehead. The silence settled over us, gradually growing heavier until I couldn't stand it any longer. I closed my eyes, drew in a deep breath and blurted, "I just…feel like I don't want you to touch me, like you're going to find something you don't like." See something inside that I didn't want her to, know the thing I was desperately trying to hide while I figured out how to make it better.

We'd made love once since I'd come home five weeks ago. Once. We for who *once* was our per day quota, not our per month. And the more I pulled away, the worse the feeling became because I was the one withholding from her. She deserved so much more. So much better.

"I don't think that's going to happen," she mused quietly. "There is nothing about you that I don't love, Sabine. Not inside or outside."

My breath came out in an exasperated huff. "I want you, I love you, I want to make love with you, but I just…it's, I think it's that *thing*."

"What thing?" she asked, propping herself up on an elbow as she studied my face. She wasn't going to let me get away with vaguely skimming over the facts. Not this time.

"It's my PTSD," I finally said, quietly, as though that would somehow give the word less weight.

"Have you talked to Andrew Pace about it?"

"Yes."

It wasn't a lie, we had skimmed over it in our sessions, but I didn't need to tell him intimate details because I already knew the issue. The same one I'd had after The Incident where I'd been so terrified of making love with Bec that I tensed every time she tried to initiate it. Back then I was afraid of hurting myself. Now I was afraid of her touching me, of running her hands over my body…over my scars. Which was absurd because she'd touched me, touched them, thousands of times. One night back then, all the fear had melted away and I'd been fine. Would it happen that way this time too?

"What did he say?"

"Basically we'll just keep working at it." That was the nutshell version. The only version I wanted to get into at the moment.

"That sounds like a good plan." After a pause, she added, "You know, it's not just about sex." She used her fingertips to brush hair from my forehead. "You're struggling, darling. Please, let me help you."

"That's not the first time you've said that to me," I murmured. It seemed like an eternity ago. After my ex left me, and I'd fallen into a state so mentally and physically exhausted that I'd frozen during surgery, Bec—in her capacity as my boss—had made me medicate myself so I could sleep and recuperate.

Bec smiled. "No, it's not. But that time I didn't call you darling. As much as I wanted to."

"Are you going to tell me to drug myself now?"

"No, I'm not going to tell you what to do even though I think medication is a good idea." Before I could even open my mouth, she shushed me quietly. She knew me too well. "Sabine, there's nothing shameful about what you're feeling, and I know your feelings are real. But at the same time, I'm worried that you could be reacting to things you think *might* happen rather than things that are actually happening. Medication to help settle those thoughts would be beneficial."

I huffed out a sigh. Bec was right of course—I always embraced the worst-case scenario. Worrying about what she *might* think or do instead of focusing on what she *was* doing.

Bec spoke with quiet conviction. "Trust me, please. Trust Andrew. And trust yourself."

Nodding, I agreed, "Okay. I just, I can't help but worry… how many times can I ask you to wait for me to get better? How many times do I have to beg you to stick with me while this thing is overshadowing *everything* in our lives?"

"You can ask me again and again, and I will always say yes, Sabine." The words came out with an edge of panic, like she couldn't say it fast enough. Did she really mean it?

I couldn't do anything but nod, the lump in my throat making my response stick. So I kissed her, lightly, intending it as nothing more than to signal the end of the conversation so we could sleep. Or so I could insomnia. But when her hands came to cup my face as they usually did, something familiar but unexpected stirred in my belly. Need. Desire.

I rolled her over, pressing her gently down to the bed, settling carefully on top of her with my forearms resting flat on the mattress either side of her shoulders. Aside from her mouth moving against mine with familiar warmth, she was still. Almost as though she was afraid to move and break the mood. I slid my tongue against her lower lip and with a quiet sigh, she opened her mouth to me. Bec's leg slid between mine until I was straddling her thigh, and the effect was almost instantaneous—a low deep curl of arousal in my belly that spread heat through my legs. I lifted my head to look down at her, wanting to see what I felt in my body mirrored in her eyes.

And I found it—the heat and need in those familiar blue depths. Bec raised her head, seeking another kiss and when I gave it to her, she tangled her hand in my hair, fingers brushing my scalp. After a careful stroke of her tongue against mine, she pulled back. "Are you sure?" Her expression could only be described as hopeful, and it smothered some of my gnawing doubt. She was hopeful I wouldn't bail again, hopeful we'd actually have sex, hopeful I'd behave like a normal partner.

I loved Bec. I loved sex. I loved sex with Bec. It wasn't like the whole thing was a hardship or not pleasurable on some level. Just do it, Sabine. She's not going to hurt you, she's not going to be repulsed. I answered her with another kiss, this one deeper and lingering until I felt her press harder against me. A soft groan followed, but Bec pulled away again, though this time I could feel her reluctance. "I don't want to push, if you're not comfortable."

I rested my forehead against hers. "You're not pushing me, baby." I'm pushing myself, Bec. I have to, or I'm going to fall apart, never to be put back together again.

She let out a soft exclamation when I dipped my head to suck the skin where neck met collarbone, then moved the soft cotton tee aside to kiss the swell of her breast. Bec reached to turn out the light but I grasped her arm. "No. Leave it on please. I want to see you." Needed to know it was her. And that I was safe.

She slid her hands over my shoulders, likely intending to continue a leisurely trek down my back to my ass, but I tensed when her fingers brushed the slightly cratered exit-wound scar on my scapula. And she withdrew. Just like that. Without pushing or questioning.

Our foreplay was long and slow, the kind that usually heralded hours of lovemaking and a connection so exquisitely sweet I could almost cry. Now I felt awkward, shy almost as though I wanted to second-guess every kiss and touch, and each sound she made.

Stop it, Sabine. Not the time, not—

"Baby…"

I blinked a few times. "Mmm?"

"Come back to me," she begged.

"I'm sorry," I whispered.

She kissed me softly. "It's okay, sweetheart." Bec let me guide her until she was lying on her stomach and I gently drew her arms up above her head, then lowered myself until her body was covered by mine. She let out a soft exhalation as I began a slow, thorough worship, reminding myself of all the things she willingly gave to me. God I loved her body, all womanly curves and soft skin. I could spend hours exploring her, letting my hands and mouth roam to all her hidden places. *My* places. They were mine. She was mine.

She clutched the pillow tightly, moaning as my tongue traced the curve of her buttocks. My fingers dipped closer to her tantalizing wetness and I gave in, indulging myself by stroking her. Bec's moan turned low and ever so sexy, turning the quiet hum of pleasure in my depths to a deep, dull throb. Without taking my hand away, I inched my way back up her body, leaving soft kisses over her back and shoulders.

"I love it when you do that," she murmured.

I lightly bit her shoulder. "I know." My fingers were still playing through her folds and teasing her clit, and with every stroke she panted and twitched under me.

"Know what else I love?" Bec came up on her elbows, twisting around slightly to face me. Though I had a fairly good idea, I shook my head, wanting her to say it. She continued hoarsely,

"I love it when you finger fuck me." Unlike me, Bec rarely used profanity and when she did it was wielded with precision. The things she said in bed egged me on like nothing else, and she knew it.

I groaned. She was so wet that two fingers slid into her with only the barest push. Bec exhaled loudly and spread her legs for me, arching her back. I withdrew and thrust again, deeper. "Like this?"

Her only response was another moan. I straddled the back of her thigh, desperate for friction, and with every thrust inside her, I ground myself against the smooth skin of her leg. My abundant wetness coated her, and I slipped an arm under her armpit, reaching around to cradle her breast while I fucked her.

Bec clenched tight around my fingers, and I felt the familiar fluttering of her muscles coupled with the hitch in her breathing that meant she was close to climax. With effort, I stilled my fingers and Bec exhaled sharply, her frustration clear. She bent her head and bit my forearm. "Tease," she gasped.

I smiled against her skin, pressing open mouth kisses to her neck. "Can I lick you?" I mumbled against her skin. "I want you to come in my mouth."

Bec managed a strangled, desperate, "Please."

I withdrew carefully and repositioned myself so I could turn her onto her back. Her skin glistened with a light sheen of sweat, nipples plump and so delicious I couldn't help but take one then the other into my mouth. Her hands came to my face, holding me in place as I licked and sucked her breasts, remembering every centimeter of them. Bec squirmed underneath me, pushing herself up into me, painting her wetness onto my skin.

Unhurriedly, I made my way down her body and pulled one of her legs over my shoulder, spreading her wide. I loved her like this, so open and needing, unashamed in her desire. Her hand tightened in my hair, pushing my head to guide me, and I had to suppress a low growl as I took her in my mouth. I'd never considered myself to be a particularly jealous person but when we were making love, I often felt a fierce sort of possessiveness layered on top of all my other emotions.

Now, with everything else in my head, I felt I might come apart. I slid a hand between my thighs, stroking myself furiously, and when Bec's breathing rose and her cries reached the exact pitch I knew heralded her imminent climax, I let myself fall over the edge with her. It was a pleasant enough release, but not earth-shattering, and somehow I felt better for that. I shouldn't have a bone-melting orgasm when I hadn't allowed her to touch me.

Her grip in my hair was firm, almost rough, and once she'd finished shuddering, she released me to let the hand drift down to stroke my face. Bec drew in a long, rejuvenating breath then murmured in a low, throaty voice, "You are so fucking sexy when you come." There was no trace of upset or annoyance that I'd finished myself off, or that aside from kisses she'd barely touched me except to tangle fingers in my hair, or lightly caress my face and neck.

She kept caressing my skin and I closed my eyes, focusing on the brief moment as we'd climaxed together, when I'd felt like we were back where we were meant to be. Connected. Existing together in the same place at the same time, instead of me trying to stay tethered to the earth while Bec tried to hold on to me. It was nothing more than a tiny pinpoint of light in the dark, but nevertheless it was still light. It was a fragment of hope that maybe things would be okay.

CHAPTER FOURTEEN

Rebecca

Moments after I'd finished lunch—eaten at my desk while working through a stack of paperwork—I was paged. MVA, multiple vehicles with one entrapment who'd arrested while they were cutting him free, one coming in without vitals and three status-critical. Afternoon rounds would have to wait. So would more coffee. And returning Jana's voicemail from early this morning.

I raced toward the elevators and the continuation of what had already been a hectic, upsetting day. As I tried to do whenever overwhelmed, I focused on something pleasant—in this case, the promise of a nice evening out tonight with Sabine to celebrate our two-year anniversary.

With practiced ease the head of triage directed the onslaught of paramedics. I donned disposable gown and gloves, going through the motions with mindless efficiency. One of my team was already in the room, bent forward at the waist with his arms dangling. It was a pose I knew well and adopted myself at least once a day in an attempt to alleviate a back sore from hours on my feet.

I slipped on protective glasses. "Matt, how are you?"

He straightened with an audible groan. "Rebecca. Can't complain." A pause and a half-hearted smirk. "Nobody listens."

I grinned at his standard response and resumed assessment of the casualties. Two passed by on gurneys, almost crashing into young James Felton jogging up the hallway. "Good afternoon, Doctor Keane," he huffed, face red and sweat-sheened. "My apologies, I was coming to find you but you'd already gone." Before I could answer, he went straight to work getting himself gowned up.

Two male paramedics wheeled a casualty into the exam room. "Katie Housten, twelve-year-old female front-seat passenger, vehicle took the brunt of the impact on her side. Complained of abdominal pain. Altered consciousness at the scene, but pupils were equal and reactive. Then full loss of consciousness three minutes ago. BP eighty over fifty, respiration thirty-four, heart rate one-sixty, Glasgow coma score five. Compound tib fracture, cuts, abrasions and some *nasty* abdominal contusions."

I glanced up at the odd tone, noting right away the raised eyebrows and look of unease on the paramedic's face. "Thank you. Let's transfer one, two, three." The girl was lifted onto the gurney and I opened her eyelids with my thumb and forefinger. Her eyes were dark brown and I could barely see her pupils. I swiped my light back and forth. "Pupils are reactive but not equal. Page neuro please."

"Yes, Doctor."

The usual sound of the working team was interrupted by a gasp and a low expletive. I turned sideways to glance down the length of the girl's body, and was pulled up immediately by what I saw. Her clothing had been partially removed, and in addition to the large purple mark caused by the seatbelt and internal bleeding, her barely-adolescent torso and arms were marked by dozens of fading bruises, uneven scars and small circular marks—some raw red wounds, some older. Everyone was suddenly very still and silent.

Finally, Matt spoke, revulsion touching every word. "They aren't…is that?"

The muscles in my jaw quivered as I answered, "Yes, I think so." Her injuries were consistent with long term physical abuse. I schooled my face to a calm expression. Child Protective Services would be notified and the police would be involved. My simple case just got a whole lot more involved. And my day just got a whole lot longer.

"Christ," Matt muttered.

"What is it?" James asked timidly from behind me.

I turned around. "Doctor Felton, once we've finished here, you're going to learn the protocol for making a report to CPS." The breath I took didn't reach the bottom of my lungs. I caught the eye of one of the nurses. "Gwen, I need you to document *everything* to the letter. And page pediatrics too, please. Quickly."

After a few hours in surgery, we sent Katie Housten to ICU to monitor a brain bleed associated with her skull fracture. It was only when I'd finished my afternoon rounds with James that I realized with dismay just how close it was to the end of my shift. And how much I still had to do.

"Rebecca?"

I stopped and leaned against the wall, waiting for Vanessa to catch up. Still in scrubs and cap, she rushed over to ask breathlessly, "I'm glad I caught you. I'm just about to go up and check on Katie Housten. Have you done post-ops?"

"Not yet. I'm running a little behind," I explained wearily. "I asked them to keep me updated, and she's stable."

Felton made a noise like he was about to expand on my explanation, then at Vanessa's withering stare, he melted away around the corner.

"Frightening our residents, tsk," I said good-naturedly once he was out of sight.

"Please, that was nothing. Besides, it makes them tough. Or have you forgotten what it was like?" She smiled and gave an exaggerated shudder. "I don't know how I made it with my attendings pulling me up for everything, including how loudly I walked. I mean, of all the things to criticize me for…" Absently she pulled her scrub cap off, shaking her head as if shaking the memory of her residency away. "Have you heard from CPS?"

"Not yet. Apparently they're on their way." In CPS-speak, *on their way* usually meant any time in the next four or five hours. And that was almost an hour and a half ago. I was going to be cutting it fine to get out of here and home in time for our anniversary dinner date. I rubbed a hand over my face as though I could expunge my mental fatigue.

Vanessa's intense gaze lingered, a line appearing at the edge of her mouth. Her expression turned to concern. "Is there something else wrong?"

"No, I just have an appointment I need to keep."

"You can't reschedule?"

I shook my head, unable to speak around the sudden lump in my throat. It wasn't only that I wanted badly to go out for dinner, but that our dinner plans were also an *outing*. We'd planned to take a cab, sit in a crowded space and softly chip away at one of Sabine's fears. It had even been her suggestion.

On the surface I knew Sabine would act as though she didn't care that I was late—she knew firsthand how it was—but deep down she'd be hurt. Then she would try not to let it show, and fail.

"Well if you suddenly find your evening free, would you like to have dinner with me? You still owe me some more stories about your time in the Army."

"Vanessa, I'm sorry but I can't." I could have left it at that but felt the sudden urge to explain, to remind her about Sabine. "It's our two-year anniversary today."

"Oh, well in that case I hope you make it out of here soon. Shall we go check on this patient?"

"Sure." I collected my resident hiding around the corner, and the three of us made our way toward the elevators. Vanessa's pager began an insistent melody. She tugged it from her waistband and frowning, began to backtrack. "Dammit, I have to go. I'll get to her later. If I don't catch up to you, Rebecca, could you let me know her status and how it goes with CPS?"

"Will do," I called at her departing form.

Katie Housten was stable but still unconscious, and after a brief handover meeting, then post-ops and getting a message to

Vanessa as requested, I escaped to my office to wait for Child Services and continue attacking my paperwork pile. I'd messaged Sabine to let her know things were hectic and that I would meet her at the restaurant a little later than our reservation time. It would be in the skirt and blouse I'd worn to work that morning, instead of the lingerie and dress I had ready at home. Clock-watching only increased my anxiety about leaving on time, and after five minutes, I pulled it from the wall and left it face down on my desk.

Sabine called fifteen minutes later, slightly breathless. "Is everything all right, honey?"

"Yes, but I have a case that's going to keep me here a while. I'm so sorry."

"Sure, okay." The sound of her car starting was an uncomfortable pause. "I canceled the reservation."

I thought I'd been clear that though I would be late, I would certainly be there, and canceling seemed unnecessary. I had let her down again. I forced cheer into my voice. "Oh. We'll just have to go another time then."

"Sounds good," she said neutrally. Neutral from Sabine, who usually lived her life with all her emotions at full intensity, was not good.

A knock on my closed office door interrupted my response, though I had no idea what I would have said to her. "Sweetheart, I have to go. I think CPS is here."

"CPS? Shit, that really sucks." Sabine cleared her throat. "I guess I'll just see you at home then."

Crossing the floor, I agreed, then said goodbye with another apology and an *I love you* before focusing on the woman at the door. "Sheila," I breathed, grateful that the CPS liaison was someone I'd worked with before. Child services cases were hard enough, and anything to make the process easier was welcome. "Come in."

Sheila, a short stocky woman in her early fifties with a wonderfully eccentric sense of fashion, stepped into my office and went straight to the leather chair on the short side of my desk. After I'd closed the door and sat down, she launched right in. "The family is known to us I'm afraid. This might take a little while."

As calmly as I could, I said, "All right then." I'd be lucky if I made it home for any dinner at all.

* * *

The lights in the front room were off when I turned into the driveway just after eight thirty p.m. Once I'd parked, I glanced over at Sabine's car, half-expecting to find her sitting in the backseat of it reading or listening to music as she had been five or six times when I'd come home the past few weeks. The first time, when I'd asked what she was doing, I'd received a nonchalant shrug and "Brain homework" in response.

Before I could gather my things from the passenger seat, my phone rang. Jana. I answered, tucking the phone under my cheek. "Hey, sweetie. Sorry, I was getting around to calling you but the day ran away from me."

"No worries, I get it. Everything okay?"

"Mhmm. Just hectic and then some." As I gathered my coat and briefcase, I asked, "What's up?"

There was an uncharacteristic pause from Sabine's sister, who I'd never known to be lost for words. "Uh, I was talking to Mom and Dad last night. About Sabbie."

My hand hovered near the car door handle. "Yes?"

"The other day when we had coffee she seemed kind of off, upset. She said a few things that made me think maybe things weren't going that great."

"The day you guys saw the homeless veteran?" I pushed the car door open, recalling Sabine's breakdown later that day. To say things weren't going great was an understatement.

"Yeah. And the other night when you guys came around for dinner she didn't really seem like herself, more than the usual stuff. Look, Bec, I know she's not the easiest person to deal with, especially when she's not...feeling well. But we're really worried about her, that she's not doing the things she should. Can you do something, talk to her?"

Do something. Talk to her. I'd been trying to *do something*, trying to *talk to her* for the past month, and all the months before. And nothing seemed to be helping. "What exactly do you want me to do, Jana? She's seeing her appointed Behavioral Health contact, I'm trying to get her to open up and share with me, and short of forcing medication down her throat I'm not sure what else I can do." By the end of my monologue, my dismay and annoyance had risen until I was close to yelling. Though I knew Jana didn't mean it this way, the implication that I wasn't taking care of Sabine stung. With immense effort, I lowered my voice. "I'm doing the best I can."

"I know," she said immediately. "It's just…she should be getting better."

"She's not going to just get better, Jana. It's not something that has a quick and easy fix."

"I know," she said quietly, and I could hear her struggling to keep her tears at bay. "But I just thought being back home with you, and me…that she'd be different. That it'd be easier." After inhaling quickly she said, "Bec, I know you've got your own shit going on and I know things aren't easy, but she's my sister."

"And she's the woman I want to spend my life with," I said simply. "Jana, look, I get it. You're worried. So am I. But I've literally just got home, I've had a very long and upsetting day, and I missed our anniversary dinner because of it. Can we talk about this again in a day or two?"

She took a few seconds before answering, "Of course, sure. Love you."

"You too. Talk soon."

Jesus! Though I knew Jana wasn't accusing me of not being there for Sabine, there was still the hint that she thought I should be doing more. And the notion both angered and upset me. It was easy for anyone who wasn't trudging up a seemingly never-ending hill day in and day out to tell us how to fix everything.

This was our anniversary and I was already hours late. Being in a foul mood wouldn't help anything. I leaned back against the car, waiting to settle down before I went inside.

After a quick, unsuccessful sweep of the semi-dark lower floor, I shed my coat and bags on the kitchen table and continued the search for my girlfriend. At the edge of the back-porch cone of light I could make out Sabine on the swinging bench that hung from the thick tree beside the vegetable garden. She had one leg drawn up so her Ugg-clad foot was flat on the seat, the other foot hanging so she could push the seat back and forth. Beside her thigh sat a heavy crystal glass with her left hand resting on top of it.

At my approach, she dropped her other foot to the grass and shuffled over to the edge of the seat. "Hey."

Being near her immediately eased some of my tension. This *was* the woman I wanted to spend my life with, and I needed to remember that every time things were hard. "Hello, my darling."

She stretched down to set her glass on the grass beside the swing, causing strands of hair to fall across her face. She pushed them away and almost immediately they fell back again. With a huff, Sabine pulled the band from her ponytail and gathered her hair into a messy topknot. Her movements were jerky and impatient, and more telling than any words as to how she was feeling. Once she was done, I bent down for a light kiss.

Sabine's arm stole around the back of my neck as she kissed me, soft but lingering, and I tasted the warmth of the scotch, mixed with vanilla. For a moment, I was transported back to our first night together, both of us drinking scotch. Our first kiss. The taste of her, and how she'd been so hungry and yet at the same time so tender. There was the same gut feeling now as I'd had then, of want and need but also discomfort. Our first time, it was guilt. Now it was knowing there was something not right. With her. With me. With us.

I settled beside her, my arm resting across her lap as I leaned into her, planting kisses on the side of her neck. Sabine twisted her head so my kisses fell on her mouth again. "I love you," she said, once we'd parted.

"I love you too. I'm so sorry I missed dinner."

Sabine shrugged, the movement one of practiced nonchalance. "It happens. I know you didn't mean to. Did you get everything sorted out with CPS?"

"Yes. We'll probably have another meeting later this week." I sat up, turning sideways to face her. "Have you eaten?"

"Not yet, I was waiting for you." She smiled wryly. "I was going to cook, but I wanted it to be something special, and you know…"

I did know. Sabine enjoyed cooking and was very good at it. But only with a handful of dishes she'd perfected. She'd follow a new recipe, but I always sensed an uneasiness if she had to make something unfamiliar, whereas most of my meals were improvised or something new.

I stood and held out a hand. "Come inside then, let's make dinner together and you can tell me about your day."

After dinner, an almost telepathic thought had passed between us and we both snuck away to collect our respective anniversary gifts from where we'd hidden them. Sabine blinked away tears when she unwrapped the book I'd spent hours on the Internet to find—a German-language first edition of Kafka's *The Castle*. I knew she'd never read it, despite her familiarity with *The Metamorphosis* which she could almost quote word for word. In German and English.

Sabine carefully ran her fingers over the cover. "It's so perfect, I almost don't want to read it," she said, then held it close to her chest as she would something precious she was afraid of having taken away.

She stood beside me, hip touching mine as she brushed her teeth while I removed my contacts. By the time I'd put my glasses on, Sabine was done and staring at me, a small crooked smile turning her lips up.

"What?"

"I was just thinking that I love that watch on you." Her anniversary gift was a delicate white-gold wristwatch, slightly too big because she knew I liked wearing my watches that way. On the underside she'd had engraved B - *all the time in the world*, S. Sabine took my left hand and rotated the watch so the face rested on top of my wrist again. Then with slow, careful strokes, her fingers traced the back of my hand and down my fingers.

"Me too. It's beautiful, thank you." A sudden thought popped into my head, likely a consequence of her lovely gift of jewelry, her intense examination of my hand and my earlier thoughts of spending my life with her. "Maybe, sometime soon, we could exchange commitment rings. They don't have to be fancy, but I'd like people to know that I'm with you."

Sabine's eyes widened and her voice lifted half an octave. "Sure, that sounds great." Her left eyebrow was slightly arched. She wasn't as enthusiastic as she was trying to have me believe. No matter how hard she tried, this tell always gave her away.

Her lack of excitement had me both surprised and upset. "We don't have to if you don't want, I just thought…"

"No, Bec. I want," she said forcefully. "You just took me by surprise, that's all." Sabine kissed me quickly then almost as an afterthought leaned over for a second, deeper kiss. She left the bathroom ahead of me, striding toward our walk-in closet before stopping abruptly with her back to me. After a few seconds, she turned around again and stood at the foot of our bed, an undecipherable expression on her face. "I want," she said again, more quietly this time.

I turned off the bathroom light. "Great, maybe we can go and look sometime in the next few months?" At her confirmatory nod, I moved to her side. "Are you sure you're okay about tonight? You seem upset."

She paused, then almost reluctantly, nodded. "Mhmm, I am a little. And I'm upset that I'm upset. And I'm annoyed with myself, because a kid's been abused and I'm here feeling sorry for myself about a dinner reservation."

I ran my hand up and down her back, massaging the tense muscle. "I'm upset too. I was really looking forward to tonight and I'm so sorry."

"I know it's not your fault, Bec." She drew herself up and smiled. "But it's not about where we go or what we do, right? It's about us. And I had a really nice night staying in with you."

I made a musing sound at the back of my throat and she hastened to add, "I think it's just, like I've been psyching myself up for this all day and now I'm kinda wired. Like I don't know where to put all this energy and I just feel a little off, that's all." She gave me one of her easy smiles. "The deployment, coming home and the…PTSD, talking to the shrink and doing my brain homework. There's just a lot of shit already underneath what happened tonight, that's all, but it's fine. Honest."

I was reluctant to challenge her, not when she'd just freely given me a handful of her thoughts, which I knew was difficult for her. "Okay then, darling. If you're sure." I flexed my fingers, cracked my knuckles.

Sabine tapped my hand with a forefinger. "Don't. You'll get arthritis."

"That's not true. They've done studies, you know."

"Still. It's gross." She took my left hand again, studying it intently. Sabine lifted her eyes to mine, raised my hand and unhurriedly kissed each finger. When she was done, she murmured, "You're right. I could see a ring on that finger."

The low, husky tone and what she was implying made my stomach churn with a sudden rush of excitement. Once she'd dropped my hand, I pushed both under her tee and ran my nails over her stomach. Her abdominals tensed, and not in the way I recognized as desire, but something more like discomfort.

I withdrew my hands. "Did you see Andrew Pace today?" I sensed there was something more she wasn't telling me, some other explanation for her distance.

"Mhmm."

"How was it? Do you think he's helping?"

"Yep."

"Is he happy with your progress?"

"He is." The deflection was obvious. Carefully, she stepped out of my reach and drew back the bed covers.

I held onto my sigh. "Sabine, can we talk?" My decision moments before to not push her had faded along with her brief bout of openness.

"We're talking right now." She flashed me a facetious smile.

"That's not what I meant." I slipped around to her side of the bed and pulled her down, then sat beside her. She dropped her hands flat to the bed, but I kept hold of one of her wrists, my grip gentle enough that she could disengage if she wanted to. "Every time I ask you what's happening, you avoid the subject. I'm kind of at a loss here about what to do. I don't know if I should push, or let it go or what I need to do to get you to talk to me about these things."

I felt her muscles tense as though she was going to try and get away, but she remained sitting, clutching the duvet in tight fists. Her expression was resignation, bordering on defiance. "Really, Bec? It's our anniversary and you're…attacking me."

I couldn't pass judgment on how she felt, but the reaction seemed extreme and with Jana's *Can't you do something?* echoing in my head my answer came out harsher than I'd intended. "I'm sorry if you feel *attacked*, I really am. Obviously that's not my intention, but clearly something is up that you're not telling me."

Sabine drew in a long slow breath, then conceded softly, "It's okay, I get it. I'm sorry too." She raised her free hand to rub at the right side of her ribs.

"You know I'm just concerned about you."

Her swallow was audible. "I know."

"I don't want to push, but I think maybe we need to try something else."

"Like what? What do you want from me, Bec?"

"For starters, like I said, I just want you to talk to me, to include me in your treatment. To be honest and open with me. And I really think you need to revisit taking medication."

Sabine squirmed, breaking my grip. She twisted herself right around so we were face-to-face. "I'm trying," she ground out before turning away to stare at the wall.

I had to close my mouth to stop my rebuttal flying out. To tell her I thought she wasn't trying hard enough would not only be unfair, but counterproductive. "I know you are, sweetheart." I stroked her cheek. When she remained unmoving, I gently turned her face back to me. "Do you understand where I'm coming from? Why this is important?"

Mutely, she nodded.

"Okay then." I took a breath, trying to calm down and think of another angle to come at it. "I don't want you to be overwhelmed. I just want to help, but I don't know what to do. Will you let me help you, will you tell me *how*? Please?"

She murmured her assent then slid from beside me, standing unsteadily. Tucking her left arm under her right armpit, the muscles of her forearm danced as though pressing as hard as she could. Sabine let out a soft gasp, and bent to the right, still holding her side.

I pushed up from the bed, reaching for her. "Are you all right?"

"I'm fine," she said breathlessly. "I need to make sure Titus is locked in the house."

"Sabine!"

"Please don't, Bec. I'm fine. I swear. Just drop it. Please."

I was left stunned as she strode from the room, still bent to the side, a quiet stream of expletives following in her wake. I blinked, trying unsuccessfully to force the brimming tears away. It had been a long time since I felt this helpless, and the unfamiliar sensation had me almost paralyzed.

Should I just trust that she was working through it, that the treatment plan an old friend had worked out for my life partner was the right one? I had to. What else could I do when she was blocking me at every turn? Closing my eyes, I let out a breath. I'd drop it, for now, but I was not going to let her just walk away from me, and I wasn't going to leave her alone with whatever was in her head. Swiping at my face, I squared my shoulders and hurried to catch up to her.

CHAPTER FIFTEEN

Sabine

Bus trip day. Yay…

There'd been no text from Bec advising me as she usually did if she thought she'd be late getting home. Assuming she hadn't been caught up in a last-minute emergency, and factoring in time for her to clear up paperwork and change back into street clothes, I should be waiting for her when she came out. If I missed her then I'd just take the bus or Metro home. Awesome.

Buildings, cars, trees and people outside the window flashed by as the bus wound its way through the streets. Just ordinary stuff on an ordinary day. For everyone else, maybe. The jiggling of my leg accompanied the beat of the music in my ears, which was intentionally loud enough to make it hard to focus on anything else. Yep, I was the asshole with the music everyone around me could hear, but this time I was unapologetic—it was helping suppress my anxiety and I hadn't felt like peeing for almost fifteen minutes. Whatever it takes, right?

As the bus approached my stop, I stood, grabbing the rail above my head when the vehicle lurched to a halt. I yanked an earpiece from my ear, thanked the driver and jumped from the top step to the sidewalk to land lightly on the balls of my feet. Should have done a backflip. It was only when I had my feet firmly on the ground that I realized what I'd just done.

Yeah! You took a planned fucking bus trip, Sabine. A long one. Unmedicated. You sat in the back of a vehicle with a bunch of people you didn't know and you let someone drive you somewhere. And nothing happened. Except that guy coughing on you. Self-fixing regime is working. Just forget what happened the other night with Bec pushing and nearly making you spill just how really, really weird things are in your head. You're practically cured! I fist-bumped myself, hiked the backpack holding my uniform and boots higher on my shoulder, and strode toward the hospital entrance.

In the parking lot to the right of the path, I spotted Bec's dark blue convertible. My girlfriend leaned against her car with a hand on the soft-top, and next to her stood a tall, elegantly-dressed blond woman, close enough to seem like they knew one another. Closer actually. Or maybe the blonde was just an aggressive invader of personal space. I paused near a bench seat, far enough away that I couldn't hear the exact content of their conversation, and waited for a lull where I could step in.

I fished out a small notebook and added "Riding the bus" along with the date, time and a scaled anxiety level. Six-point-two-five out of ten. Uncomfortable, but not puke-inducingly unbearable. In another few weeks I might have some chartable data to use and show Pace in support of my self-imposed therapy. With all the extra I was making myself do to get better, surely some sort of breakthrough was imminent.

I scanned the pages listing all my other forced activities. Letting Bec drive, sitting in the backseat of the car while it was in the garage, checking my weight, most definitely not counting my steps at work, deliberately pushing my surgical instruments out of alignment on trays. And then there was the one I hated. The one that made me feel sick to my stomach because it should *not* be on a list of things causing me anxiety—twice making love with my girlfriend when I wanted to but some part of me also hadn't wanted to.

We hadn't even had sex on our anniversary last week, because I'd panicked when she'd talked about rings, and for a few seconds I thought I might ask her, until I realized I couldn't. Then we'd kinda sorta argued because I'm an idiot, and despite her obvious frustration, the whole time she was trying to tell me how much she loved me and how much she wanted to help. And instead of staying and talking it through, I'd had to leave the room because her probing me about my brain shit made the pain in my torso so bad I could barely breathe.

Standing at the kitchen counter with my hands resting on top of it, stretched forward to try and get some air into my lungs had helped. Unexpectedly, Bec followed me downstairs and I'd panicked, unable to stop the paranoia that insisted she was about to tell me she was done, that she'd finally reached the point where she couldn't deal with my shit anymore.

Instead, she'd wordlessly put her arms around me, with her breasts pressed to my back while she held me from behind. She'd kissed my neck, the soft spot under my ear, the edge of my jaw and murmured again and again that she loved me and that she would always be here for me. Within minutes my panic had frayed at the edges and fallen away. But I still hadn't been able to let myself go enough to take her to bed and show her all the ways I loved her.

My butt vibrated, and after a quick glance at Bec, still conversing with Tall Beautiful Blonde, I fished my phone from my jeans. Text from Mitch. *Rumor is they've moved promotions forward to within the next few months. Sorry Sabs, but it's time to get used to saying Major Fleischer.*

Shit. Double shit. There was no excitement or pleasure, or even a sense of accomplishment to accompany this news. Just dread. I didn't want this automatic promotion, and in a childish way, I'd hoped I could somehow slink out of the Army before it happened. The promotion wasn't unexpected, in fact it was guaranteed because Mitch and I had entered the Army as Commissioned Officers, but I thought I'd have more time to psych myself up into a believably excited reaction.

Thankfully Mitch's elation would be more than enough for both of us. This was one more rank on his way to Lieutenant

General and his dream of becoming Surgeon General of the United States Army. But for me, the thought of the upcoming promotion, and all it would entail, turned my stomach. It would be a huge deal, especially to my ex-military father, and my parents were certain to attend the ceremony. Bec would be excited and trying to pretend she wasn't because she knew how I felt about the whole thing.

For me, the military was nothing more than a means to an end, and the fact I didn't enjoy it more had always bothered me. I was the last Fleischer in line and while I loved being a surgeon, I didn't love the Army. Despite Dad's reassurances to the contrary, I always felt I'd let him down by not being a gung-ho Army-loving daughter. Not to mention the fact I wouldn't have a child to carry on the tradition for a fifth generation Fleischer in the armed services—and the way Jana was going, she probably wouldn't either.

Bec's laughter snapped my eyes up from my phone just in time to see the other woman smirk and grasp my girlfriend's arm. She held it for a few seconds, and a strange nervous sensation snaked into my stomach, overriding my dread at the news I'd just received. Lull or not, that was my opening.

I strode over and Bec glanced my way, as anyone would to note a newcomer. Then she half-started. A genuine, dimpled smile of pleasure followed a fraction later and she dropped her hand from the roof to reach out to me. The blonde took a step back, and I felt her eyes on me as I grasped Bec's hand. I tugged my girlfriend closer and in a childish display of possessiveness, kissed her hard and long. Brilliant, Sabine. While you're at it, why not pee on her leg to mark your territory?

When I let her come up for air, Bec murmured, "Hi, I wasn't expecting to see you here."

"Thought I'd surprise you. Looks like I did," I couldn't help but add.

"Mmm." She pulled back slightly and gestured between me and the blonde. "Vanessa, this is my partner, Sabine Fleischer." Bec turned to me. "Darling, this is Vanessa Moore. It's her son who's considering joining the military."

"Oh, wonderful." I looked back to this very attractive woman. She was checking me out, but not entirely in a sexual way. It felt like she was checking me out as a rival. Hmmph. I slipped my arm around Bec's waist, waiting until Vanessa's eyes returned to mine. I held eye contact, refusing to back away. "Has Nicholas made a decision?" The name drop *was* a bit of dick move, but I couldn't suppress the urge to remind this woman that Bec and I would have talked about this. To remind her that Bec and I were a thing.

"I think his decision was already made and talking with Rebecca simply cemented it." Even her voice was elegant, a soft alto, and for the first time I could recall, I felt self-conscious about the fact that when I spoke I sounded like someone battling a wicked case of laryngitis. Vanessa smiled at Bec. "She could talk a man into donating his last penny."

Bec smiled a private smile as Vanessa turned her attention back to me. "So, what do you do, Sabine?"

I straightened up, squaring my shoulders. "I'm a surgeon too, still in the Army." I had the sudden urge to big-note myself, so swallowed the dread of my promotion and added, "And according to a text I just received, apparently soon to be promoted to Major."

Bec's surprised O turned quickly to a broad smile. "Congratulations, sweetheart." She stretched up to kiss my cheek, her hand tightening on my hip.

"Thanks." Despite my micro ego-trip, I was suddenly hit with a wave of discomfort. Next to these two, I looked like a scruffy college student in my hoodie, jeans and Converse. Bec looked as beautiful and well-dressed as always, but Vanessa looked like she'd just come from a photo shoot for a couture catalogue. Well you know what, lady? You might be elegant and cultured and attractive and clearly rich, and maybe even into my girlfriend but I just rode a bus. So beat that.

Vanessa's second appraising up and down look said it all. What the hell is Rebecca Keane doing with you? After another glance at Bec, she turned her attention back to me. "What specialty?"

"General, but once I'm finished with my Army contract I'm considering a change. Perhaps a trauma and critical care fellowship."

"I see," she said evenly. "From what I've witnessed, the Army turns out excellent surgeons. Are you as good as Rebecca?"

Before I could answer her borderline-rude question, Bec piped up, "Better actually." Her hand made its way under my hoodie to scratch my back softly. "I'm sorry, Vanessa, it's been a long day. We're going to excuse ourselves and go home."

"Of course, I'm sorry to have kept you." She raised her leather tote and fished keys from the outer pocket. "I'll see you tomorrow, Rebecca."

Bec smiled. "Tomorrow, yes."

"Nice to meet you," I said cheerfully. Mental high five for fake enthusiasm.

"You too, Sabine." Vanessa Moore nodded, then spun and walked off, her expensive heels rapping sharply on the asphalt. Guess she didn't really think it was all that nice to meet me. Bec turned and pressed herself against me in a tight hug. "This is a wonderful surprise."

The warm comfort of her filled me, pushing some of that strange feeling aside. "I couldn't wait to see you." I smoothed my thumbs under her eyes as though I could smudge some of the tiredness away.

Bec glanced over my shoulder. "Where's your car?"

"At work."

Her brows knitted together. "Is there a problem with it?"

"No, it's fine. Mitch is going to drive me in tomorrow and I'll collect it then." After a beat, I added, "I took the bus here." I tried to make it sound casual but the excitement slipped out on that word. Bus.

All Bec's emotions flashed over her face in quick succession before she launched at me, wrapping her arms around my neck for another hug. Her lips pressed against my neck, and she made a low sound of delight. When Bec pulled back, she took my face between her hands and kissed me. "I am so proud of you."

I couldn't help the stupid, childish grin. "I'm proud of me too." I loved her so much in that moment, for not asking how

I was, or how the ride had gone. She made it an important moment, but not a big deal.

She stroked my cheek and with a small smile, pulled out her keys. "Do you want to drive, or…?"

"Yes please. I think one adventure is enough for today." I held the passenger door open for her then slipped quickly back around to get in the driver's side, leaning over to dump my backpack on the small backseat.

"How was therapy today?"

After what had happened on our anniversary, I'd sworn to myself that I'd try harder in therapy and harder at including Bec. "It was fine, helpful." I started the car. "We talked more about rerouting my pathways." Or rather, Andrew Pace had talked at me and I tried to take it in.

"That's good, baby. I'm pleased." She leaned back against the headrest as I pulled out of the lot. "God, I'm so tired. Today's been crazy."

I came to a stop at the set of lights just outside the hospital and glanced over at her. "Wanna talk about it?"

Bec turned her head, which still rested against the headrest, giving the movement an odd windup toy-like jerkiness. "Not yet. I do want to take a long hot bath with you, and a glass of wine."

"All of that can be arranged."

She squeezed my thigh, then left her hand resting lightly on my leg. Bec's eyes were closed, her breathing steady as she sat half-slumped in the passenger seat. We drove in silence for a few minutes until I couldn't stand it any longer, couldn't push that niggling feeling aside. I tried a casual, "Vanessa seemed nice."

"Yes, she is," Bec said without moving, or opening her eyes.

"She's quite attractive. Elegant as hell."

Her eyes opened slowly. "You think so?" At my nod, she made a musing sound, pushing herself up in the seat. "I suppose you're right."

"Seems like she thinks you're pretty great too. I was surprised she didn't whip out a cheerleading banner with your name on it."

Bec laughed, a genuine sound of amusement and surprise. "That's a little farfetched, darling."

"Come on, Bec. Don't tell me you don't see the way she looks at you, how close she stands. It's obvious she's into you." I chanced a quick look at her. "I thought she was going to challenge me to a duel for your hand."

"I don't think she has any interest in me other than as a work friend, and I certainly didn't get the impression she was challenging you in any way."

"Seriously, she was," I insisted. How could Bec not see it?

After a long silence, Bec said, "Darling, I think maybe you're misconstruing what was likely just curiosity. I've mentioned you at work, so it's natural she'd be interested."

"You talk about me? Why?" The thought of Bec discussing me with her coworkers, and especially fancy Vanessa Moore, made me annoyed, which in turn made me feel foolish.

"Because I love you and you're a very important part of my life," she said simply. Her eyebrows furrowed. "Look, sweetheart, Vanessa knows you and I are together. If she thinks something else then that's her problem." Bec turned slightly toward me. "Are you jealous?"

"No," I answered automatically. I wasn't jealous as such, but I was uneasy and uncomfortable. Standard state these days, really. In the back of my mind, I could hear Colonel Pace reminding me that *evasiveness is dishonesty*. As I pulled into our street, I took a deep breath and admitted, "I'm not jealous but she made me feel weird…and small, and that made me think about some stuff."

"What kind of stuff?"

"Irrational things as usual." Goddammit. Not thirty minutes before I'd been surfing a wave of self-congratulatory euphoria.

Bec reached into the center console for the remote. The garage door rolled up with agonizing slowness and the whole time she remained silent. I wanted to peek at her, so I could tell if she was angry or just thinking. But I chickened out and kept my gaze straight ahead.

Once I'd parked and we'd gathered our bags, she slipped around the front of the car. I followed, and tried again, attempting to spin it in a nonchalant way. "Look, all I'm saying is I can see why you'd enjoy, and return, flirting from a woman like that." I could barely believe I'd even thought it, let alone just said it. You're a fucking idiot, Sabine. Shut up. Just shut your damned mouth.

"Do not even go there." Bec's voice was quiet but with an edge I recognized and did not like. It'd been years since I'd heard that tone—the last time was when she was my boss, kicking me out of an OR. "I am *not* your ex," she said firmly. "And that's the only time I'm ever going to say it." She unlocked the door that led into the laundry and stepped into our house.

I stared at her fleeing form, wanting to chase after her, but unable to make my feet move. "Bec? Stop, wait please."

She did as I asked, then turned to face me. Bec said nothing, just looked at me in that calmly expectant way that made me want to reveal all my secrets.

Instead I blurted the first thing that came to mind. "I'm sorry."

"I know you are," she answered, and though this time her tone was gentler, the tension around her eyes was unmistakable. "You should be. It was a really shitty thing to imply."

"I know. I don't even know why I said it. I'm sorry. Every time I think I've got something under control, another thing falls apart. Fuck, I don't know what's wrong with me."

"I do," she said quietly. "Or not *wrong* rather, but why you're feeling this way." But she didn't elaborate and I knew she wouldn't. It was up to me to voice my feelings.

I took my time and eventually came up with a mumbled, "I just feel so inadequate at the moment, Bec. I'm trying so hard and just not getting anywhere. Like before, I was on top of the world because I rode a bus." I snorted out a laugh. "Just a bus, like a normal person. And now, I feel like I just dug a great big hole and jumped into it. Nothing is steady, it's always up and down."

She came to me then, and the moment her arm came around my waist, I could move again. Bec ushered me into the house with her hand resting on the waistband of my jeans. "You're used to being on top of everything, and when you're not it really messes up your equilibrium."

"I guess. I don't know, maybe I'm just tired. I'm not sleeping very well."

She tilted her head to study me. "What do you mean? Restless or nightmares?"

After a long pause I said, "Both."

"You haven't said anything." Her voice was soft and without accusation. "How frequently?"

"I didn't want you to worry and…I thought they'd settle. It's happening maybe every few nights."

"What about?" Bec unloaded her leather tote, laptop bag and coat onto the kitchen table.

I swallowed. *Evasion is dishonesty.* "The accident mostly. The stuff when I woke up intubated. You're there, the way you were, but in the nightmares, you're smothering me." An unconscious shiver slid down my spine. "Sometimes it morphs into me holding *you* down and smothering you. And then I wake up, or the dream flips into something else."

She blinked, and for a moment her mask slipped and I caught her horror before it disappeared again. "You've been talking to Andrew about it?"

I smiled my best smile. "Of course."

Her eyebrow dipped ever so slightly. "What does he think?"

"He's mentioned Prazosin." Prazosin. Ugh. Blocks adrenaline and can help with PTSD, anxiety and associated nightmares. Side effects can include orthostatic hypotension, syncope and nasal congestion. So I'd be getting a head rush and fainting while my nose is blocked. Wouldn't that be wonderful at work? Assuming I'd even be allowed to continue working, and hadn't been declared medically unfit. Oh, of course then there's the possible dreaming while awake or hallucinations of wakefulness. No, thank you very much.

"What do you think?"

I shrugged. "I think that's a very last resort." Carefully, I hooked my backpack over a kitchen chair.

She raised her chin, her gaze steady. "Why are you being so stubborn about this? You were taking medication, Sabine, and it helped."

"I know!" I shot back defensively. Trying to rein back my temper, I added, "I have that prescription for Zoloft." An as yet unfilled prescription. Baby steps.

Bec jumped on that right away. "A prescription is pointless unless you use it. You know, I wish you hadn't just decided to take yourself off the medication in the first place," she said, her anger sharp and unmistakable and totally unexpected.

It stopped me in my tracks. I'd never seen or heard her like this. During our very few arguments, Bec had never raised her voice. I'd be loud and ranting, and she'd be calm and quiet.

Even when emotional, Rebecca was usually composed. From the moment I'd met her, she'd always seemed so thoughtful and measured. It wasn't that she bottled her emotions, quite the opposite, but she had an uncanny ability to put things away until she needed them. It was such a contrast to my brain which had free rein to think whatever it wanted and then shove it out of my mouth.

Right on schedule, as if determined to highlight the chasm between us, my mouth jumped ahead of my brain. "I fucking told you why I stopped!"

"Yes you did, and I'm sorry but I don't agree with your reasoning," she said, even calmer now. "I know it's hard for you but utilizing everything that's available to you is important. And you haven't done that."

My stomach dropped. I'm the problem. Of course. "Well, it's done," I managed to say. "Old news. Why are we arguing about this?" Again. Two arguments in less than a week about pretty much the same thing. Well done, Sabine. You're doing great with keeping domestic harmony.

"We're *arguing* because you keep thinking, despite everything I've said and done, that you have to take all this on yourself. It's unfair, and after the other night—" She clamped her lips together as though to stop herself saying whatever it was she'd been about to say next. After a deep breath she said, "After all we've been through together, it really hurts to be excluded like this."

Her words stuck a pin in my indignant outrage. I'd been puffed up and ready to rebut everything, but with the simple truth she'd deflated me. There was nothing I could do except offer yet another useless, "I'm sorry."

Bec pulled her hair from the loose ponytail at the nape of her neck, the curls falling freely. "Look, I've had a long day and I want to shower and change out of my work clothes. We can finish this discussion later."

"Sure. I'll start dinner," I said perfunctorily, watching her walk away.

I knew she was right. I'd handled myself poorly. I'd done the wrong thing. I'd been throwing her breadcrumbs and pretending it was enough. I *had* been excluding her from my decisions, keeping secrets about what I was doing and pushing her away while at the same time begging her to stick with me. It wasn't working. You're a piece of crap, Sabine.

Hey, Bec…you wanna marry me?

* * *

Rebecca drove while I sat in the backseat on the passenger side, leaning my head against the window and watching the landscape rush past—familiar city buildings growing out of dust and rocky rubble. It looked like home but in my gut I knew it wasn't. She moved the radio dial back and forth until the tune settled on "Bohemian Rhapsody".

Bile rose up my throat. "Bec, can you change the station please?" She should have known better than to leave it on this song. Had she forgotten, or did she just not care anymore? I'd had a freak-out a few months into my recovery when it had come on the radio. When I'd calmed down enough to stop shaking and puking, I'd told her that it was the song Richards had sung badly and hilariously on the second-last Humvee ride of his too-short life.

"Fleischer!" The brigadier general beside me spoke up, his voice as gruff as I remembered from my interview. "Maybe that's why he died, why hajji got off the round that hit ya, why y'all got shot to shit. Because the specialist was fucking around singing goddamned songs instead of patrolling from the turret like he was supposed to."

From the driver's seat, Bec made a musing sound and slung her arm over the back of the passenger seat so she could turn and watch the exchange. My throat was dry, scratchy and when I coughed, dirt shot out of my mouth. So desperate for a drink of water but there was nothing in the vehicle. "I don't know, General," I croaked out. "I have no fucking idea if singing is or isn't allowed on patrol. Sir!" I leaned forward again, and around the dry lump in my throat reminded Rebecca, "I'm a surgeon, Bec. Not a soldier."

"No, Sabine, you're both." Her eyes found mine in the rearview mirror. "Are you dressed, Captain?"

I blinked. Please, Bec, no. Don't ask me that. Always that question, every nightmare. One of the last things Richards said to me before the explosion that killed him. It was how I knew I was dreaming. Wake up, Sabine.

Offhandedly, I said, "I'm almost a major now. And of course I'm dressed." I glanced down at myself. Scrubs. Blue, my favorite color. Where had my uniform gone? I patted my torso, trying to feel if I'd hidden a vest under my scrub top.

Bec turned around and smiled at me, with all the patience of a parent trying to explain something to a dense child. "No, darling. You're not." She wore full combat uniform and was trying to take her vest off. My hands moved over her torso, batting her hands away and making sure the vest was secure. I yanked it tight and double-checked that all the SAPI plates were in place to stop the rounds that would ping through the vehicle in less than a minute. Don't unbuckle it, don't loosen it because it's uncomfortable. Keep it on. Please keep it on.

"What was that, sweetheart? You have to speak instead of just thinking." Before I could answer out loud, Rebecca continued, "Could you maybe move or do something so you don't get shot? I really can't be bothered with your surgery."

A disembodied voice came from behind me. "She thinks you're worthless, Fleischer. Spends her whole life saving people that got blown and shot up but can't be bothered with you."

A nerve under my eye flickered. "Thank you for that information, sir."

Bec tsked. "I'm just so disappointed in you, Sabine…"

"Why?" I choked out.

"Because you're not going to do anything. You're just going to let yourself get hurt and won't even shoot back. Highest rank in the vehicle and you're going to lie there like an idiot."

"I'm not a soldier," I whispered. Something pressed down on my tongue and I choked. I tried to get a grasp on the thing in my mouth but I couldn't. Couldn't breathe.

"Leave it alone, Sabine. Stop trying to breathe over the ventilation tube," Bec snapped. She reached over, touched my lips and when she drew her hand back, the sensation of something sliding up my trachea had me gagging. My girlfriend sighed. "Look, can you…just hide or something then? Get your weapon."

Panic rising, I cast my gaze around the interior. It was just her and me, and stacked everywhere were medkits and cooler bags of vaccines. "There's nowhere I can go," I whispered. "I can't see my weapon."

Bec began to unfasten the chin strap on her helmet. "Here, then you should take this. You're going to hit your head, remember?"

I reached up to refasten the strap. "Leave it on—you need it." My hands were making sure the helmet was secure under her chin. I had to keep her safe. I placed my hands on the helmet at her temples and stared into her eyes. They were the wrong color, like that strange azure blue in the crack of an iceberg instead of the usual deep blue I loved.

Rebecca shrugged. "Okay, if you're sure."

"I'm sure." In my peripheral vision, a shadow moved. Something flashed. "…because we're going to be blown up. You should get out of the Humvee."

But she didn't move, didn't speak, just kept smiling her dimpled smile at me. The projectile was almost on us but I couldn't move my head to look at it. I could only look at her, knowing exactly what was about to happen. Desperately I shoved at her. "Bec! *Please* get out!"

CHAPTER SIXTEEN

Rebecca

My glasses had slipped to the end of my nose, the frames about to slide off completely. I pushed them back up and glanced at the clock on my bedside table, noting with displeasure that the display read 2:14 a.m. I couldn't have been asleep for more than an hour or two. Following our terse conversation after work, Sabine and I had eaten dinner and watched TV. She'd pushed herself up from the couch a little before ten and murmured that she was going up. I'd followed, because I didn't want her to go to bed alone after we'd had an argument. Or rather, after we'd had *another* argument.

They were more frequent lately, always about the same thing—her reluctance to do all that was possible to get better, to embrace a prescribed therapeutic plan, to take the recommended drugs—and I was disappointed in myself for the way I'd been handling it all. But it was growing ever more difficult to know what to do, when every attempt I made to help was met by her emotional brick wall. I couldn't keep acting like it wasn't affecting me.

We'd kissed good night as always, then she'd rolled onto her side facing away from me. After ten minutes or so, she'd turned over and wrapped a loose arm around my waist as I sat up against the pillows, reading. I'd stroked her hair lightly as I read and despite our truce, the tension in her body had been obvious.

Her feet had moved rhythmically back and forth under the sheets the way she always did as she drifted off. It was like she couldn't even be still while falling asleep. Eventually the movement slowed, her legs relaxed and arms went slack until she'd finally let herself go. And I'd kept reading, kept my fingers tangled loosely in her hair, kept trying to figure out what the hell we were going to do.

Now she lay still, facing me with an arm slung under the pillow, and for a moment I considered staying in bed and curling up to her, trying to forget we'd argued. But I needed the bathroom. When I pulled my legs from under the duvet, my book dropped to the floor with a loud thud. I froze, waiting to see if Sabine shifted, but she didn't stir, soundly asleep at last. Leaning down, I picked up my book and the now broken clip-on reading light from the floor, and placed both on the bedside table.

There was a sliver of moonlight stealing through the curtains, just enough for me to see her. I loved watching her sleep—slumber seemed to give her permission to finally let go. Sabine is a constantly moving thing, frenetic and electric. But I see a change in her sometimes. When we make love. The change comes over quickly, like a shutter being yanked down, and she slows and steadies to a meandering river instead of her usual set of rapids.

In these unguarded moments, it's as if she turns inward, eyes semi-focused. I can imagine the back and forth inside her head as though she's debating if she should allow herself this fleeting peace. I watch it happen, the way her eyebrows rise and fall in minute degrees, then the relaxation of her shoulders as though she's just thrown off a cumbersome load. But those moments had been infrequent since her return home and without any respite, the weariness that had been creeping up seemed to be suffocating her. Suffocating both of us.

I had to blink hard to stop crying. It was time to accept that this had gone beyond me. I needed help—help with Sabine and help for myself—because nothing I'd done was working. But I had to be careful. Contacting her commanding officer because I had concerns about her mental health would have serious professional ramifications. I could call Andrew, but that had its own issues given our work history. Amy and Mitch were the obvious, and probably best, starting point.

Sighing, I admitted that no matter what I did, Sabine would probably think of it as a betrayal, or that I thought her incompetent. At this point, I almost didn't care. This thing had grown too big for me to hold all on my own and now it was crushing me. I'd start with the softest touch first then escalate as necessary. Amy and Mitch, then Andrew, and as a last resort Henry Collings. A plan. But I wouldn't do it in secret. I would tell her and bear her upset if it came to that.

I grabbed my pajamas from the chair in the corner of the bedroom and padded across the cool floor to the bathroom. My toothbrush had been moved. When I picked it up to place it back in the right spot, the damp handle and bristles increased my confusion. I ran my thumb over the bristles and concluded Sabine must have used mine instead of hers. How bizarre. I brushed my teeth, turned out the light and closed the door partway.

And was face-to-face with Sabine. Aiming my gun at me.

Unconsciously, my hands went up to shoulder height. "Sabine...what are you doing?" Shadows from the moonlight cast a strange glow over her face, giving her features an even darker, macabre tint. Her eyes were wide, unfocused pools. She didn't answer me. Mentally I raced through possible reasons for what was happening. Was she sleepwalking? Lucid dreaming? Was she actually taking prescription meds I didn't know about, and having hallucinatory side effects?

The strangest thing, aside from the unreal situation, was that the pistol was in her left hand. Sabine was left-handed, but she shot both pistol and rifle with her right, because as a teenager she'd been taught with her father's right-handed guns. Her hands shook erratically, the pistol wavering with each jerk. Sabine's hands *never* trembled.

I glanced at her hands, unable to tell if the Beretta was on safe or not. But I could see that her forefinger rested against the trigger guard, not on the trigger. A fragment of the fear I had for myself let go. The fear I had for her remained, sharp and dangerous. Desperately, I shoved it down. I couldn't be afraid. If I was afraid then I couldn't think, and I needed to think. I needed to process and help her.

"Sabine?" The tightness in my gut made the word come out breathy and soft. "Sweetheart, what are you doing?" I asked again.

The voice that replied was flat, dark and completely unlike hers. "Something's wrong. You're not supposed to be here. Why are you here?"

Despite my panic, words slid from my mouth like silk. "What do you mean?"

"You got out of the Army and left me here." She didn't lower the gun. "You should be back home in the States. Why are you at the FOB?"

I drew on every ounce of willpower I had to stay calm. "Sabine, we're both in the States, remember? You finished your deployment about six weeks ago. This afternoon you caught the bus to surprise me after work, then we came home, you made my favorite pasta dish for dinner, we watched television and went to bed. Sabine, you're home."

She stared at me, her mouth moving but no sound escaping. Her expression was unlike anything I'd ever seen before—blank, eyes glazed. She was looking at me but she wasn't looking at me.

I covered the remainder of my fear with a mask, willing my voice to remain steady. "Darling, can you put down the gun please? You're frightening me."

She didn't. "Rebecca…" The word stretched, as though she was tasting it, testing it.

"Yes." I kept my hands up and took a small step toward her. My eyes found hers, but they were still unfocused. "It's just me. It's Rebecca. I'm meant to be here." Choking back a sob, I repeated myself. "I'm meant to be here."

"No…"

"Yes, sweetheart." I was close, but not close enough to grab the gun and I couldn't risk startling her.

I took a chance, mustered up my parade command voice and said firmly, "Fleischer! Secure your weapon."

Her arms dropped suddenly, as though she was a puppet and someone had cut her strings. They hung slack at her sides, the Beretta still gripped in her left hand. Quickly, I closed the two feet between us and grasped Sabine's bare forearm. Despite the cool air, her skin was hot, clammy. She didn't resist when I took the gun from her.

I ejected the magazine and racked the slide to remove the cartridge from the chamber. The bullet fell from my hand, and the sound of the metal rolling along the wooden floorboards was deafening. I set the gun on the dresser and slipped the magazine into the top drawer, then spun back to her.

"Bec?"

"Yes, darling," I murmured soothingly. "It's me."

Each breath came out a noisy gasp as Sabine swallowed convulsively. She pushed her hair back from her face, clapped a hand over her mouth and rushed toward the bathroom, almost making it past me before she stopped to retch. Vomit seeped through her fingers and inexplicably, Sabine pulled her hand away from her mouth. The rest of the vomit cascaded over her tee and fell to the floor to splash our feet. She raised her head, her expression one of absolute, wide-eyed horror. "Oh my—I'm sorry. Fuck, I'm s-so s-s-sorry."

I wasn't sure if she was apologizing for pointing a loaded gun at me or throwing up on the floor. Inside, I was screaming but forced my voice to a neutral tone and took her arm. "It's okay, we're all right. Come on, sweetheart, let's get you into the shower and cleaned up."

She let me guide her into the bathroom where I stripped her and turned on the shower. Now I'd moved into familiar detachment, the mindset I needed in order to deal with this terrifying thing. I'd been here in this zone so many times before and the familiarity was almost comforting. Every movement was mechanical and methodical, thinking about nothing beyond the next step. Sabine behaved like a mute child, letting me move her around without protest.

I pulled off my vomit-spattered pajama bottoms and tossed them into the hamper with Sabine's clothes. I dipped a hand into the stream of water to check the temperature then stuck my feet in one at a time to clean them off. Then I gently pulled her forward and with a hand on her back, told her to, "Hop in."

Sabine stepped under the spray, turning away from me to adjust the showerhead. My eyes inevitably strayed to the fist-sized scar on her back, the skin puckered and uneven in the crater left by the bullet exiting her body. When she turned around again, her head bowed under the water, my eyes were drawn like magnets to the other marks on her torso. I knew each one like I knew my own face. Had felt every one under my fingertips more times than I could count.

Her childhood appendectomy. Bullet entry wound under her right armpit. Chest tube scar made by Mitch. My surgical incision, too long because I was almost mad with panic. Shrapnel marks on her thighs, arms, face and neck. All those wounds were hers but also forever mine, even now when I knew she didn't want me touching them.

She didn't wash herself, just stood under the shower, shaking even though the water was hot. Sabine angled her head to catch water in her mouth, then spat it out again over and over. I rubbed my thumb and forefinger back and forth, trying to calm myself, trying to focus on the present, on this terrifying event. I felt as if we were back in Afghanistan, just like that fateful, awful day, and I was trying to put Sabine back together again. I wanted to talk to her, to ask her what was going on, but the look on her face made it clear she was in no shape for a discussion right now.

Sabine shut off the shower and stood with her arms crossed over her chest, still shivering. I wrapped the towel around her, and after a few brisk rubs, left her to dry herself. It took an enormous effort to not rub the fluffy towel over her body. I wanted desperately to comfort her, and at another time she'd have enjoyed being taken care of, but now I sensed she'd take my action as some indication that I thought she wasn't capable. Or that I meant her harm.

After a final glance to make sure she seemed okay by herself for a minute, I hopped around the mess on the floor to fetch a pair of sweats for myself and something for her to wear. The Beretta on the dresser was a dark and menacing shape, a sharp contrast to the sweet, light-filled photographs of Sabine and me. I bent to retrieve the stray bullet from where it'd rolled away to rest against a bed leg. "Sabine? Are you okay in there?"

"I'm fine," she responded crisply. After a long pause she added less bitingly, "Thank you."

Fine was a lie.

I crossed the floor, picked up the Beretta and robotically broke it down into harmless pieces, just as I'd done a million times before. After a quick glance at the bathroom door, I retrieved the magazine from the dresser drawer, opened the window overlooking our back yard and flung both the magazine and slide out into the darkness. Then I locked the rest of the gun parts and that stray bullet back in the safe, closing the closet door as quietly as I could. When I came back into the bathroom, Sabine was standing at the sink, my toothbrush in hand.

"Sabine? That's my toothbrush."

She turned to me, her eyebrows jammed downwards. "What? No..."

My heart raced. I pasted a smile on my face and set the pile of clothes on the closed toilet lid. "Yes, sweetheart. Mine's the green one." Since I'd moved in, my toothbrushes had always been green, the same way hers were always blue because she loved blue.

Sabine stood motionless, her head drooping to stare at the toothbrush in her hand. Eventually, she set down my toothbrush and picked up hers. She squeezed toothpaste with a steady hand and shoved her brush into her mouth.

I tried to catch her eye in the mirror. "I'm just going to go down and get the mop. Will you be all right for a few minutes?"

She looked up, the reflection of her dark eyes finding mine, and nodded.

"There's some clothes here for you."

She nodded again. I grabbed the wicker basket of soiled clothes and raced downstairs into the laundry. It only took a few minutes to rinse off our clothes, toss them in to wash, and grab the mop and bucket.

When I came back into the bedroom, Sabine was in bed, still and quiet under the covers. She watched me clean the floor, her expression unreadable, and I couldn't tell if she was scared, embarrassed, horrified or sorry. Perhaps it was a combination, and possibly more.

I flipped off the light and slid into bed to cradle her from behind. Sabine stiffened at my touch, then after few moments relaxed and moved her arm to rest over mine. Her fingertip ran over my forefinger, all the way up, then down the back of my hand to my wrist. She did this to one finger at a time until all of my fingers had been touched. Then she started again. And she never said a word.

My head swirled. Had she taken something? No, she wouldn't. We'd argued about prescribed medications. Repeatedly. PTSD was the obvious but no less terrifying explanation, but it generally manifested in nightmares and anxiety about loud noises and being in the car, not this. Was it our fight that'd set her off? My harsh words? My pushing her?

I opened my mouth, flexing my jaw to dispel the tears pooling at the corners of my eyes. "Sabine? Darling, what's going on?"

Her fingertip stopped halfway along my left ring finger. "I don't know," she whispered. After a shuddering breath, she choked out, "I am so sorry, Bec. I don't know what to do."

"I know. It's okay. We're okay." I kissed her neck gently then pulled myself closer to her, burying my face in her hair. My eyes strayed to the closet, the closed door and hidden safe before I glanced at the window where I'd tossed the only magazine and the pistol's slide.

But I didn't sleep again.

CHAPTER SEVENTEEN

Sabine

Horror.
Self-loathing.
Fear.

I lay awake for the rest of the night and when Bec shifted just after five a.m., I closed my eyes and feigned sleep, even as soft lips brushed against my cheek and temple. She moved to the bathroom then the closet, and I heard her changing before she left our bedroom. The back door opened, and after a few minutes closed again. I waited for the drone of the treadmill downstairs before I rolled over and buried my face in her pillow.

Bec's scent was one of the most comforting things I knew— shampoo and lotion, her perfume and the thing that was just *Bec*. I'd always clung to it, even before all of this. Before we belonged to one another, I always knew if she'd been in the room recently, and knowing she was nearby helped soothe some of the discomfort of being deployed. When we were finally together, and my PTSD would overwhelm me, I would lie in bed and breathe her in until I was calm again.

I pulled the pillow tighter to my face. What the hell had I done last night? It was unacceptable, unforgivable, terrifying, and the worst part was I still had no idea what exactly had happened. Had I had a psychotic episode? Was I really losing my mind? I'd been trying desperately for hours to connect the dots. To figure out how I'd done…that. But all I could remember was waking up, hearing a loud noise and being afraid, and that was it. Nothing. Blank. Until I woke up again, standing near the bathroom door. With a gun in my hand.

The look on Bec's face had told me everything. I'd threatened her. With a gun. Who the fuck does that? The whole experience was akin to watching myself in a dream, until I kind of snapped from one place to another and I was looking through my eyes again. After the argument we'd had last night, anxiety had remained like a lump of stone deep in my stomach, but I never would have thought it would ever lead to—

Don't cry.

I squeezed my eyelids closed until I was certain no tears would escape. Downstairs, the treadmill continued its rhythmic whine. I had no idea how she'd just gotten up and gone downstairs for a jog, as though this was an everyday morning when it was anything but. If she stuck to her schedule, Bec would finish in fifteen minutes or so. She would want to talk about what happened. But I *couldn't*, because I just didn't know. I stretched off the side of the bed and reached for my Uggs.

I'd brewed coffee, set things for Bec's breakfast on the table and was forcing down granola when she emerged from the hallway. She rested a hand on my shoulder, leaning down to kiss my temple. "I'm just going to shower." Bec seemed calm, unconcerned, but I knew her well enough to know how good she was at setting aside her feelings. My girlfriend was an expert in compartmentalization.

My skin was electrified, my body twitchy. I felt like I was back at school, outside the principal's office. When Bec returned, she was in a robe, not her work clothes. Her hair lay in wet curls against her neck as though she'd barely taken the time to towel it dry. She picked up my nearly empty coffee mug. "I'm going to call in today."

"Why?" I straightened up from my hunched position and rested my hands on top of the table.

"Because of what happened last night. I'm worried about you, darling." The statement was matter-of-fact but still gentle. "And I don't want you to be home alone," she added from her position by the coffee machine.

I ran my tongue along my lower lip. "I won't be home alone, Bec. I'm going to work."

"Oh," she said on an exhalation. "Is that a good idea?" Rebecca poured coffee for both of us and sat in her usual spot to my right.

I had no idea what was a good idea and what wasn't. The correct course of action, how I should act, what I should say. But I knew one thing. "I have to tell Colonel Collings what happened."

"Okay then. Yes. That's the right thing." An awkward silence descended as she trickled sugar into her coffee, poured cereal and began slicing a banana over her bowl.

I added milk to my mug and stirred for exactly thirty seconds then stared into my bowl and counted to fifteen. Spoonful of soggy granola. Chew for fifteen seconds. Swallow. Wait fifteen seconds. Spoonful. The pattern was comforting. I repeated it. Then told myself to stop repeating it and ate while staring out the window at the yellow and red oak leaves moving in the light breeze. One leaf...two. My neck tightened. I dropped my eyes back to my breakfast.

I was desperate to break the quiet but had no idea what to say. *Sorry I held a loaded gun on you* didn't really seem to cut it. The sound of Rebecca setting her knife on the side plate dragged my eyes away from the mess in my bowl.

"Sweetheart, are you all right?" She dipped her spoon into her breakfast and my main thought as she put it in her mouth was that she had a disproportionate ratio of banana to Special K.

I pushed my breakfast to the side. "I don't think so, no."

Bec swallowed and gave me a small smile, reaching out to touch my arm. She curled her fingers around my wrist, holding me in a gentle cage. "Do you want me to come with you to talk to Collings?"

"I think I need to see him by myself first." I drew in a long, shaky breath. "Bec, I'm so *so* sorry. I don't even know what happened. I wasn't…I would *never* sh-sh—" Jesus, I couldn't even make myself say it. Shoot you. I would never shoot you.

"I know, darling," she soothed, stroking my forearm. "Tell me about it, tell me what you think happened." She casually ate another spoonful, as though she wasn't really that interested in what I had to say but was being polite. It was almost like we were talking about whether to cook or order in for dinner tonight.

I knew she was trying to keep me relaxed and open to discussion. At the same time, I almost wished she wasn't so calm. I didn't deserve this acceptance. I reached for my mug, wrapped my hands around the warm ceramic and chanced a look at her. Bec chewed slowly, her eyes focused on me. Desperate to relieve my dry mouth, I swallowed a gulp of too-hot coffee, scalding my tongue in the process. "I'm really not sure I can explain it."

"Try, Sabine," she urged gently.

I tried to order my thoughts. "It sounds so fucking stupid, but I woke up and heard a loud noise, and I just knew I was over there, not here, and something bad was about to happen." My voice broke. "I was so scared, so I got the gun out of the safe, but it was kind of fuzzy, like watching me do it, not actually me doing it, and…then it was like I was just me again."

"Did you think it was an intruder? Or something else?"

"I'm really not sure." Gritting my teeth, I tried to fight the defensiveness, that deep indignation which stemmed from knowing I'd done something wrong, however unintentional. My question came out as a forced whisper. "There's something really wrong with me, isn't there?"

Bec's eyes softened and she blinked rapidly a few times before answering, "No, not wrong *with* you, but I do think there's something wrong. And I don't think it's anything that we can't work through, darling. But…I think it's time to admit that we need some help."

Nothing we can't work through. But I'd have to come to the party. I thought I'd been at the party but apparently I was just standing outside by myself while everyone else mingled. "I'm just so…" I threw my hands up, unable to even find a strong enough word to express how I felt. Devastated came pretty close.

She reached over to softly thumb the edge of my mouth. "I know, I can imagine. How are you feeling now?"

I ticked off emotions like a list of things I was supposed to get from the grocery store. "Mortified. Scared. Embarrassed. Anxious."

"That all seems reasonable, sweetheart." After another mouthful Bec added, almost absently, "You were holding it in your left hand."

"Pardon me?"

"The gun. It was in your left hand."

Left hand. I couldn't breathe and had to suck in a sharp breath to kick-start my diaphragm. That day came flashing back, my thoughts as clear as they had been while I was sprawled in the foot well of the Humvee, hiding from enemy fire. Entry wound under my right armpit. Exit wound near my right scapula. I couldn't move my right arm to handle my rifle or pistol as I usually did. My lips moved soundlessly as the exact thought I'd had in that moment overtook everything else in my head.

It's going to have to be southpaw.

"Sabine?" Bec grabbed my hand, her tight grip bringing me back.

"It's going to have to be southpaw," I repeated aloud. The rush of clarity was swift. It was a nightmare, that's what had happened last night. If I was dreaming about *that*, acting on that, then I couldn't be trusted. The choking intensified until my breathing was nothing more than ragged gasps. Breathe in, count to five. Breathe...out, count...to five. But trying to control my breathing had no effect on the panic smothering me.

Bec pushed out of her chair and crouched in front of me. "Look at me."

I couldn't. Couldn't do anything but try ineffectually to draw in oxygen. She took my face in both hands, forcing me to look at her. There was just the faintest quaver in her voice. "I'm okay. You're okay. I promise, sweetheart. Breathe in and hold on to it. Do it for me, Sabine, even just a little bit of air. You can do it."

I tried to do as she asked, felt the tiniest amount of oxygen hit the bottom of my lungs, then hiccupped it out.

"Good," Bec murmured. "Now breathe in again for me, darling."

After a few minutes of her coaching me to stop the panic-induced hyperventilation, I finally managed to ask, "Bec, can you please change the gun safe combo?" If I couldn't get in there, I couldn't hurt her. But she would know it and could protect herself from…whoever she might need to.

"I've already taken care of it," she said quickly. "I'm getting rid of it today. I…I should have thought about it sooner but…" Her voice dropped until I had to strain to hear her. "I was so busy focusing on everything else, and we'd talked about…I never thought—"

"Thank you. I can't take the chance that I might do something like that again." I sucked in another gulp of air. "I'm so afraid of what I might do when I'm not myself that I can barely breathe."

It took her a while to answer, and when she did, it looked like the words actually hurt her to say them. "Sabine, you're not thinking about doing anything, uh, dangerous?"

I knew right away what she was asking. "No. Never," I said forcefully. I was a lot of things, but I'd never been suicidal, not even during my darkest times after The Incident. "I promise I'm not, I swear."

Her exhalation was audible. "Okay. I didn't think so, but…I…" She stuttered to a stop like a car running out of gas.

"Maybe at night we could lock the sharp knives in there." After a shuddering breath, I suggested, "And maybe you should talk to the police."

For the briefest moment I saw her mask slip before she schooled her face back into neutrality. "I don't think that's going to help, Sabine. It's already happened. Let's talk to Collings first, and we'll take it from there." She looked down, her jaw working back and forth. "Your CO will help you. Commanding officers always know what to do," she said tightly.

"I could have hurt you, Bec. I could have *killed* you," I cried. "Do you get that? Do you understand?"

Her head came up, eyes brimming with tears. "Of course I do, but you didn't. I know what happened wasn't really you. You didn't hurt me, I promise."

My gorge rose, and I pressed my mouth to the crook of my elbow, willing my stomach to settle. God, why? Rebecca stood from between my knees, and I slid my chair back to stand too. Before I could, she sat sideways on my lap, smoothing hair away from my face.

I wrapped my arms loosely around her waist. "I'm so sorry." I only just managed to get the words out before sobs overwhelmed me.

Bec's arms were around my neck, her lips against my cheek, then my ear as she murmured, "I know, darling, I know."

I clung to her, crying noisily as all the worry and anxiety and fear of the past few years finally overcame me. Everything I hadn't done, everything I'd held back from her, everything I'd taken on all on my own. Then the guilt and fear and the gut-clenching horror of what I could have done last night. Burying my face in her neck, I sought comfort from her familiar warmth as Bec soothed me, gently stroking the back of my neck. "Would you take something for the anxiety?"

I bit my lip and finally, nodded. She drew back slightly, and her fingertips traced over my eyebrows, my cheeks and down over my lips. She cupped my face gently and leaned in for a soft kiss. "I still trust you, I always have. Trust *me*, please. Let me help you."

Dipping my head, I used my shoulder to wipe the sticky tears from my face. "Okay."

She cuddled into me so her cheek rested against my ear. Bec's light, even breathing whispered over my neck as we sat together in silence and I could feel her tears against my skin. After a few minutes, she leaned back, then glanced down to where her new watch had slipped to the underside of her delicate wrist. The edge of her mouth turned down for a fraction of a second and then it was gone. "Will you see Andrew today?"

"Yes, I will." The posters in his waiting area were sharp in my mind—the onus was on me to report any mental health concerns. This was a pretty fucking big concern. With every fiber in my body I didn't want to, didn't want to have to tell him what I'd done. But more importantly, I didn't want to admit what I suspected—it was my own fault. Which meant that layered on top of everything was the crushing feeling that I'd failed completely at trying to fix this myself. Perfect. Fuck you, Sabine, for letting yourself get this bad.

"Would you like me to speak with him? Explain from my perspective?"

I laughed wearily. "Yes, I would. I wish you could just call him and fix it for me." More than anything I wanted her to put on her command hat and just make this whole thing better. Make it all go away. "But…I have to do this one for myself too, Bec. But maybe, if he thinks it's a good idea, later we could have some sessions together?"

She smiled, a little relief breaking through the tension. "I think that's a good idea, sweetheart. Let's just see what he says first." Bec leaned her forehead against mine, kissed the tip of my nose. "I love you."

I turned my head so our lips brushed in a kiss that was so fleeting it could have been imagined. "Love you too."

As Rebecca readied to go to work, she gave me a look that told me clearly she wasn't happy about it. But she left after making me promise I'd call her to let her know what both Collings and Pace said. After I heard her car pulling away, I swallowed five milligrams of diazepam, then took a scalding shower. Wiping steam from the mirror, I leaned closer to my reflection and rubbed the hair at my temples, as though I could smudge the gray away. It was a fairly recent addition and oh-so-noticeable in my hair which was almost black. Bec hadn't said anything about my streaks. It was just another thing about me that'd changed.

You pointed a loaded gun at her, Sabine.

I'd been deployed for Christ's sake, back to where The Incident had occurred, right in the thick of it. I'd had some issues—okay, I was a mess—but nothing like that had happened. Yet the moment I came home to my safe place everything was all ass-backward again. I wanted nothing more than to collapse into a puddle on the bathroom floor and lie there for the rest of the day. Perhaps forever.

Stand up, go to work, talk to your boss and the shrink and sort your shit out, Sabine. If you don't, you're not going to have anything left. They'll lock you up. She'll leave if you don't get this sorted out. She deserves so much better than this.

I dressed for work, hastily threw some clothes in a duffel and ran downstairs. As arranged yesterday when I had so "bravely" caught the bus to meet Bec, Mitch would be here any moment to take me to work. It only took a minute to write a note, which I placed on the kitchen counter with a can of Titus's dinner.

Then I left the home I shared with my girlfriend.

CHAPTER EIGHTEEN

Rebecca

Gridlock on the way to work had the back of my neck tight with strain, and the headache nestled in my temples had gone from barely there to permanent resident. I scrunched my shoulders and rolled my neck, trying and failing to release the knots. There was not enough coffee in the world to help me after last night's scant sleep, the waking nightmare, then lying in bed worrying about Sabine. Not enough of anything that would help.

Though she'd insisted I go in for my shift because she had to go to work to talk to her mental health contact and explain the situation to her boss—both things she absolutely had to do—it felt so counterintuitive. As though I was letting her down and trying to pretend nothing had happened.

My fear from last night had multiplied exponentially. It was abundantly clear it was all a result of her PTSD, but I didn't feel better for understanding that. I'd seen her trying with her therapy homework and believed her when she said the things that made her anxious were slowly becoming easier. Stupidly,

I'd thought she would get things under control. I gave myself a mental slap. PTSD wasn't something to *get under control*. It would always be there, another piece in the wonderful mix of things that now made up the woman I loved.

An uncomfortable thought stuck with me. After she'd stopped taking her medication in Afghanistan, she'd told me it was because she felt great, the PTSD symptoms were pretty much gone, and she didn't need it any more. And though I didn't agree with her actions, I'd understood her reasoning, because I loved and trusted her. But...perhaps the PTSD had never become *dormant* and she'd only told me it had to ease my mind. To do something like that was so Sabine, to bulldoze through and pretend things were fine.

She'd shrugged the PTSD off time and time again, rationalizing that she had to complete the remaining time she owed the Army. She was afraid that if she let on how bad it could be they would force her to take long-term psych leave and then they might extend her contract. For Sabine, who was counting the seconds until she finished her active duty, this was unthinkable. I could not convince her of how unlikely that was. Sabine couldn't stand personal weakness or imperfection or what she regarded as failure and went immediately to the worst-case scenario.

My knuckles tightened on the wheel. I dismissed the idea that she'd skimmed over the truth, because I had to believe she wouldn't lie to me about something like this. We'd been through too much to keep secrets of this magnitude. I'd handled everything the wrong way, thinking if I pushed too hard, she would push right back and then run right through me to get away. But that approach hadn't worked. For the first time since leaving the Army, I wished I was still her boss so I could just give her an order and have her follow it.

Sabine just needed more help. She needed to use the medication that she'd initially found beneficial, continue her counseling, maybe take a real vacation. And I needed to do better. I just needed to *do something*. It was my fault that she'd had access to a firearm in the first place. With everything that'd been going on since she came home, I'd completely forgotten about removing it from the house. Yet again, I'd failed her, put her in a situation she shouldn't have been in. She could have taken it, used it on herself—

No, she'd never...she'd promised, numerous times and I believed her. I had to believe her. I was almost at my limit, and I wanted nothing more than to pull over, bury my face in my hands and weep.

But I couldn't.

I made it to my office, and after changing into scrubs checked my in tray and emails. There was nothing requiring my urgent attention, and I still had ten minutes before rounds, so I signed in to PubMed and typed in three words—PTSD delusions psychosis. An article caught my eye. *Psychosis and associated indicators in post-traumatic stress disorder (PTSD).*

...prevalence of psychotic...depression and anxiety...evidence of personality disorder...similarity to clinical diagnosis of chronic schizophrenia...

Schizophrenia? Personality disorder? Was that Sabine now? I bookmarked the page and kept skimming abstracts and bookmarking. My concern grew with every new abstract, until the buzzing of my pager against the waistband of my scrubs interrupted my research. This would have to wait. Gulping the rest of my coffee, I responded to the page, closed my office door and hurried down the hallway toward the elevator and my first case of the day.

After two surgeries and a lunch of bland cafeteria food, I was making my way back to my office, hoping desperately for half an hour of solace. Vanessa Moore's call from behind me had me stop just a few feet from my office door. Almost made it. I waited for her to catch up, marveling that even rushing up the hallway she looked poised. Sabine was right—Vanessa was elegant as hell.

"Rebecca! Are you free next Tuesday for dinner?"

Recalling Sabine's consternation about Vanessa yesterday brought everything else she'd implied to the forefront, and it was on the tip of my tongue to decline. But a niggling thought that I could really use a friend who was outside the sphere of my worries with Sabine stopped me. I nodded. "Tuesday…"

My personal phone rang as I was about to clarify that I'd need to check my schedule. I glanced at the caller ID. Sabine. I held up an unsteady just-one-moment finger. "Sorry, Vanessa. I need to take this." I turned and walked a short distance away, leaning against the wall outside my office to stop myself from sliding to the floor in an anxious heap. "Hello, darling. How are you?"

"I'm fine. I spoke to Collings," she added quickly.

I tried to mask my relief. "Oh, that's good. What did he say?"

"He's going to talk to Pace about my treatment plan after I see him this afternoon, but for now it will be psych leave and mandatory counseling. And a mark in my file."

Pretty much as I'd expected. "That sounds like the right course," I said carefully. "How are you feeling?"

"Sick." She laughed dryly. "Situation normal. But I'm all right."

"Are you sure?"

"Mhmm."

"Okay, then…I'll see you tonight and we can talk some more. I love you. Call me again if there's anything else?"

"Mhmm. Love you too." Then there was nothing but silence in my ear. I stared at the phone as though it could help explain things. I pushed off the wall and took a few steps toward Vanessa. "Sorry, family emergency."

"Yes, so it seemed." She studied me intently, then without preamble asked, "How is Sabine doing?"

I opened my mouth to respond and was mortified when instead of words, a loud sob came out. Quickly, I clapped one hand over my mouth to stifle it, but before I could control myself I was crying great, gulping sobs. Vanessa's look of alarm turned quickly to sympathy. We both reached into pockets for ever-present tissues and when Vanessa found hers first she offered me the package with a gentle smile.

"Thank you." After wiping my eyes, I balled the tissue into my pocket. "I'm so sorry. I don't know where that came from." I did not cry in public, especially not at work.

Wordlessly, she took my elbow and I let myself be guided into my office. She closed the door and once I'd slumped into my chair and wiped away the fresh tears, Vanessa settled in one of the two chairs on the other side of my desk. She crossed her legs, folded her hands in her lap and studied me with a gently expectant expression. "Would you like to talk about it?"

I rested my hands on my desk blotter, studying them as I considered what to say, what to share. I'd spent so many years keeping my own counsel, hiding a part of myself from the Army, moderating what I said and did, and still found it unnatural to share things with people I wasn't close to. But I *really* needed to talk to someone, and Vanessa was so calm and open. And she was there. "Just a rough night, that's all. Sabine's…struggling with PTSD and things kind of boiled over last night."

"Oh my, that's awful." Vanessa reached over to clasp one of my hands. "Are you all right? Is she?" After a wry smile she added, "Silly question I know, given your reaction just now."

"I'm not really all right, no. And neither is she." I had to stop and regain control. "I just thought we'd been making progress and now she seems to have regressed." Annoyed with my careless wording, I shook my head. "Not *regressed*, because treatment for PTSD isn't linear but she seemed better and now she's worse than before."

"I don't believe that's unusual with that diagnosis?"

"No, of course not. I know that and so does she, but knowing it intellectually and knowing it emotionally are two completely separate things."

"Ah yes. It's easy to forget everything we know when someone we love is involved." With a final squeeze of my hand, she released me. "Is she getting help?"

"Yes, to some degree. She's never been particularly enthused by therapy in any form, and I'm not sure how honest she's being, which obviously defeats the purpose of it. I just don't know what else to do for her. I've been trying so hard and just feel helpless really."

"Maybe there is nothing else," Vanessa said quietly.

"Sorry?"

"What I mean is, if she's attending therapy, medicating appropriately and doing all that's required then all you can do is just support that." Her smile was gentle. "But if you're going to support her then *you* need support, Rebecca. Are you seeing anyone yourself?"

"I am." Frowning, I amended, "I was. Before…life, I guess. It's been a few months." I'd worked extensively with my own therapist to move past my feelings of guilt and responsibility, but clearly something still lingered somewhere in my psyche.

"Perhaps it would be beneficial to revisit therapy."

I nodded. "You're right. I know I'm too close to it all." Glancing up, I spilled one of my horrible truths. "I was her boss, and I sent her on the errand that led to all this, so…"

"Oh, Rebecca, I'm sorry. I imagine that must add another incredibly difficult layer to an already horrible situation." She reached for her waistband and after a glance at her phone, frowned and stood. "Goddammit, what crappy timing. I'm so sorry, but I have to go."

I pushed myself up and slipped around to the front of my desk. "Of course. Thanks for, you know."

"Absolutely." After a light hug, she backed away, pausing at my office door. Her gaze was soft, understanding. "I'm here, if you need to talk or cry or whatever. Any time."

I could only nod, not trusting myself to speak. I closed my door and sank onto the brown leather two-seater couch against the far wall. Leaning my head back against the wall, I closed my eyes. Just be there. Support her. I'd been doing all that and it hadn't worked. Hadn't helped.

I almost wept with gratitude when my work cell buzzed. Distraction was exactly what I needed. After closing my office door behind me, I pulled out my personal phone and tapped out a quick message. *Remember when I told you I love you, no matter what? I mean it. See you tonight.*

CHAPTER NINETEEN

Sabine

After meeting with my CO and catching Bec up, I finished some paperwork, spent a few hours in the gym then wandered aimlessly around the grounds because Collings had instructed that I was to be hands-off for the rest of the day. After another session of psyching myself up, it was almost 1500 by the time I made my way toward Behavioral Health. My meeting with Collings had gone as I'd expected, and a sick kind of dread had lingered in my gut all day.

When I knocked on Pace's open door he jumped, then rose from behind his desk. After a quick glance at his blotter, he looked back to me, an uncertain smile tilting his mouth. "Captain Fleischer. We're not scheduled until next week, or do I have my days mixed up?" Clearly, Collings hadn't contacted him yet.

I forced myself to smile in response. "No, sir, you're correct. I wondered if you had a little time for me now?" Knowing what I was about to tell him made my mouth desert-dry, and my words sounded strained.

He closed his folder and gestured that I should come in. "Of course. Take a seat."

"Thank you, Colonel." I closed the door and crossed the floor quickly to one of the now-familiar chairs. No big deal, just going to be honest, honesty is good. Even when honesty means you might lose your job. Great. No, not great. And stop overreacting, you're not going to be discharged. Plenty of people in the military have PTSD to some degree and they're still working. They can't afford to bench too many surgeons. Just going to take some psych leave, that's all.

Pace settled in the chair beside me, reached for a notepad and flipped to a fresh page. "What can I help you with, Captain?"

My stomach was so tight and painful I felt like I'd torn an abdominal muscle. Truth time, Sabine. Spit it out. "Sir, I haven't been totally honest with you."

"What do you mean, Sabine?"

Don't cry, don't cry. "I'm…struggling, Colonel. I've been struggling for a while."

Pace nodded slowly, those bushy eyebrows drawing together. "Struggling how?" he asked quietly. "With what?"

I shrugged, gulped, and lost the battle with my tears. "Everything." I pulled a gun on the woman I love.

Pace reached over to his desk, then set a box of tissues on the table between us. I pulled out a wad and wiped my eyes.

"*Everything* is a lot, Sabine." His smile was indulgent. "Let's get a little more specific. I think we can agree whatever you're struggling with is related to your PTSD?"

"Yes, I would say that's correct."

"So, why don't you tell me exactly what you mean?"

"I mean, aside from the anxiety, I just feel like I can't get a grip on my thoughts. Some days it's fine and others I'm just a mess, like I don't know how to respond to something without overreacting. I'm worried all the time if something is going to set me off."

"Have you noticed a pattern? Only on Wednesdays? Only on days when you eat pasta?"

I smiled slightly at his attempt at levity. "I think it's usually when something upsets me, or I'm anxious. Which is more frequent lately." I reached into my pocket for my notebook I'd been using to track my progress. "As well as your homework, I've been doing some more exposure therapy, and keeping a list of all the things I've been doing that make me uncomfortable and how I feel, to see if I can find a pattern."

"Of course you've been tracking your progress." Pace grinned and took the notebook from me, flipping through the pages. The grin faded until it was more like a frown. He glanced up, both eyebrows lifted. "This is *a lot* of extra exposure therapy, Sabine."

"I know, sir. I just wanted to get it done."

"I see," he said carefully. "Do you think these exercises have helped you make progress?"

"Yes, sir. A little." After a sigh I added an admission. "But in some cases it's also caused more anxiety."

Thankfully there was no *told you so*, or anything like that. Just a calm, "How are you resetting your thoughts when the anxiety comes?"

"Usually I close my eyes and do my breathing exercises or make my lists. It also helps if I can do something else."

"Something like what?"

"Surgery, workout, talking to Bec, that kind of thing."

Pace made some more notes. "So working, surgery, is beneficial then?"

"Yes, sir. Absolutely," I said quickly.

"And do you feel your relationship is solid?"

"Mhmm." As solid as it can be after what I'd done last night. "I've been having issues with intimacy, sir, feeling strange about it, about…being touched. We've also had some arguments over me withholding things."

"I think we both know that feeling disconnected from intimacy with your significant other is unfortunately something that can happen with PTSD." He leaned forward. "Did you resolve the arguments? Were you honest with your partner?"

"I've been trying to be honest, sir, trying to communicate better but it's difficult for me. The most recent argument, um, it's well, I think it's mostly resolved." My heart began to race, thudding hard against my ribs.

"Good. What about the medication? I know it's still early, but have you noticed any positive effects on your thoughts or behaviors?"

I made the same noncommittal sound I always made when he asked if I was having any side effects.

Pace stared at me for a long moment until understanding dawned on his face. He expelled a long sigh. "You're not taking it, are you?"

"No, sir," I whispered.

"Why not?"

"Because I don't want to." Don't want to admit I'm not able to handle this myself. Don't want to admit that this thing is still with me.

"Could you explain why?" Though he wasn't confrontational, his tone was all business—I was as close to being in trouble as I could be for not following his treatment directives.

"I'm not sure I could even put it into words that would make sense to you, sir." I closed my eyes, and pushed out, "It makes me feel like I'm stuck on that day, every time I take a pill I'm reminded of every awful thing and all those awful thoughts."

There was no answer, and when I opened my eyes I realized it was because Colonel Pace was writing. He took his time finishing five and a half lines on his notepad, and when he was done, he looked back up to me. "You're not the first person to have said that to me," he said gently. "Believe it or not, those words make perfect sense."

"Thank you, sir," I whispered.

"You know, Sabine, we may never get the anxiety element of your PTSD one hundred percent under control, but I'm confident we can get it to a level where you can deal with it without medication. The medication is just a tool. A step toward the endgame. It's not a punishment, or an indication of weakness."

"Yes, sir. Okay." My leg was trembling, and I began to tap my heel on the floor to help cover it up.

Pace glanced at my foot. "Captain?" he asked gently. "What else?"

My mouth remained closed, teeth clenched hard on the words. Say it, Sabine. She deserves so much better than you diminishing what you've done. "Last night. I had a…" A what? An incident? A psychotic episode? A complete brain snap? I felt utterly sick at the thought of what I might have done if she hadn't taken the gun from me. I could easily have shot her. Killed her. Not *her*, not just anyone. Bec. You could have killed Bec. Your girlfriend. The best thing in your life. "I think I threatened my girlfriend with a firearm."

"You think? Can you explain what happened to me, Sabine?"

"I woke up, thought I was still at the FOB. But I don't think I was really awake." My voice cracked. "I heard a noise and I was so scared that I got her pistol from the safe, and I uh…I, kind of woke up again and I was pointing the weapon at—at…" I couldn't continue.

"I see. What happened then?" he asked neutrally.

"I just need a moment please, sir," I pushed out. Turning sideways on the chair, I covered my mouth with a hand as my stomach convulsed. Pace toed his wastebasket closer and I thanked the universe that I had been too busy and anxious to eat lunch.

Once I'd stopped dry heaving, he scrawled just a few words. "Are you able to continue? I'd like to know the rest."

I pressed a fist to my mouth and when I was certain I wasn't going to start gagging again, nodded. "It sounds so stupid, sir, but it really was like I was watching myself do it. Like those dreams you have when you're an observer rather than a participant. She disarmed me and I sort of just came to. And I vomited."

Another word joined the few he'd just written. "Would you call it dissociative?"

I frowned, mulling it over. "I guess that's a good way to describe it. Talking it through with her this morning, I realized that I'd had a nightmare about the attack before I woke up, or sleepwalked, or whatever and…did that."

"How did you feel when you discovered what had happened?"

"Disgusted. Embarrassed. Utterly terrified. Grateful that somehow I hadn't actually physically harmed her."

"May I ask why there was a gun in the house? You're aware of guidelines that strongly recommend against that for people with PTSD."

"Yes, sir, I know. I insisted Rebecca have it while I was deployed, sir. It made me feel better knowing she could protect herself while I wasn't there. It made me feel much less anxious about leaving, so she went along with it." I blew out a breath and offered him the only explanation I could think of, flimsy as it was. "I think with everything else that's been happening since I got back, we just forgot about it."

Three-quarters of a line of scribble. "Tell me, Captain Fleischer, how many sessions have we had since you came back from this most recent deployment?"

I raised my eyes to the ceiling, rushing through the math. "Seven. Eight if we're counting today."

His study of me was intense. "So why now? Why, in seven sessions haven't you told me how bad things were? I know you're naturally reticent, Sabine, but I can only help you based on what you tell me." He was still calm, not at all angry. Why was everyone being so goddamned nice?

I could feel my lower lip trembling and I wedged it between my teeth as I thought. Pace sat quietly, waiting for me to answer. After a minute or two, I managed to murmur, "Fear. Embarrassment. Guilt, I guess. I was scared."

"Of what?"

"Being discharged before I can finish my contract to repay my debt to the Army for med school. Being judged unfit. Losing my license. I knew I could still work, regardless, so I thought I could just charge forward and get on with it."

His smile was wry. "You and half the Army. So Rebecca knows about the PTSD and has been very supportive, right?"

"Yes, sir." After a shuddering breath I admitted, "She's basically keeping me together." And I resented that she had to, that instead of a partner she was having to mother me as I fumbled through the new version of my life.

"Then why have you been withholding from her too? Isn't an important part of a relationship honesty and communication?"

I couldn't tell him how Bec was entwined with The Incident, and how that affected the way I shared, or didn't share with her. I didn't want any trouble for her because what we did was wrong at the time. And still would be. Despite the extra complication of DADT, she had been my superior officer. This was still the Army, after all. I sighed. "I guess I just didn't want to bother her. I didn't want her to think I was useless. I thought if I could just figure it out by myself it would be easier."

"And has it been easier?"

Grimacing, I admitted, "Not really, no."

"Well, there you go." He glanced up from his notes. "Is Rebecca seeking help? I'm sure you've read the literature citing a high incidence of depression and mental illness in Army spouses. If she's been with you since your accident, then I would think she needs a great deal of support as well."

"Mhmm. She has a therapist." Depression? Mental illness? No…not my Bec.

"Good. Now, I've asked you before if you've ever felt like harming yourself or others, but I'm going to ask again. Do you?"

I shook my head emphatically. "Absolutely not, sir. No." Each word was spoken in absolute truth. "Which makes this whole thing so unbelievable. I've never even been in a fight or thought about hitting someone or *anything* remotely resembling violence."

"Has Rebecca expressed any fears for her safety?"

"No," I choked out. But just because she hadn't said it out loud didn't mean she wasn't afraid of me, or what I might do. I clenched my jaw. She seemed okay. Surely she wasn't afraid of me?

"I'm glad to hear that," he said seriously. Then he added a casual, "And where is this firearm now?"

"Gone, sir. She took it this morning to get rid of it." And sold it or gave it to a friend or tossed it in the river.

"Okay then, good." His pen stilled. "How do you feel now that you have a few hours distance from the event?"

"Appalled. I'm incredibly upset with myself, and not just at what I did." Understatement. "I'm upset that it took something like almost harming one of the most important people in my life to get this out in the open."

"Unfortunately, sometimes it takes a major event to spur us into action, Captain."

Just yesterday I'd thought something had to give soon, something had to cause a breakthrough so I could get better. Was this it? "Everything in my head is just all confused and messed up and I don't know what to do with it. I'm a surgeon, sir. If there's something that needs repairing then I do that. If there is something in there that shouldn't be, then I take it out. But I can't repair or remove this thing."

"That's true, but it doesn't mean we can't make it smaller, make it easier for you to live with." He mused quietly. "It's possible that your attempt to force yourself to unpack and confront your trauma in such a large way has had the opposite effect and opened a floodgate. Sabine, I think these symptoms are tied to stress, both personal and work-related. Last night you had an argument about what you've been struggling with—your feelings of shame and inadequacy surrounding your accident, and your inability to fully express your emotions about it. I believe the combination is what triggered this episode."

Pretty much what I thought. I'd fucked up. "Sir, what's going to happen now? I have a HPSP debt, and I can't afford to be discharged, or forced to take extended psychiatric leave, or—"

Pace held up a hand. "One step at a time. Firstly, have you spoken to your CO?"

"Yes, sir. He said he's going to contact you." I cleared my throat. "Tomorrow, I start one week of mandatory personal leave, to be extended at your discretion."

Pace glanced at the stack of call notes on his desk. "Good. Given your history, Sabine, our previous conversations and the circumstances surrounding this event, I believe this was an isolated incident brought on by extreme stress. I am going to make a report, which will go in your medical file but for now I don't expect there to be any professional ramifications. That's assuming you follow our treatment plan." He eyed me over the top of his bifocals. "All of our treatment plan…"

"Yes, sir. Of course." I fought the bristling down my neck. "With respect, Colonel, I would like to state for the record that I feel that a long period *not* working would be detrimental to me right now." A few days or a week, sure. But weeks or a month of sitting around thinking about everything that'd happened was not going to help.

"I'll take that under advisement. As for the medication that you *are* going to start taking, you may notice some minor side effects, but I'm sure you know how it goes." He clasped his hands on top of the notepad. "For now, we'll see if psychotherapy combined with medication helps. In addition to your Zoloft, I'm prescribing Prazosin to see if we can't help with your nightmares."

Clearly my expression gave my thoughts away and Pace raised his hand, smiling. "You know how this goes, we start with the lowest therapeutic dose and work from there. But we need to get serious, Sabine. And you need start being totally honest with me, and yourself."

He didn't have to say it. If I hadn't been so evasive, if I hadn't lied to everyone, including myself, if I'd taken the medication then this would probably not be happening. Now I was joining the ranks of deployed personnel on medication to help them with their issues caused by being deployed. Delicious irony. But I couldn't blame anyone but myself. I exhaled to cover the sigh. "Yes, sir. I will."

"Good. You know, Captain, people who go through their entire military career without incident still suffer from PTSD. You experienced a particularly traumatic event. There's no shame here."

"I know, Colonel. I just don't want my life to be defined by this one thing, sir."

"I understand, but at the same time I think we need to accept there's a possibility it may always be a small thing in the background. We need to work on helping you cope with that, minimizing it, which I believe will help you move back toward normalcy." He capped his pen, signaling the end of our impromptu session. Slipping around to the other side of his desk, he typed quickly and then after scrawling his name on the piece of paper that had just spat out of the printer, handed it to me. "Please go to the dispensary and have your prescriptions filled. Start the medication. I'll talk to your CO and be in touch before your appointment next week. But if you need to see me before then, about *anything*, you know where I am. Remember, you can still come in, even if you're on leave."

"I will. Thank you, Colonel."

He stood again, and I hastened to my feet too, standing at loose attention. Pace smiled, this time a little sadly. "Sabine? I'm glad you told me."

"Me too, sir."

* * *

I texted Mitch and Amy to ask them to meet me in the hospital garden. Maybe pretending I was immersed in nature would help me spill my metaphorical guts again. Maybe if I said it enough, I'd stop feeling like I was about to vomit every time I thought about what I'd done.

They both did an excellent job of not appearing too incredulous when I explained and outlined my strategy for moving forward. In typical style, they practically fell over themselves when I told them that I needed their help—Amy sang a few off-key lines from "With a Little Help From My Friends", while Mitch nodded silently, his face a mask of *gonna fix this good* determination.

I felt fractionally better after my second retelling, but by the time I left work, the guilt and self-loathing had reintensified. Knowing I had to face Bec again eventually and admit exactly why I'd had a brain snap made my nausea even worse. I'd filled my prescriptions, and the bottles lay in my backpack, taunting me. No, Sabine. Not taunting…waiting to help you.

When I let myself into Jana's condo just before seven p.m., she was seated at the table, working on her laptop, piles of papers strewn across the surface and a half-full glass of red by her right hand. Time for retelling number three. My abdominals tensed, as though readying for a punch.

"You busy?" I asked inanely as I set my duffel and backpack on the floor beside her couch.

"No, I'm just working at home because I love it so much." She grinned, and sing-songed, "Billable hours!"

"Lucky you." I bent to kiss the top of her head, and when I slung an arm around her shoulders Jana leaned into me.

She looked up, her head still pressed to my side. "Did I forget we had dinner tonight? Is Bec stuck at work?"

With a final brush of my hand over her hair, I pulled away and fumbled behind myself for a kitchen chair. "No, no dinner planned. Bec's not coming. I just, I think I need to crash here for a little while. If that's okay…" Dammit, almost got it out without losing my shit.

With deliberate care, Jana tapped some keys on her laptop, closed it and pushed it away. She leaned close and grasped both my hands in hers. "What's going on, Sabs?"

"I fucked up, Jannie. Like really fucked up. Big time." I managed to hold the tears away for another few seconds before they erupted. Again. It took almost twenty minutes to tell her the horror of the night before, why it'd happened and give her a brief rundown of the issues Bec and I had been having. The whole time, Jana just watched me, her eyes wide and her hands clutching mine.

When I'd finally finished, I offered a helpless shrug and a hoarse, "So, that's it."

And my younger sister said something *so Jana* that it eased a fraction of the tightness in my chest. "Well. Shit. That *is* pretty fucked up. More than I'd thought." She kissed my temple, gave my shoulders a light squeeze, and went to fetch a glass of water. When she handed it to me, she elaborated a little, "You've always been an internalizer, Sabs. Maybe it's time to start letting things out?"

Even after a mouthful of water to ease the dryness of my throat, my question came out small and childlike. "What the hell am I supposed to do?"

Jana blew out a breath. "Do what the shrink says. Surround yourself with people you trust, people you love and who love you. And let us help you. And take your fucking medication."

Her expression turned from earnest and pleading to one I knew well—still supportive but with an edge that meant she was about to push and probe. "Seriously, why are you here and not at home with Bec? Shouldn't you two be talking about this?"

I shrugged and was about to leave it at that. Nope, say it, be truthful. "Because I'm afraid," I whispered.

"Of what?"

"Afraid of what I did, what I could have done. I'm afraid she hates me, that she's scared of me, that I'm *really* too big of a fuckup now for her to want to be with me. It's not just what I did last night, Jannie, it's everything before it too. All the withholding and weirdness." If I'd been completely honest and open from the start, included Bec as I should have, then this would never have come about.

"No," Jana said emphatically. "Sabs, that's never going to happen. She loves you." She leaned forward, her dark eyes wide. "What's worse? The discomfort of having to talk about it and telling her what's in your head, or losing her because of this?"

"Losing her, obviously."

"Yeah. Exactly. So you need to tell her the truth, from the start. All of it."

"I guess." I gulped down a quarter of the glass of water. "I'm not sure I know how to. How to explain all those deep-down things."

"Like what, sweetie?"

I set the glass down, gripping it tightly in both hands. "Like…how I can't get around the fact that Bec's so tied up in all this."

"How so?" Using her knuckles, she gently brushed under my eyes, then handed me another tissue.

"She was there, like right fucking there when I was open and exposed on her table. And every now and then I have this thought about her hands inside my chest and what she had to do and how hard that must have been for her, and I can't put those images in the right place. She's forever in all of it. The bad part of when it happened and then with me after, helping me get better." I took another sip of water. "I mean it was always going to be people I knew, but it was *Bec*. And that's really hard. Hard to know she saw me like that, so completely fucking ruined. And now she's still seeing me that way while we're trying to move past that to just being together like a couple."

"Oh, honey. You know she doesn't think that." Jana sighed in fond exasperation. "Nobody is as hard on you as you are with yourself, Sabs. You always assume that people are seeing you as a failure and we aren't."

My sister knew me better than anyone, knew all my secrets. And I both loved and resented her for the fact she always had my measure. "I can't help being that way," I mumbled indignantly.

"I know." Jana sat back in her chair. "You should really tell Bec what you just told me."

"That's a little unfair, don't you think? How is that going to make her feel, knowing that's how I feel?" We'd never really discussed it in detail, only skirted the edges, and bringing it up after all this time felt pointless and cruel. It felt too late.

"Upset, probably because you're upset. But doesn't she deserve to know everything?"

"I guess." My throat was raw, eyes scratchy and sore from crying. "It wasn't supposed to be like this, Jannie."

"No," she agreed, her voice tight. "But it is, and you have to decide what you're going to do about it. Either you let it devour you, or you face it and do whatever you have to do to beat it." She grabbed me by the shoulders, the emotion in her voice now offset by familiar fierceness. "I'm not losing you to this thing, Sabs. I won't. I'm going to kick it in the balls if I have to, but it can't have you."

CHAPTER TWENTY

Rebecca

By the time I turned into our driveway, my anxiety had coalesced into a hard ball in the pit of my stomach. The day had been a constant up and down, trying to balance concentrating on work with the memory of the night before, and worrying about Sabine all day. During the trip home—which was interrupted by a detour to a firearms dealer to get rid of the Beretta and remaining ammunition—I'd thought about the inevitable conversation awaiting me.

This wasn't the time to be confrontational or accusatory. This was the time to be loving, supportive and strategic so we could work out a plan. Sabine loved guidelines and could handle anything if she had a concrete plan. We'd lay everything out, look at all the options and where we wanted to be, and then figure out how to get there.

As the garage door rolled up, I noticed right away that her Honda was missing. Had she been caught up in a last-minute case? But she was supposed to be on leave. Completing paperwork before her break? Or…was she avoiding us?

On my way through the house, Titus wound insistently around my feet until I nudged him out of the way with a gentle foot under his belly. It was only when I'd set my bags down that I noticed a piece of paper on the kitchen counter, anchored exactly in the middle by a can of cat food. I picked up the can, sliding my finger under the tab as I read the few lines penned in Sabine's neat hand. My finger stilled as the impact of her words hit.

Bec,
I'm going to stay at Jana's for a while, until I can sort this out and trust myself with you again. I'm sorry but I can't be here, not when I'm like this. I don't want to hurt you.
I love you so much.
Sabine xxoo

Didn't want to hurt me… Though intellectually I understood, emotionally I was shattered. Couldn't she see that excluding me while she tried to deal with this on her own hurt me just as much as any physical threat? That this was part of our problem? I dumped the cat's dinner in his bowl, checked his water, then gathered my purse and coat again.

The drive to Jana's was automatic, my brain stuck in a numb loop. Jana opened the door, a sad smile tilting her lips. She drew me in for a hug. "Hello, gorgeous."

I melted against her, absorbing her unwavering love and support. "Is she here?"

"Mhmm." Jana released me. "She's in the den."

I knew the answer even before I asked the question. "She told you?" I was surprised at how flat my words sounded.

"Yes."

"Is she okay?" I hung my coat and set my handbag on the sideboard.

"She's coping. In a very Sabine way." Gentle hands came to my cheeks. "Are *you* all right?"

"I'm…unharmed." Physically at least.

"Good. I'm so sorry, Bec. I didn't realize it'd gotten this bad." Jana kept her hands on my cheeks, and I welcomed the grounding sensation of her warm touch. "Look, I don't know everything, but what I do know scares the shit out of me. I love you, but she's my sister and she's not doing very well. Be careful with her. Please."

At another time, I might have come back with a rebuttal or reassurance that I'd never intentionally hurt Sabine, but I didn't have the mental energy to tell Jana something she should already know. So I smiled in weary agreement and made my way through her apartment. As I walked into the den, I heard a door closing down the hallway.

Sabine sat curled on Jana's comfy leather couch with her knees drawn up under a blanket. She wore a gray soft knit grandpa shirt, the sleeves pulled over her hands and thumbs poking through the holes she always made in her long-sleeved tees. Her gaze remained fixed on the blank television screen until I approached, when she looked up and smiled. But the lift of her mouth didn't reach her dark eyes. Usually so expressive, now they were flat and rimmed in red. "Hey," she said hoarsely.

"Hello, sweetheart. Can I sit?"

"Mhmm, of course."

I lowered myself beside her, leaving six inches between us. Reaching out cautiously to tuck a wayward strand of dark hair behind her ear, I asked, "Darling, what are you doing?"

One shoulder came up in an uncertain shrug, and when she eventually answered me it was with a question of her own. "Are you afraid of me?"

My response was a forceful and immediate, "No. Never."

"I am," she said simply. Her mouth worked for a few moments before she spoke again. "I'm afraid of this new me. I'm such a fucking basket case, Bec. I don't even know where to start." She paused, swallowed, and when she spoke again it was barely audible. "I haven't been honest with you."

I tilted my head. Honest about what exactly? It sounded almost sinister. I placed a hand on my stomach, pressing against my diaphragm as though that would stop its spasming. A few deep breaths settled me enough to ask, "What do you mean?"

She stared across the room, her throat bobbing irregularly. Sabine always held intense eye contact, and on the rare occasion I'd had cause to discipline her in the Army, throughout all our difficult conversations, the painful moments we'd shared, she had always looked me directly in the eyes.

Now, they were focused on everything except me.

"I haven't been totally honest about what's going on with me, Bec. I tried everything I could think of to make things better and it didn't work."

"What do you mean, darling?" I asked again.

"Doing all those things I didn't want to do just made it all worse." She let out a raw, hiccupping cry. "I screwed up, Bec. Like, *really* screwed up. All I did was overwhelm myself so much that I got worse instead of better. And then...last night happened."

Gently, I rubbed her arm, relieved when she accepted my caress. "I'm not sure I'm following, Sabine. I thought that you were supposed to be working on gentle exposure therapy?"

"*Gentle*, yes. Small things, baby steps, yeah. But all those things I was doing, the forcing and stuff was way more than what I should have done. It was all me, Bec. *I* made that decision. Not my therapist. It was me and it was too much, and it was the wrong thing."

A wave of nausea crashed over me as the implication hit. She'd made herself a treatment plan, all on her own the same way she'd decided to stop taking her medication. Independently of her therapist was one thing, but to not tell me and to make out that it was what she was supposed to be doing was... unimaginable. It was a lie.

My throat tightened, and tears slid down my cheeks. "I'm upset that you didn't share that with me. I can't help you if you don't tell me." The words were distorted by my crying. "And maybe I could have helped you."

She was crying freely herself, great hiccupping sobs between her words. "I know, I'm so sorry. I thought I could just deal with it by myself, my own way."

I had no answer, no argument.

It took me a minute to organize my thoughts. I suddenly knew exactly what had been niggling at me since I'd first realized she was in trouble. "I think I've been coming at this all wrong."

Sabine pulled the bottom of her tee up to wipe her eyes. "What do you mean?"

"I've been approaching this like a CO, not a girlfriend." I raised helpless hands. "Part of being a leader is stepping back and letting those under you find their feet, especially when you see them struggling. And all you want to do is fix it, but sometimes you have to let them fail at the small stuff so they learn how to handle the big stuff." I reached across the back of the couch to take her hand. "I didn't want to push you, and make you pull away from me so I held back. But I've been standing too far away. I shouldn't have left you so alone in this and I'm sorry."

"You haven't left me alone, Bec," she insisted. "It's like I want your help, but needing it just feels awful. And you've been there the whole time, trying and I haven't let you see what's happening."

"Well, yes…I suppose that's true too. I guess we've both made mistakes." I drew her hand to my mouth and kissed the butt of her thumb. "Do you remember the last time we were in Afghanistan together? That afternoon on the bench when we spoke about your relationship breakup?"

"Mhmm." Her thumb briefly brushed the edge of my mouth.

"You told me you felt helpless because you were there and she was here. I feel helpless now, Sabine. I just don't know what to do. Please, let me help you now. I love you so much."

"I love you too, I'm so sorry, Bec. I just need you to be here. Please don't run away." She gripped the front of my blouse.

"You'll always belong with me. I promise I'm not going to leave. This is too important to me." Tears ran uninhibited down my cheeks. "You're too important to me."

Frantically, she wiped at my face with the edge of her sleeve. "I'm going to fix this. I promise."

I leaned forward to kiss her forehead and we stayed close, foreheads lightly touching. "Okay, so where do we go from here? What's the plan?"

"Tomorrow I start a week of psych leave. And Pace is making me medicate again. Zoloft and now that fucking Prazosin for the…nightmares." She sounded so defeated that I wanted to gather her in my arms and never let her go. But she needed to talk. "Bec, I just…every time I take the medication it reminds me about what happened that day. It's so hard, I don't know if I can."

"I know, but it doesn't have to be forever, darling. It's just something else to make it easier for you. To help you stop constantly reliving that day. Please trust us to help you."

Sabine wiped her eyes with the palms of her hands. "I'm just so tired, like in my head, and I don't know what to do. I don't even know where to start." Her tears fell freely.

I pulled her close, held her as she cried. "We'll start with what Andrew says, okay? With following his treatment plan. One step at a time. We can do that, right?"

"Mhmm."

"Come home with me. Please."

"I can't," she choked out, now clutching my blouse so firmly that it pulled tightly against my back.

"Please," I begged again. "I love you so much." As though love was enough to fix whatever was wrong.

"I love you too, Bec. And *that's* why I can't."

"What are we talking about? A few days? A few weeks? A month?" I could barely get the words out. The thought of being separated from her again was so immensely painful.

"I'm not sure. Whatever it takes to make us feel safe." Her breathing had steadied, and she seemed a little calmer now, as though working out the details was helping her relax.

As much as I hated it, if time apart made her comfortable then I'd give it to her. "Okay, if that's what you think. But I want to see you every day, if that's all right."

Her eyes widened. "Of course."

"Even if it's just for a few minutes after work, or whatever you're comfortable with, but I need to see you." I was babbling, something I rarely did. "I've already had almost a year away from you. I can't stand any more."

"Me either," she murmured. "I just can't be with you at night, when I'm asleep and my dreams might take over."

"Sure, if that's what you want." I took a chance and quietly asked, "Can I stay here with you tonight?"

Her eyes held mine for the longest moment then flicked toward Jana's kitchen. It took a few seconds for me to make the connection. There were knives in the kitchen. Jesus Christ. "Sabine…"

When she brought her gaze back to mine, her wide, fearful eyes begged me to understand. I knew she couldn't say it, not again. She'd already brought that up this morning but the idea that she'd go into the kitchen, fetch a knife and attack me with it seemed so ludicrous I could have laughed. Or was it?

It was on the tip of my tongue to ask her what was different about her staying at her sister's instead of home, if she was worried even about that. If she was so paranoid, what was to stop her having another incident in the middle of the night and attacking Jana? Or were her night terrors only tied to me because of how intertwined I was with The Incident? Because subconsciously, maybe she did blame me? But I didn't say anything, except, "Okay then. Listen, sweetheart, I might go so you can get some sleep." Staying and continuing to push her wasn't going to do either of us any good. Leaving her felt terrible, but I knew I could trust Jana to keep her safe for me during the night. I had to.

She mumbled a barely audible, "Sure, thanks." She walked me to the door, her arms folded and hands tucked into her armpits. "Let me know you got home safely. I'll call you in the morning?"

"Please do, sweetheart. Call me whenever you want, no matter the time. I just want you to talk to me."

"I promise," she said, and for the first time in a long time I felt the conviction behind her words.

"Will you be home for dinner tomorrow night?"

"Mhmm." She moved as though she was going to touch me, then hesitated and glanced away. We never parted without a hug or kiss, usually both, and now it seemed she thought I didn't want her to touch me, or I her.

"Sabine, look at me." When she finally raised her eyes to mine, I held them for a long moment then stepped forward, drawing her into my arms. "I'm not afraid of you, and I will *never* stop wanting you to touch me." I held her close, felt her arms steal around my waist and her cheek come to rest on my temple.

She sagged against me, her breathing short and shallow. "I just need to ask you one more time, Bec. I need you to wait for me to catch up again. I promise, this is the last time."

"I've already told you, whatever you need to ask of me and however many times you ask it, I will always say yes." I kissed her, lingering against the soft fullness of her mouth. "This isn't a breakup. It's not a separation or a split. It's just taking a little time to get things in order. We are still very much together on this."

Sabine's exhalation was long, the relief palpable as though a bundle of worry left her in that one breath. "Okay."

I raised my chin. Despite everything, I found *her* in those dark, emotion-filled eyes. "A few years before we met, I took an overseas vacation and visited the Old Man of Storr, on the Isle of Skye in Scotland. Do you know it?"

Sabine shook her head.

"You've probably seen pictures at home and not realized. It's basically this big rock at the edge of a cliff by the sea that you can see for miles. He just stands there alone, weathering every storm by himself. Never moves, never breaks, never falters."

"Okaaay. But…it's a rock, honey. Rocks don't move."

I smiled, well aware that I was taking a long and roundabout way to say what I wanted. "What I'm trying to say is that you don't have to do that, darling. You don't have to stand there and be battered day in and day out. When it gets too much, remember you can come down and shelter in our harbor and we will *always* be there for you, no matter what. Because we love you. Because I love you."

"I know. I love you too," she whispered.

"Good. Remember that. Trust it." I drew my thumb down her cheek, then turned and walked out the door.

CHAPTER TWENTY-ONE

Sabine

You are not swallowing The Incident. You are just swallowing a pill. A very helpful one. Nothing to it. Zoloft's active ingredient is sertraline hydrochloride. Chemical formula C-seventeen…H-seventeen…ah, fuck it. I palmed the pill into my mouth and swallowed it with a gulp of water. Done. Now get to work, medication, I've got a whole bunch of things I need to fix.

When I made my way into the kitchen, Jana already had coffee brewed and was making breakfast. Dressed in running tights and a tank top under a linen hoodie, she was unusually perky for six thirty a.m. Suspicious. She stood at the stove, a foot resting on the opposite knee as she watched an egg sizzling in the frying pan. Jana glanced at me as I approached, but mercifully left the *How are you?* unsaid.

I fixed myself coffee then plonked down at the head of her table. "Did you already go to the gym?" Things didn't compute. One, I hadn't even heard her leave the house and two, Jana disliked early morning gym sessions, deeming them *too busy and full of the ultra-fit*.

"Mhmm. I heard morning spin class got a hot new instructor and I wanted to see for myself." She juggled whole wheat toast from the toaster onto a plate then passed it to me, along with a jar of peanut butter.

"Thanks. I can't believe I didn't hear you leave." That she'd left me alone was strangely comforting. My sister didn't think I was a danger to myself—score one for mental health.

"I'm not surprised. I heard you wandering around well after midnight. Did you get any sleep?" Jana sat to my right, with the same breakfast she'd been eating for the past twenty years—coffee, one piece of toast, one fried egg, fruit salad with yogurt. And people said I was rigid.

"Some." Some meaning *barely*. Bec had left around nine, and after sprawling on the couch trying and failing to tame my thoughts, I'd given myself a pep talk, gulped down my first dose of Prazosin and gone to bed for some more insomnia. Around one a.m., I'd emailed Gavin to tell him what'd happened—the bare bones but truthful version—and a sad but sweetly supportive response had been waiting for me when I'd checked my email before stumbling out of bed. My sleep had been fitful, broken constantly by the realization that I was alone. Then I'd remember why, and the anxiety would start all over again.

"Some isn't a quantifiable measure," Jana countered.

I raised a shoulder in a *got me* shrug then shifted my concentration to spreading peanut butter over both slices of toast. I cut each into two inexact triangles. Anxiety level? Four out of ten. There are worse things than uneven triangles. "So was this instructor worth getting out of bed at zero dark?"

Jana let out a low whistle. "Oh boy, and then some."

"You're terrible."

She stabbed her egg, letting bright yellow yolk spread over her plate like lava. "My life is full of simple pleasures. Checking out cute guys in spin-class shorts, nice wine, binge-watching trashy television, eviscerating opposing counsel when they've insisted we go to court, spending time with you."

"I'm glad to know I rate on your list, even if it is at the bottom."

She gave me a sweet smile, ate a mouthful of her breakfast then pointed her fork at me. And here we go. "How long are you planning on staying here? Not that I haven't enjoyed our little sleepover, despite the fact there was no hair braiding or nail painting. But Bec came to see you last night, Sabs. She's still here supporting and loving you, so you know, obviously she's okay with being around you."

I wrapped my hands around my coffee mug. "I don't know, as long as I need to be here."

"Sure… Obviously you can stay as long as you want to, but at some stage you're going to have to go home, Sabbie. You can't stay away forever, unless you're done."

"No, I'm not fucking done," I snapped. I was nowhere near *done*.

Both Jana's hands came up. "Okay, okay. Good."

"I just need some time to make sure I'm not going to hurt her." I shifted uncomfortably. Was I the only person who saw how fucked up what I'd done was? "And yeah, I know the chances of me doing it again are practically nonexistent because the gun is gone, and now I'm drugging my brain into submission. I know the chances of me sleep-walking, or sleep-whatevering down to the kitchen for a knife is improbable. And I know that me choking her or smothering her and all that other stuff is so unlikely it's not even worth mentioning. And even if I somehow did that, I know Bec could defend herself or immobilize me." Defend. Immobilize. Not words that should be applied to your girlfriend.

"Relax, I get it. But, Sabbie, this kind of feels like cause and effect. And you've got it back to front. You're so focused on the effect that you're not thinking about fixing the cause. If you want to fix it, you need to start having actual honest discussions with her. You can't do that if you're avoiding her."

I gritted my teeth. Beethoven, Bec, skiing, beach vacation, sunrise over the pasture behind my parents' house. Inhale. Let it out. "I fucking know, all right? But…*what if*, Jannie? What if I snap again? I can't be one hundred percent certain right now and the anxiety associated with that notion is far, far greater than making sure Bec is safe."

Her eyebrows rose in acknowledgement then, watching me the whole time, she ate a bite of toast and followed it with a forkful of egg. Her swallow was slow. A gulp of coffee chased the mouthful down. My courtroom sister was master of the dramatic pause. Finally, she got around to saying, "I get it, Sabs, but I still think you're reaching for things that aren't there to use as excuses because you're afraid."

"Of course I'm afraid!"

"No. Not of doing it again, but of finally having to face this for real. Of having to admit out loud that you're not perfect."

"I—" I blew out a breath. "I don't know what I'm afraid of exactly." I just knew that I was terrified. I stared at my toast. Thought about how much I didn't feel like eating. Remembered Bec's words. *I just want you to be healthy.* Then I took a bite, swallowing before I could have a feeling about it.

"You know I'll support you no matter what. I love you." Jana swapped empty plate for full bowl. "Sabs, last night, did you tell Bec what you told me? About how it freaks you out that she was the one to, you know." Jana made a stitching motion.

I shook my head. No way, no how could I bring that up now. Or maybe even ever.

"I swear to God, you two are so busy trying to protect each other from your own feelings about that whole damned thing that you're hurting each other instead."

"What do you mean?" When she didn't answer, a surge of annoyance made my jaw muscles twitch. "Quit screwing around, Jana, and tell me. My patience is worn so thin it's almost fucking transparent."

Jana raised her head, staring up at the ceiling for a few seconds before the stare came to my face. "You're always trying to help Bec, to make sure she's okay and not worrying about you, but, Sabbie it kind of feels like at the moment it's at the expense of your own mental health. And the same for her."

I huffed. I supposed Jana kind of knew what she was talking about, being that she was a therapy veteran and attended sessions at least once a week. She always told me if something bothered her and never seemed to have any major emotional issues. I guess talking about your feelings helps. Good thing I'm working on doing that. "Maybe you're right. But I love her, and I don't want her to worry."

"She's going to worry no matter what. So am I. That's just part of loving someone. You need to talk to her, Sabs. And maybe stop to ask a question or two about how *she* feels about what happened." Jana looked suddenly guilty, the twist of her mouth telling me very clearly that she thought she'd already said too much.

"I know how she feels. Upset, but so goddamned accepting, as usual. I wish she'd show some anger or upset or *something*. It'd make the whole thing easier than her constant kindness and understanding." Not that I wanted us to have another argument, but Bec holding this inside felt like too much control and made me wonder if everything would just explode from her one day.

"No, not about the gun thing, Sabbie. About what happened before."

About what happened before. Before…as in way before, as in The Incident? I'd never really considered anything other than that Bec was upset because I'd been hurt. What other feeling could she possibly have?

Jana shrugged, though the gesture seemed more a forced affectation than actual nonchalance. "Look, listen to me or don't but seriously, you need to go home."

"I'm going home tonight." To gauge how I felt about being in that space with Bec, and how anxious sleeping there would make me feel.

"Going to your house to have dinner with your girlfriend is not the same as going home."

"Semantics." Elbows on the table, I rested my face in my hands. My admission came out muffled. "I hate this. I hate *being* like this. I hate feeling like a disappointment to Mom and Dad. I hate that you and Bec have to deal with this shit. I hate the fact that it's taken so long for me to figure myself out, and I really *really* fucking hate the fact that I pointed a loaded weapon at my girlfriend."

"Oh, Sabs. You're not a disappointment, you've never been that. God, you're such an idiot sometimes."

No shit, Jana. I sniffed. Oh great, crying. Again.

She set down her spoon and reached for my hand. "You know what would disappoint them? You giving up."

"I'm not going to do that," I said, my tears not stifling the indignation.

"Good. Then for the last fucking time, go home to Bec. You don't have to stay there, but you do have to talk to her and be *honest*."

I bent my head to wipe my eyes on my shoulder, unable to answer with anything other than a nod.

We were quiet for a few minutes, Jana vigorously eating the remainder of her breakfast and me not so vigorously eating mine. She slid her empty bowl aside to join her empty plate and reached for her coffee. "Speaking of Mom and Dad, have you told them what happened?"

"Not yet. I guess I'll call today sometime." Hi Mom, Dad. Totally love you both, but also…I'm kinda messed up, but it's all okay because now I'm going to really try not to be. Oh, and also while I'm at it, sorry about the grandkids thing but you're flogging a dead horse and it's stressing me out. Bug Jana.

Perfect.

* * *

Bec rummaged through the pantry and fridge, setting things for dinner on the counter while I forced Titus to cuddle me before I fed him. I'd arrived only a few minutes after Bec, and she was still in the blouse and skirt with low heels combo she usually wore to work. She seemed subdued, not upset or wary but more contemplative. Good sign?

"How was your day?" I asked as I slid the kibble container back onto a high pantry shelf.

"Unusually quiet. I actually managed to get caught up on some paperwork."

"Lucky." I scooted past her to wash my hands. "Has Titus Maximus Felix been behaving himself?"

"As much as is possible for him. He slept on my neck last night." Bec glanced up, a smile already on her lips. She wore pale pink lipstick, and I knew she'd have reapplied it before leaving work. Just as I knew she had reapplied the perfume that lingered in the air, familiar and comforting. Suddenly all I could think of was how good she'd smell if I got even closer, and the way she would sometimes leave lipstick on my skin.

She touched my shoulder. "How about you? How was your day?"

"It was…full of television and naps. But I went for a walk this afternoon to the bookstore."

"Sounds like a lovely way to spend a day." Bec tilted her head, her left eyebrow slightly raised. "Did you want a glass of wine?"

"No thank you. I started my medication." After a beat, I confirmed, "Prazosin last night and then Zoloft this morning."

"How are you feeling?" The question was careful but she couldn't disguise her interest.

"Like my serotonin is being selectively inhibited," I said dryly.

Bec showed her dimples. "That must be some super-duper SSRI if it's working already." The dimples faded as she sobered. "You know what I mean. Are you okay?"

"Yeah, it was fine. Once I shut my brain up. I didn't dream last night but I think that's more because I didn't really sleep, rather than medication." I had to turn away from her, knowing I'd cry if I had to look at her sweet, hopeful expression a moment longer. I dipped into my jeans pockets to empty them of whatever I'd absently put in there during my day. A handful of coins, gum, a leaf that was in the middle of changing color and couldn't decide if it wanted to be green, yellow or red.

I held the leaf out to Bec and she took it with a quiet, "Thank you. It's pretty." She cleared her throat, set the leaf down beside the sink as though it was something precious, and passed me a small stack of envelopes. "Here's your mail from today."

"Thanks." I quickly sorted through the stack, saw nothing important and left the letters in the mail bowl to deal with another day.

Bec stared at my unopened mail, then turned away to pull a paper-wrapped package from the fridge. "I have steaks. Can you grill?"

Wrapped in a coat and scarf, I barbequed on the back porch while Bec made salad, set the table and occasionally came to the back door with apparently no other purpose than to watch me. Despite all that'd happened in the past forty-eight hours, there still seemed to be an easiness between us. An easiness that I realized had been absent since I'd come home from Afghanistan.

I set down the tongs. "Is it just me, or does this kinda feel like a date? Like I'm trying to impress you by demonstrating I can cook steak exactly how you want it, and you're trying to win me over with your mastery of dessert."

Bec crossed the deck, peering at the thick steaks I was watching carefully. "It does a little, doesn't it?"

"FYI, babe, your desserts would win anyone over."

She smiled, leaning in to kiss me. The gesture was so automatic that I barely gave it a thought as I moved to meet her halfway. At the last moment she hesitated, her eyes flicking up to mine. I closed the inch between us, letting our lips brush in a brief, soft kiss. I couldn't help myself, moving to kiss her jaw, then her neck and just under her ear to indulge in the scent I knew I'd find there.

A low groan built at the back of my throat, and I had to force myself to take a step back. Less than twenty-four hours of separation and my libido had flipped from "there but cautious" to "absolutely raging". Brilliant. And strange. Probably some weird reverse psychology thing.

There was the slightest flush on her neck and cheeks, and I drew in a long, steadying breath. I wanted nothing more than to kiss her again and had little doubt of where it would lead. Sex, while undoubtedly pleasurable, felt like an unneeded complication at the moment. Especially when I wasn't one hundred percent sure how I would react. When I felt somewhat controlled, I turned my attention back to dinner, and over my shoulder said, "We never really dated, did we?" We'd worked together for years, before a sudden switch from commanding officer and subordinate to lovers, then moved in together after The Incident.

"Not really, no," Bec murmured. "Are these impressive steaks almost done?"

I stared, prodded, assessed before declaring, "Another forty-one seconds."

"You geek." She kissed me again, quickly and unhesitatingly this time and left me to finish up.

Dinner was quiet, but the conversation still easy. Dessert was Bec showing her culinary genius by scooping ice cream into bowls and adding fruit. Michelin-Star stuff. We cleaned up together the way we always did, then settled on our couch—Bec with a glass of red, me with a glass of sparkling water. Titus noisily slurp-bathed himself on the floor behind us. Just a regular night.

There was a comfortable lull in our conversation, both of us leaning into one another. Bec's free hand played under the hair at the back of my neck and I relaxed into her caress, my hand resting on her thigh. The tension I'd been carrying drained, leaving me feeling pliant and ready to talk. Oh boy.

Out of the blue, I offered, "I feel okay being here with you now, like I'm not really anxious about it. But I'm just not ready to stay here, sorry. I think I need another few days before I'm ready to come home." A little more time apart where I could think without what I was trying to fix staring me in the face.

The fingers stroking my skin paused momentarily. "Oh?

"I…there's a couple more things I need to attend to before I'll feel comfortable enough to stay. Like, this kind of feels the same as when I wanted to go off-base *that* day. You know? When we were stuck with all the rules and shit smothering our feelings, and I just needed to get away from the thing that was causing so much anxiety and upset. Now, I feel like I need some space so I can sort through my thoughts without worrying about you seeing them." I grinned. "Not that you can see thoughts, but you always seem to know mine."

Bec's answering smile was controlled. "Oh, I hadn't realized that's why you asked to go on that unlikely mission back then. It makes sense." She was almost too calm now, her words measured.

I twisted to face her, bringing one leg up and settling it under my butt. Readying myself to bring up the topic I'd been avoiding for so long had my nerves firing. Step one—be honest and open. "Babe, about that. Jana made me realize that we've never talked about how I feel that it was you who…put me back together. She, um, she also said that we're so busy protecting each other from how we feel about The Incident that it's actually hurting us."

"I guess that's a good way to put it." Bec set her wineglass down on the coffee table, the movement exceedingly slow and cautious. "How do you feel about me being the lead on your surgery?"

I blew out a breath, my cheeks puffing with the force of it. "I don't like it. Actually, I think I hate it. It upsets me that you had to deal with it. That you saw me that way. That you had to carry the weight of such a fucked-up thing." Right on cue, my right side cramped. Stupid body.

Her gaze was unwavering, her voice steady. "I can understand why you feel that. At the same time, I'm sorry, sweetheart but I couldn't have done it any other way."

"Why not?"

Bec's answer was immediate. "Because I couldn't let anyone else do it. If they'd screwed up, if you'd died or been permanently compromised, then I would spend the rest of my life hating myself. It was me who put you in that position and it had to be me who fixed you." The words had come out in one long breath, and Bec drew in a lungful of air, twisting away from me, her body tensing perceptibly.

…maybe stop to think, and ask a question or two about how she feels about what happened…

"Bec…" I reached for her, gently touching her forearm.

She started. "Yes, darling?" Her hand came to her chest, but it didn't disguise the short, shallow rise and fall of her breasts. Was my stable, strong Bec having a panic attack? Would that be possible?

I slid my hand under hers, gently stroking up and down her sternum as though that might help her remember to breathe deeply. "How do *you* feel about what happened that day? Like, how do you feel now, not how you felt then."

She seemed almost perplexed that I'd asked. After The Incident, we'd cried together as we talked details. The horror she'd felt when she'd realized that it was me coming in. The way the explosion made my head feel like it was in a vise with my teeth being ground into dust. What the team, my friends, had said when she'd told them to prep. How I'd panicked in the Humvee and couldn't remember anything I'd learned all those years ago about being in combat. But everything we'd shared was dry facts designed to convey information, not true feelings.

It took almost a full minute for her to frame a one-word answer. "Guilty." Bec exhaled, her shoulders dropping, and I wondered just how much weight she'd felt holding that word inside for the past two years.

Her confession stole all the air from my lungs. Left my heart feeling so suddenly weak and sluggish that I feared it might cease beating. "Why?" I asked quietly. I realized then that it'd never occurred to me that she could possibly feel that way. Stupid, so fucking stupid and so caught up in my own head.

"Because I should have said no," she said simply.

CHAPTER TWENTY-TWO

Rebecca

I couldn't believe I'd actually answered Sabine's question with the whole, unpolished truth. The instinct to brush past anything regarding my part in that dreadful day, to shield her from my awful reality was so overwhelming that I wanted to take my words back. But what Jana had apparently said to Sabine was right. The way we kept doing this to one another, the way we kept trying to protect each other, was hurting not helping us.

That familiar guilt. Disgust. Self-recrimination. I took a few moments to acknowledge each emotion and then sort them into the place where I kept everything that wasn't helpful. Allowing those feelings to take over wasn't helpful. Not now, when we'd finally arrived at the place we'd been trying to get to for so long.

I looked up, transfixed by her expression of shock and horror and sadness, and my words streamed out in a torrent. "I think about that day a lot. About how you came to my office, knocked so tentatively on my open door like you didn't think I was going to let you come in. As soon as you asked if you could go off-base, my command-brain took over and I was about to say no, because why would I take a surgeon off the roster just to go and give flu vaccinations?

"I think you knew it, because you looked like you were about to beg me, which made me think about everything else you'd begged me for in those hours we were together. And it just cascaded from there. I thought about how it'd been thirteen days since I'd touched you, *really* touched you not just accidentally brushing against each other. Which made me think about the sound you made when I first kissed you, that little sigh as though I'd finally given you the answer to a question you'd been asking me for an eternity.

"I remembered how perfectly your breasts fit in my hands. How you tasted. The smell of your hair. How much I loved making love with you, and that it was exactly as I'd always imagined. I thought about how desperately I wanted to drag you to the floor behind my desk and do it again and again. I'd been in love with you for so long and making love with you had just confirmed how I felt, but I didn't know how to tell you. I was thinking all these things in the space of a few seconds, and then I thought that *this* was the reason why what was happening between us wasn't allowed."

I sucked in a breath, quickly, as though oxygen were sparse and I had to grab some before it vanished. "But I said yes and I still don't know exactly why. Maybe because I've always found it hard to not try to give you what you wanted. So I let you go when I shouldn't have, and I probably *wouldn't* have if I hadn't been so weak and hadn't already crossed that line. And for the rest of my life, Sabine, it's the only yes I'm ever going to regret saying to you."

Sabine only got one word out around her tears that'd begun falling freely halfway through my monologue. "Bec." She took a hiccuping breath at the same time as she drew her thumb under my eyes. She wiped *my* tears, not hers.

I reached up and drew her hand away, kissing her palm before twining our fingers together. "It's okay, sweetheart, really it is. I don't like it, it's upsetting and it hurts, but I've accepted my part in it." I had to, otherwise I would have drowned, and if I drowned then I couldn't keep her afloat as well.

"It's not okay, it's *not!*" Sabine gripped my hand like it was a lifeline, pulling herself closer until there was no space between us. She flung her arms around me, buried her face in my neck and sobbed. She rocked me slowly as I clutched her tee, my own tears wet against her skin as we cried together. Our shared grief was all at once both my greatest sorrow and the most comforting thing I'd ever experienced.

Around her sobs, the words came out jerky and broken. "I didn't even…I'd never thought you might feel that way or blame yourself or anything like that. Why didn't you ever tell me?"

I pulled back slightly, swiping my palms across my eyes. "Because living with the guilt was hard enough, and I couldn't stand thinking of you absorbing it on top of everything else that'd happened to you. Not when you were already struggling so much."

"But it's not your fault, Bec," she insisted hoarsely. "It's really not. It just *happened*."

"I know, but the feeling is still there. Even without all the other stuff between us, I was responsible for you, for your safety and I made a mistake." After a ragged breath, I countered, "None of this is your fault either, darling." I took her face in both my hands, forcing her tear-stained gaze to stay on me. "We both played a part in this."

She curled her fingers around my wrist, holding my hand against her face. "I'm such a selfish idiot. I'm so sorry, Bec." Her apology broke apart. "I didn't mean to make you carry that on your own. These past few years, I thought I was doing the right thing but really I've just been screwing up. Why do you keep giving me all these chances? I'm not saying I don't want you to, or that I'm not so fucking thankful you've stuck by me. But sometimes I can't figure it out."

I kissed her then, because I couldn't help myself. Her lips were salty from crying, and as warm and soft as ever. "I do it because I love you. Because you and your family are the most important things in my life. Maybe the only thing that's ever felt right. I stay, I fight, I try because I love you."

A warm palm came to my tear-wet cheek, warmer lips touched mine. Sabine tugged me close, drawing me almost into her lap and cradling me in strong arms. She kissed my neck, along my jaw, my damp cheeks and finally both of my closed eyelids. I moved closer, burying my face in her neck.

We sat snuggled together, my hand playing up and down her stomach, until our tears eased and our breathing steadied. I let my eyes close again and felt her slow, measured breathing under my hand. She drew in a few short, almost stuttering breaths then exhaled, the sound catching in her throat. I opened my eyes in time to see her twisting away from me. It looked as if she was trying to fold herself in half, and her left hand came up to press against the ribs on her right side. The posture was vaguely familiar, like the one I'd seen her adopt when we were having one of our arguments.

Alarmed, I drew back. "What's wrong, sweetheart?"

Sabine sucked in another quick breath. "It just *hurts*."

"Where? What kind of pain?"

Another sharp inhalation. "My ribs. It's not real, Bec. It's just a fucking fake pain."

"How bad? How long has this been happening?"

She paused, and the flicker of emotion on her face told me she didn't want to answer. But after a beat she said, "Ever since, you know."

"Why didn't you tell me this before?"

"Because it's not real and it's not relevant."

I moved to touch her torso, and she pulled back out of my reach. I didn't chase. "It *is* relevant and what you're feeling is real. What does it feel like?"

"Like a twingey kind of ache…" Her voice dropped. "Sort of how it was when the tube was there."

"Have you told Andrew?"

"Yes. He agrees it's psychosomatic and that it might ease over time, or it might not." Her jaw muscles bunched. "I'm upset, Bec. That's all. Just my brain, reminding me. As if I could forget."

"Please, may I look?" Even as I asked the question, I readied for her to say no. Instead, she nodded, the movement short and jerky. I lifted her shirt and she tensed as my fingers brushed over the scar from the chest tube incision. But she didn't move away. I gently examined the surrounding area, certain I wouldn't find any physical cause but needing to be sure. "Does that hurt?"

"No. It's inside." She flashed me a facetious Sabine grin, her usual response to something difficult she didn't want to discuss. "Inside my head."

I bent down, ducked under her arm and kissed the scar lightly. She sighed, a long drawn out exhalation, and I took my time, softly kissing the area around it, deliberately avoiding the actual scar tissue. My fingers stroked the tense muscles of her abdomen until eventually I felt them relax. Her hand came to the back of my head and when I sat up again, her expression had changed from irreverent to so serious I thought she was about to drop another bombshell on me. "I know I'm not totally okay, Bec, but are *we* okay?"

"Absolutely," I said without hesitation, and her relief was so palpable, I could have touched it.

She shifted on the couch until she was lying down on the edge, facing away from me. "Come here."

I slid in behind her, pulling her close with an arm over her waist and the other under her neck to curve around until my hand rested below her breasts. Burying my face in her soft, fragrant hair, I said, "I'm sorry if I made you uncomfortable or if the way I tried to help made it worse."

"It's okay, baby. I know. I'm sorry I find it so hard to let you help." Sabine reached down for the hand I had across her waist, gently kissing my fingertips before guiding it under her shirt to her right armpit. I stayed quiet as she used my fingers to trace the edges of the scar where a bullet had torn into her. She was tense in the way I knew meant she was unsure about something, rather than fearful and I kept silent, my lips against her neck. With deliberate movements she drew my fingers over every part of the small, ragged mark and the associated surgical scars surrounding it.

"What do you think changed your thinking?"

Sabine rolled over until we were face-to-face. "Acceptance." She raised a shoulder in a lazy shrug. "I can't be perfect, I never could be. But I can try to be what you need and what you deserve." She rested her head on my breasts. A hand found its way under my shirt, fingertips gently stroking my stomach. After a long sigh, she murmured, "Can I stay here a little while before I go?"

Stay. Go. The two words clashed against each other. I kissed her forehead. "Of course you can. As long as you want."

* * *

Thursday night after I'd watched Sabine drive away back to her sister's, I made a mug of herbal tea, and took the cat upstairs with me to read in the hope it would help me relax enough that I could sleep. Even after the ten months of Sabine's deployment, I'd never grown used to sleeping alone, and the past few days had been a fresh kind of torture.

She hadn't spent a night in our house since the gun incident. The night we'd shared our truths, we'd lain on the couch, curled up together talking until almost midnight. Yawning, Sabine had sat up again, glancing out of the den to the stairs that led up to our bedroom.

She'd murmured her apology, told me she just couldn't do it, and with a tight hug and soft kiss we'd said our good nights. And she'd left me. The next few nights had been more of the same— Sabine coming for dinner, playing with the cat, us watching television together, and talking. I didn't push because every time I'd seen her, I could see a change—the slight relaxation, an openness and willingness to talk. These nights apart were helping her, and that made it worth it.

After half an hour I gave up trying to read, unable to concentrate and slid off the bed to put the novel back. One of the books on the middle shelf sat back to front, the pages facing out instead of the spine. I eased it out and flipped it around to check the cover. Sabine's beloved Kafka.

I traced the worn embossed title. *Die Verwandlung.*
The Metamorphosis.

Fitting really that this would be the book I picked up. The past few years had been a metamorphosis of sorts. I pushed the

book back onto the shelf, the right way around. The right way…
Why was it the *wrong* way around in the first place? Sabine was
meticulous to the point of OCD, and it made no sense that she'd
put one of her most treasured possessions away so carelessly.
Especially not a book that didn't usually live on the shelf, but on
her bedside table.

As I stared at the rows of books, I made an uneasy connection
with the plot of the classic and why she'd hidden this particular
book from view. Did Sabine think *she'd* undergone some
metamorphosis, and was now so changed that the people who
loved her would somehow be happier or better off without her?

God, it'd been right there in front of me the whole time,
she'd practically left me a goddamned note telling me what
the problem was. I could have seen it earlier, if I hadn't been
so hyper-focused on all the tiny things. On trying to *fix her*,
rather than doing what she needed. I could only hope that after
everything we'd shared, she now knew that I needed her. That I
trusted her to hear *my* truth.

CHAPTER TWENTY-THREE

Sabine

Semi-awake, I fumbled my phone from the coffee table and clumsily swiped a few times to accept the call. "Sabine Fleischer."

Mitch laughed. "What kinda formal shit is that?"

"I was sleeping." On the couch like a grandma after dinner. I cleared my throat, trying to push away the just-woken gravel.

"At eight on a Friday night? Darlin', that is the saddest thing I ever heard."

"Leave me alone. Doing nothing all day makes me tired," I mumbled. "What's up?"

"Mike and me are goin' to Seventeenth Street. And you, sugar, are comin' along to blow off some steam."

Perfect, a night of dancing with Mitch and his boyfriend. Third wheel much? I rolled over, flinging an arm over my eyes. "Mmmph. I'm still at Jana's and I don't have anything here I can wear." Flimsy excuses are flimsy.

"Borrow somethin' of hers. Come on, angel. Dancin' is just what the doctor ordered." He was almost pleading. "It's been ages since we went out."

I knew well enough that if I said no, he'd turn up anyway, paw through the closet and practically dress me before carrying me out. He'd done that exact thing quite a few times during med school, somehow seeming to know when I needed a break from study.

I made a noncommittal musing sound which my best friend took as acquiescence. "We'll be there in twenty."

I sat up, swinging my legs off the couch. "Don't bother, I'm not drinking so I'll drive. Gimme forty-five minutes."

I wrote a note and left it on the fridge to let Jana know I was going out. She hadn't messaged me for a rescue call, so clearly her date was going well, and I didn't want to interrupt. I borrowed some of her makeup and pawed through her drawers and closet. We were close enough in size that there should be something for me, especially considering I wasn't dressing to impress anyone, only for dancing.

I found a green tank top and pulled on brown Cuban-heel cowboy boots that Jana bought in Texas last year, with my own jeans carefully smoothed over the top. Jana's butter-soft leather jacket would ward off the cool night air. I might have to *borrow* that one more often.

My M 'n' Ms were waiting arm in arm at the end of their driveway when I arrived, right when I'd said I would. Mike slipped into the front seat. "You look delicious. I should have brought a stick to fend off women with." He cupped my cheek fondly, kissing the other one.

"New perfume, angel?" Mitch asked after he'd leaned over from the backseat to kiss my cheek too.

"Jana's. Surprised you can smell it around that aftershave you've poured on. You drop the bottle on your face again?"

Mike laughed. "I tried to tell him."

"I thought you liked it," Mitch spluttered.

"I do, sweetie. Just not choking on it."

"Told you," I said smugly.

"I fuckin' hate the way you two gang up on me." Mitch poked me in the shoulder. "First round's on you, Sabs."

Asshole, I wasn't even drinking.

I parked a block away, linked arms with the boys and we strolled to the club. Every now and then, Mitch would count a loud "One…two…three!" and they would lift me between them the way parents do with kids. By the time we made it to the club, the three of us were laughing. The boys paid my cover—fair's fair for dragging me out—and I received a bright purple teddy bear stamp on the back of my hand.

We made our way upstairs to the bar and dance floor, and I barely had time to drink a glass of water before Mike had dragged me out to dance, clutching my hands tightly as he spun me in a dramatic circle. I'd forgotten what a great dancer he was—the kind of fluid, natural dancer you can't help but watch. He spent most of his time trying to make me laugh with outrageous moves. He and Mitch didn't leave me for an instant, forming a dance-floor circle, and the three of us gently fended off women moving in on me since I was clearly not *with* anyone.

After a few hours, Mike was pleasantly tipsy and Mitch was well on his way to drunk. I was still completely sober but buzzed from dancing, with sides that hurt from laughing. Just what the doctor ordered indeed, though of course I couldn't admit to Mitch that he'd been right. Letting off a little steam and just forgetting myself for a few hours *was* enjoyable but something still felt wrong, a little piece of me missing, and it didn't take a rocket scientist to figure out what it was.

Bec.

She wasn't big on clubs but had come out a few times to dance, and I knew she'd done it just to make me happy. Bec preferred intimate restaurant dinners, or drinks at a pub with friends. We weren't so codependent that we couldn't be out alone, and on occasion I had even gone out dancing while she'd stayed home. But I couldn't ignore my unease at being out without her now. At being without her, period.

When the beat changed to something a little too quick for me, I slipped my hands from Mike's. "Just going to the bathroom, I'll meet you guys at the bar. Can you grab me a sparkling water, please?"

Waiting in line at the restrooms, I pulled out my phone to message Bec. A flu was running rampant through her staff, even the long-suffering residents. Most unusually, she was covering, and currently in the middle of a twenty-four-hour shift. We'd had to skip our dinner date but I'd talked to her this afternoon during a break and sometime during her work night, she'd get my message that I'd been dragged out dancing, was bored, sober and that I missed her.

I pushed my phone into my back pocket, accidentally elbowing the person behind me. When I turned around, I found a pretty brunette wearing a sleeveless scoop-necked top that advertised both cleavage and toned yoga arms. She was cute, in a fresh-faced, just-turned-twenty-one-yesterday kind of way.

I flashed an apologetic smile. "Sorry."

She gave me a bright smile in return. "No problem." She leaned against the wall, folding her arms under her breasts. "Maybe they'll be done sometime tonight and we'll actually get to use the bathroom."

"Pardon?"

The smile grew and she indicated the stalls with a casual flick of her fingers. "Listen."

I cocked my head, and heard something I hadn't noticed while I'd been engrossed in texting Bec. The unmistakable sound of a bathroom stall hook-up. I snorted. "Good thing I'm not desperate to pee then." I glanced at the other two stalls. Very quiet puking in one and in the other was what sounded like a tearful break-up conversation. Oh dear on both counts.

"I am, and I'm not sure how much longer I'll last." She gestured to her chest. "I'm Amelia."

"Sabine."

"I saw you dancing with the big bear and the other guy who makes Justin Timberlake's dance moves look like amateur hour."

"Ah, yeah. Good friends. You're right, Mike dances like he's trying to qualify for Dance Olympics or something."

"Mmm, I prefer your moves though." She made no effort to moderate her full up-and-down inspection of me.

I grinned. "Well, if you like vague flailing on dance floors then I'm not surprised."

Amelia let out an honest-to-goodness giggle. "Actually, I think I do."

"Noted. How about you? Here with friends? Girlfriend?"

"Friends. No girlfriend." She lowered her voice. "I like to keep my options open."

Nodding, I agreed, "Good call, especially when you're young." Oh my God when did I become one of those "when I was your age" people?

"Not that young," she countered cheekily.

A particularly loud gasp, followed by a low moan from the far stall grabbed our attention, and Amelia and I caught each other's eye before bursting into shared laughter. How fun it must be to go out with no other intention than to get as drunk as you want, pick up a random stranger to screw senseless and then wake up without a care. Actually, I knew how fun it was but I was long past that now.

Amelia shook her head, still laughing. "You know, I'm all for hook-ups but sex in a bathroom? I'm not sure I'm down for that."

"Well I'm all for sex in bathrooms, but not random hook-ups." *All for* was an understatement. A Technicolor replay of Bec and me in a restaurant bathroom on her birthday last year flashed through my head—her with her leg slung around my ass, me with my teeth buried in the soft skin of her shoulder to muffle the sound of my pleasure. A shudder slid down my spine.

Amelia's laughing smile turned ever so slightly seductive. "Between the two of us I'm sure we could work something out."

Before I could answer, the middle stall opened and Puker exited, looking pale but otherwise okay as she made her way to the sinks. I gestured to the stalls. "You go, I can wait."

"Thank you. Lifesaver." Amelia squeezed my forearm and dashed into the stall.

Puker didn't seem in any need of help, so I left her to wash up and kept waiting for my turn. The end stall opened thirty seconds later and two supremely satisfied but very apologetic-looking women slid by. I heard their murmured *sorry* all the way down the line.

I finished up in the bathroom, and had just begun my trek back to the dance floor when a hand closed around my wrist with surprising gentleness, considering it was designed to slow me down and hold me in place. "Sabine! Can I buy you a drink?"

I carefully disengaged myself from Amelia's grasp. "Sorry, I'm not drinking, but thank you."

"How about a dance then? Cup of tea? Fortune telling? I know some great knock-knock jokes."

I couldn't help smiling at her persistence which was both flattering and mildly uncomfortable for reasons I couldn't quite pin down. "I'm good, but thanks."

She leaned in, not touching me, and murmured against my ear, "Okay, so you're not interested in any of my other skills. How about you come back into the bathroom, and maybe we can meet somewhere in the middle on that bathroom stall hook-up thing..."

Clearly *persistence* was an understatement. Laughing quietly, I declined again. "No thank you. I'm really flattered, but I have a girlfriend."

She straightened fractionally, her eyes widening. "And she let you come out alone? If you were mine, I think I'd put you on a leash."

I winked. "Some nights, she does. Have a good night, Amelia." As I strode away a sudden inexplicable rush of anxiety made my stomach turn over. Relax, Sabine. Everything's fine, you're safe here. But the awful sensation refused to go away. Bec, Titus lying upside down in his sun patch, drinking coffee from my favorite mug, sunbaking on the beach, Bec's cuddles.

What's the issue? What's making you upset? Deep breath. It was just meaningless flirting, not unusual for a club and certainly not the first time it's happened. It's not going to go anywhere, it never has because you never want it to. It's always just been innocuous teasing fun and then you go home to Bec.

Bec.

My brain skipped like a record scratch, then looped back. Home. To Bec. Focus, Sabine, think. You have Bec. At home. But…I'd always had Bec, hadn't I? Whenever I felt upset or anxious, who was the one thing that was always on my calming mantras, usually twice? She'd always been there, helping me, even when I hadn't consciously realized. I was such an idiot.

I was in the wrong place, and with the wrong people.

I rushed across the worn wooden floor, weaving around people dancing and making out. The press of bodies which had been exciting earlier now felt claustrophobic. I found the boys leaning against a crowded area of the bar and Mitch pulled me in for a tight drunken hug, lifting me from the ground. His breath was hot on my ear when he asked exuberantly, "Havin' fun yet, sugar?"

"I am, thanks for bringing me out." I held on around his shoulders and spoke right against his ear over the music. "But I've gotta go."

He set me down, looking like a scolded puppy. "'S'everythin' awwright?"

Reassuringly, I squeezed his arms. "Mhmm, it's fine. Promise. I just have to go, I need to see Bec. Sorry, can you guys get a cab home?"

Mike set down his drink. "We'll come too."

I stopped him with a hand on his chest. "Noooo, stay and have fun, seriously. I'll be fine."

Mitch grasped my shoulder with surprising gentleness. His words were slow and measured, in the way of the drunk trying to seem sober. "Sure you're good? Wha's up? Is 'Becca okay?"

"Mhmm. I realized that I'm…look, I gotta go." Spit it out, Sabine. "I just love her and I need to be with her," I said simply. I gave them each a quick cheek kiss then slipped away, winding my way through the crowd and downstairs until I was outside in the cool early morning air. Before I started toward my car, I pulled out my phone again to text Bec.

Hope you're not too busy. I love you, and I'll see you when you get home.

Home.

Everything I needed was at home. I'd been trying to get there for so long, struggling against everything in my head. Trying to make my way back to Bec, to the place where we were meant to be. I'd taken the long route, over obstacles both external and self-made, but for the first time I felt like I might make it. And Bec would be there waiting at the end for me.

* * *

When I arrived home a little after one in the morning the house was still and quiet. I texted Jana to let her know where I was, put on a load of laundry, played with Titus then showered and climbed into bed. I pulled Bec's pillow close, hugging it to me, breathing her in and felt that surge of rightness. This was where I belonged. I closed my eyes, and thought about everything I wanted to say to her when she came home.

Home…

I woke, tugged gently from sleep. Our curtains diffused the morning light, but I could easily make out Bec moving quietly around the bedroom. I rolled onto my back and propped myself up on an elbow. "Hey."

She halted like a burglar caught mid-theft. "Hey, I was trying not to wake you."

"It's okay. What time is it?" I murmured.

"Almost nine a.m."

I stretched. "How was work? Did you get some sleep?"

"The usual. I managed a few naps before things got hectic around midnight. I only just got your messages when I finished my shift." She grinned, her delight evident. "I can't even begin to tell you how glad I am that you're here, darling. Seeing your car in the garage was like Christmas morning." She pulled on her pajama bottoms. "I was just thinking on the drive home how much I love the way you stagger in tipsy and horny as hell after going out dancing. I'm very sorry I missed the staggering." Abruptly, she stopped speaking and I could tell she was rethinking what was obviously just an unconscious teasing quip.

"Well I wasn't drinking, so you didn't miss any staggering." I bounced both eyebrows. "But you might benefit from the horny part."

Her grin turned to one of relief, and she leaned down to kiss me. "Did you have a good night?"

"Kinda, yeah but also not really, no," I admitted.

Bec's forehead wrinkled. "Why not? Is everything okay?"

"Everything's fine. Except I got hit on by someone who looked like she was twelve. And I just…realized I didn't want to be there. I finally realized where I'm supposed to be."

She pulled her hair up into a loose bun, and her frown was slight but unmistakable. "I'm not following."

I sat up, pushing the covers aside. "All this time, Bec, I've been trying to figure out where I fit, where my place is now that everything in my head is different. I've been trying so hard that I've completely overlooked it. The answer isn't out there."

"Where is it?" she asked softly.

"It's here. With you." I held out my hand and when she took it, I pulled her down to the bed. "I know it's not going to change right away, and the medication is going to take a while to kick in and I need to work hard and do my therapy, and some nights if I've had a bad day I might have to sleep in the spare room."

When I paused to breathe, Bec answered calmly, "Okay, sweetheart. That's okay."

"But I *have* to be here, Bec. I have to be here so you can help me, and so I can help you. I need your help. And you need mine." Saying it aloud was easier than I'd expected, and the truth gave me strength. "I can't do this without you. I'm sorry it's taken me all this time to see what was right in front of me." Softly, I traced the outline of her knuckles. "I'm such a dumbass sometimes."

She laughed, the sound soft and musical. "Maybe. But you're my dumbass." Bec kissed me again and as she drew away, I curled my hand around the back of her neck and brought our lips together again. I welcomed the familiar need tingling in my belly and without a second thought, I allowed it to take over.

I let my tongue suggest what I wanted, a teasing slide along her lower lip before I gently pressed inside. The way she opened her mouth to me, and the tangle of hands in my hair told me she wanted this as much as I did. Her hands skimmed down my neck, over the front of my shoulders then paused in silent question. I drew her hands to my breasts, mine on top of hers and Bec's low groan of pleasure at my wordless assent melted any residual fear.

Our kisses were slow, our touches knowing and unerring as we helped each other get naked, unhurried in the knowledge that we had forever together. Our passion seemed endless, nothing but pure simple pleasure. She was warm and soft, her curves so familiar and comforting that I let myself fall completely into her. Some small part of me still wanted to shy away from her touch, to recoil and hide, but with every passing moment, every one of her soft and knowing caresses, pieces of my fear broke up and floated away.

This was Bec. *My* Bec who loved me and kept me safe and had never hurt me. She pushed me onto my back and lay full length against me. Lips on my neck, teeth grazed my skin, she licked and kissed her way down to suck my nipples before continuing her worship down my body.

I let her lead, revelling in the way she took her time, and how with each rediscovered place, she'd pause and wait for me to nod or encourage her with a quiet moan before her mouth and hands drew pleasure from where it'd been hiding inside me. The excitement was so sweetly familiar that I couldn't help but push up into her, now desperate for her touch.

Bec came back up until we were face-to-face. A thigh came between mine and she rocked against me, pleasuring herself and driving against my clit, until I was nearly on fire with the sensation. Her kiss was featherlight. "Is this okay?"

"Oh yes," I whispered, settling her fully on top of me. "More than okay." My hands ran up and down the damp skin of her back, and I had to blink away a sudden onset of tears. *This* was the same, the way our bodies communicated the things we couldn't find words for, the things we didn't need words for. If I'd only let myself see that earlier, I could have avoided so much pain.

Bec's mouth found mine again for a kiss that started as something so achingly sweet that my anguish fell away and finished as something sensual. The drumbeat of excitement between my thighs picked up. I hitched her leg over my hip until Bec straddled me, her arousal painting my stomach as she ground against my skin. She pressed forward, and I reached between us to draw my thumb over her clit in long slow strokes, delighting in the way her hips matched the movement. "You first," I murmured. "I want to watch you come."

Bracing her hands on my shoulders, her nails digging in lightly, she rocked back and forth against me. Her breaths came in erratic gasps, and when I brought my other hand to her breast, teasing her nipple between my thumb and forefinger, she drew in a sharp breath then let it out with a barely audible, "Sabine..." Bec arched backward, the muscles in her legs and stomach quivering with each of my strokes. Her eyes were half-lidded, the movement of her hips becoming more frantic as she rode me. So fucking beautiful.

I brought both hands around to her ass, slapping her lightly before pressing her forward. She took the cue, sliding up me to settle her knees on either side of my shoulders. Bec spread herself open, lowering herself onto my face until she was so close I could smell her desire. Looking up, I could see the glistening fluid of her sex, the sweat sheening her skin. I kissed the inside of her thighs, tasting the salt of her, and let my tongue glide up toward her heat.

She fisted my hair hard, almost forcing herself into my mouth. I slicked my tongue through her valley, taking my time exploring every wet fold and couldn't help groaning when she begged, "Lick me, please. Tongue fuck me."

My arousal climbed again, the heavy beat between my legs picking up tempo. Bec's knees tightened on my shoulders, the hand in my hair pulled hard and her murmured encouragement grew loud and so fucking sexy that the pounding in my clit became almost unbearable. But I kept my hands away from my own desire, letting them focus only on drawing *her* pleasure out.

I would know her cues anywhere. Every gasp, moan and pant was a marker along the path to her climax—a path she followed nearly every time. She brought her hand away from my shoulder, grasped her breast and let out an exclamation of, "Oh, God yes. Please, like that."

Closing my lips around her clit, I sucked gently and Bec bucked and shuddered, rewarding me with a low moan and an almost wondrous cry of, "Sabine, oh God…I'm coming." She fell forward to grab the headboard, her arousal flooding my mouth. I didn't dare move, except to keep lightly stroking her with my tongue and hands.

Bec's breathing slowed and steadied, and after a minute she unclamped her knees from my shoulders to slide back down my body. Her kiss was soft, almost chaste before she moved down to lick and suck my neck. Her explorations were new and exciting, but at the same time sweet and familiar. A hand trailed down my belly, lightly touched me and again she asked, "Is this okay?"

"Yes…please. Yes," I choked out, covering her hand with mine and pressing her fingers harder against my clit. Bec made a sound that was half-moan, half-desperate mewling and pushed inside me. Her exhalation was long and I had to strain to hear her when she said, "Oh, darling…"

Bec's thrusts were shallow but measured, hitting all the right places until I was incoherent with pleasure. When I thought I might shatter from the intensity of her ministrations, Bec withdrew to lightly circle my clit before entering me again. She kissed my breasts, taking her time to suck my nipples into hard, aching peaks before she kissed her way down my belly and settled her shoulders between my thighs. She placed a line of kisses from my belly to the top of my thigh where it dipped toward my sex, and then she paused a final time. "Can I?" Bec asked, her question needy and tentative.

I answered her with a single, desperate, "Please."

The first touch of her tongue was soft, just the barest pressure sliding up and down through my labia, and it had me pressing against her to seek more. "I've missed this," she murmured, kissing my thigh before burying her face back between my legs.

The silken warmth of her mouth and knowing strokes of her tongue drew my climax ever closer until I felt the heat spreading through my body. She could have withheld her touch, teased and tortured and punished me for the way I'd withheld my body from her. But of course she didn't. Wouldn't. She took me exactly the way she knew I needed it.

I raised my head, about to ask her to come back to me, to hold me as I climaxed but as though reading my thoughts, Bec pulled away and quickly climbed up to lie beside me. Before I could beg her to let me come, she reached down and cupped me, fingers gliding easily into my heat. God, she always knew just what I needed. "Bec, I—"

"I know, baby. That's it," she murmured, still stroking. "Come for me, sweetheart."

I gasped, my lips moving feverishly against her neck as my orgasm claimed me. Waves rolled through my body, spreading from groin to stomach to limbs, carrying white-hot pleasure to every cell. Burying my face in her neck, I couldn't help the words spilling from my mouth in a breathless rush. "I love you. I love you." Clinging to her, I waited for the full-body tingling to disperse and when I finally managed to collect my thoughts into words, all I could think of to say was, "Bec, I need you."

"I'm here," she said quietly, kissing my chin, my cheeks, my lips.

I pressed my forehead to hers, trying to suppress the shudder building at the base of my spine, but it came anyway. I closed my eyes, hoping she'd understand what I was saying went beyond just this moment. It was more than just lust or desire. It was us. "No, Bec. I *need* you."

She stroked my back, my neck, my face. "I know, darling." Her hands came to rest on my cheeks. "I'm here. I'll always be here." She kissed me again, gently possessive.

We lay curled around one another with limbs intertwined, and there were no words, only soft caresses and sweet kisses. With my head pillowed on her breasts, her smooth warm skin under my cheek, I grew dull and drowsy. Safe with her. Always. I absently stroked her palm and the underside of her fingers. Her finger…

Wake up, Sabine.

I mumbled something indistinct and when Bec shifted in response, carefully extricated myself from her arms, swung from the bed and crossed the floor to our closet. When I turned around, Bec had sat up, drawing the sheet over her breasts to cover herself against the cool morning air. "Are you okay?"

"Mhmm, very totally okay." When both her eyebrows shot up, I laughed quietly and raised both hands. "I'm awake and totally lucid, I promise."

Her smile was sheepish, but still a smile. "I believe you."

She trusted me. She knew, even when I didn't. When I was certain I wasn't about to burst into tears, I crossed back to the bed and kissed her. Bec curled a hand around the back of my neck, holding me close. The kiss was soft and unhurried, the kind that made my stomach flutter with sweet pleasure rather than fierce desire. Her hand slipped gently from my neck to my jaw, and when she pulled back, she brushed her thumb over my lips. "I love you," she whispered.

"Love you too. Give me a minute?"

I unlocked the safe and pulled out that small velvet box from where I'd hidden it almost two months ago. There was a choking sensation in my gut but it wasn't fear or discomfort. It was excitement, urgency. I held the box behind my back and then when I sat on the bed, moved it to rest beside my thigh where she wouldn't be able to see it.

"What are you up to?" she asked, a delicate eyebrow arching.

Instead of answering her outright, I said, "I had everything planned you know, the day I came home from Afghanistan? Then I froze and I just couldn't get it right."

"Get what right, darling?" Bec asked quietly.

I lifted the box up and cracked it open to expose a brilliant-cut sapphire set in a platinum band. When I tilted the box, the diamonds extending down the band glittered like stars on a clear winter's night. "While I was wandering the mall that day I saw this, and it reminded me of your eyes, so I had to buy it. And every day since then, I've thought about you wearing it."

Bec's mouth fell open, and her intake of breath was audible. Her hand dropped away from where she was clutching the sheet and the fabric fell, exposing her body. But she made no move to pull it up again. She just stared at the ring, her eyes widening.

I cleared my throat. "I was totally going to ask you the moment I got home. Then I turned on the light, and I saw you and how incredibly gorgeous you are, and I completely forgot what I wanted to say. So I just blurted stuff instead. And while I rambled, I thought I can't do it like this, blathering and feeling weird and not all back together the way I was supposed to be. Not worthy of you. So I didn't ask." I laughed softly. "I'm blathering now. I'm sorry, babe, this is so not romantic."

Bec lifted her eyes to mine, her pupils expanding into the blue I loved. "Sabine…" Then her gaze moved back to the ring nestled amongst black velvet. "It's beautiful."

"Mmm, yes. But not nearly as beautiful as you." I drew my thumb over the band. "Every time after that when I tried to find the perfect moment to ask, it all seemed wrong. I felt wrong. Not about asking you, but about me. Then tonight I realized that every moment *with you* is the perfect moment. I know I've been off since The Incident, and worse these past months and I'm so sorry, but…I never feel more like myself than when I'm with you." I had to draw in a shaky breath before I could continue in a voice tight with threatening tears, "Bec, you still feel like home to me."

The edge of her mouth curved upward a fraction, and she blinked rapidly but her eyes remained on the ring. It was as though she'd been hypnotized by it, and sudden irrational panic rose up to swallow me. Maybe she didn't want this. Maybe I still wasn't going to be fixed enough for her. Maybe I wasn't enough for her. "I'm sorry, this is stupid. I can't get the words right and it's coming out all wrong."

"No, darling," she whispered. "It's coming out perfectly."

Her words gave me courage, certainty, and I reached for her hand, holding it tightly. Bec tore her gaze from the ring to find mine, and those loving eyes swam with her own unshed tears.

"Bec, I love you. So much that obviously I can't even figure out how to tell you. I'm probably going to mess up again, but I know now that I can deal with it because you'll be there with me. Your love gives me strength and makes me weak at the knees all at the same time." I swallowed, trying hard to push the emotion down, but the words still came out choked and hoarse when I asked the question that'd burned inside me for so long.

"Will you marry me?"

She smiled, shyly at first, then it grew until both dimples were showing and the edges of her eyes were creased with delight. "Ask me again. Those four words are so perfect, I want to hear you say them again."

An excited sob slipped out of my mouth before I could stop it. "Really?"

She nodded vigorously. "Mhmm."

After stealing a kiss, I forced away the inane grin and excited laugh trying to take me over—the ones that would make it impossible for me to say anything—and schooled my expression to earnestness. "Bec, you take all my dark places and fill them with light. I love you. Will you marry me?"

She leaned in so our faces were an inch apart and the words I needed to hear rushed from her lips like water over a spillway. "Yes. I already told you, no matter what you have to ask me, or how many times, the answer is always yes." Bec held out her left hand. "Now please hurry up and put that on me."

Laughing, I slid the ring from the box and took her hand. Unhurriedly, I kissed each one of the knuckles of her left hand before carefully sliding the band up her ring finger. I swallowed. I stared. "That…looks really good," I finally managed to say dumbly.

Bec stared at the engagement ring, almost as though she couldn't quite believe it was really there. "It does, but you know what's going to look even better?" She looked up, eyes sparkling like the gems I'd just put on her hand. "My ring on your finger."

CHAPTER TWENTY-FOUR

Rebecca

Given the elaborate engagement party Carolyn and Jana were planning for April, I half-agreed with Sabine that us going out to dinner on the two-month anniversary of our engagement was probably unnecessary. But I'd pushed, because it would be so much more than a celebration of our decision to join our lives legally. The celebration was for the way she was trying so damned hard and actually seemed to be making progress with managing her PTSD.

Though we still had ups and downs, still battled with sporadic nightmares and occasional anxiety, as well as my omnipresent guilt, I wanted to acknowledge how we were learning to communicate our needs and how much it was helping us to heal, together. More frequently now I could see *her*, clear moments when she was fully herself, and the lightness in her filled me with such gratitude and love that I felt I could cry.

A few nights ago as we'd readied for bedtime, Sabine had palmed her medication into her mouth, and spun to face me. Grinning, she'd planted a smacking kiss on my mouth then declared completely out of the blue and with an abundance of glee, "I'm rebuilding myself, babe! I estimate a ninety-seven-point-four percent success rate."

After I'd laughed at her typically nerdy and precise explanation, she'd pressed herself to my back, kissing my neck and running her hands up and down my belly while I tried to concentrate on my pre-bed routine. A light suck on my earlobe and a whisper of, "I know something that might add a few decimal places…" had me hastening. The moment I'd finished cleaning my contacts, she'd turned me around and hoisted me up, her hands under my ass to carry me to our bed. She'd been so attentive and receptive, so uninhibited, so *Sabine* that days later I still felt the flutter of arousal when I thought of our hours of lovemaking.

I spun my watch around and checked how much time we had before the cab arrived to take us to dinner. Not much. I'd been waiting downstairs, dressed in a simple emerald-green sheath dress, for the past five minutes for Sabine.

The sound of her on the top step made me glance up and the moment I saw her, I knew the true meaning of breathtaking. She was glorious. Watching her walk downstairs, her body healthy and strong, and her face relaxed and free of the shadows that'd been present for so many months, I knew *celebration* was exactly right. I wanted to celebrate her. I wanted to celebrate us.

She wore a burgundy cowl-neck dress that clung to her body, ending just above her knees. Her dark features were set off by the silver adorning her ears, neck and wrist. Her smudged, smoky-eye makeup made her eyes appear almost black and it took everything I had not to kiss the deep red lipstick from her mouth the moment she was in reach. I settled for a light peck, having to stretch because she too wore heels. "Darling, you look incredible. When did you get that dress?"

As a rule, Sabine hardly bought anything in a shade resembling red, because she had a long-held and inexplicable loathing of the color. A few times when she'd worn old red college tees, I'd mentioned that the color suited her, and I liked it on her, but had usually received a nose wrinkle in response.

Now it seemed she'd bought this dress for no other reason than to please me.

"Yesterday after work." She pulled me close, bending to kiss the spot under my ear that made me shiver. "And you look absolutely ravishing."

"Thank you." I drew my hand up and down her back. "Our ride should be here any minute."

"Mhmm." Sabine helped me into my coat, then shrugged into hers as a horn sounded outside. She glanced at the door. "Chariot's here." This would be the first time we'd taken a cab since The Incident, and it'd even been Sabine who'd suggested it, jokingly saying that she'd mastered being a passenger in my car and it was time to go to the next level.

Seated in the backseat, the only sign of her discomfort was some leg bouncing every few minutes. But her hand in mine was warm and dry, her breathing relaxed and steady. I leaned into her as she stared out the window during the twenty-minute ride. A few blocks from our destination, she turned to me. "Where are we going exactly?"

"It's a secret." I'd booked us a table at a nice steak restaurant in the city and had told her nothing other than she should dress up a little. The driver dropped us right outside and Sabine slipped out first. While I paid, she stood on the sidewalk, facing the restaurant with both hands in her coat pockets and her breath steaming in the cold night air.

I fumbled, almost dropping my purse as I exited the cab and realized she was wearing seamed stockings. When I thought of the curves of her ass waiting atop each of those black lines, my mouth went dry. I would certainly be asking her to keep both heels and stockings on when we got home. For a short while at least. I stepped in beside her, and Sabine turned to me, her eyes wide with delight. "Charlie Palmer Steak? Bec, this is fantastic, thank you. I've been wanting to come here for ages."

"I know, that's why I chose it." Her glee drew me in like a magnet, and I couldn't help but stretch up for a kiss. "I'm courting you."

She threw her head back and laughed. "Honey, you've already caught me." Sabine dropped her head to nuzzle my hair, and I heard her gentle inhalation as her arm stole around my waist.

"Good," I said against her shoulder. "I don't intend to let you go."

Seated in front of a large window with a view of the Capitol, she seemed relaxed and happy, her inane chattering leading the conversation in all directions. Once we'd chosen wine and each had a glass poured, we were left alone with menus. Sabine peered at me over the top of hers. "Will you make it to watch me bowl tomorrow night?"

She'd joined a women's social bowling team, and a few weeks ago had attended her first games with only the barest hint of anxiety at her *new activity*. So many small accomplishments, but they all added up. She'd also promised she'd join my flag football league next season, and I couldn't deny my excitement at sharing something that'd been such a big part of our lives when we'd worked together.

"Absolutely, I'll come straight from work. I might miss some of your first game, but I'll definitely be there. There's no way I'd give up a chance to see you in those, uh…sexy bowling shoes."

Sabine snorted. "Noted for future roleplays. You know, with you watching me as incentive, I might even get four strikes this week." With a smirk she added, "I think there's a most valuable player trophy in my future."

"A trophy? Well, darling, that will certainly earn you a reward," I murmured. The banter was natural and sweet, another reminder of our shift back to that place of easiness.

Smiling, Sabine returned to her menu and after a minute or so, glanced up and said, "Oh! I almost forgot, Gavin emailed today. They've set the wedding date for next October, and he wanted to double-check my contract end date, so he could be sure we'd make it."

"That's lovely of him. Did you tell him we'd be there regardless?"

"Mhmm, and I reminded him he'd better not be deployed on our wedding da—" Sabine, like me and most of the restaurant, started when a patron who wasn't watching where he was going plowed into one of the poor waitstaff, scattering his double armload of empty plates.

The crash echoed sharply through the restaurant and I tensed, waiting for Sabine's reaction and readying myself to help her if needed. Aside from working on communication, part of our couple's counseling had been both of us learning how to give and receive help. I felt confident that if needed, she would accept it from me now, and for what it was, not as an indicator of imagined disappointment or something demeaning.

Her long, dark eyelashes fluttered while she drew in a few deep breaths. Then she raised her head and smiled knowingly at me. "On our wedding day," she finished calmly before returning to the menu.

My emotion welled up so strongly that I blurted, "I love you, sweetheart and I'm so proud of you." Just as I'd trusted her to receive my help if I'd offered it, I trusted her to receive those words as I'd intended them to be taken.

"Thanks." She reached across the table to squeeze my hand, turning it over and studying my finger intently. Every time she looked at my sapphire and diamond engagement ring—which was frequently—the same expression of awe and something akin to pride came over her face. I knew the feeling, and felt it echoed in my own body when I looked at her ring finger.

A neatly presented server sidled up beside me and waited for our acknowledgement. When I smiled up at her, she apologized for the loud disruption to our evening, offered a complimentary glass of wine each, and launched into a spiel about seasonal offerings and recommendations. Once we'd ordered, Sabine turned slightly sideways in her chair, crossing one leg over the other. "I meant to tell you, I lost a hundred bucks today," she said conversationally.

"Really? How'd you manage that?" I swallowed a small mouthful of Zinfandel.

"I made a bad bet." At my confused expression, Sabine clarified, "For the deployment pool at work."

"Ah, yes. That secret betting pool you all think we don't know about?" One year, I'd put in a secret bet by proxy and won over two thousand dollars, and I knew some of my friends and fellow commanding officers had done the same over the years.

Her smile was sheepish. "That's the one."

"Mmm. So who won?"

"Mitch. He's such an ass, I don't know how he did it because nobody else came close. I've already told him he's taking us out for dinner and drinks."

I laughed shortly, until the sudden realization of the betting pool having been paid out meant that the decision had been made, and orders given for her next posting. The thought of her leaving me again made my breath catch. "So what did you put down for your entry?" I asked as nonchalantly as I could.

"Landstuhl in seven months and thirteen days."

"And...what is it?" I desperately hoped that I didn't appear as panicked as I felt.

She turned her as-yet-untouched wine in slow circles. "Walter Reed National Military Medical Center in Bethesda. Until the end of my contract." A cheeky, insouciant shrug. "So I guess we're celebrating that tonight too."

The wash of relief was so sudden that I almost sagged in the chair. "You're staying here?" I breathed. More than staying in the area, she would finish out her contract at the facility where she was working now.

"Yes, I'm staying home." She grinned. "Sorry, Bec, now you're really stuck with me."

The grin was contagious and I felt my cheeks lift in response. I took her left hand, my thumb playing over the platinum band with a double line of inset diamonds that I'd slid onto her finger a few days after she'd proposed to me. "Darling, I thought you already knew that from the moment we met, all I've wanted is to be *stuck* with you." Raising her hand to my mouth, I slowly kissed each of her knuckles and finally, the ring.

Bella Books, Inc.

Women. Books. Even Better Together.

P.O. Box 10543
Tallahassee, FL 32302

Phone: 800-729-4992
www.bellabooks.com